NO
ESCAPE

Novelist, traveller and fresh air enthusiast, Lucy Clarke, is the author of four novels, including the Richard & Judy Book Club pick, *The Sea Sisters*. Lucy is married to a professional windsurfer and, together with their two young children, they spend their winters travelling and their summers at home on the south coast of England. Lucy writes from a beach hut.

Keep in touch with Lucy:

www.lucy-clarke.com
@lucyclarke_author
@lucyclarkebooks
/lucyclarkeauthor

Also by Lucy Clarke

The Sea Sisters
A Single Breath
Last Seen

NO ESCAPE

LUCY CLARKE

Previously published as *The Blue*

HarperCollins*Publishers*

HarperCollins*Publishers* Ltd
1 London Bridge Street,
London SE1 9GF

www.harpercollins.co.uk

HarperCollins*Publishers*
1st Floor, Watemarque Building, Ringsend Road,
Dublin 4, Ireland

First published as *The Blue* by HarperCollins*Publishers* 2015

5

This paperback edition published by HarperCollins*Publishers* 2018

A catalogue record for this book is available from the British Library

ISBN: 978-0-00-829340-6

Set in Birka by Palimpsest Book Production Limited, Falkirk, Stirlingshire

Printed and bound in the UK using 100% renewable electricity at
CPI Group (UK) Ltd

MIX
Paper from
responsible sources
FSC™ C007454

This book is produced from independently certified FSC™ paper to ensure
responsible forest management.
For more information visit: www.harpercollins.co.uk/green

For Thomas Oak, who was growing inside me during much of the writing of this novel. My world is so much richer because of you.

ACKNOWLEDGEMENTS

While writing *No Escape*, I've been lucky enough to have the sage council of many salty sea dogs. Firstly, thanks to Sue and John Woods, who I met during a research trip in the Philippines. When interviewing them about their sailing lifestyle, they said the only way to really understand it was to experience it. My husband and I spent the next five nights on their yacht, MV *Solita*, and much of the novel stemmed from those wonderful days anchoring in deserted coves, snorkelling over pristine reefs, and sleeping on deck beneath the stars.

Much thanks also goes to the other sailors who have given me varying degrees of advice, from beach-side interviews, to a peaceful sail on *Sea Spine*: with thanks to Alan and Caroline Crockard, Steve Hammond, Will Satterly, Mick Wood and Bill Lack. Please let it be known that any nautical mistakes within the novel are entirely my own!

Thank you to all at Greene & Heaton Literary Agency who do such an excellent job – in particular, my wonderful agent,

Judith Murray, who is my literary rock. I also want to thank my publishing team at HarperCollins UK, headed by the brilliant Kim Young, who worked tirelessly with me on the editing of *No Escape*. Thanks also goes to my fantastic US editor at Touchstone/ Simon & Schuster, Sally Kim.

A wonderful group of friends and family kindly volunteered to read working drafts of *No Escape*, and their feedback proved invaluable – so a big THANKS to you all (especially my mum who has read every draft of this novel – and there were many!).

The final mention is reserved for my husband, James. Thank you for joining me on various research quests in the Philippines; thank you for the motivational chats on long evenings in the beach hut; thank you for taking time off work to help brainstorm plot problems when I'd hit a wall. Thank you for being *you*. For being everything.

PROLOGUE

A body floats, unseeing eyes fixed on the brooding sky. A pair of cotton shorts has darkened, pockets gulping with water. A shirt billows, then clings to the unmoving chest. The streak of blood across the right temple has washed away now, leaving the skin clear and greying.

Below, the sea teems with darting fish carving through the water in great shoals, while tiny flecks of nutrient-rich plankton spin in the light. Deeper still, milky-eyed predators patrol the sunless depths where the seabed is scarred with the markings of currents, and broken coral lies as hard as bone.

But above there is only a body.

And a yacht.

On board, as bare feet move across the sun-bleached deck, a thread of fear begins to weave amongst the crew. Within minutes the pitch of voices becomes raised; footsteps turn hurried; eyes narrow as they press against the dark rings of binoculars scanning the horizon.

It doesn't take long for the fragile film of order to begin to tear, slowly working itself loose in the breeze. As a pair of hands reaches for the wheel, turning the yacht into the wind, the sail flapping loose, the truth is already drifting out of reach.

1

NOW

The paintbrush slips from Lana's fingers, turning through the air as it falls. It clatters to the floor at the foot of the easel, splattering tiny flecks of blue acrylic paint against her ankle.

Lana doesn't glance down, doesn't notice the spots of paint that decorate the small tattoo of a wing inked on her ankle. Her gaze remains fixed on the radio that sits on the windowsill, her fingers raised as if still holding the brush to the canvas. That silver box of metal and wires holds the entire sum of her concentration as she focuses on the voice of a news presenter.

'*. . . has sunk a hundred nautical miles off the north coast of New Zealand. The yacht – The Blue – was believed to have left Fiji eight days ago with a crew of five on board, including two New Zealanders. A search-and-rescue operation has been launched from the Maritime Rescue Centre at the Bay of Islands. The coastguard has described the sea state as moderate with wind speeds of up to twenty knots.*'

Lana blinks, struggling to absorb the information, as if it's rain running off hard, scorched earth. Her gaze bores into the radio, willing it to disclose something more, but the newscaster has already moved on to the next story.

She turns on the spot, lifting a hand to her head. She feels the cool silk of her headscarf keeping her hair off her face. It has been eight months since she stepped from that yacht, her skin tanned, her feet bare, a backpack heaved on her shoulders. She'd walked along the shoreline with dark hollows beneath her eyes, and hadn't looked back. She couldn't.

As she turns, she catches sight of herself in the long mirror that leans against her apartment wall. She stares: her face has paled and large green eyes glare back at her, wide with questions. Was Kitty still on board after all this time? Had she stayed even after Lana left? It's possible that Kitty could have returned to England. Lana tries to picture her riding the Tube with a script in her hand, glossy dark hair loose over her shoulders, her lips painted red. But the image won't form, not clearly. She knows that Kitty wouldn't have left the yacht, because how could either of them go home after what'd happened?

It has been eight months since they've last seen each other – the longest time in their friendship they've ever spent apart. She thinks about Kitty's emails still sitting unread in her inbox. At first, they came in thick and fast; then there were gaps – a few days, sometimes a week. Lana began imagining the patterns of the yacht as it sailed through remote island chains, wondering what was happening on board, who Kitty was spending her time with. Eventually, with her head too full of images, she stopped reading the emails. Stopped thinking about Kitty.

Now a beautiful memory gusts into her thoughts, bright as a kite. She and Kitty, eleven years old, sitting cross-legged on her bedroom floor plaiting friendship bracelets. 'This is yours,' Kitty had said, holding up a slim cotton bracelet woven with turquoise and yellow threads – Lana's favourite colours. Kitty tied it firmly over Lana's wrist, using her teeth to get the knot in exactly the right position. When Kitty pulled away, there was a small smear of strawberry lipgloss on the back of Lana's wrist.

In return Lana had plaited a pink and white bracelet for Kitty, and the two of them had held their wrists side by side and made the promise, 'Friends for ever.'

Lana had worn her bracelet for eighteen months, until it had faded and frayed to a dishwater-grey. It had eventually snapped in the bath, so she'd hooked it out and dried it over the towel rail. Then she'd put it away in her memory box with the photo of her mother.

Friends for ever, they'd agreed.

A guilty heat crawls across Lana's skin as she thinks of that failed promise: she's cut Kitty out of her life, like slicing a bowline and letting a boat drift out to the open ocean.

*

Lana waits desperately for another news bulletin. She needs to hear exactly what's happening out on the water – whether the crew have made it to the life raft, whether any of them is injured – but the radio station is playing a soft rock song that comes strumming into her apartment. She paces to the windowsill and snaps off the radio.

She stays by the open window. Outside, the morning light is thin and hazy, a salt breeze drifting into the room. She pushes up onto her tiptoes, peering beyond the treeline to where she can glimpse the sea. It's one of the reasons she agreed to rent the apartment with its cracked wooden floorboards and noisy electric heaters that she has to huddle against in the depths of the New Zealand winter to feel any warmth.

Now that summer is on its way, she's grateful for the wide windows that let the light flood in, as she sets up her easel in front of them so she can paint before work. She's made a life of sorts here: she has a job, a place to live, an old car. Her days may not be filled with friends and laughter and noise as they once were, but perhaps it's better this way.

Sometimes she thinks of her father back in England in his tired terraced house, spending his evenings alone doing the crossword or watching the news. After all those years of riling against his quiet routines, the irony of how her life has taken on the same lonely rhythm as his hasn't escaped her. She writes to him every couple of months – just brief letters to reassure him that she's safe – but she never includes her address. She's still not ready for that.

Lana arrived in New Zealand eight months ago now, stepping from the plane into the start of autumn, shivering in a sun-bleached cotton dress, her salt-matted hair loose over her shoulders. She'd had a backpack on her shoulders and $500 left of her savings.

She'd spent that first night in an Auckland hostel, lying on a bunk with her eyes closed, waiting to feel it sway and shudder. If someone had walked into her dorm, laid a hand on her shoulder and asked, *Are you okay? Has something happened?* she would have told them – told them everything; about the canvas backpack thrown from the side of the yacht, drifting in the sea like a body; about how a horizon curves and wavers when there is no land to break it; about the red sarong pooled on the floor of the cabin, soft beneath Lana's feet; about a kiss in a cave carved from lime-stone; about how you can look at your best friend and no longer recognize her. But no one had asked. And, as the minutes had crept into hours, and the hours stretched through the night, Lana had pushed down each of those memories, sealing them off.

When dawn had arrived, she'd showered the salt from her skin, letting the water run long and hard, marvelling at its seemingly endless supply. Then she'd pulled on her dress, followed by her backpack, and started to walk. The rubber V of her flip-flops rubbed between her toes; she'd been barefoot for weeks. She'd stopped at a sidewalk café and ordered break-fast and a coffee. As she'd wolfed down a salty bacon-and-egg bagel, a car had pulled up with a surfboard strapped to its roof and a handwritten sign taped to the back window, reading, '*For sale. $500.*' Lana had got up from her table and asked the car's owner, a young Spanish guy whose visa was expiring in two days' time, if he'd take $300. He said if she dropped him at the airport first she had a deal.

Afterwards, she'd driven north with no map, no plan, and no one sitting beside her. It had been odd to be behind the wheel of a car after so long and she kept over-steering into bends, having grown accustomed to the yacht's helm. The speed and smoothness of road travel unnerved her so much that she'd wound down all the windows to feel the wind against her face.

On that first drive across New Zealand, she'd passed serene dark lakes, endless undulating vineyards and staggering hillsides, eventually arriving at the coast. That's where she'd pulled up – on a gravel track that overlooked a bay. She'd parked facing the sea and watched as the waves rolled in, beaching themselves on the shore. When the sun had lowered itself into the sea, she'd climbed onto the back seat, pulled out her sleeping bag from the bottom of her backpack and wriggled into it, lying with her neck cricked against the door.

If anyone had asked, *Why New Zealand?* she could have told them that she'd always wanted to travel here – but that would only have been part of the story.

The truth was, Lana had always known that the yacht was going to return here eventually – just as she'd known that New Zealand was where *he* was from. Perhaps she'd been waiting all these months because, no matter how hard she tried to forget, she still wasn't ready to let go of *The Blue*.

2

THEN

Lana found the sketchbook tucked at the back of the stall between bags of cashew nuts and a stack of sun hats. She eased it from the shelf and wiped the film of dust from its cover. The pages were thinner than she'd have liked, but at least they were a bright, crisp white. She took it to the counter where a Filipino boy with crooked front teeth grinned as he searched for the price.

'Artist?' he asked.

She was about to answer, *No*, when on a whim, she smiled and said, 'Yes. Artist.' *Why the hell not?* She was travelling; no one – except Kitty – knew her over here. She could be whoever she wanted to be.

She left the shade of the stall with the sketchbook under her arm. The streets were busy, the heat of the day stored in the roads which seemed to radiate warmth and dust. Her thick amber hair was piled up in a loose knot, and she used the back of her arm to wipe away the sheen of sweat on her forehead.

The heat in the Philippines was like a wall, unmovable and solid, both day and night.

She wove through the crowds, skirting a man who stood in the centre of the pavement wafting a straw fan over the embers of a grill. A smoky charred aroma rose into the air.

Beyond him, a diesel generator whirred outside a stall and she felt the heat kicked out from its exhaust against her bare legs. She dodged two crates of glass bottles stacked on the pavement, then navigated a map of cracks and gouges in the concrete. She was a little disappointed with the stalls, having imagined trailing through them and discovering quirky print dresses or interesting handmade jewellery – but most of the stalls sold the same range of bland T-shirts and sarongs.

On the opposite side of the street a young Filipino boy padded along carrying a cockerel, a dog trotting behind him with a coconut husk in its mouth. Beyond the boy she saw Kitty standing in the queue for the bakery, her dark hair snaking over one shoulder. From behind she could almost pass as a local with her petite figure and her skin tanned a rich mahogany. She was talking to an elderly man with a stooped posture who was laughing at something she was saying. Kitty had a wonderful knack of making friends wherever they went, drawing strangers into conversation with her inexhaustible supply of stories and questions.

Lana slowed to cross the road and meet Kitty, a tide of people moving and bustling around her. The sweet, yeasty smell of bread drifted towards her on a warm wind as she waited for a gap in the procession of brightly painted tricycles. There were no cars in Norappi, only tricycles weaving, racing and beeping their way along the streets. They made her think of the Bangkok tuk-tuks she'd seen pictures of, with their decorated metal side-cars attached to the driver's motorbike.

Across the street there was a sudden blur of movement and noise. The boy carrying the cockerel gave a high-pitched yelp of surprise as the bird burst free from his grip and made a dash for it across the road. A tricycle coming towards it swerved sharply in a squeal of brakes, and the passenger – a young Western man with large headphones clamped over his ears – was shot out of his seat, slamming to the other side of the vehicle, making it veer further off course.

The tricycle careered onto the pavement, crashing into a street grill, and dragging it along the roadside towards Lana, metal raging on concrete in a hideous cacophony of noise. Stunned by the eruption of chaos, she didn't manage to move back swiftly enough and the grill caught her foot, pulling it out from under her.

Suddenly the ground was spinning towards her – her bag and sketchbook flying away. She felt the smack of concrete against her palms, the side of her knee, her ankle bone. Her nostrils filled with grit and dust. Beneath her the concrete thrummed with heat.

There was more shouting, and she lifted her head to see the young boy making a grab for the cockerel. He caught a fistful of tail feathers and yanked it, squawking, towards him, clasping it roughly within both arms. The tricycle was now parked haphazardly on the side of the road, and its driver clipped the boy over the head, scolding him demonstratively.

Lana blinked, bringing her gaze back to the ground. She needed to get up, but couldn't seem to make herself move. She was aware of her belongings tossed aside, the fresh pages of her sketchbook splayed in the dirt.

As she lay there, a young man in a bright T-shirt crouched to the ground and gathered up her things. He came towards her, fanning the dust from the pages, asking, 'You okay?'

'Yes,' she said, finally heaving herself upright. Her head swam and she touched her forehead with her fingertips.

'Here,' he said, taking her by the elbow, and carefully helping her to her feet.

As she stood, he kept hold of her, turning his back to the flow of the crowd to give Lana space while she regained her balance. Her ankle throbbed painfully and she looked down and saw a small patch of blood beginning to bloom just above the bone.

'I was in the tricycle. The driver was trying to miss the cockerel, but . . .' He paused, looking at her again. A faint beat of music slid from the headphones around his neck. 'You sure you're okay?'

'I'm fine—'

'Lana! Jesus!' Kitty was pushing her way through the flow of people, sunglasses askew on her head, a bag bouncing against her hip. Reaching Lana, she threw her arms around her neck. 'I heard the noise. Saw you! Are you hurt? How bad is it?' Kitty pulled away, her hands holding onto Lana's upper arms as she scanned her. 'Your ankle. It's bleeding.'

'I'll be fine,' Lana said, wanting to get off the street and sit for a moment. She brushed half-heartedly at the dust on her dress.

'I think these are yours,' the stranger said, holding out Lana's belongings.

Lana thanked him.

'Take it easy, eh?'

As she turned to move away, her vision seemed to swerve. Everything felt louder and closer: horns honking, quick bursts of Tagalog, the banging of a hammer against metal. She was aware of the hot trickle of blood winding its way down her foot and the sensation made her want to gag. People wove around her, scents of washing powder, food, sweat, rising from their skin. *Just walk. Move slowly. Get out of this street.*

But as she walked, her legs felt unsteady and her balance seemed to falter. She reached out a hand to find something solid she could rest against, but there was only air.

'Oh shit!' she heard Kitty cry, her voice seeming far away.

Then the man was at Lana's other side, gripping her by the upper arm – steadying her. 'Here,' he said calmly. 'We've got you.'

*

They steered her along the street, cutting through a narrow gap between two stalls that led down a shaded alleyway. Chickens roamed and bleached washing was drying stiff in the heat. An elderly woman sat with an empty plate in front of her, watching them through milky brown eyes.

He took a left, crossing a rickety bridge that stretched over a waterway, towards what appeared to be a dead end of rocks. 'It's just up here.'

A group of travellers appeared from a gap between the rocks, talking in loud voices, laughing, bashing each other over the shoulders. Lana followed the direction they had come from, hobbling slowly along a cool, stone passageway.

Eventually she found herself standing at the top of a stairway made of hundreds of white pebbles set neatly into concrete. From here a view of a bar opened out below. It was built on stilts over the water, its sides open to the softening blue sky, and almost everything she could see was made of bamboo or drift-wood. Backpackers in T-shirts and board shorts, sundresses and colourful tops, lounged in low chairs or on floor cushions, playing cards, smoking, talking. Two girls sat at the very edge of the bar drinking beers with their tanned legs dangling towards the water. The pulse of music throbbed through the space, intermingled with voices and laughter.

The man found them a spot by the water, where a cool breeze drifted in. Lana set her sketchbook on the table, then lowered herself down into one of the wide wooden chairs that sat only inches from the floor. She stretched her legs in front of her, pleased to take the weight off her ankle.

'I'll get some ice,' Kitty said, 'and drinks. Lana, you need something medicinal.' Turning to the man, she asked, 'Beer?'

He held a hand up, saying, 'You guys go ahead. I'll sort myself out. I'm meeting some mates here soon.'

'Just a quick one – to say thanks,' Kitty insisted.

He hesitated for a moment and then shrugged, saying, 'Sure, why not?'

He introduced himself as Denny, and when Kitty went to the bar he told Lana he was from New Zealand. He had an even, golden tan, which set off the pale blue of his eyes, and his hair – a bed of tight sandy curls – seemed to grow upwards. She imagined that if she reached out a hand it would feel springy to the touch.

He unhooked the headphones from around his neck and set them on the table beside her sketchbook. 'You draw?'

'A little,' she replied.

'What type of thing?'

'Oh, anything really. Whatever captures me.'

'And what captures you?' he said, looking at her with interest.

She thought for a moment. In the month she and Kitty had been travelling in the Philippines, she'd already filled two sketchbooks with illustrations. She pictured her most recent sketches – a group of boys sitting on a crumbling wall, legs swinging; a goat tethered in the shade chewing the cud; a doorway shrouded by a sun-bleached yellow sheet; a lone shoe discarded at the roadside. 'I like to sketch ordinary things that pinpoint a moment.'

He nodded thoughtfully. 'Something that has a story.'

'Yes, that's exactly it.'

Kitty returned with three beers sweating on a bamboo tray, slices of lime sticking out of each bottle neck. She passed them around, then handed Lana a bundle of napkins and a glass of ice. 'Best they could do in the first-aid department.'

Lana wrapped the ice cubes in a napkin and placed them against her ankle, wincing at the cold.

Kitty used a finger to push the lime into the belly of her beer bottle, then they all clinked bottles.

Behind them there was a crash of wood, followed by the sound of laughter, and Lana turned to see a giant Jenga tower had collapsed. Its builders were collecting the blocks, rebuking each other in Italian. Kitty turned back to the table and said, 'Great bar. Didn't even know it was here.'

'Real nice couple run it,' Denny said. 'They've definitely picked the right location.' He glanced out across the water to where the sun was getting lower, painting the water rose-gold. As he turned back, his gaze moved to the entrance. 'Ah,' he said. 'Here they are.'

Two men in their late twenties strolled across the bar, a younger blonde woman with bare feet walking between them. Denny waved them over and made the introductions.

Aaron, another Kiwi, who was square-jawed and thick-necked, stood with his hands gripped over the back of a chair. 'I picked up the part,' he told Denny, 'but I had to go to the mechanic's cousin's brother's shop.'

Denny rolled his eyes. 'What did they charge you?'

'Six thousand pesos.'

'Pretty good.'

Aaron nodded.

'No Joseph?'

Aaron raised an eyebrow, communicating something that Lana didn't understand. 'Right, I'll get the beers in.'

Heinrich, a German with even white teeth and a sensible haircut, pulled up a chair for the blonde girl, Shell, and set his next to it.

'What happened?' Shell asked, looking at the ice pressed to Lana's ankle.

'I got in the path of a runaway cockerel,' Lana said, lifting the napkin to reveal the swelling skin.

'Bloody kamikaze cockerels,' Kitty added.

Shell leant forward and pressed the backs of her fingers very gently against Lana's skin, a flock of slim silver bangles jangling on her wrist. She drew her fingers lightly around the edges of the swelling. 'Looks like a sprain. Keep topping up the ice tonight.'

Lana liked Shell immediately, sensing warmth in the wideness of her smile. She tried to decide whether Shell and Heinrich were a couple, but couldn't tell if their easy manner with one another was familiarity or intimacy.

Aaron returned with the drinks and conversation began to flow. Kitty was entertaining the table with a story of a love tryst she'd witnessed earlier between a slight Filipino woman and an ageing American. Lana was content to sit back and listen, trying to place the accents and dynamics of the friends who explained that they'd travelled through South-East Asia together.

A heady blend of beers and rum on a warm evening meant conversation flowed easily from one topic to another. Lana forgot the pain in her ankle and grinned at the colourful details she learnt about the others: Denny would only fall asleep in a Spider-Man outfit until he was nine years old; Heinrich was so competitive that he used to beg his brother to score him on how long he peed for; Shell's parents owned a cattle-feed store in Ontario and she used to go sledging on the wide plastic sacks the feed was delivered in; Aaron had once got lost in a rainforest on Réunion island and taken a badly aimed crap on an ants' nest.

Several more rounds of drinks were bought and drunk. Candles were lit and streams of white fairy lights began to twinkle around the bar as night arrived. When it was Kitty's round she ordered more beers, with a tray of chasers, and the noise around the table rose even louder.

'So what made you decide to travel? Why the Philippines?' Shell asked Lana, the group's attention turning to her.

Lana glanced down at her drink, her mouth turning dry as she thought about what led to her decision to leave England. She remembered her father's expression when he'd found her kneeling on the threadbare carpet of his bedroom with a Manila envelope in her hands: his features seemed to slide downwards, as if weighted by guilt.

Later the same night, she'd waited on Kitty's doorstep, rain dripping down the collar of her coat, her shoulders hunched against the biting wind. At her centre was a hollow, raw feeling, as if her insides had been carved out. Kitty had opened the door, taken one look at Lana and tugged her indoors, saying, 'Jesus! What the fuck's happened?'

At the time, Kitty had been renting a poky studio-flat in Ealing above a florist, and she'd led Lana into the cluttered main room where a double bed heaved with cushions and crochet throws. Kitty's clothes hung on two rails at the side of the room and her shoes were thrown in a trunk at the end of the bed. Her dressing table was covered with make-up, body lotions and bottles of perfume, and the whole place had the feel of a costume department.

Kitty plucked a fleecy dressing gown from the back of the door and wrapped it around Lana, who was trembling all over. She squeezed Lana's red hands. 'You're freezing. What's happened? Are you okay?'

'Can I stay?' Lana asked, her voice edged with tears.

'Of course! What's going on? Sorry it's so cold in here. Pissing landlord hasn't fixed the heating,' Kitty said, moving a hand to the plug-in radiator where two thongs and a tea towel were drying. 'I'll do us a hot-water bottle. And tea.'

A few minutes later they were sitting in bed with the covers pulled up, a hot-water bottle tucked between their feet. Lana cupped a mug of steaming tea to her chest, feeling her heart pounding against it. A tension headache pulsed at her temples as she began to talk. She told Kitty everything – about discovering the envelope hidden in her father's room, about the truth it contained, about how her father had no words to deny what he'd done.

Kitty listened with her eyes fixed on Lana's, her lips pressed together. Neither of them drank their tea.

By the time Lana finished talking, her face was streaked with tears. 'I'll never forgive him.'

'No!' Kitty had said suddenly, sitting forward. 'Don't say that. He made a mistake. A terrible mistake. But you mustn't hate him. You mustn't!' She spoke with such vehemence that her hands shook, a dribble of cold tea spilling onto the duvet.

Lana pushed the memory away now. She couldn't think about that day. Not out here. When she looked up, she realized everyone was watching her, still waiting for an answer.

'Spin of a globe,' Kitty said, coming to Lana's rescue. 'That's how we chose the Philippines, wasn't it?'

Lana nodded.

'I spun it – and Lana closed her eyes and pointed.'

Heinrich laughed. 'Really? That's brilliant.'

It was true – at least in part. It might not have been *why* they'd left, but it was *how* they'd chosen to come here. Lana had been sitting cross-legged on Kitty's bed with the globe in front of her. She'd closed her eyes and felt the lightest breath of air move against her fingertips as the globe spun. Then, as it slowed, she pressed her forefinger against its cool surface.

When she opened her eyes, her fingertip was placed in the centre of a mass of islands near the equator. She lifted her hand and read the name aloud: 'The Philippines.'

*

'More drinks?' the waitress asked, a tray propped against her hip.

The bar was crammed now, voices clamouring to be heard above the thudding music.

Aaron glanced at the watch on his thick wrist, then pushed back his chair and stood. 'I think we're done here, thank you.'

When the waitress left, Aaron turned to Lana and Kitty and said, 'We've got some rum back at ours that needs drinking. Gonna join us?'

*

Lana and Kitty wove behind the others with their arms linked, Lana trying to put little weight on her injured ankle. She'd tugged her hairband free, and her hair fell loose over one shoulder in thick waves of amber.

Ahead of them the group came to a stop by the shoreline. Lana could feel the effect of the beers she'd drunk – had it been five, or perhaps six? In the darkness she watched as Aaron untied a rope from a wooden post. The other end was attached to a small metal dinghy with an outboard engine, which he walked out into the shallows.

'What are you doing?' Kitty asked, a light slur to her question.

'Preparing your taxi.'

Shell, Heinrich and Denny kicked off their flip-flops and waded into the harbour. They climbed into the dinghy, which rocked from side to side, sending small waves rippling to shore.

'Where are we going?' Kitty asked, a grin spreading across her face.

'Back to our place,' Aaron told her.

'Your place is . . . a boat?'

In the moonlight, Lana caught Aaron's smile.

'Come on,' Denny called from the dinghy. 'You'll like it, we promise.'

Lana shrugged, then slipped off her sandals. The seabed was slimy beneath her soles and she tried not to think about what could be lurking in the dark, silent water.

It was a squeeze on board and Lana sat on a damp plank of wood, squashed between Shell and Kitty with her satchel and sketchbook on her lap.

Aaron yanked at the start cord and the motor spluttered to life.

The smell of diesel and fish rose from the harbour as they motored forward, clouds of cooler air brushing their skin. With the weight of them all, the dinghy sank close to the waterline, and Lana thought that if she reached a hand over the side she'd be able to trail her fingers across the surface.

The night was still and quiet as they passed fishing *bangkas*, which looked like colourful dugout canoes, drifting on their anchors. The others talked amongst themselves in an easy rhythm, but Lana and Kitty said nothing. They stared ahead as, through layers of darkness, the shadow of a yacht began to emerge, moonlight illuminating the curve of a dark-blue hull.

Lana widened her gaze to absorb it more fully. The yacht was elegant and long, with two masts standing guard. In the moonlight the name of the yacht, painted in a curling white script, came into focus. *The Blue.*

Lana turned those two words over on her tongue and, as she did so, a surge of something she couldn't quite define – excitement, anticipation, fear – pushed through her heart.

*

They were sitting towards the back of the yacht – the cockpit, someone called it, which had made Kitty giggle – drinking tall glasses of rum and Coke. Lana held a joint between her fingers that she couldn't remember being passed, and music played from a speaker somewhere on deck. The yacht rocked gently, like a lullaby from the sea, and Lana felt her body relaxing into its rhythm.

Shell had given them a tour below deck, showing them the main living area, which she called the saloon, and the narrow galley kitchen that was neatly kept except for a stack of empty beer bottles on the side. There were three cramped cabins at the front of the yacht, which contained bunks, and then two slightly larger cabins at the rear with double beds where Aaron and Denny slept.

Lana liked the simplicity of their living quarters, where everything smelt of warm wood and varnish. She'd never set foot on a yacht before and kept pausing, noticing details she wanted to sketch: the row of salt-curled paperbacks squashed together on a shelf in the saloon, bookended by a sturdy copy of *The Encyclopaedia of Cruising*; the two small hammocks attached to the galley ceiling filled with fruit; a pile of charts spread out on a table with a beautiful conch shell set on top as a paperweight.

Kitty finished her drink, then set down the glass, saying, 'I still can't believe you all live on a boat. Whose is it?'

'I'm the skipper,' Aaron said, who was sitting with his feet wide apart, a drink held easily in his large hands. That made sense; Lana had noticed the way he'd run his palm carefully over the wheel when they came aboard, his gaze moving across the deck – as if checking that everything was as it should be.

'So you just sail around from place to place, deciding where you want to stop?' Kitty asked.

He nodded. 'Pretty much.'

From what Lana could tell there were five crew: Aaron, Denny, Heinrich, Shell and then a fifth member, Joseph, who'd been smoking alone at the bow when they'd arrived. Denny had asked if he wanted to join them, but Joseph had waved a hand in the air as he sloped by, saying in a lilting French accent that sleep was calling.

As the night wore on, more rum was poured – and then more still. Lana let the conversations wash around her, hearing bursts of Kitty's laughter, which had taken on a loose, almost liquid sound. As the yacht turned lazily on its anchor, she watched the lights from the town flickering in the distance across the inky water. She had no idea that this was only the beginning.

3

THEN

Lana woke to the sensation that she was swaying. A deep throbbing resonated through her skull and she lifted a hand, rubbing the heel of it against her forehead. Though her eyes were closed, she could sense sunlight and became distantly aware of an engine running and the sound of water nearby.

Gradually her eyelids peeled open – and she saw not walls or a ceiling, but sky. She blinked, squinting against searing daylight. A breeze brushed against her face and she tried to push herself upright, but everything seemed to move, tilt, swing. She struggled – but it was as if the bed, the very ground, was sinking away from her. Then she realized: she and Kitty were in a hammock. She turned her head, sending a new shock of pain around her skull, and saw sea, sky, the deck of a yacht.

'Kit . . .' she croaked.

Kitty came out of sleep as if she'd been plugged into the mains. She sat bolt upright, her hair wild, eyes wide. 'Yes? What?'

Lana blinked again, searching out the harbour, the fishing

bangkas, the town – but land was just a blur of muted shadows behind them. 'We're moving.'

'Holy fucking shit! What happened last night?' Kitty exclaimed, half-laughing.

'Tanduay Rhum happened,' Shell said, gliding across the deck barefoot, holding out two mugs of coffee.

Lana reached for one. 'My God, you lifesaver.'

'Have you kidnapped us?' Kitty asked, taking her coffee.

Shell smiled. 'Aaron wanted to sail to a spot up the coast on high tide, so he set out early. You'll be back at the harbour by lunchtime.'

Kitty ran a knuckle beneath each eye and pulled on her sunglasses, which had miraculously survived a night on the hammock.

'Were you okay up here?' Shell asked. 'I use the hammock when it's too hot below deck, but it can get a little damp.'

'I don't think we'd have noticed where we slept,' Lana said, looking out to sea as they were motoring forward. Then she manoeuvred her legs out of the hammock, wincing at the hot ache in her ankle as she stood.

'How is it?' Kitty asked.

Lana experimented with putting weight on it. 'Not too bad.'

'Good morning.'

Lana and Kitty both turned to see the Frenchman, Joseph, approaching. He had a thin, angular face and wore a rumpled shirt over a pair of shorts, his dark hair foppish and uncut.

'Sorry I didn't stay and meet you properly last night,' Joseph said on reaching them. 'You had a good time, yes?'

'I think so – from what we can remember of it,' Kitty replied.

'We're still trying to get our heads round the fact that you all live here, on this boat,' Lana added.

'Yes, me also.' Joseph smiled. 'We're all lucky to have found it.'

She nodded in agreement. 'How long have you been on board?'

'Me – only five weeks. But very good five weeks. The others have been here much longer—'

Joseph was interrupted by a shout from Aaron. 'Shell! Joseph!'

They all turned. Aaron was standing at the helm wearing a sun-faded cap and polarized glasses. There was something authoritative about his stance, the widely planted feet, the single hand resting on the wheel, the lift of his chin. 'Let's get the sails up.'

Joseph turned back to Lana and Kitty. 'Time to see us at work.'

*

Sound filled Lana's ears: the wild flapping of the sail as it was hoisted, the creak and strain of the sheets then the rush of wind as it filled the sail, making it snap out full and proud. The yacht heeled to the side and Lana gripped tightly to the wire lifeline that ran around the perimeter of the deck.

A moment later the engine was cut and the noise of the motor slipped away so that all that remained was wind and waves. She craned her neck, mesmerized by the muscular curve of the sail as it stretched into a cloudless blue sky.

Lana had never been on a boat – let alone a yacht like this – and she was awed by the sheer magnificence of being propelled through the sea by the power of wind. There was something so elemental, so stunningly powerful, about it. The wind toyed with the hem of her dress and mussed through her hair – and she breathed in deeply, filling her lungs with the warm salt air.

She looked down the length of the yacht, taking in the weathered teak deck where swathes of rope were neatly coiled, and a paddleboard and two surfboards were lashed to the railings with bungee cords. She thought, *This is another life – another world.*

Denny appeared from below deck wearing a faded grey trucker's cap, his tight curls pinging out at the sides. His gaze found Lana and he smiled. 'Joining us?'

'Looks that way.'

Kitty and Lana watched as the crew moved expertly around the yacht – an effortless dance in which everyone knew their role. Barefoot and tanned, they seemed like an exotic race of travellers blown in from a faraway shore.

They'd been sailing for an hour when Denny pointed towards the front of the boat and said to Lana and Kitty, 'You two should stand at the bow. We'll be going close in.'

They picked their way carefully forwards, the breeze gently buffeting them both. Kitty slipped an arm around Lana's waist, leaning her head against her shoulder. They watched the coast reveal itself until they were sailing towards a towering rocky pinnacle where trees and bushes grew at odd angles from cracks in the limestone.

'Isn't this insane?' Kitty said. 'Can you believe we woke up on a fucking yacht?'

'I know,' Lana grinned. 'Beats waking up on a bus.' Last

summer they'd gone to a gig in London, and afterwards Kitty had talked their way onto the tour bus. They'd woken eight hours later at Wolverhampton Services with atrocious hangovers and only £23 between them to get home.

Beneath the sun, the sea glistened. Lana leant over, peering down at the shallowing water, which lightened to an aquamarine – coral wavering in and out of view as they glided forwards. 'God, I'm so pleased we're not in England.'

Kitty glanced at her sideways. 'You feeling okay about everything?'

By *everything*, Lana knew that Kitty was referring to her father. 'I am right now.'

The nose of the yacht drew so close to the rocks that Kitty suddenly stretched her hands into the air as if she could touch them. The yacht hugged the cliff line, and then it edged around a craggy point.

There, opening up before them, was an emerald-green lagoon framed by dramatic pinnacles rising out of the water. A serene white-sand beach curved between the pinnacles, backed by an impenetrable forest.

Kitty turned to Lana, grinning. 'I think we've just stumbled across paradise.'

*

They anchored in the lagoon, then all crammed into the dinghy to go on shore.

When they stepped onto the beach, Lana dug her fingers

through the sand, which was made of thousands of beautiful, tiny shells and fragments of white coral.

Shell lay a blanket in the shade beneath a palm tree, and Lana and Kitty joined her. They were still in yesterday's clothes and were thankful to have been wearing their bikinis beneath them. Kitty tugged off her shorts and edged into the sun, lying back using her arms as a pillow, her stomach stretching taut. Lana remained sitting, propping her elbows on her knees as she listened to Shell, who was telling them the story of *The Blue* as she plaited fine strands of leather into a bracelet.

'The first I heard of it was from a group of travellers in Vietnam. There'd been rumours about this floating commune of sailors, wanderers and adventurers. They said that they'd seen the yacht travelling around, and the crew were stopping at remote bays, anchoring off empty shores, sleeping under the stars, surfing crowdless breaks, fishing for their meals. To me it sounded like heaven,' she said, her facing blooming into a smile.

'So I travelled from Vietnam, heading west for Thailand in search of *The Blue*. I'm not sure I truly believed that it existed – but miraculously, I found her. She was anchored in a quiet bay in the west of Ko Samui. The moment I saw her I knew I had to find a way to get on board.'

Shell put down the leather she'd been plaiting and told them, 'I swam out to the yacht and introduced myself to this guy sitting in the cockpit mending a sail – who happened to be Aaron. He was making a hash of the sail, so I showed him how to make a stronger pattern of stitches. My dad's a sailor,' she added, 'so I've done my fair share of sail repairs. I spent the afternoon helping, and once the sail was fixed, I asked Aaron if I could join *The Blue*.

'There weren't any free berths at the time, but I said I was happy with the hammock. I spent the first three weeks sleeping beneath the stars, waking up covered in dew and mosquito bites – but I loved every moment. Then a Danish guy left and I took over his berth. That was fourteen months ago now.

'Denny's been here the longest: he joined Aaron in Australia. After him a couple of lovely Swiss girls joined. They left about three months ago.' Shell confided, 'I'm heartbroken. I was rather in love with one of them, Lea. Totally one-sided of course – she had a boyfriend back in Switzerland – but still, she was wonderful. There've been a few other crew – some stay for weeks, others for months. Heinrich's been with us for almost six months now. He's a good guy. Great to have around the boat. I swear he can fix anything – engine parts, cupboard doors, bilge pumps – you name it. Joseph is our newest crew member. He tends to keep himself to himself, but from what I can see, he loves being out here.' Shell opened her hands and said, 'So that's all of us.'

Lana glanced across at Kitty. They held each other's eye, a current of excitement firing between them as they both under-stood: they had to find a way of becoming part of this.

*

Lana fell asleep in the shade. She was awoken some time later by a dig in the ribs from Kitty, who whispered, 'Where is everyone?'

Lana sat up, rubbing her eyes and squinting against the bright

31

sun. Shell was gone from beside them and, as Lana took in the empty bay – the hard white of the coral sand, the clear blue water fringing the beach – she realized she couldn't see any of the crew. The shoreline was empty. She and Kitty were on a deserted stretch of coastline, only accessible by boat.

Just as the first sparks of fear were beginning to ignite, Kitty suddenly pointed towards the left-hand side of the cove. 'The dinghy. It's still there.'

'Jesus,' Lana said, placing a hand to her chest. 'You almost gave me a heart attack – I thought they'd left us.'

On the far side of the dinghy the crew were gathered in a circle, talking. Lana watched as each took turns to speak, their expressions serious. Denny sat with his arms folded over his lean chest, nodding. When Joseph was talking, Aaron turned to glance in Lana and Kitty's direction. Lana wasn't sure if he was looking at them or not, so she lifted her hand in an awkward half-wave. He didn't acknowledge her, simply turned back to the others.

Shell had described the crew as wanderers and adventurers but, as Lana watched them, she wondered whether it was a thirst for adventure that had brought them out here – or whether they all had a reason for leaving their old lives behind.

'It was the right thing, wasn't it?' Lana said suddenly, facing Kitty. 'Leaving.'

The night that Lana had turned up at Kitty's flat in a state of shock about her father, she'd made a decision that she was going to leave England. Kitty had held Lana's shoulders, looked at her squarely and told her, 'Then I'm coming, too.'

They'd talked further the following morning, Kitty ladling

pancake mixture into a pan of hot oil as she confided, 'I've been thinking for a while of giving up on the acting. It's getting me down,' she explained, tilting the pan so the batter spread evenly to the edges. 'The auditions. The rejections. The bitching. Last week I turned up at an audition for a vacuum-cleaner advert – a fucking *advert* – and the guy said, "Come back when you're not hungover."' Kitty had snorted. 'I hadn't even had a bloody drink! Can you believe that?'

'What, that you hadn't had a drink?'

Kitty had flicked out a hand and bashed Lana's arm. 'I'm just not sure I can face it any more.'

'But you're amazing at what you do.'

'Am I?' Kitty had said, loosening the edges of the pancake with a wooden spatula. 'Maybe I thought I was at school, but in London every attention-seeking twenty-something seems like they're trying to make it – and believe me, there are a lot of us. It's hard, Lana. The constant rejections are crushing me. And . . . well, the thing is, I don't even know what else I'd do. I'm not good at anything.' Kitty flipped the pancake and it landed neatly back in the pan.

'You're a good pancake tosser.'

'Curriculum vitae of Kitty Berry – experienced tosser.'

Over that long weekend in Kitty's dingy studio-flat, while the rain fell in thick sweeps against the window panes, they'd spun the globe and concocted their plan to leave.

Lana had been surprised at how easy it was to dismantle her life. It'd taken a month to work her notice, move out of her shared flat, and sell her car. She and Kitty planned to start in the

Philippines, and then travel on from there. They pooled their savings, then drew up a budget to see how long it would last them both, deciding to apply for work visas when the money ran out. They booked travel insurance, bought suncream, flip-flops and mosquito repellent, and had vaccinations for diphtheria and hepatitis A. The frenzy of activity was so consuming that Lana felt as if she hadn't paused for breath until suddenly they were clanking down the metal plane stairway into the dense Filipino heat.

Now Kitty turned towards Lana, sunlight making her eyes glitter. 'Leaving?' Kitty repeated. Then her face bloomed into a smile as she said, 'Best decision we've ever made.'

*

Lana waded into the shallows, feeling the cool grasp of the sea around her legs. Kitty hadn't wanted to swim, so Lana pushed away from the shoreline alone, marvelling at the incredible feeling of weightlessness. When she was a little deeper, she ducked below the surface letting her body trail close to the seabed until her breath ran out.

She surfaced, then swam hard for a few minutes, feeling the muscles in her shoulders and legs tighten. When she reached a cluster of low-lying rocks, she pulled herself onto them, wrung the salt water from her long hair and leant back against the sun-warmed limestone.

Sometime later she saw a tanned back skimming along the surface, a snorkel pipe in the air. Denny lifted his head and, noticing her, he pulled the mask from his face, treading water.

'See much?' she asked.

'Some amazing brain coral. Plenty of angelfish around, too.' He clambered up the rock and plonked himself beside her, his shorts sending rivulets of water streaming towards her legs.

Looking down the line of her shins towards her feet, he asked, 'How's the ankle?'

'Pretty good, thanks.'

His gaze shifted to her other ankle and he asked, 'How long you had the ink?'

Lana looked at the black tattoo of a single wing of long black feathers. 'Since I was seventeen. Kitty and I were supposed to get matching wings – but she fainted when she saw the tattoo-ist's needle.'

He laughed. 'But you had yours done anyway.'

As they'd walked out of the parlour, Kitty had been bouncing around on the spot, saying, 'I can't believe you did it! Lana, you have a fucking tattoo! How cool is that? Your dad is going to go ballistic!' But her dad said nothing. She wasn't even sure he'd seen it. She went barefoot around the house, putting her feet up on the coffee table, but he either didn't notice or simply chose not to pass comment.

Denny leant forward and placed his damp fingers on the tattoo. She felt heat spread from the point at which his skin connected with hers, and she stared at the spot as if she'd find it aglow.

'It's different,' he said, looking at her sideways, and she couldn't work out if he meant different-good or different-bad. She could feel warmth beginning to creep into her cheeks, and scrabbled to think of something to say. 'Do you and Aaron know each other from back home? You're both from New Zealand, aren't you?'

'New Zealand's a big place,' Denny said with an easy smile. 'I joined *The Blue* in Australia.'

She nodded. 'How do you all do this? This lifestyle that you have – sailing around the world with friends, living from one day to the next. It seems so . . .' She paused, looking for the word. '. . . intangible.'

'Intangible?' Denny smiled, the sun catching in the golden hairs of his eyebrows. 'I like that.'

'But how do any of you afford it?' she asked, then wondered if the question sounded rude.

'We try and keep costs down, live simply. We all put in a hundred and fifty dollars a week to cover food, water, fuel and marina fees when there are any. If there's anything left over it goes into the repairs fund. Some people had savings, plus we pick up work where we can. Like Shell – she makes jewellery and sells it in the tourist spots, and when we're in port she teaches a few yoga classes, too. I know Joseph had some money put aside from before. I'm not too sure what Heinrich's set up is; he said he's going to be running dry soon. And then me – I work while I'm out here.'

'Doing what?' Lana asked.

'I'm a translator. Of novels. French into English.'

'I've never met a translator. What an interesting job,' she said, looking at him afresh. 'Is there an art to it? I can't imagine how you go about replicating an author's meaning in a different language.'

'That's what I love – trying to find the author's voice and then convey it. Humour's the hardest. It's all wordplay and timing, which doesn't always translate so easily.'

'Where did you learn French?'

'Went on a family trip to Réunion island as a teenager. It's French-speaking. Loved it so much that I decided to study French for my degree as I got to spend a year of it on Réunion. After I graduated I worked in-house for a technical firm translating documents, but it didn't suit me. Too much looking out a window longing to be someplace else, y'know? So I moved to fiction, went freelance.'

Lana nodded, understanding that longing to be somewhere else. She thought of the endless grey days at the insurance firm where she worked following her art degree – any hint of creative ambition stifled by the need to pay rent. She'd lived for her lunch breaks just so she could walk through the park and see daylight.

A loud whistle sounded from the shore. She turned and saw Aaron gesturing to the dinghy.

Denny glanced at her with something like regret in his expression. 'Looks like it's time to head back.'

*

It was mid-afternoon when *The Blue* returned to harbour. There was no mention of the girls joining the crew, and neither Lana nor Kitty felt comfortable asking. Aaron ran them ashore in the dinghy, and they sat together watching silently as the yacht shrank in their wake.

Lucy Clarke

The noise and heat of town seemed to thicken the closer they drew to land, like a gathering thunderstorm. Lana's earlier ebullience deflated as she thought of the sweltering heat of their guest room and the stringy kebabs they'd probably pick up for dinner in town after fighting their way through the crowds, street dogs and litter.

Aaron tied up the dinghy and held it steady as the girls climbed out. The ground seemed unstable after a night and day at sea and Lana felt as if she were swaying.

She hooked her bag across her shoulders, glancing at *The Blue* for a final time. The day had taken on a surreal quality – as if Lana and Kitty had swum into a dream from which they were only now waking.

Lana pushed her hands into the wide pockets of her dress and faced Aaron. 'Thank you. It's been an incredible day.'

'Yes!' Kitty chimed at her shoulder. 'Amazing. Literally the best day of our entire trip. That beach was just . . . unreal. We'll never—'

'Be back here in two hours with your stuff,' Aaron interrupted. 'We set sail at eighteen hundred hours.'

Lana blinked, staring at Aaron. He was leaning back against the nose of the dinghy, arms folded across his chest, his face expressionless. 'Sorry?'

Beside her, Kitty's mouth was beginning to split into a smile. 'Are you saying . . . we can join the crew?'

'We took a vote on it and you're in. Joseph is going to bunk in with Heinrich, so there's a free cabin if you want it.'

'Holy shit!' Kitty exclaimed, clamping her hands over her mouth.

'Are you serious? We can join the crew?' Lana asked.

He nodded. 'But I haven't told you the conditions yet.'

'Anything,' Kitty said.

'There are four rules. You break them, you're out.'

They nodded vigorously.

'One. Everyone pulls their weight – that includes cooking, cleaning, laundry, sailing, night watches – anything that needs doing. Don't wait to be asked. Get stuck in. I know you don't have any sailing experience, but I expect you to learn. Fast. Two. All important decisions are made by group vote – where we travel, what we buy, who comes aboard. Once made, the vote stands. Three. No relationships between the crew. We don't need the complication.'

Kitty arched an eyebrow. 'You run a celibate boat?'

'I never said anything about celibacy. I just said no *relationships*.'

Kitty grinned.

'And four,' Aaron continued. 'I'm not a nanny so don't expect me to act like one. Everyone's responsible for their own safety – we've got life jackets, harnesses, a life raft, flares and an EPIRB on board. Ask one of the crew to show you how they all work, and wear your life jacket or safety harness whenever you see fit.'

He ran a hand over the back of his head, the stubble of his shaven head scraping against his palm. 'So what d'you reckon? Still coming?'

Lana turned and looked over her shoulder towards the yacht, a bright, effervescent sensation filling her. She found Kitty's fingers and squeezed them tightly between her own. 'We're coming.'

4

NOW

Lana paces through her apartment, her fingers buried deep in the pockets of her dress. The painting she was working on is drying, unfinished. On a normal day, she would be getting ready for work by this time. But she can't even think about going into the gallery and making coffees for customers. She can't think of anything but *The Blue*.

She knows that the Maritime Rescue Centre, which will be dealing with the rescue of the crew, is only 30 kilometres away – she passes the sign for it each month when she goes to the art supplies wholesaler for her boss. She grabs her mobile and searches the Internet for the number.

When she finds it, she sits on the edge of her bed and makes the call. It takes several minutes to be connected to anyone associated with the rescue of *The Blue*. Eventually she is transferred to Paul Carter, the Operations Coordinator, who has a broad New Zealand accent and tells her that they are not at liberty to give out any details.

'Look,' she says, banging the heel of her hand against the wooden bed frame, making a dull thud. 'Just tell me if Kitty Berry was on board. She's British. She's got no family out here. I can get in touch with them.'

Lana doesn't know where the authority in her tone has sprung from, but she knows she will not be ending this call until she has an answer.

After a moment she hears the sigh of someone acquiescing. 'Okay, give me a minute.'

As she waits, she bites the edge of her thumbnail, her skin tasting faintly of turpentine. She finds herself thinking of the first time she met Kitty. They were eleven years old and the summer term had just begun. Lana was grateful for the warmer weather because it meant that at lunchtimes she could sit alone in a sunny corner of the playing fields, and didn't need to stand around in the courtyard trying to make herself look invisible. She'd take out her exercise book and fill the back pages with wild shapes – swirls of smoke, twisting currents of water, clouds that billowed and bloomed from the pages.

She had seen Kitty around – they lived in the same street and took the same bus to school – but they'd never spoken. Kitty styled her glossy dark hair in a high ponytail, pulling thin wisps of it loose around her temples. She was often followed around by a loud group of boys who wore their backpacks so low that they bounced against their bony arses.

Lana had been sitting cross-legged, watching a feathery seed from a dandelion drifting towards her on a whisper of breeze. She was mesmerized as it turned through the air, daylight catching in its white softness. She wondered what it would feel like to be that weightless. She reached a hand up into the air and caught it gently in the palm of her hand, imagining its tickle against her skin. Then she closed her eyes and made a wish. She wasn't sure that you were meant to wish on dandelions, but she'd done it anyway.

When she opened her eyes, she carefully unfurled her fingers and – for a moment – it rested right there on the centre of her palm, as if she had tamed it. A few seconds later it lifted off, carried upwards on a current of air.

'What you doing?' Kitty was standing nearby, her school bag hanging off one shoulder.

'Making a wish,' she said. She felt her cheeks flush, cross that she'd not thought of something better than the truth.

'What did you wish?'

'You can't tell people, otherwise they don't come true.'

Kitty shrugged. Then she bent down and plucked a dandelion from the long grass near the fence line and held it up to her lips. 'You can tell the time by blowing a dandelion. Watch.' She blew with short puffs of air, making the seeds whirl. By her sixth puff there was only one seed remaining. Kitty adjusted her puffs so they became gentle, until her twelfth one – when she blew with all her might, sending the remaining seed dancing into the sky.

'That was twelve.' She pushed her wrist in front of Lana to reveal her purple watch. 'Twelve o'clock. See?'

Lana laughed.

Kitty's brow dipped. 'What? It's true.'

'All right.'

They were both silent and Lana wished she hadn't laughed, thinking Kitty was going to leave now. But after a minute or so, Kitty said, 'So why d'you always sit on your own?'

Lana watched a ladybird crawl up a blade of grass near her feet, making the blade tremble and bend. 'I dunno. Why are you on your own?'

'I'm not. I'm talking to you.' Kitty shook her head a little, making her high ponytail swing. Lana wondered whether Kitty was wearing mascara as her eyelashes looked so dark and long. Lana had her father's eyelashes – auburn and short – as well as his amber hair. But her long, straight nose and olive skin came from her mother. People often remarked upon Lana's unusual colouring, and she liked telling them, *My father's a redhead, but my mother was Greek.*

'Anyway, I'm looking for daffodils,' Kitty announced.

'How come?'

'It's my mum's birthday today.' Kitty looked at her from the corners of her eyes, then added, 'She's dead though.'

Lana stared back. With their gazes pinned to each other, she found herself saying, 'Mine, too.'

If Kitty had been surprised, she hadn't shown it. 'My mum died when I was seven. Cancer. How old were you?'

'Three.'

Lana told Kitty about the car accident. Even though she hadn't been with her mother, the events of the day felt imprinted on her as if she'd lived through every frame. It was a Thursday morning; her mother was driving to the supermarket when a lorry hurtling along in the other direction had braked hard to avoid a car that pulled out in front of it. The lorry began jackknifing across the road. Tons of metal swung into Lana's mother's Renault 5, killing her on impact.

When other people heard what had happened to Lana's mother, their expressions filled with pity and they spoke to her in a soft, special voice. But not Kitty. She listened with her head tilted to one side, her eyes locked on Lana.

After a moment Kitty said, 'My mum died in a hospice. On her own. My dad was sitting in our car, smoking, and I was trying to find somewhere to change a pound coin so I could get a drink from the vending machine. When I came back to her ward, a bed sheet was pulled over her face.'

The two girls eyed one another in silence. Then Lana stood, picked up her bag and said, 'Come on. I'll show you where the best daffodils are.'

*

From the other end of the phone line Lana hears the man speak, the receiver pressed close to his mouth. 'Yes,' he says. 'Kitty Berry is on the crew list.'

Lana's heart clenches tight as a fist, her eyes squeezing shut.

So Kitty has still been on the yacht after all these months. After everything that had happened, Lana wonders if Kitty could still enjoy lying back in the hammock, watching the shooting stars blaze across the sky as they'd once done together.

She runs the heel of her hand back and forth across her forehead. 'What happened out there? How did the yacht get into trouble?'

'I'm not able to disclose any information just yet,' Paul Carter says.

Lana grits her teeth with frustration. 'Have you found her? Found any of them?'

There is a pause in which she hears the man clearing his throat. 'I'm sorry. The entire crew is missing.'

*

Lana puts down the phone and remains sitting on the edge of the bed. It is almost impossible to picture *The Blue* somewhere out there in these waters. *Sunk.*

There was a life raft, she knows. It was stored in a canister at the stern, which she'd sometimes lean against, her legs stretched out in the sun. She wonders when the raft was last checked, and whether the grab bag was properly stocked, too.

She can picture the yacht easily – the teak deck warm beneath the soles of her feet; the white mainsail billowing with wind; the light slosh and draw of waves against the hull as the yacht turns lazily on its anchor. But she cannot bring to mind that same yacht struggling in the ocean as water washes on board, creeping down the hatch into the saloon where they all used to sit together for dinner. She cannot picture the sea steadily rising up over the floor, enveloping the lockers and cupboards stocked with food, blankets, torches and ropes, then creeping higher, bleeding over the photos pinned to the saloon wall and flooding the shelves of well-thumbed books. She cannot imagine the crew wading through salt water, while sodden charts, packets of food, loose clothes and toiletries float around them.

A yacht like that just doesn't sink. It was built to handle the open ocean, rough seas. *What the hell happened?*

Lana raises herself to her feet and crosses the room to the window.

For months Lana tried her best to distance herself from the yacht and crew. She closed a door of her mind because behind it lay a beautiful, bright pain – and even opening it a crack seared. In some ways, she's succeeded. She made a fresh start here in New Zealand, yet there are moments – if she catches sight of the swoop of a sail on the horizon, or hears a wave breaking onto the shore – then *The Blue* sails back into her thoughts. Sometimes all it takes to remember is a shopkeeper's lilting accent, which sends Denny spiralling into her mind, or the sight of two friends walking with their heads pressed together, making her miss Kitty with a deep ache.

Now that she has heard this news, it feels as though each of the memories she has hidden away is unwinding, link by link, like an anchor chain dragging her downwards. She feels the weight of each memory pulling her deeper: thick fingers gripped around the pale skin of a throat; Shell's tear-stricken face as she stepped forward at the bow to speak; dark waves lashing at the deck as the rigging shrieked in the wind; Kitty's hollow-eyed gaze as she raised her hand into the air; the deep-red bloom of blood that stained the deck.

Back then, if Lana had known everything she does now, she wonders whether she'd ever have set foot on *The Blue*.

5

THEN

Lana stood at the helm, her hands resting on the sun-warmed wheel. A glowing red sun was lowering itself towards the sea, washing the water pink.

She turned to Kitty, whose skin looked a deep bronze in the evening light, the lenses of her sunglasses reflecting the fire of the sunset, and said, 'I can't help thinking that at any moment someone's going to come along and tell us we're in the wrong place.'

'I know,' Kitty agreed. 'We're out here sailing a fucking yacht together! Life doesn't get much better, does it?'

This would be their fifth night on board *The Blue,* and they'd both fallen hopelessly in love with every aspect of it: the long hours spent snorkelling over coral gardens and exploring empty coves where wild mangoes grew; learning how to handle the sails and steer a course; cooking meals in the narrow galley kitchen with the view of the sea through the porthole; talking on deck until the early hours with rum warm in their throats.

'Listen to this,' Kitty said, lifting her hands towards Lana's ear and rubbing her palms together. They made a rough scraping sound where the skin had become dry and callused from hauling the ropes – or *sheets* as Aaron had taught the girls to call them. 'That's my body's way of telling me I'm not cut out for manual work. I'm going to see if Shell's got any moisturizer.'

Kitty disappeared below deck, and Lana turned her attention to the plotter screen, checking their course and position. They were sailing to a small island Aaron had noticed on the charts, where they planned to anchor for the night. Aaron had a nose for searching out secluded bays and sheltered nooks of the coastline, preferring the adventure of discovering somewhere new rather than mooring up in a marina with the yachting crowd.

Two nights ago they'd anchored on the lee side of a tiny island that had just sixty inhabitants. Almost as soon as they'd dropped anchor, a dozen village kids swam out to the yacht. Aaron invited them on board and they'd stood dripping wet at the stern, smiling shyly and giggling. Denny had fetched a bag of sweets and within a few minutes the kids were exploring the yacht. They were mesmerized by the computer, the array of books in the saloon, and the music that played from Shell's iPod.

Lana was beginning to gain an understanding of how the yacht moved. It was less reactive than a car, with adjustments taking longer, so when she turned the wheel one way it took a few seconds for the boat to follow. It was a strange sensation to steer from the back of a vessel and she kept pushing herself up onto tiptoes, peering over the bow to check the way was clear.

Aaron came up on deck holding an apple in his wide palm. He stood beside her, slipping a knife from the sheath that was fixed to the console. It was housed there for emergencies, like cutting a trapped line, or to protect themselves should they ever be boarded. Aaron wiped the blade against his shorts, then carefully sliced the first curve of the apple, lifting it to his mouth on the blade edge.

'How you going?' Aaron asked, as he crunched through the crisp flesh of the fruit.

'Good, I think. We've been averaging about six to seven knots.'

He nodded, then didn't say anything for some time. He watched the water, a peaceful expression settling into his features and softening the deep grooves that lined his forehead.

She wondered how old Aaron must be. The rest of the crew were in their twenties – Shell being the baby of the group at twenty-two – but Aaron seemed more life-worn: in his early thirties perhaps. It was still a young age to own a yacht the size of *The Blue*. Even though the yacht wasn't one of the modern, expensive new models they occasionally passed, it was sizeable at 50 feet. Aaron had told her it was an ex-charter yacht that he'd bought in New Zealand. It had the feel of a well-loved family home where each corner had a story to tell. She liked the rustic charm of the heavily varnished wood below deck that had turned an orangey colour over the years, and the quirks of how certain latches and doors had to be opened at a precise angle to make them work. He'd set up solar panels on deck, and a wind turbine too, and was eager that their travels left as little wake as possible.

'Shell was telling me that your first voyage on *The Blue* was from New Zealand to Australia?'

He nodded slowly.

'Some journey. Brave to do it single-handedly.'

'Or foolish.' He cut another slice of apple, crunching it between his teeth as he looked at the line of islands ahead, which were beginning to reveal craggy rock faces.

'What made you decide to do it?'

'Wanted a new experience, I guess.'

Lana thought about his answer: Aaron had bought a yacht, spent six months refitting it, then sailed off single-handedly. There must have been a compelling reason to make him take on such a challenge. Or, she thought, a compelling reason to make him want to leave New Zealand. 'What did you do before this? Before setting sail?'

Aaron looked steadily ahead. He spoke slowly and clearly as he said, 'I did a lot of things before this, Lana. But what I do now is sail.' He cut a final slice of apple, then returned the knife to its sheaf before wandering away to the bow. He stood alone, one hand on the lifeline, his gaze on the water.

The wind continued to blow.

*

It was dusk by the time they'd finally finished anchoring in a spot Aaron was comfortable with. Once everything was done, he called the crew into the saloon, where they all squeezed around the main table.

Aaron remained standing, saying, 'We need a quick group vote. We're spending the night here – possibly tomorrow night, too. After that I wanted to find out where people would like to go next. We've got a couple of options.' Flattening out a chart in the centre of the table, Aaron explained how they could tour the islands north-east of here where there were some great surf breaks, but that the sailing might be rough – or they could head south-east into more protected waters, where the snorkelling and diving were meant to be spectacular.

When he'd finished explaining the options, he asked for everyone's vote, giving his own first. 'I'm in favour of going north. It'd be good to see if there's any swell running.'

Shell, who was sitting beside him, voted next. 'Sorry, but I'm going to say south. I'd rather be snorkelling than wave-hunting.'

Heinrich voted in agreement with Shell, while Denny and Joseph voted with Aaron. Then it was just Lana and Kitty remaining.

'North or south?' Aaron asked them.

Lana felt oddly privileged to be included in the voting, as if it made them valued members of the crew. It was a fair and democratic system, and she respected Aaron for implementing it when, as skipper, he'd have been within his rights to make all the decisions himself.

'Both routes sound amazing, but I'd love to do some more snorkelling, so I'm going to vote south,' Lana said.

Kitty agreed – and so the decision was made.

'You ever get the impression,' Denny said to Aaron as everyone started getting to their feet, 'that we're not going to make the pro surf tour after all?'

'Tough break,' Aaron said, slapping a hand on Denny's shoulder.

*

After the group vote, Lana and Kitty made dinner for the crew, stir-frying shellfish that Denny had gathered earlier in the day.

They served the food in plastic bowls and carried them up on deck, where a light breeze stirred the moonlit bay. Lana sat with her back against the lifeline, studying the curved shadow of the island ahead. The island, Topeu, shown on the charts as being less than 0.5 kilometres wide, was reputed to have fantastic rock formations and cliffs, which Lana was looking forward to exploring in the morning.

After dinner, Shell and Heinrich cleared the bowls, rinsing them in a large bucket of sea water and then taking them below deck to finish them off with fresh water. Aaron was fastidious about saving water; showers were a luxury that usually lasted three minutes, and washing up was done in an inch of water. They had a tank on board that was filled up whenever possible, but in the remote areas they sailed through, it wasn't always easy to find somewhere to do so. Catching rainwater was helpful, but they had a desalinator installed as a backup, though the pump was noisy and drained a lot of energy and the small amounts of water it produced tasted flat.

Heinrich returned to the deck with a bottle of rum and a tray of glasses and, like most nights, the crew talked and drank and laughed as the yacht dozed at its anchor. Lana sat a little way apart from the others, her gaze cast at the sky, which was a deep velvet black, shot through with starlight. The warm breeze, scented with salt and earth, moved her hair against her shoulders, and she could hear crickets calling from somewhere on land.

There was a roar of laughter, and Lana looked around. Kitty was at the centre of the group recounting a story from the last play she'd been in. 'That,' she said, pausing theatrically, 'was when I realized – he wasn't wearing *anything*. Stark. Bollock. Naked!'

Shell clapped her hands together. Heinrich snorted.

Denny leant across the table and picked up the rum. He topped up the glasses of those nearest him, then stood and walked over to Lana with the bottle. 'More?'

'Thank you,' she said, holding out her glass.

Once he'd refilled it, he sat down beside her, pressing his back against the guardrail.

Lana turned to him. 'Does it ever wear off? The beauty of doing this?'

He took a drink and considered the question. 'Maybe the freshness fades a little – you know, that excitement of the *first* time you anchor, the *first* night swim, the *first* time you're out of sight of land. But, no, I don't think the beauty wears off.'

She nodded, pleased with the answer. She tried to imagine being out of sight of land, wondering how many miles you'd need to sail before the coast slipped away completely.

Denny asked, 'How long d'you think you and Kitty will stay on?'

The Blue was heading for its home port in the Bay of Islands,

New Zealand, which Aaron wanted to reach by November or December at the latest because of the cyclone season. The loose route they were aiming for was sailing east from the Philippines to Palau. Then they'd head south-east to Papua New Guinea, Fiji and finally New Zealand. Everything was dependent upon the weather, so nothing was fixed. Lana would love to stay for the entire journey, which would take around eight months, but realistically their money would only last another three months or so – and that's if they were careful. 'I suppose we'll travel as far as we can afford.'

He nodded.

Up ahead at the bow, Lana noticed a flicker of light as Joseph lit a cigarette. Most evenings he sat alone, writing in a slim leather notebook that he kept tucked in his shirt pocket. She could relate to his need for some time to himself because, much as she loved being on the yacht, there was almost no privacy: you shared cabins, ate meals as a group, worked together, social-ized together, and if you walked twenty paces you'd have crossed from one end of the boat to the other.

She asked Denny, 'What's Joseph's story?'

'We picked him up on this remote little island, five or six weeks back – it was Christmas Eve actually. There aren't many tourists down that way and we'd moored at this cove out of town. On the beach was a tarpaulin draped between the trees – looked like a fisherman's shelter or something. In it, we found Joseph sleeping rough. He was bone thin, didn't look like he'd eaten properly in days. I invited him on the yacht for some food. Afterwards he asked if he could sail on with us. We voted – and here he is.'

'What was he doing out there?'

'The way he was living, we thought he was homeless. But he has money – inheritance, I think.' He lifted his shoulders saying, 'Maybe he just needed some space for a while, or wanted to get away from the tourist belt. Who knows?'

Lana watched the beam of Joseph's head torch moving across a notebook he was writing in. 'I suppose everyone's got their story.'

Denny turned to her with a smile and said, 'So tell me, Lana, what's yours?'

'Mine?'

He nodded. 'You spun a globe, picked a destination, ended up here. You put your life in the hands of chance. Why?'

An image of her father – shoulders rounded as he stood in the doorway of his room – flashed into her thoughts. She shook her head, pushing the memory away.

'Why not?' Lana said, immediately regretting the defensive edge to her voice.

He looked at her for a long moment, then said lightly, 'I guess then I'll just be thankful to the gods of Chance – because if it hadn't been for that globe you spun, or for that kamikaze cockerel back in Norappi – we might never have met.'

She glanced at Denny. He was smiling at her and she felt warmth flood to her cheeks. He took a drink and, as he lowered his arm again, it rested against Lana's. She became aware of the place where their bare skin met, and felt a low stirring in the base of her stomach.

There was a sudden splash in the water, followed by the

sound of laughter. Lana peered over the side of the yacht to see Shell treading water, her blonde hair pasted to her head. 'Who's coming in?'

*

Lana slipped from her dress, tightened her bikini, and dived.

She loved that split second before she hit the water when she was falling forwards, completely committed, her hair blown back by the motion, her body straightening out as it plummeted downwards.

She cut through the surface and the sea wrapped around her, bubbled song filling her ears. She didn't kick or move, just let herself fall deeper and deeper. There was a moment of pause and then the sea began to lift her up, raising her to the surface, to the air, to the night.

She could hear the voices of others already in the water. Only Kitty was still on deck. 'Lana?' she called from the bow, where she was pacing in her bikini. 'What's it like?'

'Beautiful. I'll swim around to the stern. Lower yourself in from there.'

Lana swam with smooth, easy strokes, enjoying the magic of being in the sea at night, feeling the water slip over her skin. Since joining the yacht, they had been in and out of the sea all day and she was finding that her muscles were beginning to tone. When she reached the stern, Kitty was standing there, arms wrapped around her middle. 'I'll count you in,' Lana said.

'Okay.'

'One, two, three . . . three and a half . . . four—'

There was a splash and suddenly Kitty was in the water too, squealing and laughing and coughing. Kitty had always been a nervous swimmer and she paddled madly towards Lana, looping her arms around her neck whilst she caught her breath. 'Do you think there's seaweed and stuff below us?' Kitty whispered, blinking salt water from her eyes.

'No, it's fine. Just clear water,' she answered. 'Happy to swim a bit further out?'

'Not too far.'

They swam slowly, Kitty doing breaststroke with her chin raised above the waterline, Lana keeping level with her. When they were a short way from the yacht they stopped, treading water.

The Blue looked even more beautiful from here, the yacht lights casting a twinkling reflection in the water. There was barely a breeze tonight and they lolled on their backs, watching the stars and hearing birds call from hidden nooks within the island beyond them.

'This is incredible,' Kitty said, reaching out a hand and finding Lana's. They drifted on their backs, hands held, hair swirling around their faces. There was the light sound of splashing as the rest of the crew swam towards them, their voices carrying across the water.

'Did someone check the steps?' Heinrich said.

'Nope,' Shell said.

'Me neither,' Denny added.

'No,' Joseph responded.

Aaron spoke then. 'Are you serious? No one put them down?'

'What?' Kitty asked, treading water now. 'What is it?'

'You must've heard about that couple in the doldrums?' Heinrich said.

Kitty shook her head. 'What couple?'

'They decided to go swimming off their yacht. It was still – like this – and they both dived in. They were messing around in the water, enjoying themselves, cooling off. After a while, they started to get tired, so they swam back to the yacht – only they realized that neither of them had thought to put down the ladder. They couldn't get back on the boat.'

'There must've been some way,' Kitty said.

'No ladder, no footholds, nothing to grab onto except the smooth shining surface of the hull.'

'But they got back on eventually, though?' Kitty asked.

In the darkness Aaron shook his head. 'The empty yacht was found six weeks later – with their fingernail marks scarred into the hull.'

'But . . . what . . . are the steps down now? Someone must've put them down.' Kitty's voice was cut with panic.

'Kit,' Lana said gently, 'remember you jumped off the swim platform. It's low enough to pull ourselves back on. They're winding us up.'

Heinrich and Aaron laughed.

Kitty splashed them both. 'Arseholes!'

'Just trying to distract you from the sharks and sea snakes,' Aaron said, deadpan.

She snorted. 'I'm swimming back.'

The others joined Kitty, but Lana said she'd catch up, wanting a few moments alone. She floated on her back, letting the dark sea bear her weight. She felt a surge of freedom, a sense of possibility, a feeling that she and Kitty were part of something bold and wonderful that was so much more than the life they'd left in England. She wanted to seal this feeling in her heart. She closed her eyes, suspended in the sea, the voices of her friends slipping further away.

She became aware of a shift in the water, a new vibration in the liquid stillness. There was the brush of something against her skin, as if a hand was sliding down the length of her back and over the rise of her buttocks. She kicked out in surprise, waiting for whoever it was to surface laughing. After a while . . . thirty seconds, then a minute . . . there was no one.

She turned in the water, glancing about her, a trail of goosebumps spreading down her neck. It looked as though the rest of the crew had reached the stern and were pulling themselves out of the sea, although she couldn't clearly make out if they were all there.

Had she imagined it? If one of the others had been fooling around, surely they would have grabbed her ankle or leg, pretending to be a shark – whereas this was insidious, just the breath of a touch, like a dark eel slithering against her skin.

Lana shivered. She swam hard towards the yacht, and scrambled up onto the stern, scraping her shin on the metal edge in her hurry.

Kitty had fetched a towel and, when she saw Lana, she

wrapped it around them both so their cool bodies were pressed together.

'Kit,' she whispered, 'did you see anyone just swim over to me?'

'No. Why?'

'Just now it felt like . . . like someone ran a hand along my back underwater.'

'You sure?' Kitty said, looking bemused.

Glancing about her, Lana could see all of the crew – Shell, Heinrich, Denny, Aaron and Joseph – drying off on deck. Had one of them managed to swim back here before her?

She looked out across the dark water. But the sea was eerily still, not a ripple in its surface.

6

THEN

'Some of us don't have legs that can stretch that far!' Kitty yelled.

Lana paused, glancing over her shoulder at Kitty, who was standing barefoot on a boulder, arms folded over her chest. Her cheeks had pinkened and there was a gleam of sweat across her forehead. 'Want a leg up?'

'No, I bloody don't!'

Lana grinned. Then she watched as Kitty hauled herself up the rock, puffing and cursing.

They climbed the last part together, finally reaching the others who were at the top of the rocky cliff face, standing on a wide ledge that jutted out above the water. A warm breeze stirred the air, carrying the chalky scent of the rocks.

'Guess I'd better test out this dive board,' Denny said, moving to the edge of the cliff face and peering down. A 40-foot drop ended in a still blue lagoon, where he'd been snorkelling earlier to check the depth.

Denny removed his T-shirt and knotted the string on his board shorts. His body was lean and tanned and Lana's gaze followed the contours of his wiry muscles, imagining how she'd sketch him, where she'd shade, and which lines she'd follow. He was fit and seemed to have boundless energy; every morning he swam before breakfast, and if Lana sloped into the saloon before dawn for a glass of water, she'd find Denny awake, a coffee and his laptop in front of him as he worked on a translation.

Denny turned his neck from side to side, then performed a series of elaborate leg stretches.

'Get on with it!' Aaron called.

Denny took a few steps back from the cliff edge and then ran forwards, launching himself into the air. Lana was expecting something impressive, but he bunched his knees up towards his chest and bombed downwards, a boulder of limbs. There was a thunderous white splash as he hit the water. A moment or two later, he erupted through the surface to whoops and cheers.

Lana heard the flick of a lighter and turned to see Joseph smiling in the shade, lighting a roll-up.

'Do me one, Joe-Joe?' Kitty asked.

'Thought you only smoked when you were drinking?' Lana said.

'How do you know I haven't been drinking?' Kitty said with a wink.

Kitty reached across as Joseph passed her his lit cigarette. 'Thanks, honey.'

They spent the day hanging out on the cliff top where the breeze was at its coolest. The dives became more ambitious, with Denny and Heinrich trying to outdo each other with somersaults, inelegant back flips, and swallow dives – landing with slaps that seemed to echo off the rocks.

Lana noticed the competitive edge to Heinrich, who sought out the others' praise when he returned to the cliff top after a successful dive. Shell teased him that his formation was a little off, losing points for bent legs on entry. He looked genuinely disappointed by her verdict, until Shell's face broke into an easy grin.

When the heat became too much for Lana, she jumped from the ledge too, enjoying the burst of adrenalin that pumped hard through her veins in that moment when her feet left the rock. When it came, the smack of water was an exhilarating white burst that filled her nose and mouth with salt water, and she surfaced coughing and laughing.

Around lunchtime, Shell took the dinghy back to the yacht, and returned with a bag full of sandwiches, fruit, and bottles of chilled water. They ate looking out over the incredible view. Not a single boat was sighted and, apart from a plane flying overhead, they were entirely alone.

As the sun began to lower, one by one the crew made their way back to the yacht, until only Joseph, Aaron and Lana remained on the cliff top. Joseph wandered to the edge with another cigarette, peering down at the drop. The breeze flattened his shirt against his body and Lana noticed for the first time how thin he was. She could see the sharp jut of his shoulder blades and the ridges of his spine.

'Going to jump?' Aaron said from behind him.

Joseph just shrugged, his gaze on the water.

'You're not going to give it a go?' Aaron asked slyly.

Joseph turned to face Aaron, his back to the cliff edge. Very slowly he drew the cigarette to his mouth and took a long drag. He blew the smoke upwards to the sky, then he dropped his cigarette and stubbed it out with his bare heel. He placed his glasses carefully on the ground and took a step back so that his heels were at the lip of the cliff.

'Careful,' Lana said.

Joseph crouched down, and then in a shock of movement, he flung himself up and back, his body arching. His arms were outstretched at his sides and he seemed to float silently through an inverse world. His shirt filled with air, rising away from his chest and exposing the pale skin of his stomach. As he neared the surface, he brought his arms together in a neat point, piercing through the blue water.

Lana gasped. White water bubbled on the surface, cloaking Joseph from view. Then suddenly there was a rush of movement as he surfaced.

'Yeeaaah!' Denny bellowed from down below, his voice echoing off the rock. The rest of the crew, who were still in the lagoon, whooped and cheered, too.

Joseph trod water for a moment, his blue shirt clinging to his body – and Lana was certain she could see him smiling. Then he turned and swam calmly back towards the yacht.

'I'll be damned,' Aaron said, shaking his head. He looked at Lana for a moment and said, 'Did that actually just happen?'

'It did.' She grinned.

Without another word Aaron walked to the cliff edge, then dived forward, his chest expanded, arms stretched out. It looked for a moment as though he was suspended in the air, offering himself to the sky. When he landed, he didn't come up for breath but swam underwater, his dark shape visible below the clear surface as he ploughed hard in the direction of the yacht.

Lana picked up Joseph's glasses from the cliff edge and gathered her things. Before beginning the climb back down, she stood on the cliff edge watching the rest of the crew swimming towards the yacht, Joseph at their centre. She found herself smiling, pleased for him.

Standing there, she felt a strange longing, as if she were watching the scene, not part of it. Somehow she knew these golden moments couldn't stretch out endlessly. She yearned to press 'pause', to freeze this exact point in her life and hold onto it tightly.

*

Later that evening, the crew sat in the cockpit in the glow of a few candles, the cliff casting a dark shadow in the background. The wind had changed direction and small waves shivered through the bay, making the yacht rock. It was a rare, almost perfect evening, conversation moving fluidly from topic to topic and laughter rippling out over the dark water.

Up at the bow, Joseph was sitting alone again, writing in his notebook by head torch. Lana picked up her beer and moved along the deck towards him. 'Mind if I join you?'

As he turned, the beam of the head torch swung over her face. She squinted, holding a hand up to her eyes.

'Of course,' he said, turning off the torch. He closed the notebook and slipped it away into the breast pocket of his shirt.

'Impressive dive you made earlier,' she said, lowering herself down beside him. 'Where did you learn?'

'Paris. Years ago I join a diving club. Many nights' practice on the high board.'

'Do you do any diving now?'

'No. Not now.'

They sat in silence, the noise and laughter of the others drifting towards them. Lana was comfortable in the absence of words, having grown used to it in her own home. She felt a strange allegiance to Joseph – perhaps because she sensed his isolation from the rest of the crew and knew what it was to be an outsider, often wondering how lonely her teenage years would have been if she hadn't met Kitty.

She watched the water, noticing how the tops of the waves glinted silver in the faint light of the moon. After some time she turned to Joseph and said, 'Do you mind me asking what you're writing?'

He thought for a moment, and then answered, 'Poetry.'

'Poetry about what you see, or what you feel?'

It was his turn to look at her. 'That is interesting question.' From the pocket of his shorts he took out a tin of tobacco and some rolling papers. His fingers were long and nimble, practised at evenly packing down the tobacco. 'I write about what I *feel*.'

She nodded.

'I see you with an art pad sometimes, yes?'

'Yes. Sketching, mostly. Out here there's so much I want to draw.'

Joseph lit his cigarette and took a long drag. As he exhaled, he asked, 'You have fun on the boat, then?'

'A lot. We're very lucky to be part of this.'

'It is different, to travel by boat. It is freedom, no?' He took another drag and then offered her the roll-up. Lana hadn't smoked regularly since university, but she still had the occasional yearning. 'Thanks,' she said, lifting it to her lips and inhaling. Nicotine flooded her head, giving her a pleasing rush.

'Who did you leave behind at home?' he asked.

She passed the roll-up back, saying, 'Just my father.' She pictured him in his worn green cords and a tired office shirt, sitting in his armchair with the newspaper folded at the crossword. She was surprised to feel a stirring of pity as she thought about the lonely routine of his days, wondering who visited the house now. 'How about you?'

He laughed, but Lana caught the strange, sad note to it. 'There is no one.'

'What about your family?'

'None.'

'No family? None at all?'

He gave a quick shake of his head. 'My mother and father are dead. One year ago.'

'Oh, I'm sorry. What happened – if you don't mind me asking?'

In the moonlight, she saw Joseph's expression darken. 'They died in a house fire.'

'I'm so sorry,' she said with meaning. She remembered Denny telling her about how they'd found Joseph sleeping rough on a remote Filipino beach. He must've been out of his mind with grief. 'Is that what made you leave France? Come out here?'

He nodded slowly, eyes on the water. 'I had some money, so I could be anywhere. Sometimes it is better to go, yes?'

'Yes,' she agreed. 'Sometimes it is.'

*

Lana went to bed at midnight and lay sweltering on the top bunk in just a pair of cotton pants, her skin clammy with suncream and salt. She wished there was enough space between her bunk and the ceiling to sit up fully. The porthole only opened a crack, barely allowing in any breeze, and she could feel sweat beginning to bead between her breasts.

The peaceful sound of the sea sloshing against the keel did nothing to lull her thoughts: they kept circling back to her father. Since joining *The Blue* her days had been so full that she could go for hours without thinking about him, yet often at night she'd find herself examining memories from her childhood, searching them for the faint cracks where the lies ran through.

Lana pushed her hand through the slim gap in the porthole to see if it was cooler outside. It wasn't. She sighed.

From the bunk below, Kitty whispered, 'You still awake?'

'I think my organs are melting,' Lana said.

'You try this heat with sunburn,' Kitty said, who'd insisted on the cliff top that she was tanned enough not to need suncream.

Lana rolled onto her front and lay with her head hanging over the edge, her hair trailing down. Below her, Kitty propped herself up a little on her elbows. Lana's vision adjusted in the darkness so she could see the outline of Kitty's features.

'Kit, d'you remember how desperately I used to want to go to Greece?'

'Course. For an entire term your packed lunches were feta-and-olive pittas.'

Lana's mother had been brought up on the outskirts of Athens, before moving to England. Lana had only a few wisps of memories of her – like the smell of roasted aubergine and olive oil that filled their kitchen, and the strong angles of her mother's bone structure that were set in relief by her full lips.

She said to Kitty, 'My dad always claimed we couldn't afford the trip, or he wasn't able to take the time off work.' She shook her head. 'Just another of his lies. I keep on remembering all these little things – hundreds of details that were all bullshit. My whole childhood was a fucking fabrication!'

'Don't say that,' Kitty said, pushing herself up as straight as she could within the bunk. 'Your dad loves you, Lana. I know he fucked up – I know that – but he did it for the right reasons. He was trying to protect you.'

Right now all Lana wanted was to hear Kitty rage alongside

her, the way the two of them had always done. Her hurt was too raw, too full, to allow Kitty to see things from her father's perspective. She sighed. 'Think I'm going to go for a swim.'

'Now?'

'Yes.'

Lana climbed out of the bunk, which creaked and strained beneath the press of her feet. She unhooked her bikini from the back of the door, which was still damp from earlier.

'You're really going?'

'I'll stay close to the yacht.'

'But it's dark.'

'Tends to happen at night.'

As Lana moved towards the door, Kitty said, 'Lana, are you all right?'

'Fine. Sorry. Just overheating, I think.'

'Okay . . .' Kitty said. 'Just be careful, won't you?'

'Course,' Lana said. As she slipped out of the door and along the passageway, she felt herself thinking of that strange, slithering touch she'd felt a few nights ago and just for a moment she hesitated.

*

Lana crept along the passageway towards the galley, where the lingering smell of their mince dinner still hung. She heard the faint sound of snoring drifting from a cabin somewhere and the hum of the fridge.

Up on deck the air was only marginally cooler, but just being out of the narrow space of the bunk felt good. She was moving towards the stern when someone started.

'Shit!' Denny said. He was standing with his back to her. 'You always creep up on people when they're taking a piss?'

'Sorry,' she laughed, covering her mouth with her hand.

'And there's a queue if you're wanting to use the open-air bathroom.'

'Think I'll use the underwater bathroom.'

'You're swimming?'

She nodded. 'Need to cool off.'

'Fancy company?'

She shrugged. 'If you can keep up.'

*

They dived from the bow, the cool night sea closing around their bodies. Lana led, swimming away from the yacht and the shadow of the island, out towards the silver pathway of the moon.

They swam without words, hearing only the sounds of their arms cutting through the water, the rhythm of their breathing, the kicking of their feet.

The moon was almost full – a waxing moon. One of Lana's ex-boyfriends had once explained how you could tell whether it was waxing by looking at the right-hand side of it, which should be full and rounded – whereas the left edge should be flatter, making it look like a 'D' shape. When the moon was waning the edgings were the other way around.

After some minutes Lana slowed, treading water. Denny paused alongside her. The yacht floated serenely in the distance, moon-light catching on the curve of the hull and the tall line of the masts. She thought of their friends curled in their bunks, the light lapping of waves rocking them in their sleep.

'Joseph's dive,' she said, trying to shake free of the thoughts of her father that still lingered at the periphery of her mind, and think of something light-hearted to talk about. 'Wasn't it brilliant?'

Denny grinned. 'I love that he's been on board for almost two months, yet he's not breathed a word about being some Parisian diving god. He just let the rest of us get on with our hooting and gooning – and then ends the day with that manoeuvre. I was feeling pretty pleased I'd nailed the swallow dive until I saw that.'

'*Nailed?*' she said, an eyebrow arched.

'Okay. *Attempted.*'

Lana rubbed the water from her eyes and said, 'I was talking to Joseph earlier. He told me about his parents. They were killed in a fire.'

Denny nodded. 'Only last year. There's no one else either – no other family. I can't . . . I can't even imagine that.'

'You've got a big family?'

'Not huge. Just my parents and a brother. How about you?'

'It's just me and my father.'

'Are you close?'

She made a small sound, somewhere between a laugh and a scoff. 'Not right now.'

Denny waited, saying nothing. In his silence, Lana was

horrified to find that tears had sprung up on her lower lids. She wiped at them hurriedly.

Denny swam nearer. 'Hey, what is it, Lana?' he asked gently.

She didn't know whether it was the darkness cloaking them, or the anonymity of being at sea, or the open, intent way Denny was looking at her – but Lana found herself beginning to explain. She told him about the last time she'd seen her father, which was a few weeks before she'd left for the Philippines. She'd been kneeling on the floor of her father's bedroom, when she heard the front door opening downstairs.

'Lana? Is that you?' he'd called.

She hadn't answered. Hadn't moved. She'd listened to the slow tread of his feet as he climbed the stairs, sliding his palm along the banister. The floorboards creaked as he crossed the landing to the doorway of his room.

'Lana, what are you—'

He'd stopped when he saw his old leather suitcase open, and a Manila envelope in her grip. Her father lifted a hand to his throat, pinching at the loose skin around his Adam's apple. 'Lana . . .'

It scared her the way his whole face changed into something blank and fearful, and his voice sounded hollow, as if he were two people: the one she'd always known, and this new version of himself.

'You . . . you . . .' she began, but couldn't seem to make her lips work. Her tongue had felt numb and thick in her mouth. She lifted up the envelope, which contained a letter from a Greek solicitor. 'She didn't die, did she? Not when I was three.'

Her father had closed his eyes, the muscles in his face slackening so that all his features dragged downwards.

Lana told Denny that she'd always believed her mother had been killed in a car crash – but that the truth was entirely different.

Her mother had walked out on them, returning to her homeland. She had been desperately unhappy living in England, and had found comfort in a Greek doctor who was on secondment at a hospital where Lana's mother worked. When his contract was finished, she returned to Athens with him, saying nothing of the family she was leaving behind.

'I tried telling you the truth at first,' her father had said, his voice choked with emotion, 'but you were too young to understand. Some mornings I'd wake to find you sleeping on the rug by the front door waiting for her to come home.'

Eventually her father decided they needed a fresh start, so they moved to Bristol, buying a small terraced house on a street that Kitty would move to a few years later. 'When I took you for your first day at primary school, your class teacher asked that you tell her a little about yourself. Do you know what you said, Lana? You told her you were four, your birthday was in August, and that you didn't have a mummy because she'd gone away to heaven. I was horrified,' Lana's father had said. 'I'd no idea where you got that from – but your class teacher was already patting you on the arm, saying, "I'm sure your mummy is watching you from heaven." You'd beamed then, the largest smile I'd seen in months. And so . . . I didn't correct you.' Her father had simply stayed silent, and from there, the lie strengthened and grew until it became so permanent that it seemed to be the truth. Later, when Lana started asking *how* her mother died, her father had come up with the story of the car crash.

Lana's mother never wrote or phoned from Greece. Apparently she'd come back, just once, when Lana was sixteen. Lana had been out at the time and her father had explained to his ex-wife that Lana believed she was dead – and that he wasn't prepared to undo that unless she was committed to establishing a regular relationship with her daughter. Her mother had cried, saying her new husband still did not know about Lana. And then she walked away for a second time.

'I would never have found out the truth,' she said to Denny, 'except I discovered a letter from a solicitor that said my mother had passed away two years ago.' She paused, shaking her head. 'All those years I mourned her – but she was alive. And my dad knew.'

When Lana finished talking, her mouth was dry and the muscles in her legs were beginning to ache.

Denny was watching her closely, his expression fixed on her face. 'I'm so sorry, Lana,' he said, and she could hear the earnestness in his voice.

The only other person Lana had told the story to was Kitty, and she felt oddly exposed for talking like that in front of Denny. She pulled her gaze away, staring upwards. The sky was an ocean of stars and she felt the inconsequential nature of her existence – just a speck, floating. She allowed herself to be calmed by the idea that all the thoughts that consumed her, looming large in her mind, were – in the end – really nothing.

Gradually her breathing began to settle and she felt the water rise and fall over her chest with each exhalation. She wondered how far down the seabed lay – 100 feet, 200 perhaps? Seaweed and soft corals swaying below in the dark, fish feeding and resting, shells closing for the night.

When her gaze returned to Denny, he was still watching her, his hair flattened to his head. Moonlight glistened on his arms as they stirred the surface, his eyes on her.

'Well, that's my story,' she said with a forced brightness. 'What's yours?'

A fleeting tightness passed over his face. Then he rolled onto his back, spread his arms at his sides, and let the sea bear his weight. 'I don't have one,' he said to the sky, matching the brightness of her tone.

Lana pressed her lips together as she watched him, a strange feeling ebbing through her as if she'd just lost something that she hadn't quite found.

7

NOW

The Maritime Rescue Centre is set at the edge of a commercial port, and Lana drives in behind a container lorry. She parks in front of a squat, flat-roofed building, but doesn't get out immediately. Her wrists ache from where she's been gripping the steering wheel too tightly.

She's not sure what she's doing here – what she expects to happen next. All she knew was that she couldn't wait in the apartment any longer. So she scribbled a quick note of apology to her boss, which she left downstairs in the gallery, and then drove with the radio on hoping for a further update.

As she sits in the car now, she thinks there's something soothing about a stationary vehicle, the wind locked out, the warm air trapped inside, and the feeling of being sealed off from the rest of the world. Being on the yacht was different; you felt the world and the elements in all their rawness – each gust of wind hitting your face, the roll and rise of swell surging beneath you, the heat of the sun searing across your skin. The sea demanded your constant attention.

Beside her on the passenger seat are a stack of old sketchbooks and three blunt pencils. Sometimes at weekends, Lana will get in the car and drive along the coast without a plan or a specific destination, simply pulling over whenever the desire to do so takes hold. Then she'll climb into the passenger seat, prop a sketchbook on her knees, and draw for hours and hours.

It takes her back to the long afternoons in the school art room where she would sit with her elbow on the paint-stained desk, her hair falling down one side of her face, the sun slanting in through tall sash windows. The art room was a refuge from the rest of school life, which seemed drab and predictable. Apart from Kitty, Lana struggled to make friends. The other girls teased her for her quirky shoes, her thick amber hair, and the bright woollen tights she wore on home-clothes day. Her father had little money, so Lana's wardrobe was comprised of odds and ends she'd pick up from charity shops on their monthly visit to town.

In the art room Lana felt comfortable. It was a place of colour and noise and warmth, where the radio played constantly in the background, and the air smelt of turpentine, coffee and the chalky scent of cheap paint. She sat next to Kitty on a high wooden stool, enjoying her constant chatter as Kitty made swirling patterns with a palette of pinks and purples.

Lana was fourteen when her art teacher, Mrs Dano, called her back after class. She'd spent the lesson scrawling a stub of charcoal across an A3 page and ignoring the still-life display of weighing scales she was meant to be drawing. She screwed up each piece of work, lobbing them all in the bin and, when the bell went, she'd slung her bag over her shoulder and started lumbering from the room.

'Lana?' Mrs Dano had called as she stood at the sink washing up paint-streaked jam jars. 'A word, please.'

Lana had rolled her eyes at Kitty, then hung back, leaning a hip against the wall.

Once the room had emptied, Mrs Dano set aside the jam jars and wiped her hands on her apron, then went to the corner of the room, returning with three balls of screwed-up paper. She placed them on the desk in front of Lana. 'Please would you open these?'

Lana's jaw tightened as she picked up the first ball. The paper felt as crisp as dried leaves as she unscrewed the picture. It was a drawing of the windows of the art room, with an angry slash of charcoal across the centre that had torn the page.

Mrs Dano placed a finger in the left-hand corner, her amethyst ring catching in the sun. 'Here,' she said. 'The light. You've got it just right as it cuts through the glass. And here, too,' she said, sliding her finger lower. 'Hmm, no, this bit isn't quite right. The perspective is off, but if you just—' Mrs Dano pulled a piece of charcoal from the pocket of her apron – 'put the line this way,' she said, dusting the charcoal across the page, 'and applied a lighter pressure to shade it, you'd be there.'

With a change of stroke, the drawing had been transformed.

Mrs Dano rested her hands on the edge of the table. 'I don't want any more work going in the bin, Lana. There is beauty in imperfection. Remember that.'

Lana nodded. Then the wooden legs of her stool scraped across the floor as she stood.

'And Lana?'

She turned.

'If you ever want to use the art room in your lunch breaks, I'm usually in here.' Mrs Dano held her gaze. 'You've got talent. I'd like to see it grow.'

Lana had left the room, pleasure blooming hot in her cheeks. Outside the door, Kitty had been waiting, listening. She reached for Lana's hand, their fingers threading together. 'I knew it!' she whispered. 'I knew someone would notice your talent.'

*

Lana cannot delay going inside any longer. She takes a deep breath and opens the car door, stepping out onto concrete that shimmers with spilt diesel. The wind teases her dress around her thighs, making it seem as though the white sparrows of the pattern are fluttering and flying across the powder-green fabric.

The air is tinged with fumes and the scent of brine washing in from the water as she walks towards the main building. She comes to a reception desk that is unmanned and waits for a moment, peering into the back office – but the place is empty, computer screens off.

She moves beyond it, following a long corridor of rooms, all with their doors shut. She pauses outside a door that reads 'Operations Room' – then knocks.

The door is opened abruptly by a tall man with a thick black moustache, who introduces himself as Paul Carter, the man she spoke to on the phone. He wears hiking boots with brown socks pulled halfway up his calves. He strikes her as the sort of bloke who probably likes to spend his Friday evenings at one of the municipal beach-barbecue areas that are popular in New Zealand, although now his expression is strained, his brows heavy.

Behind him Lana can see a woman working in front of a computer screen. To her left is a noticeboard covered with maps, charts and printed weather reports. In the centre a sheet of white paper has been pinned, headed with the title, '*The Blue: Crew List*'.

Lana's insides tighten. The names of the crew have been written in thick black marker pen and she scans each of them, her fists balled at her sides, palms sweating.

Each and every one of those five names dredges up memories that come flooding to the surface of her thoughts. Her heart pounds. It is only when Paul Carter takes a small step to the side, blocking her view of the noticeboard, that she looks up.

'Can I help you?' he asks coolly.

She swallows. 'I'm Lana Lowe. I called earlier about *The Blue*.'

'You shouldn't be in here.'

'There wasn't anyone on reception,' she tells him.

'I'm afraid you need to leave—'

'I know the yacht,' Lana says desperately. 'I used to sail on it.'

That catches his attention. 'You did? When?'

'Earlier this year – from January to March.'

'Are you familiar with what safety equipment and communication devices they had on board? We've only had limited contact with them.'

She thinks for a moment, sweeping her mind over the yacht. 'There were just the standard things – a life raft, life jackets, a grab bag, flares, an EPIRB. There was the VHF radio, and maybe another type, too.' She can't remember the names of things any more – the details of the yacht that were once so familiar are now beginning to slip away.

'What about a satellite phone or personal locator beacons?'

'No, not that I know of. None of those.'

Paul Carter nods, taking this in.

Lana asks, 'What happened out there?'

'I'm afraid I need to get back to my desk now.'

'Please,' she says. 'My friends are on board.'

Paul Carter looks at her, then across at his female colleague. 'All I can say at the moment is that the crew got into difficulties and had to abandon the vessel.'

'Is there any news? Are the crew safe?'

'Search and Rescue are doing everything they can, but no, there's no news yet. A distress broadcast has been put out to all the vessels in the region, and a sailing yacht and merchant ship are diverting course to approach the search area.'

'Approach? No one is even there yet?'

'Both vessels were over forty miles away at the time. The Search and Rescue helicopter is already in the search area and we're expecting more news soon.'

'Did the crew make it onto the life raft?'

'We have no information about that, I'm afraid.'

'So . . . they could be in the water?'

'It is possible, yes.'

*

Lana is desperate to remain in the Operations Room, knowing that Paul Carter will be the first person to receive any news, but he tells her, 'One of my colleagues has organized a waiting room for relatives. Other family members are on their way here.'

Who, she thinks? The only crew with family in New Zealand are Aaron and Denny. She imagines Denny's parents would want to be here; she remembers him talking about how much he missed them. It would be over two years since he saw them last.

'I'll take you there now.' He looks over his shoulder. 'Fiona, which room have they allocated?'

'I think it was Twelve A,' she says, hands poised above a keyboard.

Somewhere in the office a radio begins to beep. Paul Carter moves towards a desk where a large monitor is mounted. He picks up a hand-held device attached to it. A voice at the other end is saying, 'Maritime Rescue, Maritime Rescue, this is Team One, this is Team One. Can you hear us?'

Paul Carter holds the radio handset to his mouth. 'This is Maritime Rescue. Go ahead, Team One.'

'We have been tracking the EPIRB for *The Blue* and have now located it.'

Lana holds herself still, hope rising in her chest. Denny once explained that an EPIRB is a device that is set off in any rescue situation. It is registered to a vessel and gives off the precise position via GPS, and then continues to transmit its position until the device – and hopefully crew – are located.

'Go ahead, Team One. What is the current position?'

'The position is 32*59.098'S, 173*16.662'E. I repeat, the position is 32*59.098'S, 173*16.662'E.'

Paul Carter leans over his desk, typing the coordinates into one of the three screens that are set up on the main desk. 'Copy that. Do you have a visual? Is the EPIRB aboard the life raft?'

There is a delay, then the rush of static.

Lana looks at Paul Carter's expression. His brow is furrowed and his mouth is fixed in a serious line. 'I repeat, is the EPIRB aboard the life raft?'

The reply comes over the radio, filling the room. 'There is no life raft in sight. The EPIRB is attached to a body.'

8

THEN

*T*he *Blue* turned lazily on its anchor, a light breeze stirring the water. On deck Heinrich was fiddling with a radio that he'd taken apart, the innards laid out on a tea towel, and beside him, Shell was sitting forward writing a postcard to her parents.

Lana had her sketchbook balanced on her knees, and was leaning close to the page, the tip of her tongue pressing against her front teeth. She moved the pencil in short, quick strokes, sketching a coil of rope that lay on deck in front of her. Looking at the page, she could see that the detailing at the end of the rope – where it trailed out of the coil and across the deck – wasn't quite right. She tore the edge from the rubber she held and rolled it into a sharp point so she could erase with precision.

She spent a few minutes re-drawing until she was satisfied with it. Then she lifted the sketchbook from her knee and held it at arm's length. Closing one eye, she studied it. The detailing in the curve of the rope was pleasing. She liked that the image spoke to her of order, things coiled tight, yet she'd also captured the weave of the rope where the threads had come loose – giving the suggestion of it starting to unravel.

Lana closed the sketchbook, setting her pencil on top. When she looked up, Joseph was storming down the deck, his face set in a heavy frown, his lips pinched. He came to a stop in front of Heinrich, casting him into shade.

'Hello, room-mate,' Heinrich said with a false smile. It was no secret that the two of them disliked sharing a cabin; often one of them ended up sleeping in the hammock on deck to have their own space.

'Have you been through my backpack?' Joseph demanded.

'Your backpack?'

'It is not how I left things! Someone has been through it!' His fingers clenched and unclenched around his loose shirt sleeves.

'Why would anyone want to do that?' Heinrich asked leadingly.

'Have you?'

Heinrich rolled his eyes. 'You really think I want to read those special stories you're always busy writing?'

'Heinrich!' Shell chastised.

'Course I haven't been through your things,' Heinrich said in a more conciliatory manner.

Joseph drew air deep into his lungs, steadying his breathing. After a moment he conceded, 'It must be my mistake,' although Lana noticed that his gaze lingered on Heinrich.

Eventually he turned away, took a tin of tobacco from his pocket, and swiftly made a roll-up. With his back to the others he lit it and inhaled, the tension in his shoulders beginning to soften.

In an attempt to lighten the atmosphere, Lana asked Shell, 'How's the postcard writing going?' Any time they were in a town, Shell would scour the market stalls in search of postcards to send home to her parents.

'Sometimes I feel like I'm writing a tourist brochure rather than sharing anything about how it actually *feels* to be here, you know?'

Lana nodded – although the truth was, she hadn't been in touch with her father since coming away. Kitty had sent a couple of emails home, and Lana imagined that the news would gradually filter through to her father. 'Your parents must love getting them.'

'I wouldn't know,' Shell said, lifting her shoulders. 'I never hear back from them. Not a single email. I don't even know if they read my letters.'

Lana was taken aback. 'Why wouldn't they?'

'We weren't on the best terms when I left. They didn't like my . . . life choices.' She laughed as she said, 'When I told them I was a lesbian, it was like there'd been a death. They grieved – actually *grieved* over the news.'

Joseph exhaled a drift of smoke into the clear blue sky. 'Why do you still write?'

Shell turned and looked at him. 'Because I want to at least try. They're my family.'

'Parents are not God. They are people. People who can be

. . . fucking assholes, no?' His voice was breathless with a sudden anger. 'If they do not like who you are, then, so what? Yes?'

Shell's eyes widened.

'This – this is a waste!' Joseph said, gesturing to the postcards with the roll-up.

'Joseph . . .' Heinrich said, and Lana caught the warning in his tone.

'It is true, Shell. I just tell you truth. You are very nice, very kind girl. You waste your time thinking of them, if they do not think of you!'

Shell's eyes turned glassy. Slowly, she gathered up her postcards and left the deck without a word.

Heinrich got to his feet too, glaring at Joseph. 'Why the fuck did you say that?'

'I only say what I think.'

'Next time, don't! Shell's had a hard time of it, okay?'

Joseph drew on his roll-up. 'Better to hear the truth, than live in dream, no?'

'You,' Heinrich said, pointing, 'can be a little prick.' He disappeared below deck after Shell, leaving the pieces of the dismantled radio gleaming silver in the sunlight.

Looking at Joseph, Lana could feel the bitterness and hurt locked away with his grief. She wondered what had happened between him and his parents.

He brought the roll-up to his lips, but before he inhaled he said, 'I do not mean to make Shell cry. I like her very much. But I also believe when parents tell us, "We do this for you, because we love you," they are not always right, are they?'

Lana contemplated this, thinking of her own father. 'No,' she said eventually. 'They're not.'

*

Lana returned to the cabin, where Kitty was lying in her bunk recovering from a hangover. She hadn't made it up onto deck before mid-morning all week.

'He didn't mean to upset her – it's just his manner,' Lana was saying, filling Kitty in about Joseph. She knew he sometimes acted in odd ways, but she also knew he wasn't cruel. 'But I don't think Heinrich saw it that way.'

'When it comes to Shell, Heinrich does have a tendency to be a little overprotective,' Kitty said, raising an eyebrow meaningfully.

'You've noticed, too?'

'Noticed?' Kitty said. 'He follows her around with his tongue hanging so far out that I've almost skidded over in his drool.'

'Shhh!' Lana said, laughing.

'Trust him to fall for a lesbian. *The ultimate challenge!*' Kitty said, taking off his accent perfectly.

Lana laughed again.

'Hey, you know what Heinrich told me last night?' Kitty lowered her voice and said, 'Aaron used to be a barrister.'

'Aaron? Seriously? How does Heinrich know that?'

'When they were moored up somewhere in Thailand, this huge motorboat – a gin-palace type, owned by a Swiss guy – reversed right into *The Blue*. Put a hole in the stern. Then motored off.'

'Aaron must've lost it!'

'Apparently not. He caught up with the boat a day or two later. Heinrich reckoned he was lethally cool when he confronted the owner, didn't raise his voice, didn't get angry. Just told this bloke that, unless he sorted out the repair bill, Aaron would be going to the police, and started spouting all this legal speak about operating a motorboat under the influence, endangering lives, leaving the scene of a crime. Afterwards, Heinrich asked how he knew all that stuff and Aaron told him he used to be a barrister.'

Lana pictured him in a courtroom, chest puffed out, arguing his case – and found that the image came to mind easily. If he'd been a barrister, it probably explained how he could afford to buy *The Blue* in the first place. 'Wonder why he gave it up.'

'No idea.'

There must have been some reason. Barrister to skipper was some career swerve. She mused on this as she picked up her sketchbook and slipped it under the mattress of her bunk to keep it flat.

'What've you been drawing?' Kitty asked.

'Just a coil of rope up on deck.'

'Let's have a look.'

Kitty was one of the only people Lana was happy to show her sketches to. The tutorials during her art degree had left behind a residue of fear – all those panic-inducing moments of standing in front of her peers, trying to put into words what she'd been hoping to capture in a piece. Even now she'd break out into a sweat when she had to speak to a roomful of people.

Lana slid out the sketchbook and opened it at the image of the rope.

Kitty studied it carefully. 'Lana,' she said, looking up. 'This is beautiful.'

'It's just a rope.'

'But look at the detail! It's amazing. It's how you've captured it.' She shook her head thoughtfully. 'I can't wait to see your work hanging in a gallery one day.'

Lana laughed. 'You've got a high opinion of me.'

'Yes,' she said seriously. 'I have.'

Lana was reminded how – even when they were teenagers – Kitty had always encouraged Lana's passion for art. 'Do you remember how we used to make that tepee den in my back garden and hide out in it over summer?' she said, thinking about how she'd draw in the shade, while Kitty filled the space with her chatter and the smell of drying nail polish.

Kitty said, 'We'd tie a piece of string between the shed and rotary dryer and drape a sheet over it, pegging the corners out wide. Then we'd bring out all the blankets and cushions we could find, and camp out there for hours.'

Hidden within the folds of the sheets they'd talk as if they were invisible to the rest of the world. 'We'd spend hours and hours imagining what our mothers would be like if they were still here, the things that we'd do together.'

'Think we decided they'd be best friends so they could take us on holidays together,' Kitty said with a smile.

Lana nodded, but she couldn't match Kitty's smile. 'All that time I was imagining her – fantasizing about what a perfect mother she'd have been, thinking about how deeply she must have loved me – she was alive. She was living a new life in another country.'

'Oh, Lana,' Kitty said softly.

'I just . . . I still can't get my head around it,' she said, the familiar anger rising inside her. It was always there, hovering just beneath the surface. 'Aren't mothers supposed to love their children unconditionally? Yet she . . . she just left. Fucked off. All those tears I cried for her over the years – imagining the car crash, wondering whether the medical team had arrived quickly enough, picturing the driver who caused the crash. But there was no driver, no accident, no medics – just a woman who didn't love her family enough to stay.'

'That's not true,' Kitty said.

'Isn't it? And *him*,' she said bitterly. 'He lied about it all. If I'd known the truth I could have at least tried to get in touch with her – had the chance to ask why she left. But he robbed me of that. And now it's too late. I don't think I can ever forgive him for that.'

'You mustn't say that. He was trying to protect you. He did what he thought was right.'

Lana rolled her eyes. 'Kit, sometimes you sound like him.'

'I just . . . I don't want you to lose him. He's your only family.'

Lana shook her head. 'No, *you're* my family. You always have been.'

Kitty put her arms around Lana. She smelt of rum and stale cigarettes.

'What a fuck-up,' Lana said, her mouth against Kitty's hair.

'I drag you halfway around the world to get away from my father, and here I am – on a yacht in the middle of the Philippines – still talking about him.'

'Dragged me?' Kitty said. 'You just try leaving me behind.'

*

When Lana climbed up on deck later, Denny was returning from a swim. He pulled himself onto the stern, water pouring off him. 'I've got something to show you.'

'Oh?' Lana said.

'It's on the island. Wanna swim over there?'

Lana looked across to the island. It was probably about a ten-minute swim, easily manageable when there was little wind. 'Sure,' she agreed, thinking she could use the exercise to clear her head.

Since their night swim together, Lana had found herself waking early and joining Denny in the saloon, where he'd be working. He'd close his laptop, make a fresh pot of coffee, and the two of them would sit up on deck talking as dawn broke. Those early mornings – before the rest of the crew rose – were becoming her favourite part of the day.

Together, they swam to the island. It took longer than Lana had thought but Denny stayed at her side, never overtaking her, and they covered the distance easily.

On the shoreline she rubbed the salt water from her eyes and wrung out her hair, then followed Denny along the beach, water dripping from the ties of her bikini. They kept close to the treeline where the sand was cool enough to walk on. 'Where are we going?'

He didn't answer, so she continued following him until they came to a halt by some rocks. 'Here,' he said, pointing towards a craggy gap, no larger than a cupboard door.

'A cave?'

He scrambled over a boulder, then carefully lowered himself into the dark space between the rocks.

'What can you see?' she called as Denny disappeared from sight.

There was no answer.

'Denny?'

She clambered onto the boulder and slipped her legs through the gap as he had done, feeling the scuff of rock against the backs of her thighs. She waited, gripped there until her eyes adjusted.

Below she could see the ground only a few feet away. She jumped, landing with a thud. 'Denny?'

His name came back to her, reverberating off the cave walls. She crept slowly forward. 'Where are you?'

'Over here,' he whispered. 'Come and see this, Lana.'

She moved slowly, her lungs filling with the cool, dank air.

Gradually her vision began to adjust so she could make out the shapes of the cave. There was a brighter patch of light further ahead where daylight was spilling in.

Denny was standing on top of a wide boulder in a stream of light. He turned towards her and held out his hand, helping her up onto the boulder. Standing beside him, she gasped.

Jagged arrows of limestone rose from the ground, stretching

hundreds of feet upward. They reached towards the sky like cold fingers, wanting to touch the sun. Daylight beamed in through the gaps, illuminating the incredible dusky grey and earthy shades of the pinnacles, making her feel as if they'd wandered into an ancient cathedral. All she could hear was the faint drip of water from the rocks, the beat of her heart in her chest, and the shallow draw of her breath.

Her thoughts slipped to the warmth of Denny's grip and the heat of his body at her side.

Out of the sun and in the damp half-light of the limestone cave, Lana shivered.

Denny drew Lana in front of him and wrapped his arms around her, resting his chin lightly on her bare shoulder. It was the beautifully easy motion of old lovers, their bodies settling against one another as if moulded together over time.

Lana's gaze wandered over the hidden grandeur of the cave, absorbing the natural arches and sculpted grooves. 'It's beautiful,' she whispered.

'Yes,' he said, his lips at her ear.

She felt her heart rate increasing as desire pulsed through her, sure and absolute. She turned within the space of his arms and felt the brush of his shoulder against hers. She raised her eyes to his.

The pale blue of his irises deepened as she looked into them. She became aware of the cool air at her back, and the warmth of Denny in front of her.

'You know that we shouldn't . . .' he said, but there was little conviction in his voice.

She thought of Aaron's rule: *No relationships between the crew*. But those words diffused like smoke as she lifted her face, placing her mouth against his.

There was a moment – before their lips began to move together – when time seemed suspended. Their eyes were open, fixed on each other, lips touching; it was like standing on the edge of a cliff the second before diving in – the heady anticipation, the inevitability of what was coming next. Then their lips pressed deeply together, Lana's tongue sliding into the warmth of Denny's mouth. A low sound of desire came from his throat. She felt his fingers at the base of her neck, running through her hair, tilting her head back as he kissed her more deeply.

Something tight inside Lana began to loosen and melt away. His skin was hot against hers and the heat seemed to spread through her.

Later, a lifetime later, they pulled apart and Denny rested his forehead against hers, his hands still holding her close. She could hear the raised tempo of his breathing.

'Wow, Lana Lowe,' was all he whispered.

9

NOW

Lana stands in the Maritime Rescue Centre, her gaze fixed on the radio module on the desk.

The EPIRB is attached to a body.

Paul Carter sets down the handset and his fingers drift to his moustache and hover there, uncertain.

'Whose body?' Lana says. The sound of her voice – thin and trembling – surprises her.

Paul Carter turns, blinking, as if he's forgotten she is there.

'Whose body was found with the EPIRB?' she repeats when he doesn't answer.

'They don't know,' he says, shaking his head. 'The helicopter only got a visual on it. The body hasn't been recovered yet.'

She thinks of each of the crew in turn – trying to picture one of them dead.

But, who?

It is Russian roulette and her imagination holds the bullet.

A horrific image fills her mind: Kitty face down in the water, dark hair fanning around her head like a pool of blood.

She covers her hands with her mouth. She begins to tremble, her whole body feeling cold. This can't be happening.

Not Kitty. Please, not Kitty.

Who, out of those five people, would she rather it be? The thought makes her sick. There was a time when she'd been friends with all of them – cared about them. How could she even pick one of them?

The female co-worker is asking Paul Carter something in a low voice. Lana struggles to focus on the words. 'I don't understand how the EPIRB was attached to the body.'

Paul Carter says, 'SAR think it must be inside the grab bag strapped to the individual's back.'

Why? Lana thinks. *Why wouldn't the EPIRB be with the life raft?* 'What about the others?' she demands, her voice rasped. 'Have they located the life raft? Have they located the yacht?'

He looks away from Lana. She notices that there is a sheen of sweat across his forehead. 'No, not yet,' he says, in a low, uncertain voice.

She is trying to work out why he looks so shaken – and then she realizes: even if the rest of the crew did make it to the life raft, they will now be drifting, blown by the winds, and tugged along by the currents, with no EPIRB to help locate them. The helicopter will search but Lana knows that in rough seas, waves and troughs can completely conceal an entire yacht, let alone a life raft.

'Lana,' the woman says kindly, getting to her feet. 'Why don't

I take you to the family room? You may be more comfortable waiting there?'

She shakes her head. She wants to stay here. Be right beside Paul Carter when more news comes in.

'Good idea,' Paul Carter says distractedly, pulling out a chair and returning to his desk.

Lana is led from the room, thoughts whirling.

*

At the end of a long corridor, the woman opens a door onto a sparse white room where eight plastic chairs are set in an oval formation. There is a jug of water on a table and a stack of plastic cups beside it.

Lana must be staring at them, as the woman says, 'I could make you a tea or coffee, if you prefer?'

'I'm fine,' she says, wanting to be alone.

When the woman leaves, Lana moves to the window alcove where there is a low ledge just wide enough to sit on. She sits with her knees drawn up to her chest, watching through the window as a forklift truck manoeuvres across the tarmac. Glancing up at the sky, she sees that the clouds are heavy now, *brooding* her father would say. She wonders if it might rain.

She thinks of those first few weeks on *The Blue* when the sky always seemed clear and their days were filled with swimming above stunning coral, eating fresh fish and exotic fruits, exploring hidden coves and beaches. Sometimes, on calm days, she and Kitty would explore by paddleboard, Kitty sitting at the front with her feet pressed together, wet hair dripping down her back. Lana would stand just back from the centre with her feet planted wide, knees bent, scooping the paddle through clear water.

'Let's go to the mangroves,' Kitty had said one evening as the sun fell behind them, their shadows lengthening across the water.

Lana had caught the scent of vegetation on the salt breeze as she paddled towards the forest of mangroves, staring at the twisted trunks that grew out of the shallows.

Kitty had been peering at the water, watching a shoal of tiny silver fish flex and dart. Suddenly the shoal broke through the surface, flying through the air and diving back down.

'Did you see that?' Kitty had laughed, swinging around to face Lana. The movement unsettled the paddleboard, rocking it from side to side. Kitty squealed as they capsized, the two of them sinking through the water in a tangle of limbs. They surfaced, squirting water from their mouths.

They never made it to the edge of the mangrove forest, but instead lay with their bodies draped over the board, their legs dangling in the sea. The evening sun dried the water from their shoulders, leaving whorls of salt on their skin. 'I think,' Kitty had said as they drifted, her gaze on *The Blue*, which was gilded by the lowering sun, 'this is the happiest I'll ever be.'

It is memories like those – ones that just popped into Lana's head as if sewn into the fibre of her being – that jolt her awake. They force her to remember that – despite everything that happened during those final days on *The Blue* – Kitty is her best friend.

Kitty was the one who plaited beads into Lana's hair during

the long hot summer they turned twelve, spending most of their afternoons jumping over the sprinkler in Lana's garden; Kitty was the one who hung out with her at the skate park, sitting on a concrete bench and listening to the roll of wheels in the half-pipe; Kitty was the one who Lana called to tell her she was thinking of quitting her degree, needing to hear her voice saying, 'You're too good to drop out.'

Other people collected friends like badges but Lana chose only one – and that friendship was pinned so close to her heart that removing it had left behind a jagged tear.

When Lana left *The Blue*, she didn't consider that she might never see Kitty again. But what if it is Kitty's body that the EPIRB has been found strapped to? What if the last time Lana saw her – with all the hurt and anger sharpening her words into blades – what if those are the final things she'll ever say to her?

Having Kitty in her life was like finding the one other person who could speak her secret language; it was being understood without needing to explain; it was knowing that there was someone to call in the middle of the night when the rest of the world fell dark. But now Kitty is out there at sea and Lana is sitting here on land, warm and safe.

They should be together. That was how it was always meant to be.

*

An hour passes without news. Lana takes her mobile from her pocket, wondering whether she should call Kitty's father and let him know what's happening. She imagines his voice at the other end of the line, the slight slur to his vowels depending on what time of day she caught him.

Growing up, Lana had watched Kitty's father with curiosity. He had a waterbed, played his music loud, and wore gel in his hair – even into his fifties. Sometimes he'd dance through the house, grabbing Kitty and waltzing her across the lounge, lifting her off the ground so only her toes brushed the carpet. Lana would try to imagine her own father – who listened to radio plays, and drank two ales a week at Sunday lunchtime – behaving in the same way, but couldn't. She wasn't envious, though, because Kitty's father stormed through the house more than he danced, banging doors and yelling, swear words rolling from his mouth.

Kitty never used the word 'alcoholic', but she didn't need to. She spent more time at Lana's house than she did at home, as then she didn't have to worry about what time her father would get back, or what mood he'd be in. Living with Kitty's father seemed to Lana like riding a roller coaster with your eyes closed – you didn't know when to expect the drop. When they were teenagers, sometimes he'd take them out to the pub, buy them drinks, and show off his 'beautiful Kitty' to his friends – and other times he'd call her a lazy cow, and tell her she was dreaming if she thought she'd be an actress some day. The swerve of his affections left deep grooves in Kitty, and it was Lana who had to pick up the pieces.

Now she turns her mobile over in her hands, then slips it back in her bag. She'll call Kitty's father when there is something concrete to say.

The door to the waiting room opens and Paul Carter enters, followed by a middle-aged couple. The woman has thick blonde hair tied back in a low ponytail, and she wears new plimsolls, jeans and a V-neck sweater. The man, her husband Lana imagines, pulls out a chair for his wife. The plastic chair squeaks against the metal legs as she lowers herself down.

'I'll be back as soon as we have any news,' Paul Carter says, then leaves the room before anyone has a chance to stop him.

'Hi,' Lana says, her gaze fixed on the couple. She wonders if they could be Denny's parents – she knows that they live in New Zealand – yet somehow they don't tally with her imagined picture of them. Denny had told her his mother was a primary school teacher who cycled to work on an old shopper bike she'd had for twenty years, and his father ran a small boatyard as a retirement business.

'Hello. I'm Kristel, and this is my husband, Peter.'

With a fingertip the man pushes a pair of frameless glasses up the bridge of his nose, and nods at Lana.

'Do you have family on the yacht, too?' Kristel asks.

'My best friend. Kitty.'

She nods. 'It's just so . . . unbearable. Our daughter was on board. Michelle Keyser.'

Lana doesn't recognize the name immediately. It is possible that new crew have joined in the months since Lana left – but no, she saw the crew list pinned to the office wall. She looks again at the woman, taking in the thick blonde hair, the unlined, bronzed skin, the attractive symmetry of her features. Michelle. Shell. 'You're Shell's parents. From Ontario.'

'You know Shell?' Kristel asks, her face brightening.

'We used to sail together on *The Blue*.'

'Did you? Was the boat good – was it safe? Peter taught her to sail, didn't you?' Shell's mother says, turning towards her husband.

'We live by a lake,' he says. 'Shell was out on the water before she could even walk. But she'd not sailed in the sea, not with me.' He adds, 'Still, she'd know what to do in a crisis. Lateral thinker, Shell. Doesn't panic. She'd have kept her head, I know it. She'll be fine.'

'What happened?' Shell's mother is asking. 'They haven't told us anything yet – only that the yacht got into trouble and has sunk.'

Lana thinks about the EPIRB strapped to a body. She wonders whether Shell's parents have been informed about it, and decides they probably haven't. 'I don't know much more, I'm afraid.'

'Makes no sense to me,' Shell's father says with a sharp shake of his head. 'I've checked the forecast – it wasn't terrible. No deep low pressure or particularly big swell. I just don't understand. All of them were competent sailors. I'm guessing the skipper was experienced – he would've had them all in their life jackets, followed safety protocols?'

Lana thinks of them lounging around the deck in their swimwear, their skin tanned, life jackets rarely worn. They were all relaxed in their approach to safety and protocols – too relaxed.

With a shiver, she thinks of the fatal price they've paid.

'I'm sure they'll be fine,' she says weakly. But just like Shell's parents, she is struggling to understand what could have happened out on the water. What caused the yacht to sink? And why was the EPIRB found strapped to a body?

Shell's mother asks, 'How was Shell when you travelled with her? Did she seem happy?'

Lana thinks about the postcards Shell used to send home, and the way her eyes glassed over when she spoke about her parents. 'She wrote to you,' Lana says. 'Every week.'

She realizes her tone is too abrupt by the way Shell's mother tenses, her eyes flicking to her husband.

'Yes, she did,' is all he says.

They fall into silence for some time. Shell's mother wrings her hands together in her lap, the metallic scrape of jewellery scratching into the room. After a while, her husband reaches out and places a hand over his wife's. Lana isn't sure whether it is a gesture of comfort or irritation.

Shell's mother stares out of the window, her gaze just beyond where Lana sits. 'Shell told you, I suppose, that she left . . . under difficult circumstances.'

'Yes.'

'We regret that. Deeply. That's why we're here. It was going to be a surprise, us coming out to New Zealand.'

'Shell didn't know?'

She shakes her head. 'In Shell's last postcard she told us that the boat was docking here and she'd be getting off.' She glances at her husband who is rubbing a thinning spot at the back of his head. 'We talked about it . . . realized we didn't want to miss another moment of our daughter's life. So we booked our flights here.'

Her husband tips back his head, staring at the ceiling, 'We should've let her know we were on our way. That we'd be waiting for her. Maybe it would have made a difference.'

This time it is Shell's mother who reaches out, taking his hand. 'It's okay.'

'It's not. You wanted to get in touch with Shell months ago! You didn't even want to let her go in the first place!' He swallows. 'It was me. I let my daughter disappear from our lives when I should've told her that whatever she does, whoever she becomes, I will love her.' He pauses. 'But I didn't.' His head bows under the weight of his misery. His wife pulls him into her arms. She holds him close, regret etched deep into both of their faces.

Lana turns away. She stares beyond the window, thinking about how regrets can burrow under your skin, take root inside you, so that there is no escaping them. For Lana, what happened during the passage they made from the Philippines to Palau still haunts her. She's tried to let it go – push the questions out of her mind – but no matter how hard she's worked to forget, the memories are still there, as vivid and bright as freshly drawn blood.

10

THEN

On board *The Blue*, February passed in a sun-drunk bliss of happiness. Lana spent her days snorkelling and swimming over pristine reefs; drawing in the shade with her sketchbook propped on her knees; practising yoga on the foredeck with Shell as the sun went down.

The nights on the yacht – black and looming, bursting with stars – were intoxicating. Lana and Kitty were often the last to their bunks, their thoughts loosened by rum, whispering giddily about the day. Some evenings, when there was little breeze and their cabin was stifling, they'd stay up on deck, falling asleep on the dewy cockpit cushions or swaying together in the hammock like on their first night.

'Do you think it's possible to get bored of this?' Kitty said, lying on a towel on deck.

The yacht was cruising downwind in a light south-westerly breeze with the spinnaker flying. Lana drew an arm over her face before opening her eyes a fraction, squinting up at the billowing curve of the sail. The warm sea breeze smelt of ozone and salt, and the waves rocked lightly beneath them. 'Nope.'

'Looks like you're catching the sun on your back,' Heinrich said to Shell, who was threading colourful beads onto a strand of leather. 'Want me to put some more cream on?'

'Please,' she said, stretching forward and picking up a bottle of suncream.

In easy sailing conditions like this, only one or two people were needed to man the boat so the others could lie in the sun, read, cook, exercise, play cards, or just talk.

Shell undid her bikini top and Heinrich placed his palms in the centre of her back, smoothing the cream into her skin.

Through the gap in the crook of her elbow, Lana watched Heinrich's fingers draw slow circles down the length of Shell's back. His expression was concentrated, his gaze mapping every inch of her back.

'Bliss,' Shell moaned.

Slowly, Heinrich drew his hands outwards, sliding them up the sides of Shell's body, his eyes briefly fluttering closed. There was a sheen of sweat across his forehead and Lana thought, *You poor bugger*.

Heinrich must have become aware of Lana watching because suddenly his eyes snapped open, meeting hers. His hands froze. A hint of redness bled into his cheeks.

Lana glanced away, sorry for witnessing something that Heinrich intended to keep private.

A moment later she heard him getting to his feet, saying, 'All done.'

'Really?' Shell said. 'Did you do—'

'The lines!' Aaron bellowed from the helm. 'There's something on both trolling lines!'

Everyone turned towards the stern where both fishing reels were whizzing out.

Denny, who'd been coiling a rope, dropped what he was doing and bounded down the length of the yacht, grabbing one of the rods – grinning and yelling for Heinrich to do the same.

Heinrich reached the second rod, hanging on tightly as it bowed against the pull of the fish.

Lana, Kitty and Shell went over to watch, and Joseph appeared on deck, blinking in the sunlight, asking what they thought it was.

'Could be mahi-mahi,' Denny said, the muscles in his forearms straining as he gripped the rod. 'Good size, whatever it is.' He reeled in a little way, fighting against the heavy pull.

'This one is a beast,' Heinrich said, his brow creased as he focused on the line. He glanced over his shoulder at Denny. 'First to land their fish gets ice-cold beers all day.'

'You're on!'

There was always a competition where Heinrich was involved. Shell had told Lana that he used to be a professional tennis player. Apparently his parents were highly ambitious on his behalf and from the age of ten he was thrust into a strict training schedule, with even his diet monitored. Lana could picture him on a tennis court – the starched whites, the long muscular calves, the steady gaze fixed on his opponent. Heinrich had the focus and drive to excel, she had no doubt, but an elbow injury had stopped him. He'd needed surgery three times in three years, cutting short his career in his prime. The disappointment must have been enormous, and Lana wondered whether that's why Heinrich had been drawn to *The Blue* – a lifestyle without routine, and not a tennis court in sight.

It took almost an hour to land both fish. Heinrich got his on deck first and pumped a fist into the air. The fish, mahi-mahi as Denny had guessed, had cartoonish blunt faces and yellowy-blue bodies that seemed iridescent in the sunlight. They flapped and writhed, red gills pumping, and after being admired for a few moments, the smaller of the two was released back into the water. Lana was pleased to see the sharp flick of its tail as it disappeared beneath the surface. The larger one – big enough to feed the whole crew plentifully – was killed swiftly with a blow to the head.

With all the excitement Lana hadn't looked up, and now she saw they were sailing closer to the coastline where they were hoping to anchor.

'What do you reckon?' Aaron said to Denny. 'Dinner on the beach tonight? Cook up the fish over a fire?'

*

Once anchored, they took the dinghy to shore along with the prepared fish and a cool box of beers.

'Want to help me look for wood?' Denny called to Lana as she set down a tray of plates on a blanket.

Dusk was settling and mosquitoes were just starting to dust

the sky as she followed him towards the treeline. Hardy plants grew out of crevices in the rocks, and the air was scented with earth. There was plenty of wood to collect – broken branches, driftwood washed up on a high tide, coconut husks for kindling.

Lana picked up a beautiful piece of driftwood bleached grey by the sea. She lifted it to her face, turning it through her fingers to admire its natural curves, then ran her lips against it to feel the grain of the wood. She'd love to sketch it, to try and capture the way the sea had rubbed it smooth over the years.

When she glanced up, Denny was watching her. Evening light filtered through the branches of the trees, catching the side of his face. He smiled.

After their first kiss in the limestone cathedral, they'd climbed out of the cavernous cool, blinking into the daylight. Their fingers had laced together and they'd stood at the entrance to the cave, a buzz of exhilaration whipping between them.

Since then, they'd kept managing to find excuses to be on their own – swimming together, offering to go ashore for provisions, stealing moments alone before the others woke, slipping away to make love when they reached empty coves. In the company of the crew they acted as though nothing had changed, careful not to draw attention to their growing closeness and the rule they were flouting.

Denny moved towards her, his eyes not leaving her face. He dropped the wood he'd collected, then he reached out and carefully removed the piece of driftwood from Lana's grasp. His hands moved to her waist and he drew her towards him. 'You're so beautiful,' he told her.

She had never associated herself with that word – her body too angular, the planes of her face too sharp – yet within Denny's arms, she felt it.

She kissed him, breathing in the smell of salt on his skin, and the heat of desire burnt through her. Her hands slipped under his T-shirt and she felt the warmth of his skin beneath her palms. He pulled her in to him more deeply.

They lowered themselves onto the ground, Denny's weight on top of Lana. She felt herself groan as his hands moved lower, sliding beneath the cotton of her dress.

Nearby there was the sound of rustling, as if a foot had come into contact with brittle twigs. Startled, they both looked up.

She couldn't make out anything beyond the dense trees, which had been leached of colour in the half-light of dusk.

Lana held her breath, waiting.

Then the sound came again – a snapping of twigs.

'Is someone there?' she whispered to Denny.

They waited with their heads raised, the warmth of Denny's chest pressing against her.

Nothing but silence followed. They listened for a minute or so, and gradually Lana's heart rate began to slow as she realized it must have been an animal.

Just as Denny turned back to her, there was a blur of movement between the trees – the shadow of a person disappearing into the woodland.

'Who is it?' Denny called, lurching to his feet.

The footsteps vanished and then there was silence, save for the croak of crickets. A chain of goosebumps had risen across her skin. 'Who was that?'

'No idea,' Denny said, getting to his feet.

Lana sat up, dusting dry leaves from the back of her dress. 'Do you think it was one of the crew?'

'I don't know,' he said, his brow ridged with frown lines. A moment later he stretched out a hand and helped Lana to her feet. 'Come on,' he said. 'We should get back.'

*

Lana had prepared the mahi-mahi on the yacht, seasoning the thick steaks of fish with oil and spices, then wrapping them in foil. They cooked the parcels at the edge of the fire, along with a pan of rice. Kitty made a mango-and-red-onion salad and they ate with plates on their laps and woodsmoke in their hair.

Lana sat slightly back from the heat of the fire while she was eating, pleased that the smoke was keeping the mosquitoes at bay. She couldn't shake the thought that someone had been in the woods watching her and Denny. She remembered that night they'd all been swimming together and she'd felt a cool slithering touch beneath the water, like a hand trailing down her spine. Lana shivered, pushing the memory away.

Opposite her, Joseph set down his plate – his food barely touched – and held a thin branch into the flames, lighting the end of it. Then he pulled it out and waved the flame in the sky, like a child entranced with a sparkler.

Beyond him, out in the dark bay, the yacht looked serene as it rode on its anchor, masthead light winking. She briefly wondered what would happen if the yacht came free of the anchor while they were all ashore. It would drift off with the current or tide and they'd be left stranded with a tiny dinghy and no supplies.

In the distance she saw a second light moving across the water at the edge of the bay. She stared, following the glow.

'Another boat,' Aaron said, noticing her looking.

As the yacht moved closer, she saw its pale shadow cruise beyond the edge of the beach. The deck of the yacht was lit up, but appeared empty.

'Autopilot,' Aaron said.

'Looks eerie.'

'Perhaps it is a ghost ship,' Joseph said, watching it glide over the silent water, the smoking branch still gripped in his fingers. He turned to Lana. 'You know of the story – *Mary Celeste?*'

She shook her head.

'*Mary Celeste* was a merchant ship. One day – a long time ago now – a boat came across it, but found no crew on deck. No one. But the sails were up. They shouted, wanting to get the crew's attention. But there is nothing. Nobody around. Eventually they manage to board the ship – but it was completely abandoned. They search the boat and found a life raft was missing and all of the seven crew. But there is no . . .' He struggled for a word. 'No reason. No explanation. The boat is in good condition. There is food. The sea is calm, the weather good. It is . . .' He paused for a moment. 'A ghost ship.'

From the other side of the fire, Kitty asked, 'What happened?'

Joseph pressed the branch back into the flames, his eyes glittering as he said, 'The crew was never found. There is many theory about pirates, a mutiny, sea monsters. But no one knows the truth.'

'Sea's a dangerous place,' Aaron said, setting his plate on the sand and leaning over to the ice cooler to hook out a cold beer. 'Usually it's the stupid things that cause accidents. I heard of a guy who was pissed and motoring back across the harbour in his dinghy. He fell in, stepping from the dinghy to the yacht. He hit his head, drowned.'

'Shit,' Heinrich said.

'When I was in Tahiti there was this married couple, South Africans, cruising around the South Pacific in a beautiful yacht. The man went overboard, knocked in by the boom. His wife saw it happen – threw out the life ring, logged the coordinates, did everything right. It was a calm day, perfect visibility, but by the time she managed to tack, then furl the sail and try and get to him under motor, she'd lost sight of him.'

'But she found him eventually?' Lana asked.

Aaron shook his head. 'He drowned. Most people that go overboard on passage don't make it back onto the boat alive.'

Lana said nothing more. She looked out to sea, wondering about the darker currents that ran through its depths.

*

After dinner, Kitty pulled two bottles of rum from her bag with a flourish, and passed them around the fire. Heinrich was playing the guitar, his shoulders rounded, eyes half-closed as he strummed a bluesy melody. The music seemed to soften the harder edges of his personality and, watching him, Lana felt that she still didn't know Heinrich fully, not yet.

She lay back with her head cushioned in the cool sand, feeling the rum swirling hot in her belly. She tried to picture what she'd be doing if she were in her old life but she couldn't even recall what day of the week it was. Out here the days rolled together in a bliss of free time, unpunctuated by dates or appointments.

She heard Kitty's laughter, a loud gush of it, and Lana saw she was leaning against Aaron, her hair falling over her face, her dark top slipping down from one of her shoulders.

Heinrich began playing an upbeat song and Kitty rose to her feet, dancing barefoot in the sand. Her expression was distant and her eyes glazed, but her body found the rhythm of the chords and she swung her hips. There was clapping from the group. Someone shouted, 'Go, Kitty!'

She tipped back her head and laughed, then danced harder. Her necklace swung with her, a silver bell Lana had given her, catching the firelight.

Kitty was like a lantern, burning bright on people's attentions. She could hit a high for days – socializing, staying up late, drinking, smoking, being the centre of the party – but Lana knew what she was like when her wick burnt out.

Shell was the first to be drawn to her feet by Kitty, who took her hand and tugged at her teasingly. Shell dusted the sand from the backs of her legs and began to dance, too. They looked beautiful together in the firelight, long hair swishing over their shoulders.

Joseph was next to be caught in Kitty's beam. She danced towards where he was sitting and plucked the lit cigarette from his mouth, placing it between her lips, then pulling him to his feet with both hands.

She spun him around on the spot and Joseph surprised Lana by laughing as he twirled. When Kitty let him go, he continued to dance, using his arms as vigorously as his legs in a peculiarly jerky manner.

For a few minutes, Joseph, Shell and Kitty danced together, making an odd but pleasing picture. Lana didn't join them, content to watch. When Heinrich's tune ended, he strummed a slower groove and Joseph flopped back down on the sand, sweating at the temples. Kitty wasn't done. She drew Shell close, slipping a knee between Shell's. She placed her hands on Shell's waist and set a rhythm, moving their hips together so that they danced as one. Shell's top had ridden up, exposing a glimpse of her flat, toned stomach. Kitty ran a thumb over the bare skin there, and Lana saw the way Shell's gaze focused on her.

With her hands around Shell's waist, Kitty slowly arched backwards, her body curving, the stretch of her throat exposed – lips parted, dark hair swaying towards the sand. There was clapping from around the fire and someone wolf-whistled.

Then slowly, sensually, Kitty rose back up, pressing her hips against Shell's. When she had straightened, she placed her hands around Shell's face, drawing Shell towards her and kissing her deeply. Shell responded immediately, her fingers splaying through Kitty's hair.

Oh, Kit! Lana thought, rolling her eyes.

She glanced at Heinrich who was still managing to keep a tune, while watching them kissing. She couldn't read his expression clearly in the firelight and wondered whether he was turned on – or hurt – to see Shell with Kitty. Nearby, Aaron's face was aglow with a wide grin. He gave an approving hoot, raising his beer into the air. Lana thought, *The 'No relationships' rule clearly doesn't apply here.*

Denny and Joseph had their backs to the performance, and were talking together in French. The rumble of Denny's laughter reached her across the flames.

When she'd finished her drink, she got to her feet and wandered through the cool sand down to the shore. Away from the heat of the fire the air felt pleasingly fresh. She sat cross-legged on the shoreline, listening to the sea wash in and draw out, like slow breaths.

Voices and laughter trickled over from the fire, and Lana drew her knees up to her chest, linking her arms around them. A minute or so later, there was the light tread of footsteps and she turned to see Kitty weaving towards her, the strap of her top slipping down from her shoulder, her hair loose. She came to a stop at the water's edge and turned to face Lana. 'You disappeared,' Kitty said, shifting her weight onto one foot so her hip stuck out.

Lana nodded in the direction of the fire. 'What was that about with Shell?'

'Just a bit of fun.'

'Hope that's how Shell sees it.'

'Your point being?' Kitty challenged, an eyebrow arched.

'I just don't want you to complicate things.'

Kitty tipped back her head and laughed, the sound sharp in her throat. '*Complicate?*' Kitty said, facing Lana. 'Interesting advice – coming from you.'

Occasionally, when Kitty had been drinking, Lana could see a flash of Kitty's father in her: confrontational, feisty, aiming to provoke. 'What do you mean?'

Kitty's hands opened in front of her. 'Were you ever going to tell me about him?'

Lana closed her eyes. 'Denny.'

'Why didn't you say anything? We're travelling together. We live on the same boat. We share a cabin, for fuck's sake! Why didn't you talk to me?' Kitty's eyes shone with tears.

Lana felt a stab of shame. 'I didn't know if it was anything at first . . .'

'We've always, *always*, told each other everything.'

It was true. That's what made them work. Kitty was the one person she could trust implicitly. Yet Lana hadn't breathed a word about Denny – and she knew why. What she and Kitty had found on *The Blue* was a rare, beautiful freedom to travel with friends among some of the most incredible islands in the world. Once that freedom became entangled with different loyalties and relationships, it could change everything. Kitty knew it, and Lana knew it, too. Admitting that she and Denny were breaking the 'no relationships' rule was paramount to Lana saying that she was prepared to risk what she and Kitty had found – for him.

'I'm sorry,' Lana said, digging her fingers into the damp sand. 'Really, Kit. I am. I should've told you. I don't know what I was thinking. Sorry you had to find out like that.'

'Like what?'

'Earlier. In the woods.'

Kitty looked blank. 'I haven't been in the woods. I've known for days – I've just been waiting for you to tell me.' Her head shook as she said, 'Don't look so surprised – it's obvious from the way you are around him. It won't be long before the others guess, too. What then?'

'I don't know.'

'Have you fucked each other?'

'Jesus, Kit!' Lana said, glancing over her shoulder to check they were out of earshot from the crew.

'I'll take that as a yes.'

'I like him, okay. I like Denny a lot.' It was the first time she'd admitted that – even to herself. Denny was so different from her previous boyfriends with his easy optimism and his wonderfully straightforward approach to life. She loved the way his eyes smiled even in his resting face, and that when he laughed he'd look down, rolling his head from side to side. She loved that he wasn't interested in what he wore, or owned, or how he appeared to others – but that it was everything else that captured him. He was thirsty for life – all of it.

'What about Aaron's rule?' Kitty said. 'He made it clear from the start.'

'I know . . .'

Kitty's voice was quieter, serious. 'I like what we've got going on with *The Blue*, Lana. I *really* like it. Please, don't fuck it up for us.'

11
NOW

I n the waiting room at the Maritime Rescue Centre Lana
remains seated in the window alcove, eager for news. Shell's
father paces the room, his hands locked behind his back. Every
now and then he pauses, rolling his weight from his heels to
the balls of his feet, back and forth, back and forth, chin stretched
out. Shell's mother searches in her handbag, pulling out a black
purse, a packet of mints, and finally – what she is after – a
balled-up tissue.

The door to the waiting room opens and Paul Carter is
ushering a second couple inside. Although Lana has never seen
them before, she instinctively knows who they are. The woman
has a tall, slender frame and pale-blue eyes. Her husband is
thickset, with sun-damaged skin and grey hair spun into tight
curls.

'Hello,' the man says to them all with a firm nod.

Lana's skin prickles from the nape of her neck to her fingertips: Denny's voice. Denny's accent.

Now she remembers seeing a photo of this couple pinned to the wall of Denny's cabin. In the picture the two of them were sitting together on a veranda filled with colourful pot plants. They were both laughing at whatever the person behind the camera had been saying, Denny's father wagging a finger, his other hand interlaced with his wife's.

Lana saw the photo when she went to Denny's cabin to deliver a message and he opened the door with wet hair and a towel in his hand. On seeing Lana, his face split into a wide grin. He looked past her, checking the passageway in both directions, and then pulled her into the room, kicking the door shut behind him.

He held a finger up to his lips. When he kissed her, he was smiling so hard that their teeth clashed. Her hands wrapped around him, feeling the softness of his skin, running over the hard edges of his back, shoulder blades, chest. His hair was still wet from the shower and she spread her fingers through it, drawing them downwards over his neck and shoulders. She had the sensation that their bodies slotted together – their lips, the contours of their hands, the way his knees fitted between hers when they fell onto the bed. Whichever way they lay or stood or rolled, it felt just right.

But that memory had been made a long time ago. Before the passage. Before Joseph.

Denny's parents introduce themselves as Bill and Marg.

'You're Denny's parents,' Lana says.

'Yes, that's—' Bill stops suddenly, turning.

Paul Carter is still standing in the doorway, clearing his throat to speak. 'As everyone's all together, I just wanted to give you a brief update.'

Shell's parents glance at one another.

'I'm afraid there's still no information about the crew as yet, but we do know what caused *The Blue* to go down. We only received an incomplete Mayday at eight hundred hours, but another vessel managed to pick up a further transmission. While *The Blue* was under sail, she hit a partially submerged container.'

'Jesus Christ!' Shell's father exclaims.

The muscles in Lana's neck tighten. Hitting a floating container is a skipper's worst nightmare. Aaron told them how 2,000 containers are lost from cargo ships every year. Sometimes they slip off in difficult seas, or it's rumoured that captains occasionally decide to relinquish one or two if fuel is running low, or speeds need to be increased. The containers – huge metal rectangular structures that probably weigh more than an average yacht – can float at sea for years, usually lying just below the surface, making them almost impossible to see.

Paul Carter continues, 'During the contact the second vessel had with the skipper of *The Blue*, it appears that the corner of the container struck them in the centre of the hull, piercing through it.'

Lana tries to imagine it: sailing along in good winds, focused on getting back to land. Had whoever was on watch seen part of the submerged container at the last minute and called out, hauling the wheel away from it? Or was the container completely hidden, lurking beneath the surface, and suddenly there was an almighty crash – something you never expect to hear in the open ocean – as the hull hit metal?

She imagines the crew's shock. Were some of them asleep at the time? Who was on watch? How long was it before they realized that the hull had been pierced and water was coming on board? She wonders at what point Aaron decided to put out a Mayday. Did he hesitate, wanting to deal with it alone? Or did he alert the authorities quickly?

'I'm sorry that we don't have anything more to go on right now. But we are doing everything we can, and there's a good team searching for the crew.'

'What about the life raft?' Denny's father asks. 'Did they get on it?'

'We don't know for definite, but I'd hope that yes, they would've.' He looks around the room, then nods and says, 'I hope to be back soon with more news.'

*

'I can't believe it,' Denny's father is saying. 'A gash right in the hull? Worst place for it! All those years I ran that boat and I never saw a single container.'

Shell's father asks, 'You used to run the boat?'

Denny's father nods. 'Seventeen years of charters I did on her.'

Shell's father's tone is almost accusatory as he asks, 'Was the safety equipment up to standard? They had all the correct gear, I'm assuming?'

Denny's father replies that the yacht was refitted by the

skipper before setting sail, but Lana tunes out of the details as she is focusing on the first detail Denny's father mentioned: he used to own *The Blue*.

She had known that the yacht was an ex-charter, but hadn't realized that Aaron had bought it from Denny's parents. Denny joined the yacht when Aaron was somewhere in northern Australia, and she guesses that it must have been Denny's parents who put him in touch with Aaron.

For some reason though, it makes her feel odd that she's only learnt this now. She rubs her fingers across her brow, feeling unsettled by the new knowledge, as if she's missed something important.

*

In the waiting room, time drags. Shell's parents talk together in low voices. Denny's mother tries to draw Lana into conversation, saying, 'Your accent . . . you're British?'

'Yes.'

'What brings you to New Zealand? Did you come here to meet the yacht?'

The question stalls Lana. Why is she here? Why New Zealand out of all the places she could've disappeared to?

Maybe it's no coincidence that she's built a life here, renting an apartment where she can hear the shriek of masts and rigging in an easterly, or catch the white wing of a sail on the horizon. New Zealand was always going to be where *The Blue* returned to, where the crew – and Kitty – would finally be stepping off.

'Yes,' Lana says eventually, suddenly seeing the raw truth beneath her choices. 'I came here to meet the yacht.'

Denny's mother looks at her with interest and Lana thinks she is going to have to say more – but then everyone is turning as Paul Carter re-enters the room.

His expression is serious, his mouth set in a straight line.

Shell's mother half-stands, her fingers curled tight around a tissue.

His gaze travels across each of the five people in the room. Lana's stomach curdles as she realizes he has news.

Paul Carter's gaze comes to rest on Denny's parents. His voice is grave as he says, 'Would you mind coming with me?'

12

THEN

Lana stepped out of the bank and moved along the street, passing vendors selling cooked meats and grilled corn on the cob. *The Blue* was currently moored in Toron, a busy town on the eastern edge of the Philippines that was to be their last port. They'd already been here for ten days and everyone was growing impatient as they waited for a weather window to make the passage to Palau. It would be a 1,500-nautical-mile ocean crossing, which would take around a week in good conditions – longer if the wind turned fickle.

Lana had come into town to withdraw the next week's payment for her and Kitty. They took it in turns to pay each week and, having checked their balance, Lana was disheartened to see they'd only be able to afford another couple of months with the crew – unless they came up with some way of making money. Kitty had already threatened to take out a loan if needs be, saying, 'A little detail like money isn't going to be parting me from *The Blue*.'

Town felt crowded and noisy after the yacht, and the smell of sewage and strong spices assaulted her senses. Even though it was still early, the heat was already building and she could feel the back of her dress beginning to cling to her skin.

She passed an ice-cream seller and decided to cheer herself up with a cone of home-made mango ice cream. She stepped from the busy main street into the entrance of an alley, where she ate in the shade, leaning her back against the wall.

As she was standing there, Lana saw Aaron exiting an Internet café; his laptop was under one arm, and he was pulling down his cap with his other hand. He turned, saying something to the person following behind: Denny. Lana found herself smiling as she watched Denny, taking in the way his shorts were just a little too big for him and hung boyishly from his hips.

She was about to step forward and say hello, but something made her hesitate. Aaron was striding on, his right hand balled into a fist at his side, and Denny – who was hurrying to keep up – seemed to be trying to say something, his hands opening in front of him.

It looked as if they were arguing. Denny was partially obscured by a man carrying a crate of empty glass bottles, but she could see the heightened colour in Aaron's face as they neared. She caught his voice rising above the street noise. 'I knew it! I fucking knew it! I said all along—'

'Listen, Aaron, we don't know for sure . . .' The rest of Denny's sentence was lost to a tricycle whizzing by, tinny pop music blaring.

Suddenly Aaron stopped and turned sharply to face Denny,

the flow of people having to move around them. Lana pressed herself back against the wall. She could feel the drip of melted ice cream on the back of her hand, but didn't move to lick it off. She remained still, staring at the profiles of both men: Aaron's neck was a furious red, the veins prominent. Denny's brows were furrowed together as he listened.

'I can't be here any longer,' Aaron said, his teeth clamped tight around his words.

'What do you want to do?' Denny asked.

'Leave. I can't still be fucking around in port, just waiting for it. I've got to be on the water by the fifteenth, you know that.'

Denny reached out and placed a hand on Aaron's shoulder. He held it there, applying a firm pressure. 'I know,' he said slowly. 'I know.'

Aaron nodded once, turned from Denny and marched on.

Lana heard Denny sigh as he thrust his hands deep into his shorts pockets, shaking his head. He stood for a moment, watching until Aaron disappeared. Then he turned in the other direction and was swallowed once again by the crowd.

*

When Lana returned to the yacht an hour or so later, the place was buzzing with activity. Denny was pulling the cushions from the saloon seats and checking the equipment stored beneath; Aaron was sitting at the nav station looking through the charts; Heinrich was kneeling on the floor with parts of the spare water pump in pieces in front of him; Shell and Kitty were pulling out some of the dry goods from the cupboards and decanting them into smaller containers in the galley.

'What's going on?' Lana asked Kitty.

'We're leaving for Palau. This evening.'

'What? I thought the forecast wasn't looking good?'

'It's improved,' Aaron said. 'Looks like the nor'easterlies are easing. Blowing ten to fifteen knots now. Plus, there's a low-pressure system arriving in two to three days that looks likely to hang around a while. If we don't go now, we could end up being in port another fortnight – maybe more. It's getting too near typhoon season to risk setting out much later.'

Lana thought about the conversation between Denny and Aaron that she'd overheard, guessing it had something to do with this sudden decision. *I can't still be fucking around, just waiting for it. I've got to be on the water by the fifteenth, you know that.*

'Be prepared for a busy afternoon,' Aaron said to the crew. 'We need to fill up the water tank, refuel, provision, and clear out of immigration. Shell and Heinrich, you're in charge of buying dry goods, and Lana and Kitty, you'll do the fresh produce.' He handed out lists written in a neat masculine script. 'Denny, I need you to get across town and pick up some spare water containers and batteries. We'll all meet back here at sixteen hundred hours ready to go to immigration.' He looked at the crew. 'Everyone clear?'

Without waiting for an answer, Aaron returned to his charts, a deep frown of concentration lining his face.

When Denny left the saloon, Lana followed him up onto deck. She watched him for a few moments as he concentrated on unclipping the large canopy over the boom ready to stow it for passage. His movements were sharp and hurried and she could see the tension in his jaw as he struggled with one of the clips.

'Hey,' she said, behind him.

He turned, startled. On seeing her he smiled, his expression softening a little.

'Want a hand?'

'Sure.'

Together they unclipped the rest of the canopy. The midday sun was fierce and Lana could feel the heat tingling over her shoulders as they finished removing the canopy, shaking it out over the side of the yacht. As they folded it away, Lana said, 'I saw you and Aaron in town earlier – coming out of that Internet place.'

'Did you?'

'It looked like something was up.'

Denny kept his attention fixed on the canopy. 'All's good.'

Lana glanced towards the hatch to check no one was coming. 'How did the forecast look to you? Are you happy it's the right time to leave?'

'Aaron knows what he's doing,' Denny said, taking the canopy from her, a slight rebuke in his tone.

'Denny,' she said, stepping forward and placing a hand on his forearm so that he looked up, facing her. She lowered her voice as she asked, 'Is everything okay? Really? In town Aaron looked . . . I don't know . . . troubled. And now, all of a sudden, we're leaving.'

'It's not sudden, Lana. We've been waiting to leave for almost a fortnight. Now the forecast has come good, so we're going.'

A brightly painted *bangka* motored by, trailing a cloud of dark fumes. Its wake knocked against *The Blue*, gently rocking them from side to side.

'Shouldn't there have been a group vote on it?'

'On whether to set sail? That's always the skipper's call. The rest of us haven't studied the charts or forecasts to be able to make that decision.'

It was a fair point. Denny was the next most experienced crew member on board and she knew he had an instinctive, intuitive approach to the sea. She'd noticed the way Aaron would seek out Denny's opinion, listening closely to what he said. 'If you think it's the right decision, then I'm happy with it, too,' she said, leaning forward and placing a kiss on his neck.

Denny's gaze moved from her to the hatch.

Lana turned and saw Kitty standing there. 'Ready to get these provisions?' she said coolly.

*

They took the dinghy to shore in silence. Once they got into town, Lana struggled to keep up as Kitty ducked around the back of a tricycle, then followed a narrow rubble path between two buildings where the stifling air smelt of chicken muck and spices.

Once the fruit market was in sight, Kitty said, 'I'll meet you there. I just need to pick up a couple of things.' She peeled away before Lana had a chance to ask any questions.

The fruit and vegetable stalls stood shoulder to shoulder

beneath a dusty white awning. She moved into the shaded, sweet-scented air, browsing the beautifully displayed produce. Huge bunches of deep-yellow bananas hung from the tops of the stalls; crates of watermelons hunkered together; squat pears were neatly placed in white nets.

She filled several bags with fresh vegetables and deliciously ripe fruit as per Aaron's list. It was only when she was leaving that Kitty rejoined her.

'Sorry, had a few shopping requests from the others,' Kitty said, glancing down at the bag in her hand which was clinking with bottles.

Lana said nothing.

Since their row at the beach fire, it felt as though a barrier had gone up between them. Sensing Kitty's disapproval about Denny, Lana had been wary of mentioning his name. Yesterday she and Denny had gone to pick up a spare part for one of the bilge pumps, and had a couple of hours to themselves. They'd enjoyed lunch at a dusty roadside place where they sat with their hands linked across the table, talking and laughing. When she returned to the yacht, she'd been desperate to tell Kitty about her day – but there was such frostiness in Kitty's tone as she'd asked, 'Had a good time, did you?' that Lana decided it would be best to keep quiet.

They walked in silence to the wet market, the fetid smell of the place drifting downwind towards them before they'd even reached it. Set at the edge of the harbour, the building was open-sided with a tin roof. Long stone benches ran the length of it and were covered with melting ice. An eye-boggling array of fish and meat was on display, and flies swarmed in the air.

Lana's flip-flops squelched through the blood-inked water as they peered at the fresh glassy eyes of the fish. Ahead of her a slight Filipino man weighed out fish in two buckets that were attached to a pole balanced over his shoulder. All around, people shouted and haggled, prodding and sniffing the fish, then filling plastic bags they held at their sides.

They wouldn't buy fish as the crew preferred to catch their own – so instead they moved on to the meat section, advertised by the bloodied head of a pig hanging on a hook. Dark congealed livers were laid out beside whole, pink chickens that were still bearing a few feathers.

Lana asked for four chickens, pointing at the ones she wanted. A man wearing a blood-smeared apron slung them on the scales. 'Cut?'

She nodded, and they watched as each chicken was slapped onto a plastic chopping board and then set upon with a meat cleaver, separating the wings, breasts, legs. A fragment of bone flicked into the air and landed on the floor between her and Kitty.

As they waited, Kitty asked, 'So what's happening between the two of you?'

'Denny and me?' she said, surprised by the question. 'I'm not sure . . . I guess things are good.' She turned to look at Kitty, but her gaze was fixed on the meat. 'I like him, Kit,' Lana said gently.

'Are you going to speak to Aaron about it?'

'I suppose we'll have to eventually if we want to be open about things.'

'Is that what Denny wants?' Kitty asked, turning to face her.

'What do you mean?'

Kitty said nothing.

Lana didn't like the implication in the question. 'Yes,' she answered tightly. 'It's what Denny wants, too.'

The man finished slicing the chickens. When Lana handed over the money, he took it in his bloodied hands and rummaged in his pocket for the change, returning it to Lana with a glob of blood on it.

*

Back at the yacht they began unpacking, placing the fruit in hammocks that hung bulging from the galley ceiling, and storing the meat in the freezer. Kitty slipped off, taking one of the bags to her cabin.

Shell was putting away the dried goods – pasta, rice, lentils, tins of beans and vegetables – into the lockers under the saloon seating. They had to store more food than needed for the anticipated passage, in case there were problems. *Plan for the worst and hope for the best*, was Aaron's motto.

'Did you hear?' Shell said. 'Joseph's not coming on the passage.'

'What?' Lana said, pausing.

'He's in his cabin packing. He's leaving today.'

'Why?' Lana asked, shocked. 'When was this decided? Was there a vote?'

'No. It was Joseph's decision, apparently. Aaron said he's run out of money.'

Lana left the shopping, and walked down the passageway to

Joseph's cabin. She found him pushing a neat bundle of clothes into his canvas backpack. 'What's going on? I've heard you're leaving.'

'You hear right.'

'Why?' she asked.

He shrugged. 'My money is run out.'

She shook her head. 'But . . . I thought you said you had enough money to reach New Zealand?' They'd been talking about it only a week or two ago.

He shrugged. 'Maybe I do my numbers incorrectly.'

It was almost impossible to overspend on the yacht, as they kept to a strict budget for food and fuel, and the only additional things you had to pay for were personal items or alcohol.

Lana pulled the door shut behind her. 'Really, Joseph, why are you leaving?'

He looked at her squarely. There was something completely unreadable in his eyes. 'I already tell you.'

'Does Denny know?'

He nodded.

'What are you going to do now?'

'I will think of something.'

Lana looked at him closely. She realized how thin he'd become, his face gaunt and unshaven. 'Is everything okay? I have some money. Maybe I can help.'

He smiled. 'You are very good person. But no, I will not take your money.'

'But I thought you loved being on *The Blue*.'

'I love the horizon. An empty sea.'

'I'll be sad to see you go.' She enjoyed their chats while they sat at the bow under the stars – Joseph smoking and telling her stories of little-known French poets or about the subtle difference between platform diving and cliff diving. Lana liked the dips and curves of their conversations, his thoughtful pauses, the sudden spurt of talk on a subject she knew little of.

'Clearing out in five minutes!' Aaron bellowed from the saloon.

'It is not sad for everyone,' Joseph said with a raised eyebrow.

'Is it Aaron? Did something happen?'

Joseph didn't answer. 'I should finish packing.'

'But . . . when are you leaving?'

'I go in the dinghy to shore with you all.'

It all felt wrong. Too sudden. She'd have liked to have cooked a final supper so the crew could give Joseph a proper send-off. It was too rushed. She imagined him leaving the yacht, having to check into a guest house with his canvas backpack slung over his shoulders, a group of trendy young travellers looking at him, then at each other with sly smiles.

'Let me write down your email address so we can keep in touch.'

'I don't use email.'

'But . . . how will we know you're okay?' she asked, thinking of how Joseph had been sleeping rough before joining *The Blue*.

Joseph looked at her, then smiled. 'I am always okay.'

*

The crew said goodbye to Joseph in a rush at the town jetty, Aaron and Heinrich already walking ahead in the direction of the immigration office.

Shell and Kitty kissed Joseph goodbye, giving him strict instructions to carry on diving. Denny pulled him into a big hug, and Joseph said something in French that made Denny's whole face break into a smile.

When Lana hugged Joseph, he felt desperately thin beneath his T-shirt. She didn't want to let him go, feeling as if they were somehow letting him down. 'We'll miss you.'

Joseph said nothing, just laughed his strange sad laugh. He shrugged on his backpack, which looked so heavy and full on his frame that his shoulders rounded beneath its weight. Lana watched him go, unsettled that his departure had been so sudden and unmarked. He looked somehow vulnerable as he trudged away into the heat and crowds.

She remained standing there until Denny came to her side, squeezing her fingers between his, and asking, 'You okay?'

She nodded slowly. Then after a moment they walked on and rejoined the others.

The atmosphere at immigration was muted. Aaron had already cleared the boat out of the country with Customs and the Port Authority, so now all they had to do was fill in a form each and have their passports stamped. What could have taken not much more than twenty minutes was dragged out to take over an hour as the staff casually followed their usual procedures while chatting to each other. Aaron kept checking his watch, eager to get back to the yacht to catch the outgoing tide.

Eventually they were back on board, winching the dinghy up from the water and stowing it away for the passage at sea. Final checks of supplies and equipment were made, and loose items were stowed away or strapped down. When Aaron was satisfied that everything was in order, they started the engine and hauled anchor.

Lana sat at the stern, watching over her shoulder as the busy harbour town faded into the distance. She wondered whether Joseph would be sitting in a bar, smoking, as he watched *The Blue* sail off into the dusk.

She gazed at the wake created by the yacht, a spill of white rolling across the sea's surface, trying to follow the lines of white water, watching until they levelled and knitted back together again.

The metallic taste of blood shivered across her tongue. She looked down and realized she was biting the edge of her thumbnail and had ripped away the tough skin at its edge. She snatched her hands from her mouth and pressed them against her knees.

A sharpening sense of anxiety was building in her chest, triggered by Aaron's abrupt decision to set sail, and the strange and sudden way Joseph had left the yacht. It was almost as if something was being kept from her – but she couldn't say what.

When Lana looked up again, she saw that the town had begun to shrink into the distance. Soon it would be no more than a shadow behind them as they headed for the open ocean.

13

NOW

Lana stares at the doorway through which Denny's parents have just left. What does Paul Carter want to talk to them about that couldn't be said in public?

She thinks of the body the Search and Rescue team located with the EPIRB strapped to it, and has to squeeze her eyes shut against the thought that it could be him.

'What's going on?' Shell's mother asks, her voice edged with anxiety.

Her husband answers, 'Perhaps they just want to talk to him about the boat.'

Lana cannot wait in here with speculation and guesswork breeding more anxiety. She leaves Shell's parents in the waiting room and moves along the corridor, looking for Paul Carter. She walks in the direction of the Operations Room, glancing through the open doorways as she goes.

Somewhere ahead of her she is sure she can hear his voice. A moment later, she spots him standing in a small room at the end of the corridor facing Denny's parents. Lana presses herself against the wall so as not to be seen.

Although she cannot hear what is being said, she watches intently. Paul Carter shifts from foot to foot as he touches his moustache. He looks at the floor, then at Denny's father. He does not look at Denny's mother.

He says something, turning his palms skywards, shaking his head.

Denny's mother, who has been standing with her hands held in a prayer, the tips of her fingers resting against her lips, suddenly folds. Her body doubles over and she covers her head with her hands.

Denny's father doesn't move a millimetre. He stares straight ahead as if he is frozen.

Not Denny. Please, not Denny.

Lana feels the blood drain out of her as she watches the awful tableau ahead. Denny's mother is still bent forwards, as if Paul Carter's words have sliced straight through her core and she can no longer stand upright. Then, as though a pause button has suddenly been released, sound and movement flare to life. Denny's mother rears upright, whirling around on the spot, her arms flung out at her sides. Lana catches sight of her face, and is shocked by the way pain has twisted her features.

'My boy!' she howls, her hands curling into fists.

Her husband moves then, gathering her in his arms. She struggles and writhes, fighting his hold.

Over and over again he tells her, 'I've got you. I've got you. I've got you, Marg.'

Eventually she goes limp in his arms. The awful wail of tears and grief chokes from her throat, the sound threading along the corridor until it reaches Lana, twisting at her gut.

Paul Carter stays for another minute or two, saying something that Lana can't hear. Eventually he nods solemnly and leaves.

Lana's skin feels too hot. She cannot breathe. She needs to move – get away from here. Yet she stays as she is pressed against the wall. Paul Carter is moving towards her now, the heavy tread of his footsteps approaching.

It is only when he is almost upon her that he looks up and sees her. His face is grey, eyes unfocused. It takes him a moment to place her. 'Lana.' He turns and looks back over his shoulder towards Denny's parents.

'He's dead. It was his body with the EPIRB, wasn't it?'

Paul Carter looks at her levelly. 'I'm terribly sorry.' He goes to say something else, but she is already turning, moving away from him, hurrying down the corridor, pushing open the fire exit with the heels of her hands.

She sprints across the courtyard and rushes to the side of the dock, falling onto her hands and knees. She retches into the harbour, bile swirling with oil-slick water.

*

Later, Lana wanders the port following the concrete harbour edge, skirting the huge steel cleats that tether ships to land.

The news of Denny's death is so fresh, so surreal, that she

doesn't feel it yet – not fully. It's as if the information is suspended, just hovering in the air above her.

When she thinks of him, it's impossible to picture his body face down in the sea, clothes waterlogged and dark, his beautiful hands limp at his sides. Instead what she sees is the Denny she first knew – with his head angled towards her, the sun in his eyes, grinning. How could that person – the one who'd slipped his hand into hers in a cave of limestone, who'd trod water beside her in the moonlight, who'd placed his lips at the base of her throat – be dead?

She remembers an afternoon in the Philippines when they hired a moped to explore the far side of an island where they'd moored. The rest of the crew were content to stay with the yacht, so it was just the two of them cruising along the narrow tracks of hardened earth and through fields where the long grasses whipped at Lana's bare legs. 'Okay back there?' Denny called as they sped forward, verdant scents rising from the sun-warmed earth. The track ascended up a rutted path and Lana tightened her grip around Denny's waist. She remembers the heat of his body and the hard muscles of his stomach. With the sun on her back and the warmth of Denny in front of her, she leant her cheek against him and closed her eyes, feeling an overwhelming sense of contentment.

Until today, she's not let herself think of memories like these – not for a long time – but now they burn bright across her thoughts like shooting stars, beautiful but vanishing.

She wonders about Denny's parents. How do you get in your car, drive home, and carry on with life – when your son is supposed to be sitting beside you on that journey? Had his mother stocked the fridge with his favourite foods and made up his old bed for him? Had they arranged to go out for a 'welcome home' dinner with friends and relatives?

She walks on, passing a tower block of shipping containers in rusted blues and reds. The stack looms above her, thuggish and indifferent. She tries to picture one of these containers slipping off the back of a ship, drifting alone through the oceans, its huge metal bulk lurking just below the surface. She imagines *The Blue* cutting through the waves, the wind straining in her sails – and suddenly there's an almighty impact – a clawing, metallic groan, an alarming shudder that sends the crew flying across the deck.

She wonders whether any of them were injured, or thrown overboard with the impact. At what point did the EPIRB get thrown into the grab bag on Denny's back? Was he wearing it as he tried to get on the life raft? Did he run out of time?

She moves on past the containers, pausing only when she reaches the edge of the port. She places her feet at the lip of the concrete dock, and looks down. The water is a blueish-brown, filmed with diesel. She thinks of the beautiful bays they sailed to in the Philippines where the water was so clear she could see the coral beneath her.

She wants to go back. Back to those heady first weeks on board, when the yacht was a sanctuary, a world away from real life, filled with easy laughter and good friends. Back to when she and Kitty would laugh together in their cabin with the ease of sisters. Back to when Denny would pass her in the galley and press a kiss to her neck.

In those early, blissfully simple days, the yacht was a place where death was an abstract concept entirely separate from them. It was only later that death had crept onto their deck with silent stealth.

14

THEN

Standing barefoot on deck, Lana turned slowly on the spot following the line of the horizon. It seemed to curve with her, vast and empty, broken only by the shimmering arc of the sun as it slipped away. The horizon was alight with flame-orange and magenta tones, which feathered away into muted shades of rose, finally settling into a dusky navy behind her. The colours were mesmeric; it would take a lifetime of mixing paints to be able to capture half of that palette.

She turned again, her toes pressing into the wooden deck, wind billowing through her cotton top.

Ocean.

Sky.

No land.

She breathed in deeply, filling her lungs with sea air so pure and salt-tinged that it tasted vital.

It was their second day on passage and somehow it felt

different from the previous sailing they'd done. Out here, where the land disappeared and the open ocean surged up to greet them, Lana was aware of their vulnerability. A 50-foot yacht no longer felt sizeable; it seemed no more than a fluttering leaf twirling with the breeze. Lana had the visceral sensation that, except for the five other crew, she was entirely alone. There were no boats, no land – just the weight of *The Blue* that they floated on and the power of her sails to propel them forward. It was both intoxicating and terrifying. Even the sea had a different quality away from land – it seemed thicker, darker, more alive.

In a sense, the sailing was easier. Aaron had set their course and as the sea was steady, the winds fairly light, the autopilot was able to do most of the work. The crew's time was their own to read, fish, practise yoga, cook – do as they pleased.

She felt the vibration of footsteps through the deck, and turned to see Aaron moving towards the lifeline, his gaze locked searchingly on the horizon. Over the past few weeks Lana had met other skippers and crews – some on private boats, others chartering guests, or sailing a yacht for the owner – and the majority of them managed their crews with a degree of formality, using precise sailing terms, holding daily briefings, insisting on dry passages and that life jackets be worn everywhere on deck. Aaron's approach was different. There were few set procedures or formal briefings and the crew worked together without needing to be specifically in-structed.

'Weather's been good, so far,' Lana called to Aaron.

He looked startled, as if surprised to see her standing there. Sometimes it was as if he'd forgotten that he wasn't sailing on his blue adventure alone. 'Can't complain,' he said, turning back to the horizon.

She wondered what he was looking for out there – what drew him so powerfully to the water. When she thought about his previous life in New Zealand, she could easily picture him as a barrister with his sharp intelligence and strength of conviction, and his winning poker face that gave nothing away. Yet the courts were places of bricks and mortar set deep within cities, where suits and ties and polished leather shoes were worn. It was as if Aaron were two different people: the one who'd once lived in the city, with his dusty tomes of law books and smartly pressed suits – and the one with his sun-cracked lips, callused hands, and a yacht he'd rigged to sail across oceans. It seemed that he'd let go of one life and simply stepped into another.

'Feels strange having one less crew member, don't you think?' Lana said.

He shrugged. 'Crews come and go. You get used to it.'

'All seemed quite sudden – Joseph deciding to leave like that.'

'Did it?'

Lana kept returning to Denny and Aaron's conversation outside the Internet café, wondering if it were entwined with Joseph's leaving. 'It's odd – Joseph told me he had enough money to sail until New Zealand.'

Aaron turned and looked at her. She knew no one liked having their authority questioned, but Lana had never been good at knowing when to stop. His tone was crisp as he said, 'Maybe Joseph's only been telling you part of the story.'

Or maybe, Lana thought, *you are.*

*

That evening Lana sat alone at the helm gazing up at a sky ablaze with stars. They rained from the black night so vividly that she felt as if she could stretch up and run her fingers through them.

With the slow rolling motion of the yacht and the calming sound of water moving against the hull, she could feel her eyelids beginning to close. She shook her head briskly, knowing how important it was that she stayed alert. She was on the midnight-till-2 a.m. watch, and although the autopilot was doing the work, Lana was still responsible for checking for other vessels and making sure they were keeping their course.

She unclipped her safety harness and stood, circling her shoulders and stretching her neck from side to side. Although she was comfortable being alone on deck, she'd worn the harness because she didn't like the idea that if she were to trip and fall overboard, none of the crew would know until the next person came on watch.

'Trying to keep awake?' Shell said, climbing up through the hatch carrying two mugs. 'I made us hot chocolate. Thought you might need the energy boost,' she said, passing one to Lana.

Despite the warm air, after a while the wind and salt left her skin chilled – and she hadn't dared leave her post to fetch a jumper. The sweet warmth of the milky chocolate slid down her throat, and she sighed. 'You are heaven-sent.' Lana settled herself at the helm, making room for Shell beside her. 'What are you doing up?'

'Couldn't sleep. Only another twenty minutes till my watch, so I figured I'd keep you company.'

'Perfect timing. I was just starting to hit the wall.'

'Comes on sudden, doesn't it? How are you finding the watches?'

The system was straightforward with each of the crew taking a two-hour solo watch on rotation throughout the day and night. Usually in the day there were always several crew on deck at any one time, so the sense of responsibility lessened – but at night you were very much alone. 'I'm enjoying them,' Lana said, then added, 'when the weather's like this, at least.'

'There's something magical about the water at night. Everything feels mellowed.' Shell took a sip of her hot chocolate. 'Back home, Dad kept his sailing boat at the end of our jetty, and some evenings I'd sleep out there, just watching the stars.'

'Sounds peaceful.'

'What's the shooting star count tonight?'

'We're well into double figures,' Lana answered, thinking how blasé she was becoming to the spectacle of nature. She'd barely been able to see the stars while living in the city – yet here the sky was bursting with them.

The two of them fell into silence as they finished their hot chocolates. Shell set her empty mug between her knees, and Lana heard her slowly turning the bangles she wore on her wrist, rotating each one in turn like a rosary. Lana glanced across at her, sensing there was something Shell had come up here to talk about. 'How come you couldn't sleep?'

'Guess I just wasn't that tired.'

Lana waited, not asking anything further.

Eventually Shell said, 'You and Kitty go back a long way.'

'Since we were eleven.'

'She was telling me about living in London, trying to make it as an actress.'

'It's a tough industry. Lots of people fighting for work.'

'I bet she's brilliant.'

'She was,' Lana said, thinking of all the performances she'd watched. The moment Kitty walked onto the stage, the audience was utterly rapt. She had a presence about her, something that made people want to stop and watch. But what the audience never saw was Kitty pacing the dressing room beforehand, a bottle of vodka in her hand. No matter how many performances she aced, or how many compliments were lavished upon her, she could never quite shake off her stage fright.

'Must've been hard making the decision to leave it all behind and go travelling.'

'You know, I think it was surprisingly easy. Coming away was the first thing that made clear sense – for us both.'

'Did Kitty leave anyone behind? A . . . partner?'

'No. No one.' Lana realized that this was what Shell had come up here to talk about. She felt a bolt of annoyance at Kitty who carelessly flirted with Shell whenever she craved the attention – pulling Shell onto her knee, asking her to apply her suncream, sunbathing topless together – but there was nothing more to it than that.

'Guess there's no imminent danger of me and Kitty breaking

Aaron's "No relationships" rule?' Shell said, trying to keep her tone light.

Lana could hardly say that Kitty was only interested in women when there were men around to watch. Instead, she tried to deflect the remark by saying, 'Seems a bit of an odd rule, don't you think?'

'Lots of other skippers impose it. I guess they're worried about shifting loyalties or extra tensions between the crew.'

Lana could understand that. 'So Aaron's never had a girlfriend on the yacht?'

'Never.'

'Two and a half years he's been doing this . . . Surely he must get lonely?'

Shell said, 'I'm pretty sure there was someone – before *The Blue*.'

Lana glanced at her, attention piqued.

Shell lowered her voice as she said, 'There was this night – we were in Thailand at the time – and we were all out, drinking. Aaron was talking to me one moment – and the next, he just stopped and all the colour seemed to drain from his face. I turned to see what had caught his attention, and saw a woman walking into the bar. It was like . . . I don't know . . . as if Aaron could no longer hear us, or even knew we were there. He just stared at this woman as she moved through the room. All of a sudden, Aaron was on his feet. As he approached her, the woman turned – and Aaron reared back as if he'd been slapped. She obviously wasn't who he'd been expecting.

'He didn't rejoin the rest of us – just left the bar and returned to the yacht. When we got back a few hours later, I went to check on him and he was sitting on the floor of his cabin, an empty bottle of rum at his feet. He was in a bad way . . . he was sobbing . . . kept on talking to someone he called Lydia – telling her how much he missed her and loved her – and how sorry he was.'

'What did he say the next day?' Lana asked.

'Nothing. He didn't come out of his cabin until the evening, and when he did, he never mentioned a thing – just carried on as before.'

'So who do you think Lydia is?'

'I don't know – but I've a pretty strong feeling that she's got something to do with why he set out on *The Blue*.'

Lana thought about this for a moment. 'Aaron never talks about his past, does he?'

Shell shook her head. 'Maybe *The Blue* is his way of escaping it.'

Lana nodded slowly, feeling as though Shell had touched on something important. 'What about Joseph?' she asked. 'You think Aaron threw him off?'

'No,' Shell answered without hesitation. 'We always vote about who comes on board and who leaves. Aaron would never make a decision like that without talking to the rest of us. That's not how *The Blue* works. It was Joseph's choice.'

She saw that Shell believed wholeheartedly in *The Blue*'s ideology – and in Aaron. Perhaps Lana was just a sceptic, but she wasn't convinced that everything was as democratic and transparent as Aaron would like them to believe.

15

THEN

Dawn cast a weak orange light across the water. Lana's bare feet dangled towards the sea, swaying with the motion of the yacht. White plumes of spray kicked up into the air, but only a fizz of it struck her legs. Her loose hair whipped around her face and she glanced at her wrists looking for a spare hairband, but there wasn't one.

She gathered her hair in one hand and, holding onto the lifeline with the other, she leant forward, staring down at the water as it parted around the bow. She liked sitting up here where there was nothing in front of her except ocean and wind. Perhaps that's why Joseph had chosen to write here; you could only look forward as everything else was blown behind you.

Suddenly the water split open, and the curve of a dolphin's back cut an arc through the air, glossy and dark. Lana's mouth opened in surprise. She watched as it jumped and dived through the wave created by the bow.

She got to her feet, shouting to Denny who was on watch at the stern. 'Dolphins!'

She heard his footsteps, light and fast, moving along the deck. He joined her at the bow, leaning over the lifeline. They both grinned as an entire pod – maybe twenty or so – erupted from the water. 'Just look at them!' Lana said, astounded, as they cut through the waves, then dropped back, diving and resurfacing playfully.

Denny placed his arms around her waist and rested his chin on her shoulder. It was rare to find themselves alone on deck together and she absorbed every moment of it, watching the pod until they finally disappeared.

Lana thought about the life she would otherwise be leading: a desk and a headset; a 45-minute commute spent gazing through rain-smeared windows; her daydreams doodled in the margins of an administration form. It was staggering to think of all those hours, weeks and months she'd given up to a life that didn't fulfil her, when across the world there was this. It scared her to think that she could so easily have missed it.

'How do you go back, after this? Really, how can you ever be satisfied with your old life again?' Lana asked.

'That's the thing, Lana. You don't go back. You go forwards.'

She liked that: *You don't go back. You go forwards.*

She turned in the space of his arms to face him. In the early-morning light his face was deeply tanned, the pale-blue irises looking sharper. She noticed how the ends of his eyelashes and his outer brows had been bleached by the sun and she wanted to press her lips against them, taste the salt trapped there.

'Travelling doesn't have to be an extended holiday from life,' he said. 'Maybe you use the space to take a look at things from a different perspective, work out what you want.'

'What, go travelling to find yourself?' she teased, an eyebrow cocked. She hooked a finger beneath the neckline of his T-shirt. 'You wearing a shark's-tooth necklace beneath there?'

He laughed. 'You know,' he said more seriously now, 'maybe having some time away is more about letting go of all the things you're not. Becoming the person you were always meant to be.'

When she first met Denny, it would have been easy to disregard him as another laid-back traveller coasting from one good time to the next. But she was learning how much more there was to him: he'd carved a career out of his passion *and* found a way to do it whilst maintaining a lifestyle of freedom and adventure. Denny had found what made him happy – travel, friends, languages, freedom – and he'd built his life adhering to principles that kept those things as a priority.

In contrast, Lana felt as if she'd rolled from one thing to the next, like a ball fired from a pinball machine now bouncing from one edge to the other, with no control over where she ended up.

Denny set his gaze squarely on her in his arms. 'So, Lana Lowe. What is it you want?'

You, she thought.

And, *For this to never end.*

*

Footsteps sounded up on deck and Aaron appeared.

In a flash Denny had released Lana and stepped away from her. 'Morning,' Denny called, moving down the deck to greet Aaron.

Aaron looked tired as he settled his faded cap into place, then rubbed a hand across the side of his neck. If he'd noticed Lana standing at the bow, he didn't say anything. 'What's the weather doing?' Aaron asked.

'South-westerlies still,' Denny said. 'Steady force four. Been cruising at six to eight knots.'

Aaron nodded again, looking up at the mainsail which was reefed down to the first point.

'Could make some good ground today,' Denny said.

Aaron shoved his hands in his shorts pockets, turning and surveying the sea conditions. 'Bit of cloud out east.'

Denny nodded. 'You think that low-pressure system that was brewing in Micronesia has anything to do with it?'

'The forecast didn't show anything significant.' Aaron stared at the cloud for a long while, saying nothing more.

Lana watched from the bow as Denny took a step towards Aaron, placing a hand on his shoulder. With his gaze on Aaron, he said something in a low voice that Lana couldn't make out.

Aaron's expression didn't alter. He just remained as he was, looking out to sea. After a long time, Aaron said, 'I need some coffee.'

When he disappeared below deck, Lana moved slowly towards the cockpit, where Denny was checking their position on the navigation plotter. 'Is he okay?'

'Aaron? Yeah, fine. Probably just tired.'

She nodded. 'You know, I've been thinking,' she said, glancing over her shoulder towards the hatch. 'Maybe we should have a chat to Aaron about . . . us. See what he says.'

Denny's eyes widened. 'I don't think that's a good idea.'

'Why not?'

'He's made the rule, Lana. He's not going to budge.'

'So what do we do?'

'Maybe I like sneaking around, stealing kisses,' he said, placing his lips on her neck.

'Maybe you'd like it more if I could share that great big double bed you've been hogging in your cabin,' she said with a small smile.

'I *would* like that.' He grinned.

'Then let's talk to him.'

He rubbed a hand along the back of his neck. 'It's not the right time. Not on passage.'

She remembered the remark Kitty had made about Denny when they'd been provisioning, implying that it was convenient for him to keep their relationship quiet. 'Will there be a right time?' she challenged.

'Look,' he said, his voice lowered, 'Aaron's got a lot on his mind at the moment. Bringing this sort of thing up with him isn't a good idea right now.'

'Why do you care so much about what he thinks?'

'I know how Aaron works – and I want to approach this in the right way. Trust me when I say, the right way isn't now.' His expression was set as he said, 'Let's wait till we reach Palau. Think about things when we're on land.'

She had been willing to break one of *The Blue*'s rules because, in her mind, Denny was worth the risk. But as she replayed his reluctance to make their relationship official, and the swift way he'd turned from her when Aaron had come up onto deck, she wondered whether Denny saw things differently.

'Sure. Let's leave it till we're on land,' she said curtly. She slipped out of his grasp and disappeared below deck.

*

She paced through the galley towards the bathroom and wrenched open the door. 'Shit! Sorry!' she called, realizing someone was in there.

Turning to leave, she hesitated as her mind began to process what she'd just seen.

Slowly, she pulled the door open again.

Her eyes widened. 'What the—?'

Joseph was standing with his back to the sink. He held a finger to his lips, then pulled her into the bathroom, shutting the door behind her.

'What are you doing here? You left the boat!' she whispered frantically. 'Do the others know?'

'No one.'

They stood face to face in the tiny confines of the bathroom. Up close she could see the cracked skin on his lips, and a dusting of grey hairs sprouting prematurely at his temples. 'Aaron is going to go mad when he finds out. Where've you been hiding?'

'Sail locker.'

She was stunned. The sail locker was right in the very bow of the yacht, accessed through Heinrich's cabin, and there was only enough space to lie flat. It would be like locking yourself in a coffin. She had no idea how he'd managed to stay hidden for the two days they'd been on passage.

'How did you get back on board? We all said goodbye.'

'A *bangka* drop me off while you were at immigration.'

'Why are you here?'

'I have nothing else, Lana,' he said, his gaze lowering. 'This . . . the boat . . . the crew . . . it may not seem much, but for me is very much.'

Slowly, she nodded. She understood. 'What are you eating? Are you getting enough water?'

'I have supply, yes.'

She wiped a hand across her brow thinking about the lengths Joseph had gone to in order to stay on board. Then a new thought hit her. 'You didn't clear out! When we arrive in Palau, immigration won't let you in.'

'I will explain.'

'You'll *explain*? They're not going to like it. Jesus,' she said, 'neither is Aaron.'

'Then he will have to turn us back.'

Aaron wouldn't do that – and Joseph knew it. If they turned back now it would mean they'd be days behind schedule, and then could be delayed in the Philippines as they waited for another weather window. 'You—'

A knock at the door startled them both.

'Lana? Is that you?' Denny called.

She looked despairingly at Joseph, who opened his hands, saying, 'They have to find out at some point.'

She unlocked the door and faced Denny.

'Listen, I just wanted—' He stopped. 'Joseph? What the hell?'

Before anyone had a chance to explain there was the heavy tread of footsteps along the passageway. Aaron's walk was distinctive: powerful, firm strides that made the floor vibrate. He stopped alongside Denny, and Lana watched his expression change as he saw Joseph: the muscles in his jaw tightening, his lips pulling back over his teeth. He enunciated each word acutely as he demanded, 'What the fuck are you doing on my yacht?'

'Surprise!' Joseph said drily.

Lana closed her eyes, feeling the tension knotted in the tops of her shoulder blades.

'You fucking idiot!' Aaron's glare was poisonous. 'You have no idea what you've done.' He looked at Lana. 'Want to tell me what's going on?'

She realized that Denny was staring at her, too. 'I just came in . . . and, well . . . Joseph was here.'

Lana wanted to get out of the bathroom, but Aaron was blocking the doorway. She pressed herself against the bulkhead, feeling the varnished wood against her back.

Joseph began to smile; Lana couldn't tell whether it was a reaction to the tension, or whether he was genuinely thrilled by what was happening.

Aaron took a step forward, putting only inches between himself and Joseph. 'You,' Aaron said, pointing at him, 'had better wipe that fucking smirk off your face. You got any idea how serious this is? As skipper, I am legally responsible for everyone on this yacht. I didn't clear you out – that means immigration think you're still in the Philippines. If I turn up with you in Palau, it's as good as smuggling you in.'

'I will explain there was error. And I will pay you – pay you double.'

'I don't want your fucking money!'

'I thought that was why I could not stay on your yacht, no?'

Lana heard the challenge in Joseph's tone.

Aaron's hand shot forward and he seized Joseph by the neck, thrusting him up against the bulkhead, narrowly missing the towel hook nailed into the wood. 'Do not push me.'

The wood creaked behind Joseph's head as colour rose in his face.

'We both know why I wanted you to get the fuck off my yacht. You're lucky I'm not beating the fucking shit out of you!' Aaron spat through gritted teeth, his lips twisting around his words.

Denny reached forward, placing a hand firmly on Aaron's shoulder. 'We can work this out,' he said calmly.

Aaron's expression remained taut. He leant in close to Joseph's ear and in a low, deadly voice, said, 'Don't forget, I know you, Joseph. I know what you are.'

16

NOW

Lana realizes that she hasn't eaten since yesterday evening. She drifts back through the port, and returns to the lobby of the main building where she remembers seeing a vending machine. She stands in front of the glass box, which houses rows of crisps, chocolates and nuts, and sees her own hollow-eyed reflection glaring back at her. She still can't believe that Denny is gone.

Behind her, the double doors into the building push open and she hears the click of high heels along the corridor. The sound makes her think of Kitty walking with her arm threaded through Lana's when they were teenagers, their hair straightened, lipstick painted on, sauntering in a cloud of Kitty's perfume.

A memory flashes in her mind like a camera bulb: the two of them hiding in the theatre green room after drama class. The lights had gone out and they heard the door clank shut – and then they were enclosed with rails of dusty costumes and tired theatre props. Lana felt a giggle swelling in her throat and she bit down on her lip, waiting for their teacher's footsteps to recede.

Beside her in the darkness she could feel Kitty's shoulders beginning to shake against hers, their acrylic school jumpers crackling together with static. Laughter began building in Lana's chest, bubbling up through her throat and finally bursting from her mouth in an explosion of gasps and howls.

When their drama teacher had taken out her mobile and called her husband, telling him to come home early as she had a surprise for him, she hadn't been aware that there were two pairs of ears listening from behind the props box.

Lana could barely catch her breath as she staggered towards the doorway. She felt along the wall and flicked the switch, the cold strip lights buzzing on. As her eyes adjusted, she saw that Kitty had pulled on the nearest costume – a horse's head with huge yellow teeth and a flapping dark mane – and was sitting on a stool, legs crossed, pretending to smoke a cigar. 'So, a horse comes into a bar,' Kitty said in her best New York accent, 'and the bartender asks, "Hey, why the long face?"' More laughter peeled from Lana's mouth.

After the two of them had tried on and twirled around in various other outfits – vicars, sailors, angels and chimney sweeps – Lana flopped down onto a bed of blue sheets that had been used to represent the sea in last term's production of *The Tempest*. 'Shall we bother going back to lessons?' Lana said, staring at the ceiling, amber hair fanning out beneath her.

'No,' Kitty said, lying back too, the smell of her body spray overpowering the musty sheets. 'Let's just stay here and pretend we're somewhere sunny and beautiful.'

'Greece?'

'Further.'

'Australia?'

'Yes! Australia! And the sea is warm and clear, and there are bare-chested boys bringing us ice-cold drinks.'

'I like it here,' Lana grinned.

'When we leave school,' Kitty said, rolling onto her side and looking at Lana, 'let's get away from here.'

Lana had turned towards her, their noses inches apart, their breath warm against each other's face.

'We can't stay around here for ever. I don't want that to happen to us, Lana. I don't want us to end up working on the tills or at the social club. I want more than that,' Kitty said emphatic-ally. 'I want you to be a brilliant artist,' she said with a flourish, 'and for me to be a famous actress. I want us to have adventures.'

'We will,' Lana promised her – but even then, she'd never believed it. People on their street didn't become renowned artists or actresses; they worked in shops, pubs, and cafés – and they were the lucky ones.

The staccato clacks of high heels grow closer, stopping behind Lana.

She turns and is immediately struck by the elegance of the young woman before her. She is wearing a long beige summer coat, which – on someone else – could look drab, but instead looks sophisticated and fashionable. Her dark hair is swept into a low bun, and there is a touch of colour to her lips, making her pale skin appear even smoother.

Although Lana has never met this woman before, she somehow looks familiar. Her dark eyes search Lana's face. 'I am wondering if you would help? Is this correct building for Search and Rescue?'

A strange heat pinches Lana's cheeks as she hears the European accent. 'Yes . . . it's the Maritime Rescue Centre.' She pauses, looking closely at the woman. 'Are you here about *The Blue*?'

'Yes. *The Blue* that sink. I am waiting for information about someone. My brother. I think he was a passenger on a yacht that is in problem.'

Lana blinks rapidly, suddenly placing her accent: French. A chill shivers down her spine. 'Your brother?'

The woman nods.

Lana knows exactly what is coming. She tries to swallow, to fill her lungs with air, to prepare herself.

The young Frenchwoman says, 'His name is Joseph.'

*

Sweat prickles across Lana's skin. She feels the ground softening beneath her feet, feels her mind tilting. Joseph had a sister. And she is here, standing in front of Lana.

It's not possible. Joseph said he had no family. She remembers the conversation clearly. She stares aghast at this woman.

Joseph's sister touches the back of her bun, a quick uncomfortable gesture. Then, 'You have someone you love on board, also?'

Lana seems only able to gape. She is aware of how strange she must appear. Simply moving her lips around the words, 'Yes, a friend of mine' seems to dissipate all her energy.

Joseph's sister inclines her head as if expecting more.

But Lana cannot manage anything further.

Joseph's sister waits, her eyes on Lana. 'What happened to the yacht? It sink, I am told?'

Lana nods her head a little. 'It hit a container. Put a hole in the side of the boat.'

'Have the people been rescued?'

'No. No, not yet.'

Joseph's sister nods, then pushes her hands deep into her coat pockets.

Lana's heart is hammering against her ribcage. This cannot be happening. She wants to ask, *Why did Joseph tell us he had no family? What are you doing in New Zealand? How did you hear about* The Blue? *What do you know?*

She manages to compose herself enough to ask, 'So . . . you're in New Zealand to meet your brother?'

A small, sad smile emerges on the woman's lips. 'Yes, I am – but it is . . . I don't know how to say . . . difficult with us?'

Lana waits.

'Months ago my brother write to me telling me about *The Blue*.' She pronounces the name of the yacht in the same way as Joseph – as if their tongues are only lightly brushing over the words. 'He left his home – Paris – because he had . . . troubles. He needed to be . . . how do I say? Free of himself, I think. In his letter he describe the yacht so beautifully, yes?' Her expression softens as she says, '. . . that she swept through the water, that there were people on board who he knew would become his friends, that he was going to sail with her to New

Zealand. He write that he would like me to be here when the boat docked.' She removes her hands from her pockets and clasps them together. 'So I come all this way from Paris to meet him. I ring the port this morning to ask when exactly the boat is meant to arrive, but . . . they tell me this news instead. I hope . . . I hope that he is safe.'

I hope that he is safe . . .

A dark panic builds in the pit of Lana's stomach; she feels it reaching into her throat, squeezing tight around her voice box. She wants to turn, to run, to not have this conversation, to not think of what happened to Joseph.

'We have to hope, don't we, that they will all be returned safely?' Joseph's sister says.

The blood drains from Lana's face. She already knows that the Search and Rescue team will not be bringing in Joseph.

He is anything but safe.

17

THEN

Joseph's attempt at stowing away had the effect of a heavy stone dropped into still water: tension rippled outwards and was absorbed by everyone.

Aaron stayed at the helm all day, winching the hell out of the sails to try and pick up what little speed they could. His jaw was set and he refused any efforts to engage him.

When Joseph came up on deck, Aaron glared so hard at him that everyone else fell silent until Joseph retreated. By evening, Aaron was sunburnt and exhausted, and his temper had only worsened. He didn't even touch the pasta dinner Lana had cooked, simply shaking his head as she offered the meal.

Now Lana cleared away the crew's bowls, scraping the remains overboard, then running a modest amount of fresh water to soap them with. Heinrich stood beside her in the galley, a tea towel at the ready.

'Sweltering down here tonight,' she said. The air felt close, as if it were thick with heat. With the wind being so light there was little breeze, and they'd only covered just over half the distance Aaron had wanted to by now.

She handed a washed bowl to Heinrich, who was gazing out through the porthole, a frown settled on his brow. 'You alright?' She asked.

His tone was distant as he replied, 'Even when you're in the middle of the ocean, you can't fully escape it.'

'Escape what?'

'Money.'

He wiped a teatowel unhurriedly across the plate. She said, 'By the end of the month I'm going to be flat broke.'

'And then what?' Lana asked.

'Guess I'll have to go back to Germany,' he said with a shrug.

'What will you do?'

'I've spent my life running around a tennis court. I'm not qualified to do shit.'

'Couldn't you coach?'

Heinrich squeezed his eyes shut as if the very thought of it pained him. '*Failed tennis star ends up as a coach*: what a cliché!' He shook his head. 'I couldn't stomach training other kids to have dazzling tennis careers, when mine is over. I'm an arsehole, right?'

'Can't you pick up some bar work when we get to Palau? Maybe it'd pay for a few more weeks on *The Blue*.'

'Aaron's not planning on stopping in one place for longer than a week. I would otherwise. I'd do anything to stay on board.'

For the first time, Lana saw the chink in Heinrich's armour: he needed *The Blue* just as much as they all did.

As she glanced through the porthole a light on the water caught her attention. 'Did you see that?'

Heinrich moved to her shoulder. 'You sure you saw something?'

Lana waited to see the light again, wondering if she'd imagined it. They were nowhere near land so it could only be from another vessel – a yacht or container ship, perhaps. Then a beat later, it came again 'There! A white light across the water.'

'A boat!' Heinrich exclaimed. 'How far away do you think it is?'

'Not sure. A long way,' Lana said, finding it almost impossible to judge distances at night.

They watched the light as they continued washing up, speculating about who was on board and where they were going. It was most likely a foreign shipping vessel transporting goods across the sea. She guessed the vessel was sailing away from them as she could only see the white stern light – but just knowing that there were other people out at sea gave her a strange feeling of comfort.

As she emptied the sink, passing the final clean bowl to Heinrich, Joseph wandered in, his hair flattened to one side of his head, his skin pale. He hadn't eaten up on deck with the others, and although Lana had offered to bring a bowl of pasta to his cabin, he'd refused. Now he snapped a banana from the bunch hanging in the fruit hammock.

'Eat as many as you can,' Lana said. 'They're going to turn in another day.'

Joseph peeled the banana carefully and placed the skin in

the bin. Then he flicked on the tap and started rinsing the naked banana.

Lana watched, surprised he was being so careless with the water supply.

'Hey, Joseph—' Heinrich began, but was cut off by Aaron, who was walking into the galley, his fingers curled around a rolled-up chart. When he saw Joseph at the sink, he stopped. 'What the fuck are you doing?'

Joseph didn't turn. He continued as he was, rinsing the banana.

Aaron stormed towards the sink, shouldering Joseph out of the way and snapping off the tap. 'You don't rinse a fucking banana! We're on a passage, for fuck's sake! Where do you think we get more fresh water from?'

Joseph lightly tapped the excess water from the banana, then turned, lifted it to his mouth – eyes on Aaron – and took a neat bite.

Beside her, Lana saw Heinrich's eyes widen, incredulous.

Aaron took a step closer to Joseph, his chin jutting forward. 'You,' he said, his expression livid, 'do not want to cross me. Not today. I catch you wasting water again – you'll be off this boat before we even reach land. Get it?'

Joseph said something in French as reply. Then he smiled.

The colour deepened across Aaron's face. His fingers clenched into fists at his sides and Lana watched the veins straining over the backs of his knuckles.

But Aaron didn't raise his fists. Instead, he surprised Lana by responding to Joseph in French. The sound of his gruff voice rolling together French words was so unexpected that she found it somehow shocking.

Joseph looked just as taken aback. His cheeks reddened as he held Aaron's gaze.

Then Aaron turned from him, and stalked back up to the deck.

Joseph stood there for a moment, dazed. Then he grabbed a bottle of rum from the cabinet and sloped back towards his cabin.

'God,' Lana exhaled after he was gone. 'I thought Aaron was going to kill him.'

'I wish he had,' Heinrich said, with a look of distaste.

*

As darkness thickened, Aaron sat at the edge of the stern nursing a beer, his back against the lifeline. Denny sat with him, the two of them silent.

Tension shimmered across the deck. It seemed to reach deep into Lana, stirring a headache between her eyes. She squeezed the bridge of her nose, rubbing her fingertips upwards along the arches of her eyebrows. She and Denny hadn't spoken again since their disagreement this morning, and she sensed that he somehow held her responsible for Joseph's reappearance. She was eager to just go to bed – sign out on this awful day – but she was on watch for another hour.

She was beginning to understand that on passage your existence shrunk to the 50-foot stretch of the yacht. In that small space, everyone's emotions and opinions collided, like atoms bouncing back and forth – building enough energy and motion to create an explosion. Issues that could be diffused on land by taking a walk or having some space, became enraged at sea, growing and distorting until they bore little resemblance to their original shape.

She picked up her beer and stared ahead at the black water. The boat she'd glimpsed earlier was no longer visible and she wondered whether in daylight they'd be able to see it again.

A few minutes later, Kitty climbed on deck carrying a large plastic jug and a stack of glasses. As one of the yacht's lights caught her face, Lana noticed her eyes looked glassy. 'Cocktail time!' she declared, grinning. It was Kitty's trick: pretending to be the social hostess, when really she just wanted company in her drinking.

'Skipper first,' Kitty said, sauntering towards Aaron. 'You, sir, most certainly deserve a drink,' she said, performing a small curtsey in front of him.

Aaron accepted a large drink, knocked it back, then exhaled hard. 'No half-measures in that, Kit.'

Kit? Since when had he started calling her Kit? Lana marvelled at the way Kitty worked around Aaron, able to soften his mood. Perhaps it was all the practice she'd had growing up with her volatile father.

Kitty refilled his glass and then poured drinks for the others.

'What's in it?' Lana asked, tasting rum and something citrus.

'Mostly just fruit – and a dash of rum and vodka, too. I name this cocktail *The Passage*.'

Alcohol seemed to be the answer. Within an hour, the icy tension seemed to have thawed and deep bursts of laughter erupted around the deck.

Lana glanced across to where Denny was still sitting with Aaron, his head bent close as he talked. Aaron's gaze was fixed on Denny, nodding in agreement with whatever he was saying.

Opposite, Shell and Heinrich sat at the edge of the cockpit. Kitty picked her way over to them and topped up their drinks. Shell placed a hand lightly on the small of Kitty's back as Kitty emptied the remainder of the jug into her own glass. Then she stepped aside from Shell and settled herself on Heinrich's lap, looping an arm around his shoulder.

Shell's gaze followed the line of Kitty's bare legs, which were pressed close to Heinrich's, and Lana noticed her expression tightening. A few minutes later, Shell had risen to her feet and disappeared towards the bow, Heinrich and Kitty barely seeming to notice.

*

By the time Lana's watch finished at midnight, voices and music filled the deck. Kitty was doubled over at something Heinrich was telling her, her hand stretched out over his bicep. Her words were slurred and loose, broken by her own laughter. Shell watched from a little way off, nursing another drink. In the moonlight her skin looked pale, her blonde hair glowing ghostly white. *Poor Shell*, Lana thought, pissed off at Kitty's lack of awareness.

Lana glanced at the time and realizing her night watch was now over, she got to her feet to let Aaron know he was on next. As she moved across the cockpit, she was surprised by how hard the alcohol had hit her: her legs felt light and insubstantial, and she had to hold onto the helm for balance.

'Aaron?' she said, interrupting him and Denny.

Aaron swung around, his eyes barely able to focus on her.

'Think you're on watch next.'

He glared at her and she immediately felt foolish for telling the skipper what to do. 'I'm getting another drink first,' he said, moving towards the hatch.

'You sure that's a good idea?' Denny said.

Aaron didn't answer. As he reached the hatch, Joseph appeared, coming the other way. The two men came to an abrupt halt facing one another. Neither of them moved aside, or retreated to make room for the other. Instead they squared up to each other; Joseph was an inch or two taller, but Aaron had the stocky, muscular build.

The light from below deck illuminated Aaron's face as his lips curled around a single word: 'Scum.' Then he shouldered his way past Joseph, who staggered backwards, only managing to right himself by grabbing onto the edge of the hatch. As Aaron disappeared into the saloon, Joseph whirled around on the spot, calling after him, 'You do not know me! You. Do. Not. Know. ME!'

There was no response from Aaron.

Joseph looked up to find the rest of the crew staring at him. He glared at them, bashing the palm of his hand twice against his chest. 'None of you knows me! I am nothing to you – but I am something. Remember, I am something!'

Then he wove past them, picking his way over ropes and around deck hardware to reach the bow. As he moved, there was a sudden cry. Shell was bent over clutching her ankle. Joseph staggered back against the lifeline in surprise. 'Sorry! I didn't see you!'

Heinrich tipped Kitty from his lap, and rushed towards Shell, crouching down to inspect her ankle. 'Are you okay?'

'I'm fine.'

He stared at Shell for a moment, his face close to hers, and then he straightened, turning towards Joseph. 'Watch where the hell you're going, you prick!'

'It was an accident,' Shell said.

Heinrich took a step nearer to Joseph, who was pushed up against the lifeline. *Careful,* she thought, seeing them both so close to the yacht's edge.

Joseph held a hand up in the air. 'I'm sorry! I'm sorry! I'm sorry!' Then he shook his head and walked away from Heinrich and the others, slumping down at the bow, alone.

*

Lana exhaled slowly, not having realized she'd been holding her breath.

She glanced at Denny, who was now sitting alone, watching the water. She'd had time to think about their earlier disagreement, and had decided that perhaps Denny was right to suggest waiting until they reached Palau before talking to Aaron. On passage everything felt different, too enclosed, as if every word, gesture and emotion were under a microscope being magnified and examined.

As she moved towards him, Denny got to his feet. 'Oh, I was just coming to see you,' she said, hearing the slight slur to her words.

Denny paused, a hand on the back of his neck. 'Got watch in a few hours. Thought I'd get some sleep. You're staying up for a while?'

'Yes,' she told him, thinking that he was going to say he'd join her.

'You'll take it easy, yeah?'

She blinked, not sure what he meant. Then she saw that his gaze was on the drink in her hand. 'Sure,' she said tightly.

Denny disappeared below deck leaving Lana standing alone, her cheeks smarting in the darkness. Up ahead at the bow she noticed the glow of Joseph's head torch and decided to join him. As she picked her way along the deck, thick flumes of cloud cloaked the moon, shading out the light. She paused, a hand on the lifeline. The sea seemed to close in around them, the waves just dark shadows now swelling lightly beneath them.

Save for the navigation lights, the deck was deliberately unlit to help the crew maintain their night vision. It took Lana's eyes a moment to adjust to the disappearance of the moon, and then she moved on, sliding a hand along the lifeline to steady herself against the boat's movement.

When she reached Joseph, his pale shirt was billowing, ghostly, in the wind and the beam of his head torch was illuminating a page of his notebook. He sat hunched forward, writing feverishly as the yacht rose and fell softly with the waves.

Lana stood behind him thinking of her sketchbook stowed beneath the mattress in her bunk. She would love to take it out to try and capture what it was to sail through the ocean at night. She hadn't sketched since they'd left land, the motion of the yacht too uneven for her to keep a steady hand.

She must have sighed as Joseph swung around, the beam of his head torch dazzling her. She held up a hand to block the light. 'It's just me.'

'Sorry.' He closed the notebook and slipped it into his breast pocket, turning off his torch.

Lana lowered herself down beside him, keeping an arm hooked onto the lifeline. For a while they just sat together in the darkness without speaking. Joseph pulled a joint from his top pocket. 'Smoke?'

'Sure.'

He lit the joint and passed it to Lana.

She drew it to her lips, closed her eyes and inhaled deeply. Warm smoke curled into her lungs. She held it there, concentrating on the feeling of the smoke working loose the knots of tension in her chest.

During art school she'd smoked regularly, a post-dinner routine she shared with her housemates, their lounge becoming a haze of marijuana and electronic beats. By her third year she'd grown tired of the boneless feeling it gave her, and the brain-softened daze she'd find herself in the following morning, and she began to spend more time away from the house, so as not to get sucked deeper into the lumbering habit.

Now she was grateful for the numbing tingle that spread

beneath her skin, and she tipped her head back and exhaled, a drift of smoke blown away on the salt wind.

'What do you think about love, Lana?'

'Love?' she said, bringing the joint towards her mouth, watching the glow of the ember as she sucked hard.

'Do you think it near to hate?'

She thought for a moment. 'I think that the more you love, the greater capacity there is for hurt, and yes, maybe hate, too.'

'You believe that hate comes from hurt?'

'Maybe. I don't know.' Her mind couldn't hold onto the threads of the conversation – it felt looser, as if it were drifting.

'I think sometimes you can love people too much,' Joseph said.

'Perhaps . . .'

'I think,' he said, in a low voice, 'that Aaron doesn't understand this.'

'I think,' she said conspiratorially, 'Aaron can be an arsehole sometimes.'

She saw the corners of Joseph's lips turn up.

She took a final toke on the joint and then passed it back to Joseph. 'Thank you.'

She watched the water. The white froth of the waves seemed like sunken clouds, eerie but beautiful. At night, the sea played tricks on you, creating shapes and visions. 'Do you ever feel,' she began, 'like diving in . . . and just swimming away from the yacht? Away from everything, into all that space?'

He looked out towards the horizon, the joint burning between his fingertips. 'Yes, I do. I feel that very much.'

His tone resonated with a deep sadness, and instinctively Lana reached out and put her arm around him.

He turned to her then. She thought he was going to say something more, but instead he leant forward and pressed his lips against hers.

For a moment her mind felt foggy, slow to register what was happening. His hand reached her back, his fingers spreading out, trailing down her spine – an echo of the slithering touch she'd felt underwater. Then she realised: it'd been Joseph who'd dived under and brushed his hand along her back. She hadn't imagined it.

She jerked away, knocking the joint from his fingers, which fell into his lap. He dusted at it rapidly, the orange ember disappearing into the ocean.

'What the fuck?' She scrambled to her feet, grabbing onto the lifeline.

He opened his hands, eyes wide. 'I . . . thought you . . .'

'No! No.' She shook her head. Her thoughts were loose, jumbled. She wanted to get away. 'I don't want you,' she said, the words feeling too sharp, like small pips being spat from her mouth.

Then she stumbled away from him, back towards the stern, her legs feeling disconnected from her body. She could hear the sounds of laughter and voices rising from the cockpit, but she didn't look up, didn't want to know if anyone had seen.

18

THEN

The cabin sweltered, the air heavy with heat. Lana rolled onto her side, kicking off the sheet. Her throat felt rasped and she moved her tongue against the inside of her cheeks. She could taste the stale breath of smoke.

She heaved herself from the top bunk and half-fell to the floor, landing with her bare heel on an upturned hairbrush of Kitty's. 'Fuck! Fuck it!' she cried, hopping onto her other foot.

She expected to hear Kitty's voice then, but when she looked, the lower bunk was empty. She glanced at her watch and saw it was almost ten o'clock. Lana never usually slept in this late.

She stood for a moment, a palm pressed to her forehead, feet planted wide, wondering if she was going to throw up. Somewhere beneath her the waves surged, drawing the yacht up – then releasing it. The open ocean was not the best place to wake to the mother of all hangovers. God, she wished there was a pause button. She craved stillness, land, a cup of tea that didn't slosh in its mug.

She took a deep breath and then dug around in her backpack for something to wear. Shit, her head hurt when she leant down! She yanked out a pair of salt-stiffened shorts and a vest, and shrugged them on. She found her sunglasses wedged beneath her pillow, then staggered along the passageway, passing Heinrich and Joseph's closed cabin door.

All of a sudden her cheeks flushed hot as recollections of the night before launched at her in a snapshot of images: Joseph calling to them all, *You do not know me*; Lana talking to him at the bow about love and hate; his mouth pressed to hers before she'd recoiled, aghast.

In the galley she poured a pint of water, drinking it at the sink. *Jesus, had anyone seen?* She wiped her mouth on the back of her hand and set the glass down – but it slid along the counter. She picked it back up, dried it with a damp tea towel, and put the glass away.

She lurched up the steps onto the deck. The yacht was heeled over hard and it was a surprise to find the morning sky flat grey. She remembered the clouds closing in last night, swallowing the moon. After days of blue skies, it felt oddly eerie to see the sky colourless. The wind felt as if it were gusting from a different direction, churning the sea so that the tips of waves were frosted white.

Kitty and Heinrich were sitting in the cockpit letting the autopilot do the work. Kitty had on dark glasses and was staring out to sea – but from the angle of her head it seemed as though her eyes were closed. Heinrich looked as if he hadn't slept at all; his face was unshaven and his hair stuck up at the back.

Lana slipped past them both, moving towards Denny, Shell

Lucy Clarke

and Aaron. The three of them were talking together, but as Lana reached them, they fell silent.

Lana experienced that awful insecurity that used to plague her at school that she'd just been the subject of their conversation. Her gaze trailed to Denny for reassurance, but he was staring straight ahead at the water.

'What's going on with the weather?' she asked when no one said anything.

'Wind's swung around. Blowing head on from the south-east. Just what we don't fucking need,' Aaron answered. He looked in a bad state after last night; his skin was sallow and a stale, unwashed smell rose from his skin. She shifted her position so she wasn't standing downwind of him.

'Think it'll turn again?' Shell asked. The evening had even taken its toll on Shell; her usually glowing skin looked washed out and there were dark bags beneath her eyes.

He shrugged. 'Who knows? There's a low-pressure system out that way, which we don't want heading towards us.'

Denny nodded vaguely as if his thoughts were elsewhere.

'What time did everyone call it a night?' Lana asked.

'Can barely even remember,' Shell said.

'Fucking stupid, drinking like that on a passage,' Aaron said. 'Dunno what the hell we were thinking.' He shook his head. 'I've busted my shoulder too – fell in the shower last night. Caught the edge of the clamp on the shower hose. Managed to put a pretty gash in my shoulder.'

'You cleaned it up properly?' Shell said.

'Ah, it's fine. Stuck a bit of medical tape over it. Should close

184

up with a bit of fresh air. I'm just pissed off at being so stupid. Back to dry passages.'

'You know what we all need?' Shell said, trying for a smile. 'Bacon bagels. What do you think? I'll make them.'

'Sounds good,' Lana said, thinking that some food in her stomach might be just the thing.

Aaron agreed, and followed Shell towards the stern, leaving Lana and Denny alone. They both stood with a hand hooked over the lifeline. Lana looked at the tanned spread of his fingers, the light blonde hairs at the base of them, an old pink scar across the edge of his thumb. Slowly she slid her hand along the lifeline, covering his fingers with her own.

He looked thoughtfully at her hand.

'Everything okay?' she asked.

He nodded.

'How was watch?'

He blinked, looked at the water. 'Fine.'

'When did the heavy weather come in?'

'Around five or six, I think.'

She wondered if anyone had seen what'd happened with Joseph at the bow. Denny had already gone to bed, but one of the others could have mentioned it – they were all in the cockpit at the time. She began to say something, but Denny was turning to look over his shoulder. 'Think we'd better reef the sails.'

His hand slipped from beneath hers, the explanation still hovering on Lana's lips.

*

Lana stood in the cockpit, watching the sea. The wind was moving hard across the water, quivering in dark patches and causing the sail to strain.

The greying blur of the horizon looked almost secretive, concealing something beyond the thick layer of cloud. Beneath a clear blue sky, the vast space of the ocean was exhilarating, yet now – with the sound of wind rushing across the water – she felt a shiver of unease winding its way into her thoughts.

When Shell returned to the deck with a tray of bacon bagels, Lana joined the others in the cockpit. 'Thank you,' she said, feeling the warmth of the bagel between her fingers.

Lana noticed the way Shell glared at Heinrich as she passed him a bagel, and he looked away.

Kitty hung back, not taking hers. Despite her tan, her skin looked pale. Her hair was tied back in a scruffy knot and there was something about her appearance that suggested to Lana that she hadn't gone to bed.

'Never ever let me drink one of your cocktails again,' Lana said. 'You've ruined us all. Hope you're feeling as wretched as the rest of us?'

Kitty's mouth didn't move into a smile.

'Joseph not up here?' Shell asked, looking at the spare bagel on her tray.

'Haven't seen him,' Lana answered.

'I'll wake him,' Shell said, taking the bagel with her.

Lana followed Shell below deck, in need of a painkiller.

In her cabin she snapped a white pill from its foil packet, washing it down with a glug of slightly warm bottled water. She perched on the lower bunk to finish her bagel, licking a smudge of tomato sauce from the back of her hand. Afterwards she lay back and sighed, waiting for the painkiller to kick in.

She could only have drifted off for a moment when there was a knock at the door. Shell peered around it. 'You seen Joseph? He's not in his cabin.'

'No.'

Shell still held the uneaten bagel. 'I've checked the bathrooms too, and the galley and saloon.'

Lana sat up. 'Sure he didn't pass you and is up on deck now?'

'I've just stuck my head up there.'

'Remember he's good at stowing.'

'True,' Shell said, although she didn't smile.

Lana got to her feet. 'Here, I'll look with you.'

They moved through the galley, using handholds to keep themselves steady. Last night's empties were crammed in a crate that was wedged between a cupboard and a bulkhead, the glass rattling together each time the yacht yawed.

'Let's check all the cabins,' Shell suggested.

Everyone else was up on deck so the cabins were empty. They started with Aaron's, knocking first and then letting themselves in. All his belongings were stowed, the sides of the bed folded down neatly. She thought of her and Kitty's cabin – sheets tangled in the bunks, belongings spilling out of their backpacks, traces of mascara smudged on the small rectangular mirror, the air thick with the smell of sun lotion, deodorant, wet bikinis. The only signs that Aaron slept in here were a head torch hanging from a hook above the bed and a chart of the southern hemisphere pinned to the opposite bulkhead.

They went next to Denny's cabin, and found his much the same. The bed wasn't quite so neatly made and there was a T-shirt and a pair of shorts cast on the edge of it, but other than that, the cabin was tidy. He had a row of books above his bed that were held in place by a strip of wood, so they didn't tip out in rough conditions. Lana found herself wanting to pause, run her finger along the spines of each of them, see what he was reading, but Shell was already moving on to the next cabin.

After they'd checked and re-checked each cabin Shell turned to Lana. 'That's everywhere down here.'

'He must be on deck.'

They climbed through the hatch, expecting to see Joseph sitting at the bow, perhaps having slipped up here during their search. But as Lana turned on the spot, the wind raking through her hair, she saw that the bow was empty and Joseph was nowhere to be seen.

The rest of the crew were sitting in the cockpit, and Shell asked, 'Anyone seen Joseph this morning?'

Everyone shook their heads, saying they hadn't.

That's when the first flicker of panic sparked in Lana's thoughts. 'When was the last time anyone saw him?' she asked.

'Last night,' Kitty said. 'He was sitting up at the bow around midnight.'

Shell agreed. 'That's when I saw him, too.'

'Was he still in bed when you got up?' Lana asked Heinrich, who shared a cabin with him.

Heinrich opened his mouth, then closed it again. He turned away as he said, 'I don't know. I can't remember.'

'So no one's seen him this morning?' Aaron asked.

'No,' everyone confirmed.

'Lana and I have just checked all the cabins and bathrooms,' Shell said. 'We can't find him anywhere below deck.'

'And he's not up here,' Aaron said, turning on the spot to look at the empty deck. He even cast his gaze up the mast to see if he was on the first spreader.

'What does this mean?' Lana asked.

No one spoke.

Shell's hands knotted together. 'This is crazy. He must be *somewhere*. He can't just have disappeared.'

*

Anxiety rippled through the crew as they moved around the yacht, calling Joseph's name and searching hidden nooks.

Kitty traipsed leadenly along the passageways, fingers pressed to her lips, her face white. Heinrich rushed past, tearing through cabins, patting down bunks and sleeping bags, yanking open lockers and deep cupboards, and repeating over and over to himself, 'He has to be here somewhere.' Shell stayed close to Aaron, questioning him about any areas where Joseph could have become trapped. She was intermittently calling Joseph's name, but the conviction in her tone weakened each time there was no answer.

Eventually Lana climbed back up on deck where Denny was manning the helm.

He looked at her. 'Anything?'

She shook her head.

Then she began to methodically search above deck. Although it looked empty, surely there were places someone could hide or become trapped. She checked the hammock, followed by the dinghy, in case there was any way he could have slipped inside as it hung suspended on davits at the stern. When both were shown to be empty, she began walking around the perimeter of the yacht, her hand trailing the lifeline as she looked over the side. There were stories of people who'd fallen overboard and were hanging against the hull, their lives saved by their safety harness. But as she completed a circle of the entire yacht, it was clear Joseph wasn't there. Though why would he be? None of them had been wearing safety harnesses that night, or even life jackets.

Aaron joined her up on deck. 'Nothing,' he said.

Heinrich came up behind him. 'He's not down there,' he said, moving past Lana and searching the deck in the same places that Lana had just looked, even opening the lazarette where the spare fenders and lines were kept.

Eventually the whole crew congregated in the cockpit. Shell stood beside Lana, turning the bangles on her wrist, moving them in rotation one after the other.

Aaron cleared his throat, and every pair of eyes swivelled to face him. His skin looked grey and there was a sheen of sweat across his forehead. 'I don't want to have to say this, but as none of us have managed to locate Joseph, we need to consider the possibility that he's gone overboard.'

Lana closed her eyes, swallowed. *He can't have.* But even as she told herself this, she knew perfectly well he could have. What if he'd taken a leak over the side of the boat in the middle of the night, and slipped in? What if he was so drunk that he stumbled and fell overboard? Could that have happened to Joseph? Or what if he hadn't been able to sleep and he'd come up here to write? Maybe he'd fallen asleep at the bow and then simply slipped in. She thought of the horror of it, the boat rolling or hitting a wave and sending him overboard. He would've been alone in the water, watching the yacht drift off into the distance.

Shell said, 'One of us must have seen something. What was the watch rota?'

'I was on from ten p.m. to midnight,' Lana said. 'Then I handed over to Aaron.'

'I was after Aaron,' Kitty said. 'Two a.m. to four a.m., and then it was Heinrich, then Denny.'

Both men nodded, confirming that.

'Who was the last person to see him?' Aaron asked.

'I know he was sitting at the bow – close to one in the morning,' Lana said. 'After that I went to bed.'

'I didn't notice him there later,' Aaron said. 'When I handed over to Kitty, he definitely wasn't at the bow. Anyone else see him after that?' The crew shook their heads. 'So if Lana saw him last then it's possible that he went overboard any time between one a.m. and now.'

'I've been on deck since sunrise,' Shell said, 'and I haven't seen him.'

'Okay, so we can assume then that he went missing sometime between one a.m. and around six a.m. When the sun rose,' Aaron said.

Lana tried to calculate how far they could have sailed in that time. The wind had been fairly light in the early evening, but it had strengthened throughout the night. She wasn't great with her distance calculations, but she guessed that between 1 a.m. and 6 a.m. they could've travelled anywhere between 30 and 50 nautical miles.

'We need to start searching,' Heinrich said. 'We've got to turn the yacht around and look for him.'

Aaron said nothing. As skipper he was always the one making the decisions, organizing the crew, but he seemed in shock, amazed that Joseph wasn't here.

'Yes!' Denny said, fervently. 'Let's get fucking searching!'

'Should we put out a "Man overboard" alert?' Shell asked.

'No,' Aaron said firmly. 'Not yet.'

19

THEN

Lana lowered the binoculars, rubbing a knuckle across her eyes. She blinked rapidly to try and sharpen her vision, but her eyes were burning-dry, and a dull pain was building between her eyebrows from squinting.

They'd been searching for Joseph for five hours. Aaron explained that the usual protocol would be to make an expanding-box search that covered the point from which a person went overboard, moving methodically outwards. But seeing as there was no exact time or location as to when Joseph went overboard, the best they could do was estimate the time frame in which he went missing, check the logbook, and retrace the route during this period.

Aaron's injured shoulder was preventing him from taking the helm, so he paced the deck barefoot, his dark polo shirt flattening against his body in the strengthening wind. His gaze kept flicking back towards the east in the direction they should still have been sailing in, and Lana noticed the sheen of sweat clinging to his brow.

She slid a hand along the back of her neck, where the life jacket was chafing her skin. Denny had handed them out a few hours ago and all the crew had put them on wordlessly. She felt foolish for not wearing one for the entire passage, but when the weather had been so calm she hadn't even considered it. If Joseph had been wearing one, maybe he'd have had more of a chance.

She stared hard at the sea, which glared back at her, a twitching blue eye. It felt strangely surreal to be searching for a lost crew member – the situation so stark and dreadful that she couldn't believe it was actually happening. She kept half-expecting Joseph to pop out from a hatch or cabin, shouting, *Surprise!*

How had this happened? No one had raised the question yet – as if to do so would shift the focus away from the search towards the cause. Lana had been the last one to see Joseph, and a low heat burnt at her cheeks as she recalled her reaction when he kissed her. Was that the last contact he'd had with anyone – the imprint of her rejection as the water surrounded him?

Lana raised the binoculars again, concentrating on the small circle of her vision in front of the yacht. Heinrich was searching on the port side, Shell on starboard – with the intention that between three people they could search the widest possible area.

Despite Lana's desire to be methodical and thorough, with only open ocean and no landmarks it was easy to lose track of where she'd searched. The ocean looked blank and infinite. Aaron believed the sea temperature would be around 27 to 29 degrees – warm enough to stay alive for many hours, but exhaustion would be the problem. If Joseph had gone overboard sometime between 1.00 to 6.00 a.m., he could have been in the water for up to fifteen hours by now. She wondered if he could hold himself up for that long, or whether hypothermia would have set in. It was possible that they were already too late.

She adjusted the focus on the binoculars. Ahead, the flat light was stealing definition from the sea, so that it felt almost impossible to see clearly. She thought of the light from another boat she'd briefly seen last night, and sent up a silent prayer that maybe someone else had found Joseph and pulled him to safety.

From the far side of the yacht, she heard Shell gasp.

Lana didn't even turn. When the eye is fixated on the same area for a long period of time, it's easy to become fatigued. Your mind starts playing tricks on you – simple waves transforming themselves into outstretched hands, the back of a head, the silhouette of a body drifting on the surface.

She waited for a few seconds and then heard Shell's sigh. 'Nothing.'

As Lana continued staring through the binoculars, a growing sense of hopelessness filled her: the sea had never looked so vast or so empty.

*

Lana jumped at the feel of a hand on her back.

'Hey, it's just me,' Kitty said. Wisps of loose dark hair whipped around her unmade face. 'Take a break. Drink something.'

Lana's knees felt stiff from where she'd been bracing herself against the rock of the waves. 'I need to keep looking.'

'I'll take over,' Kitty said, raising her voice above the wind. She eased the binoculars from Lana's grip, and hooked them around her neck, saying, 'Shell made sandwiches. They're in the fridge.'

Lana wasn't sure she had the stomach for it, but she knew it was important to keep up her strength if she was to be of use.

When she looked at Kitty properly, she saw that her eyes were dulled, hooded with shadows. Without the weight of mascara and eyeliner, she looked younger, frightened. Two tiny patches of eczema had cracked the skin at the corners of her lips and her eyelids were lightly swollen.

Suddenly Kitty closed her eyes, her nostrils flaring, and sucked in long, deep breaths. Lana watched as the blood seemed to drain from her body. She placed a hand on her arm, concerned that she was about to faint. 'Kit?'

After half a minute or so, Kitty opened her eyes and fixed her vision on the line of the horizon. 'Seasickness. Since we turned I haven't felt right.'

'Really? You sure it's not a hangover?'

Kitty's gaze snapped to Lana's. 'I know what a hangover feels like. This isn't it.'

Lana removed her hand from Kitty's shoulder. A few moments later, Kitty said, 'Sorry . . . I just . . . everything is so spun out right now. I just wish I hadn't . . .' Kitty trailed off.

'What is it?'

'Nothing,' she said, as if the thought had passed.

Lana asked, 'Have you taken anything for the seasickness? There are pills in with the first-aid stuff. Shall I get you some?'

'Already taken them.' Kitty drew in a deep breath, then lifted her hands to her head, rubbing her scalp.

In the brief moments that her hands were free of the lifeline, the yacht suddenly lurched as a wave smacked into the side of the hull, spray shooting across the deck. They both stumbled, Lana managing to grab Kitty by the arm, pulling her close.

They stood facing each other, eyes wide.

'I didn't see it coming,' Kitty said, her face white. 'We could've . . .'

Lana nodded, a lump of emotion filling her throat.

Kitty's fingers squeezed Lana's as they stood together, feeling the water surge between them.

It was that moment when it became real. 'It could happen so easily,' Lana said. All it would take was a sudden jarring of the yacht, a lapse of concentration, and any one of them could go over. Just like Joseph.

Slowly, Kitty nodded, tears bright in her eyes.

*

Below deck, Lana poured a glass of water and held onto the sink with one hand as she drank it. The water was flat and tasteless from the desalinator, but she filled herself a second glass and gulped that down, too. Remembering to drink enough on a passage was crucial, yet it was surprising how a whole day could slip by and it was only the baseline thud of a headache arriving that reminded her to drink.

She went next to the fridge, fetched one of the sandwiches

Shell had made, and took it to the saloon table. It was a relief to be sitting down out of the wind.

She began to peel back the crinkling silver foil covering the sandwich and, for a moment, she sat there almost dazed by it. After watching the water for hours – the fluid, movable monotony of it – she found the foil mesmerizing in its rigid, shining contrast. Her mind tripped to walking down a supermarket aisle beneath the bright, dazzling lights and feeling the smooth edges of bottles of bleach, washing-up liquid, the cardboard corners of washing powders, the soft give of kitchen roll wrapped within polythene, and then coming to the long tubes of silver foil. How many times in her life had she groaned about having to dash around the supermarket? Now the solidity of those aisles, the firm normality of it, seemed like an impossible dream, as if she'd never find herself doing anything as ordinary as walking through a supermarket again.

She took small bites of the sandwich, working them around her mouth. The bread tasted stale and the cheese was flavourless. She felt guilty being down here, resting, when she knew Joseph was still out there. But if she were honest, the search felt hopeless: the area they had to cover was enormous and it was impossible to accurately estimate how far someone could have drifted in that time, or where the currents, wind, or swell could have taken him.

Denny climbed down into the saloon, his hair wild and windswept. He slumped down beside her at the edge of the table.

Instinctively she raised her hand to his cheek, not worried

about who might see. His skin was cool against her palm, a shadow of stubble there. For a moment his eyes closed and his head tilted towards the touch of her fingers. The skin beneath his eyes looked bruised, almost sunken, and his bottom lip was cracked from the sun.

It scared Lana to see him looking so shaken. His ebullience was gone, and a wretched look had settled into his features. She had an overwhelming desire for this never to have happened; for Joseph to still be on board, and for her and Denny to slip off to his cabin, slide under the cool sheets and lie in each other's arms.

It was tempting to imagine that in a parallel world, where there are infinite options of reliving a moment with a different set of outcomes, there was one where Lana and Joseph would have been sitting at the bow together last night – and when he leant to kiss her, she'd have smiled, placed a hand lightly against his chest and said, 'I'm incredibly flattered – but I'm with Denny.' She could have reassured Joseph, stayed with him.

But instead, Joseph was missing, and Lana was the last person to have seen him.

'Denny, I need to tell you something,' she began suddenly. 'Last night . . . Joseph and I were smoking up at the bow.'

He lifted his gaze slowly, settling it on her.

'We were just talking, you know, about anything. Everyone was drunk – Joseph, too – and as we were talking, he tried to kiss me.'

Lana didn't know why she felt so compelled to tell Denny this right now. Perhaps it was that she wanted everything between them to be transparent. Or maybe she needed someone to say to her, *This is not your fault.*

Denny looked at her for a long moment. Then he glanced down at his hands, which were clasped together on the table. 'Yes, I know.'

He already knew? Lana had thought Denny was in bed by then. Perhaps someone else had seen it happen and told him. She was about to ask more, when Heinrich strode into the galley, binoculars around his neck. He poured a large glass of water and gulped it back, gasping for breath at the end.

She willed him to leave, return to the deck so she and Denny could remain alone. Denny straightened, filling his lungs with air. He placed his hands on his thighs and got to his feet, crossing the saloon and pulling a chart from the nav station.

'It's not looking good out there,' Heinrich said to them both.

'Do you think we should put out a "Man overboard" alert?' Lana asked.

'I'm not sure there's any point now,' Denny said. 'We're in the middle of the ocean. Even if we did put one out, who's going to come? No helicopters can fly this far, and we're at least three days from land whether we sail west or east.'

Heinrich nodded in agreement.

Lana saw the hopeless truth in what he was saying. There was nothing they could do. No help was on the way. Out here, they were on their own.

Gazing through the porthole at the empty horizon, she chewed the edge of her thumbnail, wishing they'd never left the Philippines. She'd had an uneasy feeling about it from the outset.

She'd seen Aaron's impatience building each day they'd spent in port; he'd sit alone in the evenings with a glass of rum, studying the charts and forecast, and writing long lists of what needed to be done. Thinking about his growing restlessness, she recalled the strange conversation she'd overheard when he and Denny had been leaving that Internet café together. There was an odd fervour in Aaron's tone as he'd said, *I've got to be on the water by the fifteenth.*

She wondered what was so important to him about that date. What day was it now? She'd lost all track of time since they'd been at sea, hours and days rolling together.

Looking to Heinrich and Denny, she asked, 'What's today's date?'

Heinrich glanced at his watch. 'Thursday the sixteenth.'

A cool, ominous feeling pressed close to Lana. Joseph had gone missing last night – on the fifteenth.

*

Heinrich returned up on deck, and Lana and Denny were alone for a few moments. They didn't talk, just sat together in silence, both lost to their own thoughts.

There was a bellow from above, followed by a loud, creaking noise. For a moment, Lana had almost forgotten where she was, why the ground was moving beneath her. The floor seemed to tilt, and she lurched in her seat. Her gaze swung to the porthole, where the horizon seemed to shift and re-form. Then she realized: the yacht was turning into the wind, the sail losing its power and making a loose flapping noise.

Then the wind must have filled the sail again on the other tack, heeling the yacht over.

'What the hell?' Denny yelled, getting to his feet. He thundered from the saloon up on deck, Lana following.

Shell was at the helm, Aaron beside her, and Heinrich was tying off the sheet.

'What are you doing?' Denny demanded, the beam of his vision on Aaron.

'Turning back,' Aaron said.

'We haven't found him yet.'

Aaron approached Denny, addressing him in a low voice so that the others couldn't hear. She could see the tension in Denny's arms, his hands curled into fists at his sides.

After a minute or so, whatever Aaron was saying seemed to soothe Denny, and his hands began to unfurl. With a nod, he disappeared below deck.

Lana stood there, still surprised. 'I don't understand. We can't have finished the search course yet.'

'Look ahead of you, Lana.'

She looked up to see a threatening horizon of blackened cloud.

'There's a low-pressure system coming in. I'm hoping we're only going to hit the shoulder of it – but if we wait any longer we could find ourselves right at its centre. It's just too dangerous. The crew are getting sick, and we provisioned for a set period. I won't put lives at risk.'

'What about Joseph?' Lana asked.

Aaron said nothing.

She shook her head. 'No. No – we can't do this. We can't leave him out there.' She turned on the spot, looking for an ally in Shell or Heinrich, but neither of them would meet her eye. 'We can't give up on him!'

'I'm sorry to say this, Lana,' Aaron said quietly, 'but I don't think there was ever much hope of finding him. Just look,' he said, gesturing with a hand to the endless expanse of water.

Her breath caught in her throat. 'So he's dead, then? That's what you're saying. Joseph is dead?'

The wind rattled against the mast, an eerie, lonely answer.

20

NOW

Lana stands facing Joseph's sister, aware of a throbbing in her temples and a sheen of sweat licking her back. It was only this morning that *The Blue* came crashing back into her world with the news that it had sunk – and in a matter of hours, it feels as if the very seams that are holding Lana together are starting to strain, rip apart.

It is just a matter of time before Aimee Melina discovers that Joseph wasn't on the yacht when it sailed to New Zealand – and she is going to want to know why.

The problem is, Lana's not even certain that she knows the truth herself.

But one of the crew does.

She still sees Joseph's face, even now. It's carved into her thoughts: the sharp angle of his nose, the darkness of his eyes with a glimmer of light at their corners, the foppish dark hair. She wonders if she'll ever get over what happened as the memory of it beats within her like a second pulse.

What if, she thinks darkly, *the crew don't return?* Lana will lose the people she once cared about – and she'll be the only living person who was there the night that Joseph disappeared.

What would she tell Aimee Melina then?

*

'Who should I speak to? Who is leading the search?' Joseph's sister asks Lana.

Lana swallows. 'Paul Carter. The Operations Room is just up ahead on the right. I'm sure he'll be able to help you.'

'Thank you.' Aimee Melina turns, and Lana watches her glide along the corridor, her posture effortlessly graceful.

Lana already knows that once she reaches the Operations Room and enquires about Joseph – that will be it. Something will be put into motion that cannot be undone.

Lana needs to get away from Joseph's sister – have a chance to think clearly. She hurries towards the exit of the building, shouldering through the double doors. Outside, the chill air breezes over her skin, cooling the red heat in her cheeks.

Across the flat plain of concrete, Lana sees her car. The urge to get in, to drive far away from the Rescue Centre, is almost overwhelming. When she walked away from *The Blue*, she thought she could let the bad memories and questions sail off with her friends. Only she was wrong. They were still here, living deep within her – just as they would be if she left now. She has no choice but to face them.

She walks towards the edge of the port where a bench is set

back from the water. She sits there, feeling the cold wood against the backs of her thighs, waiting for her breathing to settle. She can imagine the conversation Aimee Melina will be having with Paul Carter: *My brother was on board* The Blue. *Joseph Melina.*

I'm sorry, but we've no record of him. Sure you haven't made a mistake?

Certain. He wrote to me from the yacht, told me he was sailing to New Zealand.

I'll check again, Paul Carter would say, searching through the crew list – even though he'd know all their names off by heart. He'd return to her, palms opening as he said, *I'm really sorry, but no, he's not on the list. He must have got off in one of the earlier ports.*

It's not going to be long before Lana has no choice but to explain what she knows about Joseph. For months she hasn't allowed herself to think of that night – or the terrible days that followed – but now her thoughts begin to carry her back there.

An image fills her mind: a dark red bloodstain at the edge of the teak deck. She recalls the way it had seeped into the grain of the wood, the blood locked there like a memory.

21

THEN

A pair of binoculars dangled from Lana's neck like a dead weight. Gradually each crew member retreated below deck to rest. Kitty had been the first to leave after seasickness had taken a firm hold, her shoulders hunching as she heaved over the side of the yacht, her skin turning sallow. Aaron had insisted she lie down, positioning a bucket and a large bottle of water at the head of her bunk.

Lana remained alone at the helm, knowing that once she allowed herself to sit, exhaustion would claim her. The sea state was worsening, a confused mess of waves being pushed and buffeted in different directions, so that the yacht lost rhythm.

A spasm of pain tightened across the inner arch of her foot, and she breathed out sharply as it began to cramp. She crouched, grabbing her foot and rubbing at the furiously contracting knot of muscles. She breathed deeply, trying to send oxygen around her body and, after a couple of minutes, the tension began to ease and she was able to flex and stretch her toes a little.

As she straightened, a patch of something dark at the edge of the deck caught her attention. She peered at the stain, which bloomed into the wood, the size of a fist. With a start, she realized what it was: blood.

Why was there blood on the deck? They hadn't been fishing for a few days – and anyway, Aaron, fastidious about keeping the teak clean, didn't let the crew gut fish on deck.

An image of Joseph suddenly flashed into her mind: his head lying to one side, eyes open but blank. A small pool of blood trailing from his open mouth.

She blinked, shocked at the thought.

She squeezed her thumb and forefinger against the bridge of her nose, trying to push away the image.

'Hey, what's going on?'

Lana looked up. Shell had come up on deck with Aaron, and they were both looking at her quizzically as she remained crouched low.

'There's blood. Here. On the deck.'

Shell and Aaron moved closer, bending down to see.

'How odd. Where has it come from?' Shell asked. When she glanced at Lana, she must have seen the apprehension in her expression, as she added, 'You're wondering if it's something to do with—'

'Typical!' Aaron said. 'I moan at everyone else to keep the deck clean and then I go and drip my own blood all over it.'

'Yours?' Shell said.

'My shoulder.'

Lana stared at Aaron. 'I thought you hurt it in the shower?'

Shell's gaze flicked to Lana, as if surprised by the confrontation in Lana's tone.

'I did. Came up here after to get some air, sober up. Didn't realize how bad it was until Kitty said I was bleeding through my T-shirt. Actually,' Aaron said, turning to Shell, and carefully rolling up his sleeve, 'I wanted to ask, you reckon that looks all right? Like it's going to heal? I stuck a few of those tape stitches over it. You know what it's like getting cuts to dry out at sea.'

The gash on Aaron's shoulder was no more than an inch or two wide, but it looked deep. The skin around it was swollen and angry red, and had been pulled together with thin pieces of medical tape just as he'd described. It would have bled plenty – certainly enough to cause the bloodstain beside her.

But what was puzzling Lana was how anyone could get that sort of wound from stumbling in the shower.

*

The following morning, the rain arrived. Awake in her bunk, Lana had watched it sheet across the ocean, strangling visibility and making the sea boil. Now, by lunchtime, a wet sheen covered the deck, and the wet had crept inside the yacht. It was carried in on the soles of feet, and shaken from damp clothes; it rose from sodden hair and dripped through open hatches.

She lurched along the passageway towards the galley to make herself a coffee. The rough seas made Lana feel as though she was walking drunk – the stagger, the loss of balance, and the sensation that the whole world was wavering around you.

Most of the crew complained of becoming nauseous if they spent too much time below deck where everything swayed and tilted, and you couldn't see the waves coming to brace yourself for impact.

In the galley, Shell and Heinrich were standing facing each other, their eyes narrowed, speaking in quick voices. Shell's fingers cut through the air in sharp strokes and Lana caught Heinrich's urgent reply, 'We were both there, Shell.'

Shell laughed, a short mirthless sound Lana had never heard from her before.

Heinrich said, 'We can't undo what happened.'

'You think I don't know that?' she hissed in reply.

They didn't notice Lana until she was almost upon them. They both fell silent, stepping apart. Heinrich moved to the saloon table where he slumped down, pulling out a book from the shelf behind him, while Shell busied herself in the galley, her back to Lana.

Lana made her coffee in silence and, a few minutes later, Aaron strode into the saloon with a piece of paper in his hand. 'New watch rota,' he announced, pinning it to the noticeboard. 'What with the weather, plus Kitty being out of action, I've had to rejig everything. I want us to pair up for night shifts – everyone's getting knackered and the conditions could be challenging over the next forty-eight hours, so I don't want to take any risks. It's going to be three hours on, three hours off. I want everyone harnessed. In daylight, it'll resume to single shifts of two hours, so you can catch up on your sleep.'

Lana's brain felt sluggish, slow to take this in.

'What do you think the low-pressure system will do?' Shell asked.

'Difficult to say. Depends how quickly it's moving and what direction it takes. I'm hoping it drops out, or we might be lucky and stay on the shoulder of it.'

This is only the shoulder? Lana thought as she felt the yacht rise and then plunge beneath her.

*

Lana returned to her cabin, intending to get some rest before her next watch. Kitty was asleep, and Lana lay on the top bunk, staring through the porthole, watching rain slide across the glass. A gusting wind lashed the sea, squalls of dark wind charging at them.

Her mind wouldn't shut off: all she could think about was Joseph and what had happened to him. With everyone so caught up in yesterday's search, and the worsening weather, it felt as though there was no space or energy left to talk about him.

She wondered if the others were as plagued by questions as she was. She kept going over and over what had happened. *Did he slip? Was he drunk? Was he taking a leak and fell overboard? Did he shout for help? Why didn't anyone hear him?* It was all so strange: one day he was here – part of their crew – and the next he'd disappeared.

No, not disappeared. Died.

Even though no one was saying it, it was a death they were dealing with.

She kept replaying her final conversation with Joseph, remembering the look of hurt that had stung his features when she rejected him. There was something else worrying the edges of her thoughts, too. Lana had asked him, *Do you ever feel like diving in . . . and just swimming away from the yacht . . . away from everything . . . into all that space?* She'd been drunk – she hadn't meant the question to be as provocative as it sounded, but now Joseph's answer came back to her: *Yes, I do. I feel that very much.*

The crew were all assuming his death was an accident – but what if it hadn't been? What if – half-drunk and stoned – Joseph had *chosen* to go overboard that night? She thought of his situation: he'd recently lost both his parents; he'd been thrown off *The Blue* by Aaron; the rest of the crew were furious with him for stowing away – and then his closest ally on board, Lana, had rejected him.

Was it possible that it was suicide?

Her breath shortened. It felt as if there was no longer enough air in the cabin. She needed space. Air. Sweat began to crawl over her skin, climbing up the back of her neck, dampening her hairline. She scrambled from the bunk, her breath coming in quick gasps.

She yanked open the door into the passageway – but the air was no cooler there. She didn't want to go back to the saloon where the others would be, or up on deck in the pouring rain. There was nowhere – no fucking space anywhere!

Without knowing fully what she was doing, she crossed the passageway and let herself into the cabin Heinrich shared with

212

Joseph. The room was empty and felt a little cooler, the smell of stale sweat mixed with deodorant.

Joseph's sleeping bag was still laid out on the top bunk, his canvas backpack thrown on top. She placed a bare foot on the edge of the lower bunk, pushing herself up to reach it. Her hands gripped the stiff, salted fabric and she pulled it closer. She felt like a trespasser as she unbuckled it and pushed her hand inside.

Lana was surprised to find so little in there – she remembered the backpack seeming full to bursting when she'd watched Joseph heaving it onto his back as they said their goodbyes in the Philippines – but now she only pulled out a handful of items. First was a pile of clothes: two matching blue shirts, a pair of black shorts, and three pairs of boxers. They were all the clothes he travelled with. Next was a wash bag. Inside it there was a razor and shaving foam, a bar of soap in a plastic dish clouded with soap scum, a tube of insect repellent, a toothbrush and paste.

She removed a paperback from near the bottom of his bag: *The Vietnam Spy*. The battered cover showed an image of a muscular man crouched in the jungle, a gun propped on his shoulder. It was an oddly boyish book, no doubt filled with fights and explosions and gruesome war details. She would have expected something grander, and the sight of this slim, worn novel reminded her of how young Joseph was. How much life he had left to live.

There were a few other items too: a pair of sunglasses, three pens, his passport. She flicked to the back and saw his photo, a pale shot of him with a shaved head. His full name was Joseph Pierre Melina. Strange how she'd never known it until now.

There was a leather wallet pushed into a side pocket. Opening it, she found 500 US dollars. She thought of Aaron's claim that Joseph had left the yacht because he'd run out of money – but here was proof that he'd been lying. Although it wasn't a huge amount, it was enough to pay for at least three more weeks on *The Blue*. If Joseph hadn't been kicked off because of money, Lana wondered why Aaron wanted him gone so resolutely.

There was a final group of items left in the bag: a bundle of four identical black notebooks bound together with an elastic band. Lana didn't know why she was surprised to see several of them – if Joseph enjoyed writing poetry, it made sense he'd fill more than one whilst travelling.

She pictured him hunched over his notebook, writing by head torch, his brow creased with focus. As she removed the first book, she paused, wondering whether it was wrong of her to intrude on his privacy – yet what if the notebooks contained answers that would help them understand what had happened? Perhaps she could show them to Denny, ask him to translate.

She slipped the first notebook free and opened it.

The pages were covered in slanting handwriting and she peered closely at them, trying to make sense of the pattern of French words. It took her a moment to realize that the entire page was filled with just one word, repeated again and again.

Désolé.

Sorry.

She flicked to the next page – and saw exactly the same. The word began to swim before her eyes. She turned more pages, but that was all there was: thousands upon thousands of apologies.

Picking up the next notebook, she opened it at random: *Désolé. Désolé. Désolé.*

She shook her head, staggered. All four of Joseph's notebooks were filled with apologies. *What were you sorry for, Joseph?*

'Lana?'

She turned sharply to find Heinrich glaring at her from the doorway of his cabin. His gaze travelled to Joseph's belongings and his eyes widened. 'What's going on?'

Her face flushed hot at his curt tone. 'I was just looking through Joseph's things.'

'What for?'

'I . . . I don't know . . . I just needed to. I'm finding it hard to get my head around what's happened.'

Heinrich said nothing, just continued to stare at her.

'I can't quite believe he's gone – that this is actually happening. It's so sad.'

'Yes. It is,' he said without conviction.

She quickly packed away Joseph's belongings while Heinrich watched. 'Sorry, I should've checked with you before I let myself in.'

He glanced towards his own backpack, which was fastened around the end of his bunk. 'Did you find anything interesting?'

She could have told him about Joseph's notebooks painstakingly filled with 'sorry's, but she didn't want to share this personal detail when Heinrich and Joseph had never been friends. 'Not especially.'

He nodded once, then a protracted silence followed as they both struggled to think of something to say next.

'How's Shell?' Lana asked eventually.

He drew his shoulders back. 'Fine. Why?'

'I haven't seen much of her. She doesn't seem like herself at the moment.'

Heinrich shrugged. 'Everyone's finding it hard . . . since Joseph.'

'Yes,' Lana agreed.

Then Heinrich stepped aside from the doorway, making room for her to leave.

*

Lana kept to herself for the rest of the afternoon. It was too rough to read or draw, so she watched the agitated ocean through the porthole.

Just before 8 p.m., she pulled on her oilskins and went up on deck with Shell to begin their watch. Daylight had turned to darkness, but still the rain continued to lash down, heavy drops blown sideways by the wind, soaking her face and stinging against her eyes.

Denny, who they were relieving, shouted a few details to them both about the course and the wind, and told them to clip on. He waited a moment, his head torch pointed at Lana's safety harness, until she'd hooked it to the helm. Then he nodded, and clambered wordlessly below deck, his hair soaked and flattened to his head.

Shell took the wheel, fighting to keep it steady, and Lana stood close by, legs braced. The sail strained beneath the wind and waves hit the side of the yacht, slashing across the deck in ghostly sprays of white. It felt as if they were saddled to a bucking, writhing beast, all thrashing muscles and salty breath.

Beneath her oilskin, her skin was hot – sticky with sweat and salt – and she wanted to peel off her clothes and life jacket and let the rain wash her clean.

She looked towards the bow, which was barely visible in these conditions. No one would sit out there tonight as it rose and crashed through the waves. It already seemed a lifetime ago that Joseph would perch there on calm nights, his thin legs dangling towards the water, a notebook in his lap.

Désolé. That was all he'd written, over and over, every night. She wondered whether he really was considering ending it all? She pictured him standing at the edge of *The Blue* in the darkness, stepping over the lifeline and looking down at the dark water – and then letting go. If it was suicide, perhaps the sea was a good place to end things: there is no great leap from a building, or awful fixing of a noose, or buying of a gun. There is just the water and a gentle step into it. Then you are swimming, watching the faint light of the boat as it sails on, everyone on board unaware. You know you won't be found, so that is it, the decision made. You lie on your back and look at the stars and wait.

But what if it wasn't like that at all? What if it wasn't suicide? What if he'd slipped and fallen in, been desperately calling and swimming after the yacht – but with the wind and the waves, and the crew drunk, no one would have heard.

A sudden squall blew across the water and Shell tightened her grip on the wheel. Lana held onto the side of the console, bracing her legs. When the surge of wind hit, the wire shrouds shrieked and wailed, a tortured sound. A contrary swell caught them in its path, lifting the yacht, and they slid down its face into a trough, the nose of the vessel slashing through the next wave, jets of water pouring over the deck.

'You okay?' Shell shouted beside her.

'Yes!' she called back, feeling her heart rocking against her chest. She was glad to be on watch with someone else. She wouldn't want to be up on deck alone, not tonight.

*

After her watch had ended, Lana went into the saloon, pleased to be out of the wind and rain. Her clothes were soaked and, despite the warmth of the air temperature, she was cold.

The saloon felt thick with moisture and heat. The bananas had turned, their skins browning and bruised, their sickly-sweet smell permeating the galley. She briefly considered throwing them overboard, but the idea of staggering up on deck, one arm filled with bananas, the other clinging onto the bulkhead, the steps, the hatch, the lifelines – anything to keep her steady – felt like too much effort.

She unbuckled her life jacket, then shouldered off her oilskin and hung it on the back of the bathroom door with the others.

There was a pool of water on the floor that shimmered in the lamplight. She thought about mopping it up so no one slipped, but in the end she left it.

Lana drank a glass of water and ate a handful of nuts standing with a hand gripped to the kitchen counter. Then she went to the bathroom and cleaned her teeth. Glancing at her reflection in the mirror, she was unsurprised to see dark bags beneath her eyes and a tangle of damp hair hanging scraggily across her face. She spat the paste into the sink, wiped her mouth on the back of her hand, then crept into her cabin.

There was a sour, damp odour of vomit and unwashed skin, and Lana wished she could prop the door open to let air circulate, but it would only bang back and forth with the waves. Kitty slept with her bunk's lee cloth fixed in place. It was a piece of canvas that was attached along the front edge of the bunk under the mattress and fixed to hooks on the sides, so that when the yacht yawed and rolled, you wouldn't fall out.

Lana fixed her own lee cloth, climbed up onto her bunk and lay on top of her sleeping bag, the shiny material sticking against the backs of her legs. It felt horribly claustrophobic – the thick darkness, the cabin ceiling inches from her face, the lee cloth blocking her exit. She felt for the hook of the cloth, checking she could undo it easily.

She placed her hands on her stomach and exhaled a long breath, feeling the air leave her. Two hours and forty-five minutes to sleep – then another watch. She drew in a slow breath, feeling her ribcage expand. She tried to focus her thoughts only on the action of breathing – but they rolled and shuddered with the yacht.

Joseph's death loomed above her, like dank breath close to her face. Her need to understand what happened to him consumed everything, and questions filled her mind. *Did Joseph plan it? Or was it an accident? Did we search hard enough? Why was Aaron claiming that Joseph didn't have enough money to stay on* The Blue? *And why was it so important to Aaron to be on the water by the fifteenth of March?*

Her breathing became ragged and shallow and she rolled onto her side, trying to search out light on the water. The heavy rain blanketed the moon and stars, and only the faint glow of the yacht's lights illuminated the sea. It felt as though they were sailing blind, ploughing through an endless, landless body of water. She wanted to press 'pause'. To get off the yacht. To remember what it felt like to be still, to be quiet.

'Kit,' she whispered into the darkness, her voice thin. The lee cloths felt like a barrier between them, when she wanted to lean over the bunk edge, feel Kitty's fingers entwine with her own as they had done on their first nights on board. 'Kit, are you awake? I keep thinking about Joseph.'

She thought she heard Kitty move, the sound of covers being pushed back.

'Kit?' she whispered again.

Lana waited, her heartbeat elevated. But all that came was the soft sound of Kitty's breathing.

22

THEN

That night, Lana barely slept. She woke with a start, sitting bolt upright – her head smacking against the low ceiling above her bunk. 'Fuck,' she said rubbing a hand against the top of her head, where her hair felt matted and thick with salt.

She'd been having a nightmare. She couldn't pull the narrative from her thoughts clearly enough to see what it'd been about, although she could sense the water in it – an eerie feeling of nothingness deepening beneath her.

'Lana?' Kitty's voice was a thin whisper. 'You okay?'

'Bad dream.'

She glanced at the time. It was 8 a.m. She tried to think when her second night watch had ended. Two hours ago? Three, maybe? Her body clock felt utterly out of sync and exhaustion was leaden in her bones. She hauled herself out of the bunk, asking Kitty, 'How you feeling?'

Kitty was lying on her back, eyes closed, hands at her sides as if she were on an autopsy table. Her skin was the colour of chalk.

'Still bad?'

Kitty nodded.

'What about something to eat?'

'Not sure I can.'

Kitty had said that she felt as if the smallest of movements – a mouthful of food or a string of words – would be enough to tip the cautious balance between not throwing up and throwing up.

'I'll fetch you some cereal – dry. No milk. You've got to keep up your strength.'

'Okay.'

In the galley, Shell was making coffee on the stove, adding a cupful of long-life milk to the pan. Aaron was standing beside her, his back to Lana, saying, '. . . three or maybe four days till we reach Palau – depending on what this low-pressure system does.'

'What do you think will happen when we arrive? About Joseph?'

'What, and report that we had a stowaway who went overboard? We'll be in the shit, is what'll happen.' Aaron shook his head as he pulled a glass from a cupboard and filled it with juice.

'Morning,' Lana said.

Shell turned. Her gaze hovered over Lana's face for a moment, prompting her to ask, 'You need a coffee?'

Lana's heart rate seemed permanently accelerated, yet her mind felt sluggish. She nodded, 'Please.'

Aaron said to Shell, 'I've been talking to the others about this

– what we should do when we get to Palau – and I'm not sure we should say anything.'

Shell stopped stirring the coffee in the pan. 'Not say anything?'

Lana focused on Aaron, who told them both, 'Heinrich pointed out that no one knew Joseph was on *The Blue* when we left the Philippines. Not even us. His paperwork shows that he's still there. So if we say nothing, to all intents and purposes, he'll still be thought to be in the Philippines. It's not like he's got family who are going be worrying about him when he doesn't get in contact – so why report it at all?'

Lana shook her head. 'That's crazy.'

Aaron turned to face her. 'What do you think they're going to say when we arrive and tell them we've lost a crew member – but that he had no paperwork?'

Lana said nothing.

'They're not going to like it, that's for sure. *The Blue* will be impounded during the investigation. It could take months. All of us will be taken in for questioning. Think of all the press, too. They'll love this! You want your face splashed all over newspapers back home? We've got nothing to tell them – no one saw anything, no one heard anything.'

'You're serious?' Lana said.

'I'm considering all options.'

'Maybe we need to talk about it together,' Shell said diplomatically.

'I agree,' Aaron said. 'I was going to call a group meeting about it – get everyone together. Put it to the vote.'

'We're going to vote about whether to inform the authorities that one of our crew has died?' Lana said, incredulous.

When he spoke again, his voice was softer. 'Look, I know it's hard, and everyone is upset about what's happened, but we've got to deal with it. We all need some time to think things through, so we'll talk tomorrow. Eighteen hundred hours.'

In a day and a half's time they'd be deciding whether Joseph's existence would be denied or not.

*

Lana's hands were shaking as she carried her coffee and the bowl of dried cereal back to the cabin. She couldn't believe what Aaron was suggesting.

She nudged the door open with her elbow and found Kitty sitting up in her bunk and Denny perched at the other end of it.

Whatever they'd been talking about suddenly ceased, and they both turned to look at her.

There was an awkward moment of silence. Then Kitty held out her wrists. 'Denny made me seasickness bands.'

Lana looked down and sure enough on her wrists were two sweatbands, with bottle tops taped to the centre of each one, that were now pressing into the pulse points on her inner wrists.

Lana looked at Denny. 'Kind of you.'

He shrugged. 'It's worth a try if it helps.'

Lana passed Kitty the small bowl of dried cereal, then closed the cabin door, leaning her back against it. She cupped the coffee in her hands, the smell filling the cabin.

She began telling them about her conversation in the galley with Aaron. 'He wants to have a group vote tomorrow at six.'

Denny nodded. 'We heard.'

'You already knew?' she said, looking between them.

'Denny just told me,' Kitty said. She placed a piece of cereal in her mouth and began to chew it slowly.

'I've got to go,' Denny said. 'On watch in a few minutes.' As he moved past Lana, his arm brushed against her waist. She looked up and caught his eye. His pale-blue irises looked dulled as he tried to smile.

When he was gone, Lana said, 'I can't believe what Aaron's suggesting. It's completely insane. If it'd been anyone else from the crew, he wouldn't even be contemplating this.'

Kitty sank back down into the bunk, the cereal bowl pushed aside.

'We can't just pretend nothing's changed. Vote to say, "Let's forget about him."'

'No,' Kitty said quietly, her eyes closing.

'We don't even know what happened to him, for fuck's sake!'

'It was an accident,' Kitty said, her voice folding away again so that the words sounded weak enough to ring hollow.

*

When Lana's daytime shift at the helm came around, she was grateful for the solitude up on deck. The howling wind whipped her tiredness away, and she sat hunched in her oilskin, rain dripping from the hood, her hands gripped to the wheel, eyes alert on the horizon.

In big swells the autopilot system on *The Blue* was no use. The yacht needed to be manually steered so that they could hit waves at the points of least impact, and her biceps ached from the constant force on the wheel.

She'd read an article once about a woman who'd sailed single-handedly around the world, who'd said that the hardest thing of all – worse than the sleep deprivation, the lack of fresh food, the physical endurance of it – was being alone on the water with her thoughts, the way they kept on looping around and around, and there was nothing to break the cycle. Lana would never have understood that fully before they left sight of land – but now, with nothing to focus on except the sea around them, the space seemed to amplify her thoughts.

She gripped the wheel, thinking about Aaron's suggestion that Joseph's death go unreported. She understood his reasoning – of course she didn't want there to be an investigation, or for the yacht to be impounded – but how could they bury the information when none of them even knew what had happened to Joseph?

She pressed the question to her brain, trying to draw out an answer. So far she'd considered two options: first, that his death was an accident, or second, that Joseph had planned it.

But there was a third option, too, one that she'd been reluctant to let her thoughts visit: what if someone else had been involved? There were still so many things that didn't make sense, like why Aaron had been so adamant about being at sea on the very night Joseph died, or why no one was admitting to seeing anything. The deck was never unmanned, so surely someone must have noticed something? There was a strange atmosphere amongst the crew, as if behind every door people were whispering.

Lana shook her head, running a hand across her chest; maybe it was just the sleep deprivation getting to her, feeding into a sense of paranoia and shaping a tragic accident into something darker.

*

After Lana's watch ended, she checked on Kitty who was sleeping, her hands curled beneath her chin. She'd planned to climb into the top bunk and kip for a couple of hours, too, but she felt restless and edgy.

She wanted to see Denny – to slip into his room and steal a few minutes alone with him. There was a risk that she'd be seen, but with everything else that was going on, it seemed of trivial importance. Things had felt strained between them since Joseph's disappearance and she realized how much she needed him right now.

As she moved along the passageway towards the stern, she heard Aaron's voice from within his cabin. It sounded as if he was standing on the other side of the door, inches away from her.

Lana found herself pausing to listen.

'I know it's not!' Aaron said, his voice animated.

There was a muffled sound of a second male voice – Heinrich's, she thought – coming from the far side of the cabin.

'You don't *agree?*' Aaron said, his voice lifting in ridicule. 'Are you a fucking idiot? You know what'd happen, don't you?'

The yacht swayed beneath her and Lana had to grip the door frame to steady herself as she listened.

She couldn't pick out much of the conversation now because Aaron had lowered his voice, but she caught the flare in his tone as he challenged, 'Don't be ridiculous! What difference does it make?'

Heinrich's response was unclear, but he must have been talking for a while because then Aaron sighed loudly. 'Look, I don't like it any more than you do.'

Lana started at the sound of a dull thump, as if a fist had just connected with a wall.

She held her breath, waiting for them to speak again. Then Aaron's voice: 'It's for the best. Remember that.'

A moment later footsteps crossed the cabin, and Lana darted away, hurrying back along the passageway to her room. Inside, she pressed herself against the door, her heart drilling, wondering what the hell they were talking about.

*

Half an hour later Lana went into the galley to make a snack, and found herself alone with Aaron.

'Aaron,' she said, setting herself in front of him. 'When we were in the Philippines, you told us that Joseph decided to leave *The Blue* because he'd run out of money.'

'And?'

'And I know that's not true.'

'Do you?' Aaron said, his eyes meeting hers, heat in his glare.

'Oh, come on, Aaron. Cut the bullshit. Why did you really want Joseph off your boat?'

His lower jaw moved from side to side as he ground his teeth together. 'I'll tell you why,' he said, a steely edge to his tone. 'I found out some information about him. Something I didn't like at all. I didn't want someone like him on my yacht.'

'*Like him?*'

'Should've trusted my instincts. Right from the start I wasn't sure about Joseph. So I did some checking up. Found out a few things.'

Lana thinks of Aaron and Denny coming out of the Internet café just before they left the Philippines, Aaron's face a furious red. And then a few hours later, Joseph's sudden departure.

'What did you find out?'

'You claim to know Joseph so well, maybe he told you?' Aaron paused. 'Before he left France he was a suspect in a murder trial.'

'That's crazy!'

'The case got thrown out because of lack of evidence, but Joseph was the only suspect.'

Lana could feel her hands beginning to tremble at her sides. 'That can't be true. Who? Who did he supposedly murder?'

Aaron looked at her for a long moment. 'This is the really nice bit: his parents.'

'But they died in a fire.'

'Yes – a fire Joseph started.'

'No! I don't believe you.'

He shrugged. 'I don't care what you believe.'

Lana felt a strange heat building in her neck, spreading to her face as she realized Aaron's explanation made a terrible kind of sense. She thought of the black notebooks filled with the one word, *Désolé*. 'If this is true, why didn't you say anything earlier?'

'Thought I'd handled it by asking him to leave. But then of course, the idiot stowed away.' He shook his head. 'I know he was a friend of yours, Lana, and I'm sorry that Joseph is dead – I really am – but he wasn't who you thought he was.'

As she turned to leave, Aaron said, 'Oh, and Lana? One more thing. You know the crew voted on whether you and Kitty should join *The Blue*? You might be interested to know something: not everyone voted in your favour.'

23

NOW

Minutes have passed, maybe even hours, when a thrumming noise fills the sky. Lana looks up at a ceiling of dense grey cloud. She feels dazed, unsure how long she's been sitting out here. She's covered in goosebumps, her skin pale and chilled.

The thrumming sound is growing louder, the air seeming to vibrate with it. She glances around, wondering what it is – a ship engine, a motor of some sort, perhaps a—

And then she realizes: it is a helicopter.

Is it the rescue team? Has there been news? Has she missed something important while she's been wandering the port? She wants to tear away the clouds, stare right up at the sky and see inside it.

Then, as if by the power of the thought, a white-and-red helicopter lowers out of the cloud layer like a vision. Large lettering on the side reads, *Coastguard*. A bright light of hope fills her: it must be carrying the crew. Kitty will be inside.

Suddenly she is running, following the direction the helicopter is turning in. The car park is the widest flat area she's seen – it can only be going there. Her sandals clack against the concrete and her cardigan slips from one shoulder as she runs.

Lana is out of breath by the time she reaches the main building. In front of her the door opens, and Shell's parents hurry across the tarmac with Paul Carter. A man in a high-visibility vest stands in the centre of the car park waving two brightly coloured flags above his head.

Paul Carter puts his hand up, indicating that they mustn't go any closer. Shell's parents are clutching hands. Have they been told that Shell is on board? Lana wonders again how long she's been wandering the port for – an hour? Two hours? What has she missed?

She hurries to Paul Carter's side, an arm hooked over her head to keep the wind from tearing her headscarf free. 'Who is on board?' she yells above the sound of the helicopter blades.

Paul Carter doesn't turn, doesn't seem to hear. So she places her hand on his arm, shakes him. 'Who is on board?' she says, yelling louder. 'Survivors?'

Then he turns, the edges of his moustache blowing in the breeze. 'Yes!'

Her heart lifts.

The helicopter lowers, blades cutting through the hazy afternoon. The noise is astounding and Lana clamps the hem of her dress between her knees to stop it billowing in the wind.

Once the helicopter touches down there is a minute when nothing happens. Lana cannot see who is inside, no matter how hard she strains. She wants the blades to stop whirling so she can think, breathe.

Then the helicopter door opens and a man in a jumpsuit climbs out. He offers his hand to someone who steps from behind him huddled beneath a silver blanket.

Lana squints, eyes streaming, trying to see.

She recognizes the tanned, long legs, blonde hair trailing over the foil blanket.

Shell! Her hair whips wildly around her face as she climbs down the steps, holding tight to the hand of the man who helps her.

Shell's mother clamps her fingers over her mouth as if she cannot believe that this really is her daughter – alive, on solid ground – after all these months. Suddenly Shell's mother is rushing forward, the wind raking her hair free of her neat ponytail.

When Shell sees her mother she freezes, surprise making her mouth hang open. Her hands rise to her face, framing her cheeks. Her head shakes with disbelief. Then Shell is stumbling forward into her mother's arms, and they clasp each other tightly.

Shell's father stands back, watching with his arms clamped at his sides. His skin is grey and his lips are squeezed together as if containing a sob. After a moment, he begins to move towards them. When he reaches his wife and daughter his arms unfold, gathering his family to him. He holds onto them, his head resting against Shell's.

Tears sting the back of Lana's throat as she thinks of her own father; she misses him, she realizes. She pushes the thought aside and looks beyond Shell – waiting, hoping. *Please, Kitty. Please be in there.*

There is movement and Lana watches as a second person steps out.

Heinrich.

He doesn't have family waiting for him, but Shell is already turning, drawing him into the circle of her own, keeping an arm around his waist as if she is anchoring him.

Lana watches. It is so strange to see the two friends together on land. They look different away from the context of *The Blue*.

She is looking back towards the helicopter, waiting for the next person to appear, when there is a loud clanking noise. The helicopter door is shut.

She blinks. *No, that can't be it.* She steps forward, as if to stop it leaving. There must be more people to come – because Kitty is not here. Nor is Aaron.

Wait! Wait!

But the helicopter's blades seem to pick up speed, rotating faster and faster, and suddenly it is lifting off, tail first, climbing towards the clouds.

*

'The others? Where are they?' Lana cries, staring skywards as the helicopter is swallowed by the clouds.

People are beginning to move towards the main building. She wants to yell, *Stop! You can't leave!* Because, where is Kitty? Where is Aaron? She doesn't understand why they weren't in the helicopter. She turns on the spot looking for someone to explain, but Shell and Heinrich are enclosed by Shell's parents and she cannot get to them.

Her gaze lands on Paul Carter, who is moving towards the main building, and she hurries after him. 'Wait!'

He glances over his shoulder, but doesn't stop walking.

'Please! Wait!' she calls again, reaching his side. 'Where are the rest of the crew? Is the helicopter going back for them?'

He turns to face Lana. Ahead of them she is aware of Shell and Heinrich moving into the main building, still flanked by Shell's parents and two medics. She doesn't want to lose sight of them – it's as if they are not quite real yet, just apparitions drifting out of view.

'I'm sorry,' Paul Carter is saying, drawing Lana's gaze back to his face. 'You weren't in the waiting room when I updated the others. Search and Rescue located the life raft – but there were only two people on board.'

'Two?' *Shell and Heinrich.* 'Where are the others?'

He shakes his head, saying, 'We don't know just yet.'

A hot wave of fear washes through Lana as her brain scrambles to process this: if Kitty wasn't in the life raft, then all it can mean is that she and Aaron are in the sea. But it's already been several hours since *The Blue* went down. Without a life raft, was it even possible to survive?

'But the coastguard helicopter . . . it's here,' she says, glancing towards the space where it's just been. 'Who is looking for them?'

'A second helicopter is in the search area, and two boats that picked up the Mayday are searching, too. I assure you, Lana, we're doing everything we can to find them.'

24

THEN

On the evening of the group vote, Lana stood in the galley, one foot wedged against the base of the cupboard to keep her steady as she prised the lid from a can of kidney beans.

With everyone too frantic or exhausted to think about meals, hunger was exacerbating already fragile emotions. Lana decided to prepare a simple rice supper that the crew could grab when they had a moment to rest. It seemed like a lifetime ago that dinners had been taken together, all of them sitting on deck, plates on their knees, cold beers beside them, chatting as the stars shone bright in a cloudless sky.

Now she looked out through the rain-slashed porthole and saw brutish waves rolling towards *The Blue*, which hit the hull, rocking and jostling her. She was growing used to the cacophony of sounds – the wind tearing at the sails, shrouds rattling, the vibration of the crockery and glasses clinking, the creak of wood as the boat strained. The constant movement and noise had become so much part of each day that if the wind were suddenly to stop, she wasn't sure she'd be able to sleep without it.

Lana dragged her gaze away from the window and fetched a pan, holding it steady with one hand as she poured in a pack of rice. She covered it with water and a lid, then adjusted the fiddle rails on the stove to wedge the pan snugly into place. Next, she searched in the store cupboard for a tin of chopped tomatoes, clinging onto the cupboard door to stop herself stumbling as a wave hit. She was pleased to have the activity of cooking to concentrate on because, in a few minutes' time, the crew would be gathering in the saloon to talk about Joseph.

As Lana crossed the galley to fetch the final fresh pepper, her foot met a wet patch just as the yacht pitched. She was thrown backwards, her legs rising up from the floor so that, for a split second, it seemed as if they were above her head.

She landed hard on her back – the air punched from her lungs.

She lay on the floor stunned, her mouth open and gasping for air.

'Jesus!' someone exclaimed from the hatch, hurrying down the steps towards her. Suddenly Denny was crouching beside her, water from his oilskin dripping onto the warm skin of her arms. 'Are you okay?'

She wanted to tell him that she couldn't breathe, that her lungs felt compressed – as if she were underwater – but she couldn't squeeze the words from her throat.

Then all of a sudden her chest seemed to spring open, her lungs filling once again with air. She gasped, feeling the heady sensation of air rushing into her body.

'Are you hurt? Can you move okay?' Denny asked, pushing down the hood from his oilskin.

'Just . . . winded,' she managed. She lay there, letting the breath come back to her, but the sea was allowing no compensation as it continued to throw the yacht around, causing her to slide on the galley floor. Eventually she managed to scrabble upright.

Denny's face was white and he pulled her to him. 'Lana,' he said, his lips against her ear. 'You've gotta be careful. Out here there's no help . . .' He held her tightly, his hair wet against the warm skin of her cheek.

She closed her eyes and concentrated on the feeling of being within his arms. It felt as if it had been weeks since they'd last held each other. She didn't care that his oilskin was wet against her clothes, or that the zip was pressing against her cheek. She just stayed there, eyes closed, feeling the tears spilling down her face.

'Lana? What is it?' he asked softly.

She couldn't find the words to explain.

'Please,' he said after a moment, 'talk to me.'

'I . . . I don't even know what to say.' A deep, icy unease had been building in Lana since they'd left the Philippines. 'Everything feels wrong. The weather . . . Being so far from land . . . The atmosphere between everyone . . . between us.' She paused, hoping that Denny would say something, but he remained silent, his gaze on her face. 'And no one's even talking about Joseph. It's as if we can't bear to admit that we fucked up. All of us. And now we've got to *vote*,' she said with disbelief, 'about what we should do.'

Denny released his grip and Lana took a small step back, holding onto the kitchen counter. She looked at him square on as she said, 'He died, Denny. One of our crew died. How can we ignore that?'

'I . . . I . . .' He shook his head.

'If we say nothing, it would be like Joseph never existed. Like we've just decided – because it suits *us* – to erase him from history.' A lump of emotion rose in her throat, the situation stirring painful memories of her father's betrayal.

Denny looked at her intently, his gaze mapping her face.

'I won't let that happen with Joseph,' Lana said. 'I can't.'

*

Everyone was gathered around the saloon table – even Kitty, who was slumped forward with a sick bag on her lap. She still looked wretchedly pale, but there was a hint of brightness in her eyes, which Lana hadn't seen in days.

Shell and Heinrich sat apart. Aaron positioned himself at the head of the table, nearest the hatch, so that he could keep an eye on what was going on up on deck. The sails had been reefed and the autopilot was running, and hopefully it would give them a few minutes to talk all together.

'I'll keep this brief,' Aaron began. 'We all know why I've called this meeting – to talk about Joseph.' He glanced around the table at each of them. 'It's been three days since he was discovered missing. We've done our best to search for him – thank you, all of you, for your help with that – but sadly, I think we knew that the chances of finding him were always incredibly slim.'

Lana felt the yacht rise up on a wave and she braced herself. The movement as they slammed down into the trough rocked through her body, and Aaron grimaced as he stumbled against the bulkhead, his hand moving to his injured shoulder.

'We're all having a hard time over what's happened – but I don't want any of you to feel responsible. As skipper, Joseph's safety was my responsibility, not yours. I know everyone's been talking about what exactly happened. Up until this point, we've all been assuming it was an accident – that Joseph was drunk or stoned, and lost concentration somehow. It's happened to many sailors before him, that's for sure.' He paused. 'But I don't believe that's what happened to him. I think it was sadder than that.'

Lana felt a buzzing heat rise through her body.

'I believe Joseph planned to kill himself.'

The saloon fell quiet. Outside, the wind heaved against the sails, waves beating the hull, but at the table there was silence.

'But why?' Shell asked.

Aaron's gaze fell on Lana. 'Yesterday, Lana and I had words, didn't we?' he said, casting a smile at her.

She was thrown off balance by the remark and the friendly tone of it.

'Lana told me off – quite rightly – for not being open with her, and all of you, about the real reason I asked Joseph to leave *The Blue*. And she was right to question me, because there was more to it.' Aaron explained what he'd discovered about Joseph's history and the allegations that Joseph was responsible for his parents' death.

Lana glanced around the table; the others were listening, rapt. When her gaze returned to Aaron, she thought, *I can see the barrister in you.* Every detail of his tone, body language, even the inclusive vocabulary of 'we' and 'us' was all part of a performance designed to encourage an alliance with him. As he spoke he softened his voice, talking slowly as he looked each of them directly in the eye. He'd even found the time to shave and put on a clean T-shirt, making him look the epitome of a confident skipper who was in control.

Aaron continued. 'I believe – no, let me amend that. I *know* that Joseph was sorry for what he'd done. I checked through his belongings in case there was anything important that would help us unpick what'd happened, and found these.' He produced a bundle of four black leather notebooks, setting them in the middle of the table – as if laying his evidence before the jury.

'Lana's already seen these,' he said, casting another quick glance her way, 'but the rest of you will probably be surprised to hear that the notebooks are filled with page upon page of apology.'

She realized that Heinrich must have told Aaron that he'd found her going through Joseph's belongings.

The crew opened each notebook, flicking through the reams of apologies while Aaron continued, 'Knowing about Joseph's past and these notebooks, I got thinking about him stowing away. What was the point in it? He knew that once he got to Palau, I'd chuck him off. So why bother? Why put himself through the discomfort and stress of stowing away if he was only going to be on board an extra week? That's when I thought maybe he wasn't planning on reaching Palau at all. What if his plan was actually to throw himself overboard? And if no one knew he'd stowed away, no one would even know he was missing.'

He finished talking and sat for a moment, letting the others absorb what had been said. After a time, Aaron said, 'Whether Joseph's death was an accident – or something he planned – it still doesn't change the fact that one of our crew is now dead. And so we're left with the decision of what to do when we reach Palau.

'I've managed to speak to most of you about this already, and naturally everyone's got different opinions, so I called this group vote so we can decide – *together*—' he said, emphasizing the word, 'whether we inform the authorities about Joseph.'

He shifted his gaze steadily between them. 'I've been spending a great deal of time thinking about this, and I'm concerned that if we tell the authorities about his disappearance, then we will have a serious problem on our hands. Joseph was not even on the crew list. They'd wonder why he was travelling with us illegally. Then there'd be questions about his death, why we were all drinking, why he wasn't clipped on, why he wasn't wearing a life vest.

'I'm worried that the investigation could turn into a witch-hunt. *The Blue* would almost certainly be impounded until the case is resolved, which could take months. It's possible that *The Blue* would never be released.'

He paused for a moment and took a couple of steps up the hatch to check that everything was on course. He looked calm and efficient, authority oozing from him.

When he returned to the saloon table, he faced them, saying, 'The alternative is simple – we say nothing. Do nothing. No one knows. No one investigates. Joseph is dead – we can't change that. But we can affect what happens next.'

Shell's hands opened as she asked, 'But what if Joseph told someone he was sailing on *The Blue*?'

'He did sail with us around the Philippines. But the boat's papers show that he also disembarked there. To all intents and purposes, Joseph is still in the Philippines. No one would have seen him get back on the yacht since none of us realized he'd stowed away.'

Heinrich nodded.

'The bottom line is, Joseph's death was tragic – a tragedy that we all have to live with – but I don't want to make that tragedy any bigger than it needs to be by involving the authorities.'

Lana could see the sense in what Aaron was saying: what difference would telling the authorities make? Joseph would still be dead. Yet somehow it didn't feel right. 'But what if there's someone out there wondering where he is?'

'There is no other family. We know that,' Aaron answered. 'Joseph told us.'

'What about friends?' Shell asked.

'Did he ever mention any?' Aaron pitched to the crew.

They shook their heads.

Lana looked through the window over the achingly bare

ocean, where waves danced primitively beneath a sombre sky. 'Saying nothing feels wrong.'

'What's wrong is that Joseph died under our watch. We let him down,' Aaron said solemnly. 'But,' he said, 'that doesn't change things. We're still left with a decision to make. No one likes this, but we – as a crew – have to decide what happens next.'

Lana watched him, thinking again how good Aaron was at this – absorbing the responsibility and blame, claiming to share the same anxieties as the rest of the crew – yet he seemed *too* good at it.

'The fairest thing to do is put the decision to the vote,' Aaron said. 'I hope you've all had enough time to think about things, as this is the hardest group vote we'll ever make.'

25

THEN

'I think you already know what I believe we should do,' Aaron resumed from the head of the saloon table, 'but in the interests of clarity, my vote is that we don't inform the authorities of Joseph's death.'

Heinrich was the next person to vote. He was sitting with his chin raised, shoulders squared, and it didn't come as a surprise to Lana when he said, 'I agree with Aaron. I don't see that any good will come to us – or Joseph – by getting the authorities involved. What's done is done, I say.'

Convenient! Lana thought, shaking her head. It was far too easy to say that, to just walk away, pretend it hadn't happened. Except it *had* happened. Joseph was dead and she, for one, wasn't about to let that go.

'Lana, you're next,' Aaron said.

'I can't believe we're even sitting here, discussing this. It seems insane that we'd do anything other than tell the truth about what's happened. It isn't up to us to decide what's right or what's best – we should be doing what's honest.'

She glanced around the circle of crew. There were no nodding heads or murmurs of agreement as there had been when Aaron spoke. She felt as if she should be making some sort of counter-argument, at least trying to balance things, but she could feel her face growing hot beneath the crew's attention. 'I just . . . I believe . . . he was our friend, and . . .' Lana lost her stride and her sentence petered out.

She cleared her throat, and all she managed was, 'I'm voting that we tell the authorities the truth.'

Beside her, she could feel the heat of Denny's body. His hands were locked together in his lap, the veins on the backs of them standing proud. She could smell the fresh scent of sweat lifting from his skin. He was voting next, and she realized that she had no idea what he'd say.

With his gaze fixed squarely on Aaron, he said in a clear voice, 'I'm voting that we tell the authorities the truth, too.'

Aaron's eyes widened. Denny and Aaron always voted together – Lana had never known a split decision between them. She wanted to slip her hand into Denny's, squeeze tight, and say, *Thank you.*

After a moment, Aaron managed to pull his features into a vaguely neutral expression, but a vein at the side of his temple continued to throb.

There were now two votes in favour of telling the authorities the truth, and two votes against.

'Shell?' Aaron said, prompting her vote next.

Lana glanced at Shell. Tiny beads of sweat had formed across her top lip. Shell kept her gaze locked on her hands, which were gripped to the table.

When she spoke, there was a slight waver to her voice as if she was on the edge of tears. 'I'm sorry,' she said, not catching anyone's eye. 'But I vote not to tell the authorities.'

Lana's stomach clenched with disappointment. She'd thought – hoped – Shell would vote with her and Denny. She was always so level-headed and fair that Lana was genuinely surprised by her decision.

'I'm really sorry,' Shell said, her gaze still on her hands, '. . . but I just . . . I don't want to lose *The Blue*.'

Aaron nodded in agreement.

With just Kitty left, Lana wondered what would happen when the votes were equal – three for and three against. She'd never sat in on a vote where that had happened as there had always been seven of them. Did they toss a coin for the final decision?

'Kitty?' Aaron said.

Kitty's skin looked grey. She swallowed several times, and when her voice came out it was barely more than a whisper. She held Aaron's gaze as she said, 'I vote to not tell the authorities.'

'What?' Lana spluttered.

Kitty's gaze flicked to hers, then away again.

'That's four votes to two in favour of not informing the authorities,' Aaron said, 'so I believe we're decided.'

Lana's palms slammed hard against the table, making it shudder. 'No!'

Everyone stared.

'We can't do this!' she said to the crew. Then she turned to Kitty. 'How could you? I can't believe you think that's the right decision—'

'Lana,' Heinrich cut in. 'It's a vote. A democracy.' He spoke in a level but firm manner. 'It is very difficult. For everybody. But we have voted now. The decision is made.'

'But it's the wrong decision!' She exhaled hard, her hands sliding from the table, leaving behind a trail of moisture.

Out here, hundreds of miles from land, it felt as if they'd slipped down a plughole into some alternative reality where rules and integrity were something shifting and fluid.

*

'What the fuck was that about?' Lana demanded the moment she closed the door to their cabin.

Kitty slumped down in the bunk, lying flat on her back. She closed her eyes.

'I can't believe you! You voted against me!'

'It wasn't against *you*,' Kitty said, with no fight in her voice. 'I voted for what *I* think is best.'

'So concealing Joseph's death is best?' Lana asked. 'How, how can you think it's the right thing to do? You saw Aaron's bullshit barrister performance in there. It's all a fucking act! He manipulated everyone into siding with him.'

'It's not about siding with him – or with you. It's about doing what each of us thinks is best.'

'Best?' Lana said, outraged. 'Best for who? Certainly not for Joseph. No one even talks about him. It's like he never existed. I feel like I'm the only one grieving for him, the only one who cares about what happened to him.'

'You're not. Believe me, you're not,' Kitty said tightly. 'But do you know what I tell myself? I think about his parents – that poor couple were asleep in their home when he burnt it to the ground. Who does that? He would've—' she stopped abruptly, as if she'd lost her train of thought.

'So because of what *allegedly* happened in his past, it doesn't matter that he died?'

'Of course not!' Kitty said, her voice rising to match Lana's now. 'I'm trying to be pragmatic. Joseph's dead and raking it up with the authorities won't make it any better.'

'Which is what you think I'm doing? What everyone thinks I'm doing?'

'No. No, we don't. It's just Aaron says—'

'Fuck Aaron! He might be the skipper, but he doesn't make our decisions for us.'

'He's not trying to. We voted, Lana.'

'You voted wrong.'

Kitty sat up now, her face tightening. 'Did we? There were six of us around that table and four of us agreed the same decision. What if it's you who's wrong? You're the one setting people against each other. Setting yourself apart. And what for? Maybe your opinion is only as valuable as the next person's. You thought about that?'

'Aaron's hiding something.'

'You're the one who didn't tell us that you'd already seen Joseph's notebooks. You're the one who Joseph tried to kiss that night – yet you haven't even mentioned it to me. It seems to me that if anyone's been hiding something, Lana, it's you.'

26

NOW

Lana paces the corridors, biting the hard skin at the edges of her nails.

'Lana?'

Her head snaps up. Shell is standing in the doorway of the waiting room – Heinrich beside her. Shell's legs are bare and deeply tanned and she wears an oversized man's jumper. Her hair is loose, a tangle of blonde knots spilling over one shoulder.

It's been eight months. The last time Lana saw either of them was when she was climbing from *The Blue* onto another boat, tears lining her throat.

'You're both safe,' Lana says.

Shell reaches for her and they hold each other tight. Lana breathes in scents she associates with the yacht: salt, oil, a faint hint of the apricot shampoo Shell always used.

'You're in New Zealand,' Shell says, shaking her head.

'I've been here since I left *The Blue*,' Lana says, stepping back.

She and Heinrich don't hug, but he says, 'It's good to see you.'

'We're just about to go and get checked over by the medics,' Shell says.

There is a cut on the inside of her knee, raw and red, that will need stitching. Lana must be staring as Shell says, 'When we hit the container, I was knocked down. Caught my knee on a cleat.'

Lana nods as if she understands, but she doesn't understand – not any of it. Her mind seems to bend and curve beneath the weight of all her questions. 'What happened out there?'

Heinrich and Shell stand side by side as they explain in rushed bursts, the story switching between them. Shell describes how they were all up on deck when they hit the container – the impact of it knocking them from their feet. Then the water came flooding in, seeping upwards through the floor from the cracked hull.

Heinrich looks grey as he takes over, relaying the Mayday Aaron put out, and how they used the bilge pumps, fighting a losing battle against the flooding sea. Aaron instructed them to get rid of any spare weight from the yacht to slow down the sinking. 'Everything went overboard,' Heinrich says. 'Backpacks, cushions, food, spare ropes, the paddleboard, fishing gear, tools, books, computers – everything. We emptied the water tank, then the fuel tank, and even began ripping off seat panels, mattresses – anything to slow down the gush of water. But it just kept on coming . . .'

Heinrich cannot stop speaking. Lana feels his need to share every detail, to let out the horror and fear of the past few hours, retelling it from every different angle. He asks questions of Shell, of Lana even, wanting to hear the unfolding of events from the ground. He shakes his head often, lifts his hands into the air. Occasionally he slips into German, and there is a strange milk-iness behind his even tan, as if all those hours in a life raft have washed the colour from deep within him.

She hears about how Aaron got them all into the life raft and stepped aboard last. The five of them watched as *The Blue* was cast around in the sea like a rag doll, all her elegance and beauty finally swamped as she sank beneath the waves.

'Kitty?' Lana asks. 'What happened to Kitty?'

Shell's voice breaks as she describes the wave that flipped the life raft, washing out Denny, Aaron and Kitty. 'We could see them right there in the water – but the wind was blowing the life raft faster than any of them could swim. They couldn't reach us.'

Lana closes her eyes, thinking of Denny's body being pulled from the water – only found because he still had the EPIRB strapped to him.

Lana shouldn't ask this question, but she needs to know Shell and Heinrich's opinion: they were there, she wasn't. 'Do you think anyone could survive out there for this long?'

'Search and Rescue are still looking,' Heinrich says, 'and there are two boats in the area, too.'

'Yes,' Shell agrees. 'Lots of people are looking.' But even as she says this, they all know that it is possible to lose someone who's gone overboard. All the crew know this after what happened . . .

Bursting into the space between them, like rain heaving from a cloud, the memory of Joseph is there. The three of them look at one another for a long moment. It's a pause that contains so many truths and memories; the opening and shutting of cabin doors and the sharp calling of Joseph's name; the press of binoculars against the sockets of eyes; the swing of the boom as they turned away from the wind; the vote as they sat squeezed around the saloon table in silence.

The look holds so much history and weight, that their gazes eventually drop away to the floor.

*

Standing with Shell and Heinrich, Lana knows she must tell them about Joseph's sister. They've already been through so much today with the rescue, but Aimee Melina is somewhere within these walls looking for answers and Lana needs to warn them.

Her expression must give her away, because Shell is stepping forward, her head tilted to one side. 'Lana, what is it?'

She looks from one to the other. 'It's Joseph,' she says. 'He had a sister.'

Shell blinks. 'A sister?'

'No,' Heinrich is saying, shaking his head. 'He told us he didn't have any family . . . How do you know this?'

'Because she's here. Looking for him.'

The colour in Shell's face drains away. Her mouth opens, but she doesn't speak.

'Here?' Heinrich repeats, eyes wide.

Lana nods. 'Apparently Joseph wrote to her when he was in the Philippines, telling her he was going to sail to New Zealand and wanted to meet her here.'

'My God,' Shell says. 'She thinks he's still alive.'

Lana nods.

'What have you said?' Heinrich asks sharply.

'Nothing. I didn't know what to say.'

Heinrich is looking at Shell. 'Fuck. What are we going to do?'

*

Footsteps sound behind them. 'Excuse me?'

The three of them turn, startled.

A woman is standing, looking at them, smiling faintly.

'It's Heinrich, isn't it?'

He stares. Doesn't speak.

'I'm one of the medics that's been called in to check on you guys,' she says in a chirpy tone. 'Would you mind if I steal you away for a few minutes to check you're all in one piece?'

Lana sees his relief that this woman is not Joseph's sister. He looks to Shell and Lana, as if imploring them to tell him what he should do. Shell steps forward and says close to his ear, 'Come and find us afterwards.' Then she adds, 'We'll work this out.'

When Heinrich and the medic have disappeared, Shell runs a hand over her face. Beneath the strip lighting in the corridor, Lana sees how exhausted she is. 'I can't believe he had a sister. All this time she must've been . . .'

'I know,' Lana says.

They stand in silence for a moment, and then Lana says, 'She needs to be told he's dead.'

Shell nods in agreement.

'You know she'll ask what happened.'

'I know.'

'What do we tell her?' Lana says, looking at her closely.

Shell returns her gaze. 'I honestly don't know.'

'I know none of you wanted to hear this back then – and you probably don't want to right now – but I'm certain there was more to Joseph's death than just an accident.'

She waits for Shell to refute her. But she doesn't.

'What do you think happened, Shell?'

'At first I was convinced Joseph slipped. Went overboard. A hundred per cent.'

'And now?'

Shell glances down at her feet. 'Now, I don't know.'

'Did you find something out?'

'I suppose all the things you were saying . . . the doubts . . . they stayed with me.'

There's something else, Lana can see. She waits.

'Something stuck in my mind,' Shell says. 'It's probably nothing – unrelated, even – but it's about Aaron.'

27

THEN

After the group vote, the last person Lana felt like being stuck with was Aaron but, as they were on night watch together, she had little choice.

Lana positioned herself at the side of the cockpit, while he took the helm. The night-wind beating against her face burnt her eyes dry, but she stared into the darkness, letting the wind buffet away the exhaustion that was threatening to overwhelm her.

Even though she kept her gaze forward, she could feel Aaron's steely presence and imagined a self-satisfied smile on his lips, knowing the group vote had gone his way.

He was good – she'd give him that – managing to sway all but her and Denny into voting with him. She kept replaying the flow of his little speech, how he'd picked out the facts that suited him, and ignored the ones that didn't – like letting the crew drink on passage and not insisting on safety harnesses. Now he could sleep easy in knowing that *The Blue*'s journey wouldn't be sullied by the shadow of Joseph.

It pleased Lana that Denny had voted with her. She hadn't wanted to guess which way he'd vote, knowing the strong allegiance he had with Aaron – but in this he'd proved he drummed to his own beat.

Half an hour before the shift was over, Aaron shouted across to her, 'You may as well call it a night now.'

There was part of Lana that wanted to sit it out until the final minute to prove to him that he couldn't intimidate her – yet she was also exhausted. With Kitty out of action, the rest of them were doing shifts of three hours on, three hours off – and even when Lana had a chance to sleep, she felt so wretched that she was struggling to switch off.

'Sure,' she said to Aaron, unclipping her harness and standing.

As she moved towards the hatch, he said, 'Oh, and Lana? Hope there's no hard feelings about the vote.'

She stopped, wondering if she detected a smile in his tone. 'You know,' she said, turning back to face him, 'just because there was a group vote, it doesn't mean I have to stick to it. Laws aren't made on this yacht. I'd have thought you'd know that – being a barrister.'

He stiffened.

She thought of the way he'd grabbed Joseph by the throat – slamming him against the bulkhead. How far would she need to push him before he laid a finger on her? Just a swipe of his hand could knock her overboard – and who'd be here to see it?

He took a step towards her. His voice was lowered as he said, 'You're a free person, Lana. What you choose to do – or say – when we reach Palau is entirely up to you. But don't think you'd be welcome back on *The Blue*. We run a democracy and only people who understand and respect that are invited to stay.'

'A democracy with a self-serving purpose.'

She went to move past him, but Aaron stepped into her path. He leant forward, his mouth close to her ear. 'Remember, if there were to be an investigation, you were the last person to be seen with Joseph. We all saw him coming on to you, Lana. And from where I was standing it didn't look like you were too happy about it. I'm honestly not sure what the authorities would make of that.'

*

Lana's hands were trembling when she went below deck. Denny was filling a glass of water at the sink, and looked at her, asking, 'What is it?'

'Aaron just . . .' She paused, turning back towards the hatch. 'I think Aaron just threatened me.'

'What?' Denny said, becoming instantly alert. 'What did he say?' He put down his glass and listened intently as she repeated the conversation.

When she'd finished, Denny rubbed the heels of his hands over his eyes. She noticed the dark circles beneath them, as if he hadn't slept in days. 'I think you misunderstood him. Aaron can be bullish and blunt – but he would never threaten you. Sounds like he was trying to be frank – if someone goes against whatever the outcome of the group vote was, Aaron asks them to leave.'

'I know that . . . but it just felt . . . I don't know . . . like it was more than that.' She shook her head. 'He doesn't like me, Denny.'

'That's not true. It just takes a while for him to get to know people. He's had a lot on his mind lately.'

Lana didn't know whether he was talking about Joseph, or something else completely.

'Can I ask you something?'

'Sure.'

'That first day Kitty and I spent on *The Blue* – we went to that beautiful lagoon between the pinnacles – there was a group vote between you all about whether Kitty and I should be invited to join the crew.'

Denny nodded.

'Aaron told me that not everyone voted in favour of us joining.' She paused for a moment, and then asked: 'Who was it?'

'I can't answer that. You know we don't talk about the votes.'

'Please,' she said gently. 'It's important to me.'

'Why?'

'Was it Joseph?'

'Joseph?' Denny repeated, surprised. 'No, it wasn't him.'

What had Aaron meant, then? She wondered just how much bullshit was going on here . . . people withholding small facts, bending truths, letting events become blurred. 'Who was it then? Aaron?'

Denny looked up at the ceiling. She saw his Adam's apple rise and fall as he swallowed heavily. 'Look, this is going to sound terrible . . . but it was me.'

Heat flared in her cheeks. 'But, why?'

'I liked you, Lana. Right from the first moment I met you in Norappi. But I knew with you being on the yacht . . . it would be . . .' He broke off, running a hand through his hair. 'It's hard to explain . . .'

'So don't,' Lana said. She turned to leave, but he caught her by the arm, turning her around to face him.

'Please, let me at least try.' His gaze was fixed on her as he explained, 'I knew that if you joined *The Blue*, I wouldn't be able to stop myself falling for you.' He swallowed. 'But I also knew what Aaron's like. What the rules are. I've always known.'

She pulled her arm back. 'I never realized you were quite so by-the-fucking-book, Denny.'

*

In the cabin, Kitty was asleep. Lana rummaged through the front pocket of her backpack in the dark, and eventually found her head torch. She climbed up into her bunk, her pulse racing.

She couldn't believe that Denny had voted for her not to join the yacht. What was it between him and Aaron? Denny had always struck her as incredibly self-assured, so it surprised her how easily he bowed to Aaron's rule. Yet on other things – like the vote over Joseph – he stood firm.

Everything was muddled in her head. After being at sea for so long, she felt as though the continual churning and rolling of the ocean had flooded her brain, making her thoughts move with the same haphazard rhythm. She was still convinced that she didn't have the full picture over what had happened with Joseph, but she couldn't seem to hold onto information for any length of time, as if a wave buffeted each thought out of her head, another one taking its place.

Lana was learning that on a yacht there could be no single narrative – there were as many stories as crew. People slept and woke at different times, so the flow of events switched from one person to the next, and it was almost impossible to account for a forgotten detail or bent truth.

She flicked on her head torch, then grabbed her sketchbook from beneath the mattress of her bunk, and turned to a blank page. She needed to think about things logically. With a pencil she wrote down the names of who was on watch the night Joseph went missing.

20:00–22:00	Shell
22:00–00:00	Lana
00:00–02:00	Aaron
02:00–04:00	Kitty
04:00–06:00	Heinrich
06:00–08:00	Denny

Everyone seemed to agree that the last time anyone had seen Joseph was when he was sitting with Lana at the bow, which had been at roughly 1.00 in the morning, during Aaron's shift. After that, no one could remember seeing him again. Denny was the first to go to bed, followed by Lana. The others had carried on drinking until different times. It was assumed that Joseph went missing sometime between 1:00 and 6.00 a.m.

She worked through the list of names, starting with Denny. He and Joseph had been friends – she'd often seen the two of them talking in rapid French, Joseph laughing at a quip Denny had made, or asking Denny a question about a translation he was working on. He was in bed before Joseph went missing, and since he didn't have to do a watch until daylight, she was able to rule him out of the equation.

Jesus! What was she doing? She rubbed a hand across her mouth. She was lying in here like some fucking sleuth, writing her friends' names on a sheet of paper, speculating, imagining, deducing. Maybe it was she who had the problem. She didn't need to know that Denny was asleep or wasn't on night watch when Joseph was missing – because she trusted him.

She tossed her pencil onto the bed, and let her head hang forward in her hands. This had to stop – the obsession with what had happened to Joseph. She wondered how the parents of abducted children coped, or families of murder victims whose killers are never found. How does anyone live with that uncertainty? Doubt was eating her from the inside out, making her suspicious and obsessive in her search for answers.

She turned off her head torch and rolled onto her back, spending several minutes calming her breathing. Being at sea made her feel as though her world had shrunk down to the space of this yacht. Everything beyond that seemed abstract, like a dream she couldn't reach.

She was still picturing the names remaining on the list: Aaron,

Kitty, Heinrich and Shell. Perhaps she would think about each of these people and once she was done, she promised herself – that would be it. She'd let it go.

She flicked the head torch back on, and wrote Aaron's name next. He disliked Joseph and made no denial of that. By stowing away, Joseph threatened Aaron's existence, the life he'd carefully carved out on the water. If Joseph had still been with them when they arrived in Palau, Aaron would have been in serious trouble for bringing someone illegally into a country without the correct paperwork. But were those reasons enough to kill someone?

If it was true that Joseph's death had been an accident or suicide, and he'd gone overboard, she very much doubted that it would have happened on Aaron's watch. She'd seen the way Aaron responded to the yacht; if he was in the saloon, resting or reading, there only had to be the slightest movement to the boat which was out of character and suddenly he'd be up on deck checking what was happening. If there was a splash as someone went overboard or Joseph had cried out, Aaron would have been alert to it. But then, he had been drinking hard all evening – so perhaps he wouldn't have noticed.

Then she came to the next name on the list. Kitty. She knew Kitty's faults and strengths – and she knew unequivocally that Kitty was no murderer. But what Lana wasn't so sure about was how thoroughly Kitty would have conducted her solo watch. She'd been drunk that night – perhaps even more so than the rest of them. She could easily have missed something, or fallen asleep at the helm, or left her post to fetch a drink or snack.

The final two names on the list were Heinrich and Shell.

They often did night watches together as Shell had told her she'd rather do two lots with company than one on her own – so it was likely that Shell had joined Heinrich during the 04:00–06:00 watch. If that were the case, it would have doubled the chances of them noticing Joseph. What was odd, though, was that since that night there had been a strange tension between them, as if they'd had some sort of argument that neither of them would talk about. She remembered interrupting their conversation in the galley when Heinrich had said, '*We were both there, Shell. We can't undo what happened.*' She wondered what exactly had happened, and why they both seemed so clear during the vote that the authorities shouldn't be informed.

The question of what happened to Joseph turned over and over in Lana's mind, as she stared desperately at the list of names in the torchlight, looking for an answer. It was like staring into the sea for hours on end, searching: some moments you see things that aren't there – and other times you miss the very thing that is right in front of you.

28

THEN

Time at sea was something fluid; hours began to roll together, days sliding into nights, one watch chasing the other. Lana no longer knew how long it had been since they'd left the Philippines – only that it felt like for ever. She missed commonplace things: sitting on a chair that didn't move; twisting on a tap without worrying about the water supply; being able to walk more than fifteen paces in any one direction; wearing fresh clothes that didn't smell of damp; the sound of birdsong, the voices of passers-by, even the roar of traffic.

She glanced at her watch and saw it was just after dawn. How long had she slept in the past few days? No longer than two or three hours at a time, that was certain. Perhaps this was how new mothers felt – this loosening of reality, a sensation that somewhere in the folds of a deep and long sleep lies the person you used to be – but you just can't quite reach them.

She saw the sketchbook beside her, the list of the crew members' names written in her hand. She closed it and slipped it back beneath the mattress, then climbed from the bunk and pulled on a pair of shorts.

She left the cabin, yawning, and made a mug of coffee in the galley. The air in there was starting to turn foul; the bin needed emptying, packets of food had become damp and were starting to rot, and there was something in the fridge that was leaking a milky fluid. No one had had the time or energy to keep on top of housekeeping and Lana left the galley, deciding she'd do it another time.

Up on deck, she was surprised to find that the rain had stopped and the wind had eased. Looking at the sky, she noted it was still a flat grey, yet a brightness lingered behind the cloud layer as if the sun wasn't far away.

Kitty was sitting at the edge of the cockpit, her hair pulled back from her face with a headband. She wasn't alone. Denny was sitting close to her and there was something oddly intimate about the way their heads were leaning towards one another as they talked. Kitty's knees were bent to one side, her bare toes tucked just beneath Denny's thigh. His expression was intent, listening closely to something she was saying.

As Lana watched, she felt the sharp bite of jealously clench its teeth around her heart. *No, they would never . . .*

She shook her head lightly, stunned at herself.

Kitty looked up. 'Morning.' Slowly she straightened, removing her feet. 'Sleep well?'

Lana nodded. 'You're feeling better.' It came out more statement than question.

'Yes, much. I think . . .' Kitty said, leaning forward and placing her fingers on the wooden steering wheel, 'touch wood . . . the seasickness is behind me.'

'Good.'

Denny's gaze was on Lana, his lips pressed together thoughtfully, eyes unmoving. The dark shadows beneath them seemed to have deepened. He got to his feet, saying, 'I'm beat. Gonna get some rest.'

As he moved towards Lana, he looked up at her, holding her gaze, seeming to want to say something.

'You okay?' she asked in a low whisper.

He nodded, looking away again.

She stepped aside to let him pass.

*

Kitty lit a cigarette and sat hunched forward, an elbow on her knee as she smoked.

Lana sat upwind and watched Kitty lift the cigarette to her lips and inhale deeply. There was a new gauntness to her face that hardened her features.

They were both silent for a time, watching the water. They hadn't spoken since their argument over yesterday's vote, and Lana felt the tension simmering in her throat.

It was incredible how the seascape had changed, levelling out over just a few hours, as if the wind had never raged. The sun was still threatening to break through the dawn clouds, and Lana longed to feel its hopeful kiss against her skin.

Lana circled her right foot, then the left. It was nice to stretch out the tendons and muscles, which ached from balancing at strange angles during the days of rough weather.

Kitty held the cigarette between her lips, then leant down and placed her fingers on Lana's tattoo, slowly tracing the edge of the black wing. She mapped the outline three times. Then she stretched out her own leg, placing it alongside Lana's. She had to shuffle to the edge of her seat so their feet ended in the same place.

Lana looked down at their ankles side by side.

'Never got it done, did I? After all that talk.' She laughed; a strange, almost sad note to it. 'Your dad never said a thing about it, did he?'

Lana shook her head. She wondered how he must have felt watching Lana return home with a tattoo, streak her hair purple, plaster her room with angry artwork, and let music rage through the thin walls. In those late teenage years, full of temper and experimentation, Lana had been willing her father to say, just once, 'You remind me of your mother.' It was as though she was trying on different identities to see which would make her more like her mother.

His silence on the topic only made her rail harder. Sometimes she yearned to stir things up, for them to shout and scream the way they did at Kitty's house, to have that cathartic release of all the emotion that was kept sealed, weighted down with silence. She wanted to rip off the lid, scream, shout fucking swear words in their quiet house, smash things against the walls, sob. It was only recently that she understood why he had kept quiet – because every time he mentioned her mother, it further cemented his lies, so he'd decided it was easier not to speak of her at all.

'You've always been the brave one,' Kitty said.

Lana glanced at her sideways, surprised. There was something off with Kitty that she couldn't pinpoint. A breeze ran between them, loosening a section of Lana's hair, which she retied. When she looked again at Kitty, she realized she was wearing a jumper that wasn't hers. It was pale blue with a flash of green across the chest.

'Is that Denny's?'

Kitty looked down, nodded. 'I was cold.'

Lana swallowed. 'Was he up here a while?'

She nodded. 'Said he couldn't sleep.'

Lana thought of him awake and alone in his cabin last night – just as she had been.

She glanced again at Kitty, taking in Denny's jumper and the seasickness bands he'd made which she still wore on her wrists. Then she thought of the way Kitty had untucked her legs from beneath Denny when she'd noticed Lana. 'What were you and Denny talking about when I came up on deck?'

Kitty's voice was smooth as she answered, 'Nothing really. How come?'

'Looked like you were talking about something important – and stopped when you saw me.'

Kitty pulled in her chin. 'What does that mean?'

Perhaps it was what had happened to Joseph, or the boldness that comes from sailing out the other side of a storm, but Lana pressed forward: 'I mean, the two of you looked . . . close.'

Kitty's laugh was sharp and hard. 'Oh, my God! You think I'm fucking him? Is that it? Shit, Lana!' she said, getting to her feet. 'What is going on here?'

What was going on, Lana realized, was that she no longer trusted Kitty. There had been a time when they were a unit, the two of them against the rest of the world. But now their friendship seemed to have changed, and it felt insubstantial, like a shifting wind.

Kitty took a drag on her cigarette, then paced to the lifeline and flicked the butt into the water.

Lana watched, irritated.

'I'm not,' Kitty said, her back to Lana. 'Fucking him. I would never do that. I would never do that to you.'

Lana said nothing. She wondered, *Would Kitty? Was she capable of it?*

As Kitty stood at the lifeline, her shoulders began to round forward, the beads of her spine jutting through Denny's jumper as she hunched over, a low sob sounding in her throat.

'Kit? What is it?'

'It's everything. It's . . . it's that you could even think that about me. What's happened to us? What's happened to all of us? Nothing feels right any more.'

'Joseph died – that's what happened.'

'It's not just you that's feeling bad, Lana!' she snapped, swinging around to face her. 'It's all of us. We all feel fucking responsible for what happened.' Another sob rose up through her mouth, and Kitty stifled it with her hand. 'Oh, God,' she groaned.

Lana waited. 'What is it, Kit? Do you know something?'

Kitty's eyes closed.

A chill went down Lana's spine. 'Kitty, please. Tell me.'

She rubbed a hand over her face. 'I spiked the drinks, Lana. I spiked all of our drinks that night. I added a shit-load of vodka – but disguised it with juice. That's why everyone was so fucked. Why Joseph was half out of his skull. Why Aaron was . . .' she broke off, falling into another sob.

'You couldn't have known what'd happen.'

'If we hadn't been drinking so hard – maybe nothing would've happened. Maybe Joseph would still be here.'

Lana knew it was a stupid thing for Kitty to have done – but none of them could know whether it had ultimately changed the outcome of the evening.

Kitty wiped roughly at her tears. 'It's just . . . it's so hard right now. So hard. We'd found this,' she said, looking up and gesturing to the yacht. 'And now . . .' Kitty said nothing more, just shook her head as if everything was lost.

*

Later in the day, the whole crew gathered at the bow of the yacht, standing together in a loose semicircle. The deck was wet with spray and Lana held onto the lifeline, wanting to get this over with.

Aaron cleared his throat and said, 'As you all know, Shell suggested holding a sort of memorial for Joseph. These last few days have been difficult for all of us, with hard decisions to make, so I hope this is the first step in a new and positive direction.' He glanced up at the sky. 'Even the weather seems to be on our side today. Looks like the low-pressure system has dropped out, so it should keep on improving.' He ran a hand across his chest, saying, 'I'm not going to be the one doing the talking here – feels like I've been doing plenty of that recently. So if anyone wants to say anything, then please do.'

When no one moved to speak, Shell stepped forward, saying, 'I'll start.' She stood with bare feet pressed together, her hands clasped in front of her. She cleared her throat twice. 'I didn't know Joseph well – sometimes people come into your life just for one scene of it. So it means I can't talk about what Joseph was like as a boy, or what he was like as a teenager.' As she spoke, Shell looked at everyone in the group, although Lana noticed that her gaze skimmed past Heinrich.

'What I'll remember of Joseph,' Shell continued, 'were small moments tucked into the fabric of *The Blue* – like that first night he came on board and cleared three plates of food. I'll always picture him sitting right here at the bow, looking out over the water. Or the way he dived with such beauty from the cliffs back in the Philippines. I'm pretty sure I just saw a snapshot of Joseph, one tiny fraction of the person he was. And I'm sorry that none of us will get to see any more.' Shell lowered her head with her lips pressed together. After a moment she stepped back into the semicircle.

Although Shell's sentiment was kind – and a part of Lana was pleased to hear it, there was something about this whole memorial that felt forced. As Shell said, they'd barely known

Joseph, yet the six of them were the only people in the world who knew he'd died. All he got as a goodbye were a few crumbs of words on the bow of a yacht, miles from land.

Lana wouldn't be stepping forward. This memorial wasn't for Joseph; why would he want the six people who'd decided not to even report his death to be the final ones who spoke about him?

'Anyone else want to say something?' Aaron asked. 'Lana?'

'No,' she said with a firm shake of her head.

'Heinrich?'

'No, thank you,' he said, eyes on the deck.

Lana thought that would be it now, no one else would speak, but then Denny stepped forward. 'I'd like to say something.'

Aaron appeared as surprised as Lana. 'Right. Sure.'

Denny didn't look at any of them, but kept his gaze levelled at the horizon. When he spoke, it was in French. The words seemed to flow easily from his lips, and the whole crew listened in silence. Even though Lana couldn't understand what was being said, she watched Denny's eyes flickering as if he was lost in a memory with Joseph. It was as though the rest of them were no longer there, and Denny was alone on deck talking only to Joseph.

When he was finished, he dipped his head once, and stepped back.

For a long time, no one said anything. Then Aaron cleared his throat and picked up Joseph's belongings. He passed them to Shell and Heinrich, who were standing on either side of him.

Heinrich held the small pile of Joseph's black notebooks up

above the bow, and Lana had to grip her hands together to stop herself rushing forward and seizing them. She could only watch as they were tossed overboard, hundreds of pages of apologies turning sodden and unreadable in the salt water. No one would ever know what those notebooks meant to Joseph, or why he'd dedicated so many hours to religiously writing in them – and now they were gone.

His sleeping bag was thrown in next, which snaked across the ocean's surface slick and dark. She wondered where it would end up – deep on the seabed, layered with sand and silt, perhaps.

Like his body.

The final item was his canvas backpack that Shell held in her arms. She mouthed something silently and then let it drop over the side with a deep splash.

Every trace of Joseph, gone.

Together they watched the bag bobbing on the surface for some time. As Lana stared at it, the sleeve of one of Joseph's shirts worked its way loose, tugged by the water. Gradually, the rest of it was drawn from the bag and spread out across the surface of the sea. From where Lana was standing, it looked almost as if Joseph was there, floating face down in the water.

She covered her hand with her mouth as a sob heaved through her throat.

This was wrong. All of it felt wrong. 'No one will ever know Joseph was here!' she said, a shot of anger burning bright inside her.

Everyone turned.

She looked at Aaron as she said, 'You've got rid of everything. Got rid of the *evidence*.'

'Lana,' Aaron said softly. 'His belongings aren't evidence – they're just the trappings of someone's life. Letting them go is our way of honouring him. Out here, it's all we can do.'

'Honouring him? Did you honour him enough to throw *everything* overboard? What about the money?' she demanded.

Heinrich looked up.

'I mean the five hundred dollars Joseph had in his wallet when he died.'

Aaron didn't so much as flinch. 'I didn't toss the money away. That would've been stupid. I decided to put it into the repairs fund instead.'

'I?' she said, casting her gaze around the group. 'Where was the group vote about that?'

Aaron kept his voice level as he explained, 'I would never throw anyone's money away. That five hundred dollars will help towards keeping *The Blue* together so she stays on the water for as long as possible. I hoped that'd be as important to you as it is to the rest of us.'

Lana said nothing. She no longer knew any more.

*

Lana spent the rest of the afternoon in her bunk, lying on her stomach with her sketchbook propped on her pillow.

She turned through each sketch, focusing her attention on the perspective, the areas of light and dark, the detail and depth of the images: a palm tree with light slanting through the fronds; Denny's profile when he was sitting on deck reading; two pairs of flip-flops askew in a bucket; the mahi-mahi they had caught, scales glistening. It all felt so long ago, like a different trip. Flicking on, she came to one of Joseph. She paused, looking at it. The drawing captured him sitting at the bow, the nib of a roll-up held between his long fingers.

What happened to you? she wondered. *Who is it that knows something?*

She glanced out through the salt-smeared porthole. The ocean was achingly empty, an angry navy-blue. All that space, all that water and sky. It was dizzyingly bleak – and still they were three days from land.

'Lana,' Shell said, poking her head around the cabin door. She stepped inside uninvited, pulling the door behind her.

She peered up into the bunk, looking at the sketchbook open in Lana's hands. Seeing the image of Joseph, she asked, 'You okay?'

'Fine.' Lana closed the sketchbook and slipped it away under the mattress.

'I just wanted to come and see you. Check in. I know you're taking Joseph's death really hard – we all are – but I wanted to say, you don't need to see the rest of us as the enemy. We love you – you know that.' Shell reached up to Lana in the bunk, placing her hand on Lana's arm. 'I hate seeing you hurting like this.'

The unexpected proximity of Shell, the warmth of her concern, made something knotted inside Lana begin to loosen. She could feel tears gathering in her lower lids, and she blinked rapidly.

'Please, honey, you've got to try and let him go.'

'I can't – not until I know what happened.' There were so many pieces of information missing, and Lana needed to find them to have a chance of understanding.

'We all wish we'd seen something. But we didn't.' There was a hint of impatience in Shell's tone.

Lana said, 'The night Joseph went missing, what went on between you and Heinrich?'

Shell drew back. 'Why are you asking me that?'

'Because nobody is telling the full story,' Lana said.

'I don't want to talk about this.'

Lana climbed down from the bunk and stood facing her. Shell's cheeks were flushed, and her breathing was coming more rapidly. 'Can't you see, we have to? Everyone's trying to ignore what happened to Joseph – pretend he didn't exist, pretend it's okay not to tell the authorities. But it isn't. So please, Shell, be honest with me. What happened to make you and Heinrich fall out? I know you do your watches together – what did you see? What happened?'

Shell looked shocked. 'My God, you actually think we had something to do with Joseph's death?'

Lana rubbed a hand across her forehead. 'No, I'm not saying that. I just want people to start being honest, stop closing up the gaps when it's convenient for them.'

Shell's eyes narrowed. 'You've become so fixated on Joseph that maybe you're forgetting that not everything is about him. As you so desperately need to know every facet of that night, then I'll tell you what happened between Heinrich and me. We slept together! The first guy I've been with in six years.' Her eyes filled with tears as she said, 'It was a terrible, ugly mistake – for us both. Heinrich came into my cabin; he was upset, so he climbed into my bunk and I let him. We were both drunk – too drunk to think clearly . . . and now . . . now everything's ruined.'

'Oh God, Shell. I'm sorry, I didn't realize—'

'So no, I didn't do Heinrich's watch with him that night. He was out there alone. And I didn't see Joseph falling overboard – just like none of us did.' She snatched a breath. 'Maybe it's time you started believing what people are telling you.'

29

NOW

In the corridor at the Maritime Rescue Centre, Shell and Lana stand close. There was a time on board the yacht when Lana didn't fully trust Shell – didn't trust any of the crew. But what about now?

Lana asks, 'You said that at the time you believed Joseph's death was an accident. Has something changed?'

'I'm not sure . . . I just . . .'

'You mentioned Aaron,' Lana encourages.

'I don't want to talk ill of him,' Shell says, hesitating.

Lana understands. It would be wrong to sully his name when he's still missing at sea; yet it's also important that they share any facts that might help them move nearer to the truth. 'Please, just tell me what you think.'

Shell nods, tucking a strand of blonde hair behind her ear. 'Remember the morning after Joseph disappeared? Aaron came up on deck with an injured shoulder, saying he'd fallen whilst having a shower.'

Lana nods.

'It didn't strike me as odd at the time, as I knew Aaron had been drinking hard that night, so it was very possible he'd slipped and injured himself. A couple of months later, we were on our next passage and Aaron started laying into Heinrich for wasting water to wash with. It reminded me of something – Aaron never showered on passage. He couldn't bear to waste the water.' Shell shakes her head lightly. 'As I said, it's probably nothing – maybe Aaron did shower that night. The comment just niggled at me, that's all.'

Lana thinks about Aaron's appearance the morning after Joseph disappeared. He looked haggard; his face was covered in thick stubble and there were deep grooves beneath his bloodshot eyes. She vaguely recalls that there was a stale, unwashed smell around him, and she had shifted position so as not to be downwind of him.

Then she thinks of something else. 'That bloodstain I found on deck. Aaron said it was from his shoulder. But if he injured it in the shower, the water would've washed the blood away – and then he taped it up. Why would it have bled up on deck?'

Shell looks as if she has considered this too. Eventually she says, 'Maybe the blood didn't come from Aaron's shoulder.'

*

'That group vote,' Shell says. 'I've thought about it a lot since. You and Denny were right – we should've reported Joseph's death. Looking back, I think everyone was so scared of losing *The Blue* . . . of having to return to their old lives.' She pauses. 'I know I was.'

Lana feels the weight of that admission. For most of the crew, *The Blue* had become a home of sorts, an escape, and the idea of losing it was terrifying.

'The guilt affected us all. We never took on any more crew, did you know that?' she asks, looking at Lana.

'I saw the crew list when I arrived today – and was surprised to see all of your names still on it. I know Kitty's money must've run out months ago, and Heinrich said he could only afford to stay until Palau.'

Shell nodded. 'Kitty took out a loan, and one of Heinrich's relatives died and left him some money. I'm pleased they both stayed. It was like that passage bound us all and we didn't want anyone else walking in after what'd happened.' Shell pauses, looking at Lana. 'I'm sorry about the way you left *The Blue*, though. I know Kitty found it very hard afterwards. She emailed you . . .'

'I didn't read them.' She wants to explain that it was too difficult, after the way Kitty betrayed her, but Lana can't seem to find the words. Knowing that Kitty could be out in the sea right now, fighting to live, made everything that happened between them feel inconsequential.

Shell says, 'Do you remember when I used to write those post-cards to my parents? I'd try and write from every island we visited. It bothered you that my parents never responded, didn't it?'

Lana nods.

'But for me it was worth it because at least I was doing something. I was trying. That's how Kitty felt with you.'

A lump forms in the back of Lana's throat as she pictures

Kitty sitting in dimly lit Internet cafés in all corners of the world, trying to communicate how she felt.

'She was so sorry, Lana. Whatever happens, you should know that.'

Lana feels a tightening in her throat as she battles to swallow the lump of emotion.

Further down the corridor, Heinrich steps out of the room where he was seeing the medic.

'All okay?' Shell says, turning towards him.

'Fine,' he says. When he reaches them, he says in a low voice, 'What did you decide? About Joseph's sister?' He looks anxious – his eyes darting between Shell and Lana.

Shell says simply, 'Let's wait and see what the others have to say when they're rescued.'

Lana has forgotten about Shell's optimism. She wants to believe that Kitty and Aaron will survive – she has to believe that. But as time ticks on, her doubts grow and strengthen.

Shell places a hand on Lana's arm and squeezes. 'I should get back to my parents now. There's a small canteen in the next wing of the building. If you want company, that's where we'll be.'

Shell and Heinrich move away along the corridor, Heinrich leaning in close to Shell, saying something Lana cannot hear. It reminds her of how close they were on board, how protective they were of one another.

As she watches the two of them, Lana realizes she was wrong ever to doubt Shell. She was a good friend to her during her time on *The Blue*, and was always open and honest.

But could she say the same about Heinrich?

30

THEN

'Lana,' Kitty whispered, opening the cabin door a crack and peering in. 'There's land! We can see land!'

Lana woke, disorientated, to find herself lying dressed on the top bunk, a paperback bent beneath her arm. She must have fallen asleep. She propped herself up a little and, rubbing a hand over her eyes, gazed through the porthole.

At first she thought she was seeing only a cloud bank – a hazy mass on the horizon – but as her eyes began to focus, she could make out the texture of an island in the distance.

'Where are we?' she asked, shaking her head. 'Palau?'

'No. It's that island on the charts. D'you remember? Aaron showed us.'

When they were still in the Philippines, Aaron had been studying the charts and told them that it looked as though there was a tiny fleck of an island a day or two's sail from Palau. It had looked so small and isolated that he'd wondered if it were a mistake.

'How far away are we?'

'A couple of hours. Come and see it from up on deck. We're all up there.'

Lana hesitated. She'd avoided being with the rest of the group, feeling isolated by the split in their decision over Joseph. But she was grateful to Kitty for coming to fetch her.

'I'll meet you up there.' It took Lana a few minutes to shake off the lethargy that swamped her after sleeping in the day. She went to the bathroom and splashed a little cool water on her face, then retied her headscarf and smoothed down her top. She'd barely looked in the mirror since they'd been on the passage and she didn't recognize the face looking back at her; her cheeks were gaunt, and her skin had darkened with windburn. She looked older somehow. Changed.

She glanced out of the porthole in the bathroom and saw the welcome contours of the island as it grew nearer – somewhere she could at least set foot on and remind herself that there was life beyond this boat.

When they got to Palau – tomorrow, the next day? – she wondered what would happen then. Could she continue sailing on *The Blue*? Or was the only option to leave? But if she left, what about Kitty? What about Denny? And the others too – they were her friends, weren't they? Her head swam with confusion.

When she finally went up on deck, she saw that the clouds had parted and everyone was standing together in the early-afternoon sun. She paused for a moment, looking at the crew. The sea was calm, *The Blue* cutting smoothly through the water. She thought how beautiful the image was, how much she wanted to capture it. She could see the details she'd draw – Kitty's fingers holding an empty beer bottle loosely by her side; Denny standing alone facing the island, his lips pursed thoughtfully; Aaron's mouth pulled to one side in a slight smile as he talked to Heinrich; Shell sitting cross-legged on the deck, her face turned to the sun.

Kitty threw back her head and laughed, the sun catching in her dark hair. Lana wanted her to turn, to see her standing there, and to grab her by the hand and bring her to the others – the way she used to do when they were kids.

But Kitty didn't turn.

As Lana approached, it was Denny who took a beer from the cool box, snapped the lid off, and handed it to her. The others looked around then, noticing her. No one said anything and she felt an awful coolness creep over her skin. She sought out Kitty, who smiled. 'Hey, you came.' But her gaze was glassy, vacant – the look she got when she'd been drinking.

Lana glanced at the cool box and saw that almost all of the beer bottles were empty. How long had they been drinking and celebrating together as they sailed nearer to land? Only Kitty had thought to fetch her – and not until now. She wrapped her hand around the neck of the beer, noticing that her fingernails were bitten down to the flesh.

*

A couple of hours later they were anchoring at the edge of a coral cay, no longer than 200 or 300 feet. Running along the spine of the island was a cluster of spindly palm trees and scrubby foliage amid the desert-white sand. After nine days with only the sea to look at, this tiny stretch of land seemed an almost miraculous sight.

Heinrich and Shell, who appeared to have put their troubles behind them, wasted no time getting the dinghy into the water, and the rest of the crew squeezed in to join them.

'You coming?' Kitty called from the dinghy.

Lana shook her head. 'I'll keep an eye on things here.' While she yearned to feel solid ground beneath her feet again, her need to be alone was even stronger.

Kitty opened her hands and began to say something more, but it was lost beneath the sound of Aaron pulling the start cord of the outboard.

She watched as the dinghy motored over the shallow reef towards the island. Lana took several long, deep breaths, rolling her shoulders back, then stretched her neck from side to side. It felt like the first time in days that she could breathe properly. She opened another beer and sat on the bow seat, letting her legs dangle towards the water as the sea lapped against the hull.

There was a time when she'd have sat on the yacht like this – beer in hand, the sun on her face – thinking that there was nowhere else in the world she'd rather be. But now she thought of Joseph, sitting on this seat with his notebook in hand, writing a soliloquy of apologies.

'What happened to you?' she said desperately, the weight of her questions growing the closer they got to Palau. It felt as though the others were moving on, putting it behind them – but

Lana couldn't. Somewhere in this ocean was his body. She wondered whether it would sink over time, or whether the gases produced as he decomposed would make him rise to the surface, and he'd just drift and drift, until the flesh had been leached from him and only bones remained.

*

Sometime later, Lana heard the outboard motor. She looked up and watched as the dinghy cut across the water. She picked up a pair of binoculars, squinting through the two circles of glass.

As the shapes and features of the crew became clearer, Lana wondered what she'd think of each of them if she were seeing them for the first time. She'd notice Aaron's firm, tanned hand gripping the tiller, his eyes staring ahead at the water; she'd see the dark sheen of Kitty's hair as she turned towards Denny, smiling at something he was telling her; she'd admire the ladder of colourful bangles climbing Shell's wrists, and notice Heinrich's clear, even tan. She'd think they were a group of travellers, young and carefree.

What she wouldn't know was that several days earlier, one of their crew members had disappeared at sea. She wouldn't be able to tell by looking at their bronzed, relaxed faces, that all but Denny had decided to bury this information, make a secret of it so that they weren't implicated. She moved the focus of the binoculars to each person in turn. One of them knew more about Joseph's death than they were letting on. But who?

She pushed the binoculars aside and, as the dinghy motored

closer, she caught a drift of words. 'Reef', 'trigger fish', 'beer'. She heard laughter – Heinrich's or Aaron's perhaps – and wondered what was funny. Was this how Joseph had felt sitting alone in the bow seat, hearing the rest of them having fun together?

'Missed a beautiful snorkel,' Kitty said, climbing onto the deck, a towel wrapped around her hips, wet hair dripping down one shoulder. 'Amazing coral. Completely untouched. Heinrich saw a sea snake.'

'It was over a metre long,' he said, measuring the air with his hands.

'We're anchoring here tonight,' Aaron said. 'We all fancied the break from night watches. Gonna set off for Palau at first light.'

Lana felt her muscles tighten. She wanted to keep going, reach Palau. Arriving there had become a beacon, the goal. It was the place where this terrible passage finally ended – where she could be amongst other people, feel the sweep of normality again. She didn't want to wait around, anchored near a half-island. 'Are you sure? I just want to get there.'

Everyone turned to look at her.

'We all do,' Aaron said, 'but I think everyone deserves a break.'

Kitty wrung the water from her hair over the side of the boat. 'I've been in the sun too long,' she said, disappearing below deck.

'Beer?' Heinrich asked Denny.

'Sure.'

'Let's have a look over those charts, too,' Aaron said.

The men went below deck, and Shell disappeared to change.

Lana remained on deck, agitation burrowing under her skin. She looked towards the island, which was about a kilometre away. She wasn't in the right frame of mind to draw or read – her thoughts skittering and jumping too much to focus on a page. Maybe she should swim, burn off some anxious energy.

She stood at the stern and looked down at the sea. They were anchored in about 30 feet of water. The seabed shelved off deeply, the depth finder reading over 100 feet a little further out. There was something daunting, a primeval fear, about diving into the unknown, where sharks or other predators could be lurking. Without giving herself time to hesitate or delay, she unhooked her dress, tied it around the lifeline to keep it from blowing away, and dived in.

The water felt cool against her skin as she cut through it, her fingers and toes in a point. She opened her eyes underwater and blurry blue light filtered around her.

She let herself gradually float to the surface, the sea carrying her gently upwards. Then she began to swim, her arms slicing through the calm water with smooth, steady strokes. It was surprisingly wonderful to be moving – not just within the constricted space of the yacht – but freely, fluidly.

She swam away from the yacht in the direction of the island. There seemed to be no current or wind, but she hovered for a few moments, setting her gaze on a fixed point on the island as Denny had taught her so that she could check whether a current or tide was pulling in a certain direction. After a minute, she had barely moved, so she swam on, feeling the pleasing ache building in her arm muscles. It was a relief to be doing something physical, and she felt immediately better for it.

The water beneath her grew shallower as she swam over the reef, coral waving in and out of view. She should have brought the mask and snorkel. She dived under and stopped kicking, hovering there in the still blue.

She wasn't breathing, wasn't thinking, wasn't swimming – just gliding through layers of ocean and salt water. As her lungs began to tingle, she heard a rumbling sound. Her thoughts drifted around the familiar shape of the noise, wondering what it could be out here in the empty ocean. Sounds underwater travel five times faster than in air, so Lana knew that whatever it was must be further away than it appeared.

Suddenly her eyes flashed open to the salt-sting of the sea as she recognized the noise: it was the sound of the engine starting up.

She kicked hard, splashing to the surface and taking in a gulp of air. *The Blue* was still positioned as it had been before – about 500 metres away – but she could see the shape of someone standing at the bow bringing in the anchor. Perhaps it was dragging and they'd decided to re-anchor.

It was eerie to know the anchor was being pulled when she was this far from the yacht. She chided herself for swimming such a distance. Deciding to head back, she swam in front crawl, keeping the rhythm steady.

The engine noise increased, a throbbing sound that bubbled through the otherwise still air. As she watched the yacht, she became aware of the bow turning away from her, pointing in the opposite direction – out towards the horizon.

She guessed they were re-anchoring, but it was unnerving to see the yacht turning away from her. She swam harder, thrusting her arms through the water.

She kept expecting the yacht to turn back, to see its bow swinging towards her as it found a new spot to anchor – but oddly it kept its course, heading towards the open ocean, the dinghy tied to its stern.

Surely they wouldn't anchor far from the original spot where Lana was swimming. They must just be making a wide turn. She swam after it, her arms beginning to tire – but the yacht didn't swing round. It was getting further away from her.

'Hey!' she shouted. 'Wait!' She could see some of the crew on deck – just silhouettes where the sun was behind them – but no one turned. No one heard.

She was exhausted, panting from the burst of front crawl, and she had to tread water for a moment while she caught her breath. It was hard to judge distances or speeds without land-marks, but it seemed that the yacht was already 200, maybe 300, metres from where it had been anchored. She waited, still believing that the yacht was going to turn back – but a minute passed, and then another. *The Blue* didn't turn.

Then she realized: the position the yacht was now in was too deep to put down the anchor. The crew weren't finding a new spot to anchor – they were leaving.

*

'Wait! Stop! Stop!' she cried, the pleas scratching at her throat.

With a sickening sense of dread, she remembered that she hadn't told anyone she was swimming.

Her dress was tied to the lifeline – surely one of them would see it and realize?

With ragged breathing, she trod water, watching as the boat motored further away into the distance. *Come on! Notice the dress. Notice I'm missing!*

A rogue thought ratcheted up her fear: it had been hours before anyone realized Joseph was missing. For the first time, she felt the full horror of what he must have experienced – seeing *The Blue* slipping from view as it was now, being left alone in the endless sea.

Lana spun around, arms cutting through the water. Panic sparked and thickened, a thousand fear-spiked thoughts cutting into her mind: *What now – do I try and swim to the island? But it's too far! I'll never make it. I can't drown. I can't drown out here!*

'Why the fuck aren't you checking I'm on board?' she screamed across the empty ocean.

Then a shot of fear pierced her thoughts.

What if they had?

*

She shook herself into action. *Kick your legs. Move. Swim. Come on, Lana!*

She fixed her vision on the island, focusing on two palm trees that bowed towards one another, forming the shape of a heart.

A palm tree heart, she told herself. *Be positive. You'll reach the island. There's no current. You can just take your time. You're a strong swimmer, Lana. Just relax.*

She swam forwards in front crawl, trying to keep her rhythm steady, but she was surprised by how quickly she tired. She'd already been swimming for at least fifteen minutes before the yacht left; her mouth was dry from panting, and she was beginning to shiver.

She paused, treading water to catch her breath, and glanced back over her shoulder. *The Blue* had sailed so far into the distance that it was only a speck. Losing concentration, she slipped beneath the surface, the sea covering her with impersonal ease. She fought her way back up, spitting salt water from her mouth. Panic made her limbs heavy, her mind loose and hot. *Keep your head, Lana. Breathe and kick, that's all you need to do.*

She fixed her gaze on the island again. She could not look back at the vast blue emptiness behind, and she wouldn't look down into the unknown depths beneath her legs. There was only the island and the rhythm of her strokes, the sound of her breath. Anxious thoughts dived around her like hunting seabirds, but she tried to ignore them, focusing only on putting one arm in front of the other.

When cramp edged into the inner arches of her feet and tightened the muscles of her calves, she had no choice but to turn over and swim in backstroke. But seeing only empty sky above unnerved her further, and she swung around onto her front again, gritted her teeth against the cramp, and set her gaze on the heart-shaped palm trees.

Time had no measure. Sight was her only guide, and gradually, gradually, she saw that the island was growing closer, becoming richer in detail. She told herself she could smell the bark of the palms, the scent of the sand, feel the firmness of solid ground.

Eventually the water grew shallower and her toes brushed the scalloped seabed. She looked down to see clouds of sand moving around her feet. She staggered through the shallows, chest heaving, legs trembling, and hauled herself towards the beach, where she collapsed, panting. The damp sand smelt chalky and salty. She closed her eyes and dug her fingers deep into the sand, where the footsteps of her friends were already beginning to fade.

When she had the energy, she lifted her head and stared out towards the shrinking shape of *The Blue* thinking, *Now what?*

31

NOW

Lana watches Shell and Heinrich move away along the corridor until they disappear out of sight. She takes a deep breath, then slips her phone from her pocket, checking whether she can pick up the Internet in here. Talking to Shell has made her realize that she needs to read Kitty's emails.

There is very little signal, so she moves along the corridor, towards the exit. As she passes the Operations Room, the door opens behind her.

'Lana?'

Paul Carter has stepped out of his room and is addressing her. She doesn't want to stop – she knows what it'll be about. She pretends she hasn't heard and continues on.

'Lana,' he calls again. He begins to walk after her. She can hear his rubber-soled boots squeaking on the lino floor. Sweat prickles across her back as she picks up her pace.

Before she's able to reach the exit, he catches her up. She has no choice but to turn and face him. 'Oh, hi,' she says, feigning surprise. 'Sorry. I was miles away.'

'Got a moment?'

'I . . . I was just on my way to . . .'

'It'll only take a minute.'

There's no option but to go with him. Reluctantly she turns back and follows him towards the Operations Room.

Lana already knows who she is going to find in there.

*

'Lana, this is Aimee Melina,' Paul Carter says, gesturing to Joseph's sister. 'She believes that her brother, Joseph Melina, was travelling on *The Blue*.'

'Yes, we've just met.'

Tiny splotches of colour have risen on Aimee Melina's pale cheeks. 'I have this letter,' she says to Paul Carter, waving a piece of cream paper in front of her. 'Joseph wrote to me. He explained about the boat, the skipper, the people on board. He said he would be here when the boat arrived.'

Lana stares at the letter. She can see the flowing script of Joseph's hand, his name signed at the bottom with a single kiss.

Paul Carter nods cautiously, as if he's afraid of the emotion in her voice. 'But Joseph wasn't on the crew list. I have the most current one from when *The Blue* left Fiji to sail back to New Zealand. I'm afraid Joseph wasn't on it.'

'He must be,' Aimee Melina says, her voice rising a note. 'He would contact me if he left the boat. He promised he'd be here.'

Paul Carter looks at Lana, saying, 'Lana spent some time travelling on *The Blue*, didn't you?'

She sees that he is deflecting this woman's anger in her direction. Lana's mouth is dry and she has to swallow before she can answer. 'Yes.'

Aimee Melina tilts her head to one side and looks at Lana closely, most likely wondering why Lana didn't mention this earlier. 'Then, you know Joseph?'

Lana opens her mouth, but her throat seems to constrict, squeezing tight around her words.

Aimee Melina's gaze bores into her. 'Joseph was on board, yes?'

Lana's palms are sweating. She presses them against the tops of her thighs, feeling the heat through her cotton dress. She can hear her own breathing, as she sucks air in and out of her lungs.

She needs to answer.

'I must know,' Aimee Melina demands, her voice rising. 'Was he? Was my brother travelling on *The Blue*?'

*

Lana can feel a light breeze moving through the open doorway behind her. She is desperate to turn, escape the room and leave behind Aimee Melina's question.

If Lana answers, *Yes,* then it confirms that Joseph's letter was true – that he was on board. Aimee Melina stares at her with her penetrating dark gaze. Beneath Lana's dress her skin is faintly sticky with sweat.

For a moment, Lana thinks she has happened upon a solution. She will tell them that *Yes*, Joseph was still on board when *The Blue* sank, and let his sister believe he drowned today. It would be a lie, of course, but at least it would be near to the truth.

But immediately the flaw reveals itself: there will be no paper trail showing Joseph clearing in and out of immigration in any of the countries that *The Blue* has sailed through since the Philippines. It wouldn't be possible to make as many stops as *The Blue* has done without registering one of the crew.

Paul Carter and Aimee Melina stare at her, waiting for an answer.

If she were to tell them, *No, Joseph was never on board*, isn't the letter proof that she was lying? He could have named the crew, or what if he sent photos to his sister or a friend?

'Lana?' Paul Carter prompts.

'Sorry,' she says, rubbing a hand over her face.

This time there is no group vote, no sitting around the saloon table with the luxury of time to decide upon an answer. All Lana can do is be honest. 'Yes. Joseph did sail on *The Blue*.'

'Do you know if he was still on board when it sank?' Paul Carter asks.

There is a beat of a pause. 'No. Not when it sank.'

32

THEN

Lana stood on the shoreline, shivering in her bikini as dusk gathered like smoke blown in on the breeze.

'Lana! Lana!' Kitty yelled from the dinghy, waving wildly.

As soon as the dinghy was close enough, Kitty jumped from it, stumbling into the shallows, water drenching her red sarong as she came splashing up onto the shore. 'Thank God! Thank God you're safe!' she said, throwing her arms around Lana's neck. Her skin was hot and damp with sweat, and Lana could smell the yeasty scent of beer on her breath.

Denny cut the engine, beaching the dinghy. He vaulted over its side and Kitty stepped back as he pulled Lana to him. He held her tight to his chest, where she could feel the rapid beat of his heart against her skin. His lips moved against her ear as he whispered, 'I'm so sorry! We didn't know you'd gone! I'm sorry, Lana. I'm so sorry this happened . . .'

She closed her eyes, concentrating on the warmth of his body against her chilled skin. Denny stroked a hand through her damp hair, his fingers trailing down to the nape of her neck.

When they stepped apart, Kitty said, 'When we pulled anchor, we thought you were in the cabin. But then I saw your dress.' Kitty shook her head. 'I rushed down, checked the bunks, but you weren't there. You weren't there, Lana. We searched and . . . shit, it was fucking terrifying. You weren't on the yacht. You weren't anywhere. It felt like . . . like it had done with . . .'

Kitty broke off. She didn't need to finish her sentence for Lana to know it had felt like it had done with Joseph.

*

Denny fetched a beach towel from the dinghy and wrapped it around Lana's shoulders, and the three of them sat on the shoreline in the fading sun.

'What happened?' Kitty asked, her fingers entwined with Lana's.

'I went swimming. I thought we were anchoring for the night. But when I looked up – you were leaving.'

'Jesus,' Kitty said. She stared out to sea at the distance between the island and the yacht. 'It's such a long way. What if you hadn't made it? I can't bear to think—'

'Why did you leave?' The question came out sharply.

'We looked at the charts and saw Palau was closer than we thought,' Denny explained. 'We decided to sail on – see if we could make it there by morning.'

Lana could only have been waiting on the island for half an

Lucy Clarke

hour before she'd seen the yacht beginning to turn, but it was long enough to experience an overwhelmingly terrifying sensation that the entire world was tipping. Sheer white terror had filled her, keeping her frozen on the shoreline with her arms hugged to her chest. 'I thought . . .' she said, a tremor to her voice. 'I thought you'd left me. On purpose.'

'What?' Kitty said, sitting bolt upright. 'Fuck, Lana! Don't say shit like that. Just don't!'

All the fear that had been crouched inside Lana now seemed to tumble from her. 'Who suggested pulling anchor? Sailing on to Palau? Was it Aaron?'

'Lana, what are you saying?' Denny's brow furrowed. 'And no – it wasn't Aaron's idea. It was Heinrich's.'

She felt tears spilling onto her lower lids, and she rubbed them roughly with the back of her hand, grains of sand coarse against her skin.

Kitty put her arm around Lana and pulled her in close. 'I can't believe you thought we'd leave you. How could you even imagine something like that?'

There was a beat of a pause. Then Lana said, 'We left Joseph.'

*

'We didn't leave him,' Kitty said, eyes wide. 'We searched and searched.'

'Hard enough?'

Kitty and Denny said nothing.

Lana's shoulders rounded and she clutched her head in her

302

hands. She was losing it. The more she said, the further away she seemed to push people – but she couldn't leave it alone. 'Something wasn't right about his death. I know it.'

'What do you mean?' Kitty asked.

'Aaron knows something. I'm sure of it. I just . . . I don't trust him.' She turned to Denny. 'You saw the way he was when he discovered Joseph had stowed away – he pinned him to the wall. If you hadn't calmed him down, he would've hit him.'

Denny didn't deny it.

'And why was Aaron so fixed on being on the water by the fifteenth of March? He was talking to you about it just before we left the Philippines. You were coming out of the Internet café. I overheard you. Aaron kept on saying he couldn't be on land any longer – that he needed to get on the water by the fifteenth.' She paused. 'The fifteenth – that's the day Joseph died.'

Denny rubbed a hand over his mouth as he looked out towards *The Blue*.

'What was so important about the fifteenth?'

Denny drew in a long breath, then told her, 'The fifteenth of March is the anniversary of Aaron's wife's death.'

'*Wife?*'

Denny nodded. 'Lydia.'

Lana remembered the name from Shell's story about Aaron in a bar in Thailand. 'When . . . when did this happen?'

'Three years ago.' Denny's expression clouded. 'Lydia was murdered.'

'My God,' Lana whispered.

'What happened?' Kitty asked.

'She was at their home in Auckland. It was the middle of the day and she was in their back garden at the time, collecting in the washing. It should've just been an ordinary day. It could've been – except there was this guy. Mills Weaden. An addict. He was high – been up for days on some massive meth hit. When he ran out of cash for his next hit, he robbed the store at the end of the block at knifepoint. The owner gave chase, but tired out pretty quick and lost him. But this Mills Weaden, he kept running, thinking the shop owner was still after him. The police reckon his system was so loaded with drugs he would've been half out of his mind with paranoia. So when he jumped Aaron's back fence and crashed into Lydia, he thought she was fighting him, trying to stop him. There was a knife in his hand, so he used it. Stabbed her four times in the stomach and chest.' He swallowed. 'She was eight months pregnant.'

Lana closed her eyes.

'Lydia died – haemorrhaged in the hospital with Aaron right there in the room. Aaron lost them both – his wife and baby.' His mouth twisted as he said, 'How does anyone get over something like that?'

Lana shook her head, stunned by the scale of Aaron's loss. 'Is that why he left New Zealand – set sail?'

Denny nodded.

'Are you the only one who knows?' Lana asked Denny.

He nodded. 'Aaron doesn't like to talk about what happened.'

She could understand why Denny seemed so protective of Aaron. He'd been on *The Blue* almost from the beginning, and was the only person Aaron had trusted with his past.

She thought of Shell's description of Aaron sobbing in his cabin, calling out his wife's name. She could picture the way he'd have held his head in his hands, his eyes bloodshot with misery.

Gazing out towards the yacht, Lana tried to see it through Aaron's eyes: *The Blue* was a new beginning for him, a place he could live squarely in the present and not be reminded of everything he'd lost.

*

'What the fuck were you playing at?' Aaron barked the moment Lana stepped foot on deck.

Lana drew back in surprise. 'I went for a swim and—'

'You never, ever, leave the yacht without telling anyone! What if I'd started the engine when you were right by the propeller? You've got to think! We don't need two dead crew members on our fucking hands.'

If she'd begun to soften towards Aaron, now that hardness came slamming back into place. 'What about doing a fucking head count before leaving, skipper?'

Aaron went to say something else, but Denny cut in sharply. 'Lana's just had a pretty rough time of it. Give her a break, yeah?'

Aaron looked momentarily startled by Denny's tone, but then he lifted his hands in deference, saying, 'You're right.' He took a deep breath, turned to Lana and said, 'I'm sorry. I'm really glad you're safe.'

Shell and Heinrich greeted Lana with hugs and, after they'd exhausted their questions, Lana was free to slip away below deck, where she drank three glasses of water in a row, then retreated to her cabin.

Kitty was already there. 'I'm taking your watch tonight. You deserve to rest.'

'I'm fine—'

'No arguing,' Kitty said firmly. 'You covered enough of my watches when I was sicking up my guts.' She took out a pot of moisturizer and began rubbing it into her cracked heels.

Lana sank down on the edge of the bunk beside Kitty. She dipped her finger in the moisturizer and rubbed it through her callused hands, the scent of coconut lifting into the cabin. 'So we're still setting off for Palau, then?'

Kitty nodded. 'Aaron thinks we'll be there by mid-morning.'

They were both silent. Palau marked the end of the passage – could Lana really disembark and say nothing about Joseph? Once they'd been through immigration – that would be it. There would be no going back. Joseph would be erased from this passage, his death left as a mystery that the world would never hear of.

But if she decided to go against the others and inform the authorities, what would happen then? As skipper, Aaron could be arrested, or *The Blue* could be impounded indefinitely. It was likely that they'd all have to fly home. Lana might never see the crew again – or Denny.

She sighed, too exhausted to know what to think any more.

Kitty screwed the lid on the moisturizer and returned it to her backpack. When she turned back to Lana, she looked at her closely.

'What?' Lana said.

'You're going to leave, aren't you? When we get to Palau.'

'I'm not sure,' she said truthfully.

'I know this passage has been fucked up – but things will get better. They'll get back to normal, I promise you.'

'They won't, Kit. How can they? Joseph's dead. How will it ever be the same?'

Kitty had no answer to that and they were both quiet for some time.

'If I left,' Lana said, 'what would you do?'

Kitty closed her eyes. Her head shook lightly from side to side as she said, 'I can't give this up, Lana. I'm sorry. But I can't. I don't know how to explain it – but I feel comfortable here. I don't think about all the crap from before – my failed acting career, the string of shitty men, my dad's drinking. Out here I can just . . . be. And I like that, it suits me.' Kitty looked at Lana. 'I think it suits you, too. You've been thinking less about your own dad, haven't you?'

'I don't know. Perhaps. Or maybe I just don't talk about him so much because – this – it all feels so separate, you know? Like everything else back on land doesn't really exist.'

Kitty nodded.

'But I'm still angry with him. Furious. Whenever I even think about him, I'm just filled with this . . . rage.' She pushed her fingertips into her hairline. 'How will I ever let that go?'

'You have to, Lana. It'll still be there, and it'll still hurt, but you've got to try and let go.'

She shook her head. 'I used to visit her ashes, for God's sake!

Dad told me they were scattered in the woodland on the heath, so I'd walk up there with my sketchbook, and spend hours drawing and talking to her. Talking to my dead fucking mother, who was actually alive! And he *knew*. He let me go down to the woods to be near her ashes – he let me cry for her. How could he have done that, Kit?' she said, turning to face her, eyes stinging with tears.

'He was trying to protect you.'

Lana threw back her head in frustration. 'It doesn't mean it was right, though. She came to England, for fuck's sake – to see me – but he sent her away.'

'He was thinking about what was best for you. Lana, it was the day before your GCSEs – imagine how that would've messed everything up. It wasn't the right time.'

Lana sat there for a moment, the comment tripping something in her mind. She looked at Kitty, her heart beginning to pound. 'What did you just say?'

'I just said he was thinking about what was best for you.'

'No, after that.'

Kitty glanced to her left. 'I said it could've messed up your studies in your GCSE year.'

'No,' Lana said slowly. 'You said my mother visited on the day before I started my GCSEs. How could you have known that?'

Kitty blinked several times, rubbing the end of her nose. 'I don't know. I must've got it wrong. Maybe I thought you'd told me?'

Lana shook her head. 'I never told you. All Dad said to me was that my mother tried to visit me once when I was sixteen.

He didn't mention anything about GCSEs.' She stared hard at Kitty, whose face was starting to redden. 'Why did you say that?'

Kitty got to her feet and unbuckled her backpack. 'Must be just one of those random things I imagined, I guess.' Her tone was too bright, her body language evasive.

Lana's gaze bored into the back of Kitty's head. 'Why would you've imagined something so specific?'

Kitty kept her back to Lana. 'No idea!'

Lana moved towards Kitty and placed a hand on her shoulder. Kitty turned. Her cheeks were pink and tiny splotches of colour had risen on her neck. 'You're lying to me.'

Kitty tried to turn away again, but Lana kept her grip. 'Look at me.'

Kitty raised her gaze to meet Lana's. Her eyes were wide, pupils dilated.

'What do you know?'

A taut, weighted silence pulsed between them. The muscles and tendons in Lana's body felt rigid as she waited for Kitty to speak.

'I . . . I . . .' Kitty stuttered.

'What? What is it?' She wanted to shake her.

Kitty swallowed. 'Your mother . . . she . . .'

Lana suddenly realized: 'My God, you knew! You knew my mother was still alive, didn't you?'

Kitty's gaze slid away to the floor. 'I met her, Lana.'

*

Lana felt a strange tingling numbness crawl through her body. The cabin walls seemed very close all of a sudden, as if they were contracting and locking out the air. She could feel the layer of heat trapped beneath her T-shirt and skin slowly building, and imagined her blood, hot-red, pumping hard.

'I'm sorry,' Kitty whispered.

A burning sense of disbelief flamed inside Lana. She wanted to escape the cabin, escape the yacht – yet she needed to know. 'How? How did you meet her?'

'She found out the name of the street you'd moved to, but she didn't know the house number. So she went knocking on all the doors.' She paused, swallowing. 'I happened to answer ours. I didn't know who she was to begin with – she only gave her first name – but then she said she was visiting from Athens and was looking for you and your father. I didn't think it was possible – you know, that your mother was alive – but she looked so much like you, Lana.'

Her stomach contracted with the pain of those words. Lana hadn't seen her mother since she was three years old. The memory of what she looked like had faded long ago into a blur of the few old photos she had of her.

Kitty continued. 'I asked if she was your mother, and she welled up as she told me, "Yes, I am." I said, "But what about the car accident?" – but then my dad was behind me, taking over, sending me away.

'I went to my room and crouched by the window so I could listen. Dad told her that you lived four houses down. I knew you wouldn't be there – you were staying late to finish your art

310

coursework, but she thanked him and crossed the road to your house.'

Kitty looked up at Lana as she said, 'Your mother waited in front of your house for ages. She didn't knock – just stood there. I wondered if she was going to turn around, leave. But then she stepped forward and knocked. Your dad came to the door. When he saw her, he went very still. They spoke for a moment on the doorstep, and then he let her in.'

Had it been that close? Could it have been Lana who'd opened the door to her mother on a different afternoon of the week?

'That was all. That's all I know. I'm sorry, I should have—'

'Told me?' Lana said with fire. When she had finally found out the truth from her father, she'd been floored by it – utterly stunned. And the first person she'd gone to, turning up on her doorstep soaked through and bewildered, was Kitty. She remembered what Kitty had said about Lana's father: *He made a mistake. A terrible mistake. But you mustn't hate him. You mustn't!*

Her eyes fixed on Kitty. 'You bitch.'

'I'm sorry, Lana. I'm so sorry,' she gasped. 'I wished I didn't know . . . I didn't want to keep it from you. I honestly thought you'd come into school the day after your mum visited and tell me what'd happened. But then you got on the bus as normal and didn't say a word – didn't even seem any different. I wondered if your dad was waiting till the weekend – till after your first exams were over – to talk to you about it, but then the following Monday, you still didn't mention anything. And then it got to the end of exams and we broke up for summer . . . and then . . . well, I realized he wasn't going to tell you at all.'

311

'But *you* could have.'

Losing their mothers fused Kitty and Lana's friendship in a way nothing else could. When other girls were talking about shopping with their mums, or complaining of a fight they'd just had, Lana and Kitty's eyes would seek out each other's, a silent message twitching between them.

Occasionally Lana tried brokering her mother's name to her father, but the sadness and tension that hollowed his face and lingered in the house for days as silence, dissuaded her from further attempts. Instead it was Kitty she had spoken to, whispering her mother's name and sharing the thin string of memories she wore close to her heart. In return, Kitty traded stories of her own mother, and together they made up entire narratives of the lives their mothers would have had.

But all of it had been false. Lana's mother had been alive – and Kitty had known.

'Get out,' Lana said.

Kitty was beginning to cry, her hands trembling at her sides. 'We need to sort this—'

'Get the fuck out of this cabin! Now!'

33

NOW

Lana leans against the passenger door of her car. She's managed to slip away from Aimee Melina and Paul Carter before they can ask any more difficult questions, pretending she has to take an urgent phone call.

Glancing towards the main building, she is relieved to see that no one has followed her. Everything appears still: no one arrives, no one leaves.

It's already mid-afternoon and she wonders how long the search will continue. Until dark? Overnight? At what point is a search called off?

For every minute that ticks by, Kitty seems to drift further out of reach. The thought that she could already be dead – her body floating somewhere out there in the darkening sea – is unfathomable. Not after the way things were left between them.

It was never meant to be like that – not for them. Kitty was once everything to her. More than her best friend: she was her family. The script of Lana's life was written with Kitty as a main part. They were meant to be there at each other's weddings; to one day lay their hands over each other's stomachs and feel the kick of a baby; to grow older side by side, laughing at their wrinkling skin and thickening waists.

Kitty was never meant to die young.

Lana can't bear it.

Shell told her that Kitty sent dozens of emails over the months she kept sailing with *The Blue*. Lana remembers reading the first few of them when she had just arrived in New Zealand – short, broken apologies, bashed out on a keyboard in an Internet café with the clock ticking. Lana scanned them, shaking her head at the trail of clichés.

Eventually she stopped checking her account. There was nothing she wanted to hear from Kitty – and nothing Lana needed to say. She was attempting to pick up the pieces of her life, start again in New Zealand, and Kitty's emails only pulled her back to the yacht.

But now that's precisely where Lana needs to go. She needs to remember exactly what happened – try and piece it together, because she knows she's close.

She takes out her phone and tries to recall her old details for her email account. On the third attempt, she types in the correct password, and is surprised to find the account still active. Over 500 unread emails begin spilling onto her screen: messages from companies, banks, charity appeals, and newsletters.

She scrolls through five or six pages, and Kitty's name doesn't appear. Lana wonders whether Shell got it wrong – perhaps Kitty gave up emailing within a few weeks of Lana leaving *The Blue*.

She manages to click on a button that switches the view so she can see the oldest email at the top of the screen – and that's when she spots Kitty's name.

The date shows that Kitty sent it a fortnight after Lana left *The Blue*. She scans across and sees the subject header is empty. She clicks on the email and opens it.

Dear Lana,

I don't know whether you've read any of my emails – but I'm going to keep on sending them until I hear back.

I'm typing this in a shitty little Internet café where the connection keeps dropping out, so I'll have to keep it brief. I guess I've said most of it before anyway. I'm not sure how many different ways there are to say SORRY! I know I should've told you that I'd met your mother – but I want to try and explain WHY I didn't.

The bottom line is: it wasn't my secret to tell.

I wish I'd never opened the door to your mother that day. Believe me, Lana, I didn't want to know more about your family than you. Sometimes information is thrust upon us that we'd prefer never to learn.

Just so you know, I never let on to your father – or anyone – that I knew. There was no big collusion between me and him like you're probably imagining.

If you want to know, I feel sorry for your father. You've spent all this time being furious with him, not

*even giving him a chance to explain. I get why: you're
angry and hurting. But have you even tried to switch
things around and look at it from his perspective?
Because here's how I see it: his wife walked out on
him and left him heartbroken – and with a three-year-old
daughter to bring up. All he wanted was to stop you
from hurting as badly as he did – so yes, he lied, like
me – but we did it with the right intention: we wanted
to protect you. Sometimes that's what people who love
you have to do.*

Kitty x

Lana leans back against her car, her shoulder blades pressing
into the cool metal. She stares at the email, wondering whether
Kitty is right: did Lana ever pause to consider things from her
father's perspective? He lied to her out of love – but she ignored
this because it was easier to focus on her anger than to begin
the harder road towards forgiveness.

A cold shock of realisation hits as she suddenly sees the
pattern of her actions: when things get tough she closes down,
disappears to a new country, breaks all contact. She's done it to
her father, to Kitty, to Denny.

With a sickening clunk of understanding, Lana thinks: *I walk
away from the people I love – just like my mother.*

Her legs feel unsteady so she places a hand behind her, her
fingers spreading out over the metallic body of the car. All these
years she's been trying to create this perfect image of her dead
mother, so she could stand before it and see parts of herself

reflected back. But she never thought — even for one moment — that she might not like what she saw.

In all that time, what she didn't notice was that it was her father who stoically carried on, bringing Lana up, loving her, clothing her, feeding her. Doing the best he could.

Maybe, she thinks, *when all of this is over, I will call him.* She could even ask if he wants to visit her out here — she can't think when he last took a holiday. Perhaps out of the four walls of his life, he'd be someone different. Maybe it would give them a chance to try again.

Lana wonders whether she'll get that same chance with Kitty. She hopes with every fibre of her being that Kitty is still alive, fighting against the odds to survive. There is a steely determination to Kitty that people haven't always seen — and Lana just hopes it's strong enough to bring her safely back to land.

Even as Lana is focusing on this, hoping for a positive end to the day's tragedy, she is also thinking, *But would I be able to forgive her?* Because the truth Kitty withheld about Lana's mother was only the tip of her betrayal.

34

THEN

Lana didn't leave her cabin all night. A deep pressure filled her head and she lay in her bunk moving her jaw from side to side, trying to release the tension. It took hours to fall asleep and, when she finally drifted off sometime after 3.00, her dreams were a tangled knot of images surrounding her mother, Kitty, Joseph, and a yacht disappearing towards the horizon.

She woke just before dawn covered in a film of sweat. She lay still, absorbing the movement of the yacht through the water. She could feel the light vibration of the bulkhead against the backs of her fingers, and hear the splashing of swell against the hull. When she propped herself up on her elbows, she pressed her face to the open porthole, breathing in deeply.

She could smell it. Land.

The air was warm and heavy with the scent of earth, trees, sand. Now her eyes were fully open, she could see that the line of the horizon was broken by a series of curved silhouettes, like floating hills rising from the water. The light was just beginning to break, illuminating an edge of the magical tree-covered islands.

So this was Palau. The relief was immediate: in an hour or two she would be able to step off the yacht. Get away. Think.

She climbed from the bunk and pulled on a crumpled dress, then moved along the passageway to Denny's cabin. She hadn't gone to him last night when her head was still spinning from the shock of discovering Kitty had always known about her mother – but now she needed to talk. Everything had become so confused over the passage and a daunting gap had opened up between them. But yesterday, when he'd come for her on the island, she'd felt their connection still there.

It was early, so she knocked lightly on his door, then slipped inside the dim room. The air held the familiar smell of him – a pleasant salty musk – and she felt her stomach flutter at the thought of sliding into bed beside him. What did Aaron's rule matter now in the face of everything else?

As she stepped forward, the soles of her feet met with something soft. She glanced down. It took her eyes a few moments to adjust to the dimness.

Then she blinked, her throat tightening.

Beneath her bare feet a blood-red sarong was pooled on the cabin floor.

She could picture the curve of the hips around which the sarong had been wrapped, the tanned hands unknotting it with a playful flick of a wrist, the swish of fabric as the sarong fell to the floor.

Slowly, she lifted her gaze, settling on the two bodies entangled in Denny's bed.

*

Kitty was curled on her side, her back to Lana, dark hair spilling over the pillow. Her right arm was slung over Denny, who lay on his front, the sheet pulled up to his waist. Light caught on the edges of his shoulder blades and in the weave of Kitty's hair.

Lana laughed – a strange, disbelieving note that cut into the room. How stupid she'd been! She'd even had her suspicions when she'd seen Kitty sitting with her feet tucked beneath Denny's thigh. She remembered Kitty's outraged, vitriolic denial: *I would never do that to you, Lana!*

Quite the little actress.

The rhythm of Kitty's breathing changed. She sighed deeply and then there was an interval between breaths, as if she'd become aware of someone else in the room. Kitty lifted her head a fraction, looking over her shoulder.

Lana and Kitty's gazes fastened on each other.

'Lana . . .' Kitty removed her arm from Denny and sat up, pushing her hair from her face.

The movement roused Denny, who rolled over with a groan. He surfaced from sleep, rubbing a hand over his brow. When his eyes opened – those pale-blue eyes, which seemed to darken when Lana kissed him – they fixed on her. 'Lana.' His voice was husky, furred with sleep.

The guilt in his tone as he spoke her name caused Lana to hinge forward at the waist, as if she'd taken a blow to the stomach. *How could they?*

There was not a single thing she could think of saying. She managed to draw herself upright and left Denny's cabin, her teeth pressing down on the soft flesh inside her lip.

*

There was nowhere to go. Nowhere to run to.

She walked purposefully along the passageway, thinking about where to place each foot. It was as if her mind had been thrown so far off course that she couldn't quite recall how ordinary things worked. Reaching the bathroom, she stepped inside, locking the door behind her. She stood in the middle of the tiny cubicle.

An awful sob rushed out in a gasp and a tremor of air, causing her shoulders to hunch. She stuffed the corner of her fist into her mouth, her teeth pressing down on the bones of her knuckles.

She could see herself in the mirror – the sheer white of her face, the strained ugly expression, the pathetic desperation in her eyes. She sank down onto the floor with her back pressed against the door. The faint tinge of ammonia lifted off the linoleum. Tears fell hot against her cheeks and her chest shuddered.

There were footsteps along the passageway and a light knock at the door, the vibrations working through her back. Kitty's voice was a whisper. 'Can we talk?'

Lana sucked in her sob, screwing her eyes shut. She wanted

to run across the deck of the yacht, dive from the bow and sink deep into the ocean, and swim and swim until there was nothing.

'Lana, please! Let me in.'

Had Kitty retied her sarong around her hips, wiped the mascara from beneath her eyes, and turned to Denny looking stricken? Had he pulled her into his arms before she left the cabin, whispering, *We'll work it out*?

No wonder Kitty had said she'd be staying on *The Blue* if Lana left. How convenient it would be for them.

'We need to talk.'

Kitty's voice was the scraping of jagged fingernails across raw skin. Lana ducked her head low into her lap, clamping her arms over her ears. She would wait in here until they reached Palau. Until the anchor dropped.

*

There were muffled voices, footsteps, the sound of a cabin door closing. Later came the steady lope of Denny's strides along the passageway. His steps paused outside the bathroom door. She could almost feel the heat of his body through the door, his hand raised as he knocked.

She imagined his mouth pressed close to the wood as he said, 'Lana? Please, Lana. Please come out. I need to see you.'

Silence.

After more appeals, his footsteps finally retreated.

*

Later still there was a beep of the ignition, followed by the thrum of the engine starting up. Then came the pull of sheets, the rustle of the mainsail as it was lowered.

Through the porthole a glimpse of land came into view. Trees, rich and green. She could see the detail in the colours – knew that they were near.

It was thirty minutes before the anchor was dropped. She heard Heinrich doing it on Aaron's command, the heavy metal weight hitting the water with a splash, the churn of the engine as it was flicked into reverse.

There was a sudden burst of talk up on deck, everyone speaking at once. She heard Aaron's voice, deep and commanding, cutting through the others. 'Nothing! We do nothing!'

A few moments later there was a knock on the bathroom door. She was ready to ignore whoever it was.

It was Shell – her tone deadly cool. 'Lana, immigration are about to board us.'

35

THEN

Lana splashed cool water against her face, letting the tap run long and hard.

She patted her skin dry on a damp hand towel. Then she ran her tongue across her teeth and attempted a smile at the mirror.

You can do this.

She left the bathroom, grabbed a pair of sunglasses from her cabin, and drifted up onto the deck. It was mid-morning and the air was stiff with heat. Denny and Kitty were standing together. When Kitty saw Lana, she moved to step forwards, but Lana shook her head sharply, making Kitty halt.

Aaron was helping the two immigration officers tie up to *The Blue*, looping their boat's painter around a cleat. Shell was standing in the shade, her gaze fixed on the strangers, her fingers rotating a sliver bracelet on her wrist. Heinrich was sitting with his elbows on his knees, his thumbs tapping together.

It wasn't standard protocol for immigration officers to board a vessel in Palau; they'd heard from other sailors that usually the crew would report to immigration at their shore office. Lana wondered whether something suspicious had been reported and radioed ahead of them.

A thin slick of sweat was building beneath her top: this was the moment she'd spent hours thinking about – when Joseph's death was either hidden or revealed.

The immigration officers stepped aboard, wearing smartly pressed navy uniforms. 'Who is the skipper?'

Aaron, who was now standing very still, thick arms hanging at his sides, managed a nod. 'I am.'

The senior officer faced him, chin lifted, as he said, 'Welcome to Palau. You have arrived into a new country, so we ask you, the skipper, and your crew, to fill in the correct paperwork.'

'Of course,' Aaron responded.

Palau was one of the most remote island chains in the world and she imagined the immigration officers didn't get very many opportunities to perform the tasks they'd been trained to do. The senior officer pulled out a sheaf of papers from a black file tucked beneath his arm, and handed one to each of them. 'Immigration forms. You will need your passports to complete them.'

The crew separated to fetch pens and passports. Lana returned to the cabin, pushing her sunglasses on top of her head. She pulled her backpack onto the floor, unbuckled it, and rummaged in the inside pocket for her passport.

As she was crouched on the ground, Kitty came into the cabin behind her. She shut the door. 'Lana—'

'No.' Lana turned, rising. They were facing each other in the narrow space of the cabin, just inches between them. 'I'm not doing this.'

'We have to talk.' Now that Kitty had removed her sunglasses Lana could see her eyelids were swollen and mottled red. She pressed her back against the door, blocking Lana's exit. 'Nothing happened between Denny and me.'

Lana looked up at the ceiling in despair. Was she really going to have this conversation? Was she actually going to listen to Kitty regurgitate every excuse she'd ever picked up from one of her badly scripted acting jobs? 'So tell me, Kitty,' she said coldly, 'what were you doing in his bed?'

'We'd been talking. I must've fallen asleep.'

'With your clothes off?'

'I was dressed.'

'Your sarong was on the floor, Kit.'

'I'd been wearing it as a scarf.'

'Yeah, it's often scarf weather in the Philippines.' Lana shook her head, exasperated with Kitty's lies. 'Let me out, Kitty.'

'No,' Kitty said, standing squarely in front of the door. 'I need you to believe me. Nothing happened. We were just talking.'

'About?'

Kitty looked momentarily flummoxed by the question. 'I . . . I was upset.'

'You?' Lana laughed. '*You* were upset?' The idea that after their argument, Kitty had gone to Denny for his support – when it should have been Lana – was almost more painful than the thought of the two of them fucking each other.

'I'm sorry . . .' Kitty began.

'What do you want me to say? *That's okay, then? I forgive you?* Because I won't say that.' She felt her lips tightening around her words, squeezing them into sharp blades. 'You had to prove you were better than me. That you could have Denny.'

'No.'

'No? You've always needed that – to be told by men that you're beautiful. What was it, Kit? Not enough people on the boat to keep your ego topped up, so you went after Denny?'

Kitty's eyes seemed to grow larger, but Lana was on a roll and she wasn't about to stop. All the anger and resentment that had been bubbling inside her came fighting and punching into the cabin. 'You screwed me over about my mother – and then you go and screw Denny, too. You knew how I felt about him. You were the one who was warning me off – reminding me about Aaron's "No relationships" rule. Was that because you were jealous? You liked him too and wanted him for yourself?'

'Of course not!'

The thing about a best friend is that you know them so intimately, that you know exactly how to cut them deepest. 'If we met each other now, we would never be friends. You know what I'd think of you? That you were vacuous, selfish, attention-seeking.'

Kitty drew back as if Lana had slapped her.

Up on deck Lana could hear the voices of the immigration officers. They were waiting to see the crew members' passports.

'Why did you do it?' Lana hissed. 'Because you could? Because you were proving something? I don't believe you even like him, not really. Do you?'

'I . . .' She trailed off without answering.

'Did you think – even for *one moment* – how I might feel?'

'I'm sorry.'

She drew a deep breath. 'Please go.'

'I . . . I . . .'

Lana turned her back, signalling that the conversation was over.

Kitty didn't move. 'Please, Lana . . .'

'We're done. You and me, Kitty, we're done.'

*

Lana placed her passport on the bunk, then grabbed everything else she could see – the cardigan hanging on the back of the door, the headscarf tied around the bunk corner, the sketchbook laid beneath the mattress – and stuffed it all into her backpack, buckling it shut. She didn't care what she might have left behind – she couldn't stand to be on this boat a minute longer than she had to.

She came up on deck and rested her backpack beside her. Denny stared at it, his face aghast. When he raised his eyes to hers, they were bruised with sadness.

She looked away.

The senior officer collected the forms they'd completed and looked carefully through them.

'There are only six of you on board?' he asked, looking slowly around, counting the crew: Aaron, Denny, Shell, Heinrich, Kitty and Lana.

There was a long pause. The silence stretched out as the crew's gazes moved between one another and finally to the floor.

Aaron cleared his throat. 'That's right.'

The senior officer pulled another sheet of paper from a folder, reading something. 'And you say there were six of you when you left the Philippines?'

Lana felt the knot in her stomach pull tight. Did they know, after all? Was this a test? She glanced at Aaron. In the high morning sun his tan was washed out and she could see a vein throbbing in his temple. He looked up and caught her eye.

The air seemed to fizzle and crackle between them: this was the moment to be honest, to tell the truth about Joseph.

'Aaron?' Lana said, her tone telling him to speak up.

Aaron stared at Lana, then at the immigration officers. His mouth opened and closed, but he didn't speak.

'That's right,' Kitty said to the immigration officers. 'There were six of us.'

Lana's gaze snapped around. Kitty was smiling at the officers, her head tilted at a girlish angle, a hip jutting out.

'Okay, very good.' He returned Kitty's smile in the way that men often did. 'Everything seems to be in order. We hope you have a very happy time here in Palau.'

'Thank you,' the crew mumbled.

'Wait!' Lana heard herself call.

Everyone turned to look at her.

She could feel her heart beating against her ribcage, her pulse echoing in her ears. She thought of Joseph lost at sea, and of Denny and Kitty in bed. 'Can I get a lift to shore?'

The senior officer glanced at Aaron. 'Is this okay with you, skipper?'

Aaron stared hard at Lana. She saw the spike of fear in his eyes. 'Sure you don't want to go with all of us later?' A warning.

She glared back. 'I'm sure.'

The muscles in his jaw clenched as he said, 'Okay.'

Lana hauled her backpack onto her shoulders, feeling the surprising weight of it after so many weeks. She crossed the cockpit, avoiding the gazes of the others.

As she passed Denny, he reached out, his hand brushing her lightly on the shoulder. 'Please, Lana. Don't leave.'

She looked at him and felt her heart splintering within her chest. How did something so beautiful break down? She couldn't think of anything to say, so she simply moved past him and climbed into the immigration officers' boat, which rocked beneath her.

She didn't look back, didn't answer when Shell called out, 'Lana? What are you doing? Where are you going?' She just sat with her back to *The Blue*, the sun raw against her face, light searing off the water.

*

The boat sped towards land, Lana's hair flying loose behind her. One of the immigration officers pointed to the beach ahead. 'We'll drop you there?'

It was a stretch of pristine white sand, with a lip of palm trees fringing it and a handful of colourful houses set back in the treeline. She could hear the call of birds and felt dazzled by the verdant greens, the bright tropical flowers, the whiteness of the sand.

'Yes,' Lana replied.

As they neared the beach, one of the officers lifted the outboard motor and the boat glided forward into the shallows.

Lana rose to step out of the boat. The senior officer said, 'Miss? Everything okay?'

Behind her sunglasses, tears dampened her face. She wiped her cheeks and tried to smile.

'You had problems on the yacht, no?'

Lana looked back towards *The Blue*. She imagined Aaron storming up and down the deck, worrying about what she'd be saying.

The crew had voted and a decision had been made – but not one that Lana was comfortable with.

'You talk to me? Something you wanna tell me?'

Lana looked into this man's kind face. If she told him right now that they'd been lying – seven crew members had left the Philippines, and now there were only six – how would his expression change? Would he radio across for help? Would she be taken off for questioning? Would the rest of the crew be brought in, too? She might have to wait around here for days, possibly weeks, while an investigation happened. She would have to face Kitty and Denny.

She pasted on her brightest smile. 'No problems – just happy to be here.'

He looked at her for a moment and she wondered whether he believed her. Then he smiled, too. 'Yes. Beautiful Palau.'

Lana lifted her backpack onto her shoulders, then stepped from the boat onto land.

36

NOW

At the Maritime Rescue Centre Lana leans against her car door. She waits out here so she can avoid Aimee Melina and her cool, penetrating gaze that seems to say, *You know something*.

And Lana does.

She knows that, eight months ago, Joseph Melina died.

She knows that the crew withheld the information from the authorities.

She knows that one of the crew – at least one of them – knows exactly what happened to Joseph.

She knows that although she voted in favour of informing the authorities about Joseph's death, when they reached Palau and she found herself alone with the immigration officers, she stayed as silent as the others.

She thinks about this often, trying to absolve herself – but the truth is, Lana didn't speak out because she was thinking about what was best for *her*. She needed to get as far away from

The Blue – and Kitty and Denny – as possible. The truth would only have held her up, so she remained silent and walked away.

And now the past is catching them up.

She glances down at her phone still displaying Kitty's emails, and continues to scroll through them. There must be over thirty messages, all sent in staggered bursts over the past few months. She opens a few at random, reading about some of the beaches and islands where the crew moored. Kitty's descriptions of life on the yacht – jumping from the bow, drinking cool beers on deck, watching the spinnaker flying – make her yearn for something lost. Kitty is careful never to mention Denny, and Lana is relieved by this. She's not sure she could bear – even now – to picture the two of them together.

As she is scrolling down, a subject header catches Lana's attention. The title is just a single word. A name.

Joseph.

Lana looks at the date the email was sent, and sees it was written about three months after Lana left *The Blue*. Why would Kitty be writing about Joseph then? Even the act of putting his name in an email is tantamount to admitting he was on board. After Kitty's conviction that they shouldn't tell the authorities, Lana's surprised that she would take the risk of communicating about him.

She clicks 'open' and begins to read.

Dear Lana,

I've not heard anything from you. You must be getting my emails – so please, PLEASE write to me! I just want to know you're okay.

At the moment it feels like there's this one enormous space in my life. It's where YOU should be. You've always been the most important person in my world and even though I've made mistakes – BIG mistakes! – please let me at least try and undo them. BUT I CAN'T DO THAT UNLESS YOU'LL TALK TO ME, LANA!!

I'm not going to bother with any more apologies. They don't make you hit 'Reply' – but maybe what I'm about to say will do.

I wanted to write to you about Joseph. I've been thinking a lot about that passage we made to Palau. It was a hideous time. Really fucking terrible – for everyone. But I think it was especially hard on you. Looking back I can see how isolated you felt. You knew something wasn't right about Joseph's death, but no one else wanted to hear it. The rest of us wanted to sail on, try and forget. But you couldn't. You've always had a black-and-white view when it comes to the truth – it's one of the things I admire about you.

But sometimes there are shades to it, Lana.

I know you were upset that I didn't vote with you. Maybe you saw it as another mar on our friendship, but the reason I voted against telling the authorities was because I knew it'd only create more pain – wasn't Joseph's death already enough? But now I see that if there's any chance of us repairing things, you need to hear the truth about what happened to him.

So what I'm saying is, if you want to know what went on that night, I'll tell you, Lana. I can tell you everything – because I was there.

Kitty x

Sweat crawls across Lana's skin, building in her underarms and at the small of her back. Her breath comes in shallow draws.

She reads the email a second time, and a third, and then she leans back against the car. *Jesus,* she thinks. *All along Kitty knew what happened to Joseph.*

*

'Lana?'

She looks up, startled to find Aimee Melina coming towards her. Lana quickly turns off her phone and slips it into her satchel, hooking the bag over her shoulder.

When she faces Aimee Melina, she notices how exhausted she looks. Dark strands of hair from her low bun have come loose, and her smartly applied lipstick has now faded at the centre of her lips. 'Apparently,' she says, in her lilting French accent, a hand resting on her hip, 'I am getting in the way. They do not believe me, I think, when I tell them that Joseph was meant to be here.'

The words in Kitty's email fire through Lana's mind: *I can tell you everything – because I was there.* As she stands in front of Aimee Melina, all she thinks is, *Kitty knows how your brother died.*

'I hope we could talk,' Aimee Melina says. 'About Joseph. You sail on the boat with him?' There is a slight accusation in her tone.

Lana's thoughts flit and flap like a cornered bird desperate to escape – she is not ready to have this conversation. Not until she knows the truth of what happened herself.

Aimee Melina is staring at her, waiting for Lana's confirmation.

'Yes,' she answers eventually. 'We sailed together in the Philippines.'

'You know where he is now, yes?'

'I . . .'

In the face of Aimee Melina's direct question, Lana can think of nothing to reply with. Instead, she shifts the focus away, asking, 'What made Joseph leave France? When *The Blue* picked him up, he was sleeping rough.'

'Rough?' Aimee Melina repeats, her brow dipping.

'I mean he was sleeping on the beach. Not in a hotel or anything. The crew thought he was homeless – he was very thin and looked like he'd been staying on the beach for a while. They asked him on board to eat with them.'

Aimee Melina's head shakes slowly from side to side. 'So he was using again.'

'Using?'

'Drugs.'

Lana blinks, taken aback. 'No, no. I don't think so. Why do you say that?'

Aimee Melina pulls a packet of cigarettes from her coat pocket, slides one out and places it between her painted lips. She offers the pack to Lana, who declines with a shake of her head. Aimee Melina lights the cigarette, then stretches her chin upwards as she draws the smoke deep into her lungs, the gesture reminding Lana of Joseph.

'I do not know how much my brother told you about his past?' Aimee Melina says exhaling a light plume of smoke over her shoulder.

'He told me your parents died,' Lana says. She hesitates for a moment, but then adds, 'There was some . . . speculation . . . that he was involved?'

Aimee Melina's expression doesn't change. She continues to smoke as she talks. 'Joseph had difficulties with drugs. You know meth? It is a terrible drug – it changes the person who take it. They are not . . . not themselves. For many years my brother fight against it.

'Our parents – they were good people – they tried to help him many times. They gave him a place to stay, got him professional help. But it is no good. Joseph, he is not himself. All he think about is the drug – needing more of it. More, more, more! But he had no job, no money, nothing. So he steal my mother's jewellery – sell it to pay for the drugs.' She looks intently at Lana as she says, 'This is not him, not my brother. This is the drugs.'

Something is chiming in Lana's thoughts; there is something on the periphery of her vision that she cannot quite see. She tries to focus on this thing, willing it to become clearer, but before she has a chance, Aimee Melina is talking again.

'Our parents are very upset by this. They feel they have failed.

They do not know what to do next. How to help. They tried everything. So as last step they go to police. They report him for theft and hope he will spend time in an institute – away from drugs. They think – they believe sincerely – that they are helping.'

Aimee Melina shakes her head. 'But Joseph – he do not see it like that. He thinks they betray him, yes? Being in the institute is no good for him. He comes out worse. He did not talk about what happened to him there, but I know it was not good.'

She taps the ash from her cigarette. 'Joseph is very angry with them. He blames them. Wants to hurt them. When he knows my parents are away on holiday, he gets high and goes to their house. He . . . set fire to it. Only my parents – they were not on holiday as he thought. They were inside.'

Lana feels her insides tighten: what Aaron told her all those months ago had been true.

'My brother, he killed them. The police suspect this – but they find no evidence. So eventually he is freed.' She sighs. 'For much, much time I hated my brother. I thought he killed them on purpose – for the money.'

'Money?'

'A hundred thousand Euros they left Joseph. I took the cheque to him. But Joseph – he cried when I gave it to him. Said it's not what he want. Then all I know is, he leave Paris and goes to the Philippines.' Aimee Melina drops her half-smoked cigarette and stubs it out with a neat twist of her heel.

It is all starting to make a terrible kind of sense: Joseph left France carrying the knowledge that he was responsible for his parents' deaths – and went to one of the most remote island chains in the Philippines. When Denny found him on that beach all those months ago, she wonders if Joseph had isolated himself there to keep off the drugs. *The Blue* must have offered him the perfect way to stay clean, to start over.

'He wrote me one letter,' Aimee Melina says, pressing her hand against her coat pocket, where Lana hears the light crinkle of paper. 'He tells me how sorry he is. How he is starting again. He says about the boat. How he made friends. How he'd not used the drugs for many months.'

Lana nods.

'At the end of the letter, he asked me to come here, to the Bay of Islands Maritime Centre, when the boat was due to dock. He asked if I can begin to forgive him.'

Lana's temples pound with tension.

'You see, with time, I start to think about this. Whether I can forgive him, yes? I'm not sure I have the answer – even now – but I come out here because I believe that true in my heart he is sorry for what he did. That is a start?'

Lana nods. 'On the yacht he kept notebooks. He used to write in them every evening. Every page was filled with one word: *Désolé.*'

Aimee Melina blinks, looking at Lana closely. 'This is true?'

'Yes. He filled several of them.'

'He was very sorry, I think,' Aimee Melina says, her eyes glassing with tears. She looks beyond Lana over to the water. 'Joseph and I – we have no other family. There is no one. Just us. It is important not to let that go, yes? Our parents – they were good people. I know they would have wanted me to try and forgive Joseph – so that is why I'm here.'

Lana's heart clenches as she thinks, *You're too late.*

'I understand he left the yacht – that is what I am told. But I hear nothing from him. Not in months.' She looks at Lana imploringly. 'I worry that he has gone back to the drugs. Do you know where he is now? How I can find him?'

Lana swallows. She has to tell Aimee Melina the truth – or at least what she knows of it. Already she has put it off for too long, hoping to find out what really happened to him. But what if Kitty and Aaron don't make it back to land? What if the secrets of that night on the yacht go down with it?

'Aimee . . .' Lana begins, experiencing a deep and awful surge of pity for this woman, knowing her world is only a breath away from being shattered.

But Aimee Melina is turning, looking skyward.

Lana tilts her head back, listening. There is a faint buzzing sound in the air.

She waits, holding her breath, focusing entirely on that low, guttural thrum.

There is no mistaking it. Somewhere in the distance she can hear the drone of a helicopter.

*

Lana presses a hand to her chest, as if she can feel it expanding beneath her palm with hope.

As the helicopter breaks through the cloud layer, Aimee Melina is forgotten and Lana rushes towards the landing zone. Ahead of her, Paul Carter steps out of the main building, and she alters her path so that she is moving towards him, questions already forming on her lips: *Is it Kitty? Have Kitty and Aaron been found?*

Lana's pace falters: Denny's parents are stepping out of the building now. Even from here she can see the sadness etched into their faces, their shoulders rounded under the weight of their loss. She assumed they must have returned home hours ago, wanting to be alone with their grief. Denny's mother is leaning into her husband, a tight frown on her forehead as she looks up towards the sky.

Then she realizes why they're still here, and why they've come out to meet this helicopter: they've been waiting for their son's body to be brought back to land.

Lana's blood cools as the helicopter begins to lower: Denny will be inside, his body zipped within a bag.

*

All day Lana's been trying to hold Denny's death at arm's length. She's not yet felt the full, brutal blow of loss – and isn't ready to.

The helicopter touches the ground, leaves and dust swirling and scattering. She turns her back to it and the skirt of her dress swirls behind her in the churned wind. She moves towards the main building with her head down, berating herself for her weakness when Denny's parents stand shoulder to shoulder, hands clasped, waiting.

Just before she reaches the entrance doors, Shell and Heinrich step outside. Broad smiles stretch across both their faces. Lana halts, confused.

'The rescue chopper,' Shell shouts above the noise, as if Lana hasn't noticed it.

Perhaps the helicopter isn't carrying Denny's body – but has survivors inside after all. Lana stares at Shell, asking, 'Kitty? Is it Kitty?'

Shell's smile widens as she points towards the helicopter. 'Look.'

Lana turns.

The central door lifts open and a man in a jumpsuit climbs out. Lana squints into the choppy wind, peering beyond him.

Her heart thunders as she waits.

There is movement somewhere within, the flash of orange.

Suddenly, there she is: Kitty.

Lana's eyes widen in disbelief as she watches Kitty step down from the helicopter. She looks smaller than Lana remembers, as if she's shrunk in the months they've been apart. Her hair has been cropped boyishly short and strands are twisted and ruffled by the wind. She wears a bright-orange thermal suit that is too big for her, the material turned up around her ankles.

She begins to walk towards them, steered by one of the rescue workers who keeps his hand on her back, ushering her gently forwards.

It is only when Kitty is a few metres away that she looks up, noticing Lana.

Kitty stops dead. Her eyes are wide and round, glittering in her bare face. Her head shakes from side to side. In this moment, everything that has happened between them is stripped clean, discarded. All Lana feels is an overwhelming surge of love.

Then Kitty is walking forwards, and Lana is moving to meet her. She thinks of all the times they walked towards each other: after class when they'd meet in the playground, Lana's bag sloping off her shoulder; behind the cinema when they'd run towards one another, whispering about the boys they fancied; when they'd meet by the wall on their street to walk into town, the week's pocket money warming in their hands.

They both come to a stop a pace in front of one another. The air churns around them.

Without make-up and her hair cut pixie-short, Kitty looks impossibly young. All these months Lana has cast her in the role of temptress – black hair swishing down her back, the practised sway of her hips, the sultry kohl-lined stare – but that isn't the full picture. Kitty is also the girl who cried for a day when Lana was moved up a set in English class without her; she is the girl who drove from Scotland to Bristol, to be there on Lana's birthday; she is the girl who sent Lana sherbet lemons when she was working on her final art project for her degree.

As she looks at Kitty – alive, on land – she thinks, *We have a chance to make this right.*

Lana steps forwards, opening her arms. Kitty falls into them, gripping her tightly. The two of them cling to each other in the stirring air.

*

When they eventually let go, Kitty shouts above the noise of the helicopter, 'What are you doing here?'

There is a faint purplish tinge to her lips and Lana wants to wrap her in layers of fleecy blankets and pull her indoors out of the wind.

'I never went home,' she answers. 'After *The Blue*, I flew here.'

'So . . . you've been here for months?'

Lana nods.

'Why?' Kitty asks, but then turns back towards the helicopter.

Lana follows her gaze, realizing Aaron must also be inside. 'He made it?' she shouts, leaning close to Kitty, who nods.

Lana stands with her arm wrapped tightly around Kitty's waist as she watches for Aaron.

First, a pair of tanned bare feet emerge, stepping down onto the tarmac. He wears a thermal suit, like Kitty's, but when Lana's gaze reaches his face, she gasps.

It is not Aaron.

37

NOW

The blades of the landed helicopter cut through the sky and she wants to cover her ears from the noise so that she can think, so that she can see clearly. Her dress swirls around her knees and she is distantly aware that she should pin it down with her arms. But she doesn't move. All she can do is stare.

He's just as she remembers him: tanned, barefoot, wild-haired. He has grown a beard, which makes him look older somehow, but there is no mistaking him. It is Denny.

There is the rushing of feet and, from the corner of her eye, she sees his mother running towards him. When she reaches him, Denny's mother folds her arms around her son. Even though she is smaller than him, she rocks him back and forth, one hand cradling the back of his head. Denny must be saying something close to her ear, as she is nodding and sobbing, tears streaming down her face.

Denny's father follows at a walk, a thick hand rubbing back and forth across his mouth as if he can't quite believe it.

But . . . how? How did Paul Carter get it so wrong?

When Denny's father reaches them, he embraces his wife and son, his wide arms encircling them, the side of his face buried in his son's hair. The three of them stand together on the tarmac, clothes flapping madly in the helicopter's wind. They stay that way for a full minute, a locked family unit.

Eventually they untangle themselves and Denny looks up. His pale-blue gaze moves across the small group of them gathered at the edge of the tarmac – and then falls on Lana. His eyes widen, his head seeming to rise higher on his shoulders.

Denny's parents are linking their arms through his, saying something to him. But Denny doesn't answer, doesn't seem to hear – his attention fixed only on Lana.

*

They don't get a chance to speak. Denny is ushered inside the building, his parents flanking him like bodyguards. She watches in silence, absorbing the long stretch of his legs, the sun-lightened ends of his hair, the deep tan at the back of his neck. Her eyes follow him until he is completely out of sight, and then still she doesn't turn away.

Her mouth opens and closes. 'I thought . . . I thought he was . . .' The sentence trails away beneath the blaze of helicopter noise.

Then Shell and Heinrich are coming forwards, calling Kitty's name, smiling, reaching out, hugging her. Shell is in tears as she tells Kitty how scared she's been for her. Heinrich keeps on squeezing Kitty's shoulder as if to check she is really here. 'You're okay!' he says. 'You're both safe.' His smile is wide with relief.

The reunion between the crew only lasts a matter of moments as a medic interrupts, telling Kitty that she needs to be checked for signs of hypothermia.

As Kitty is being led away, she spins around, grabbing Lana's hand with cool fingers. 'Come with me.'

*

Kitty grips Lana as they walk into the main building, following the medic.

Lana turns, only now remembering Aimee Melina who she abandoned the moment the helicopter arrived. She sees that she is leaning against Lana's car, a fresh cigarette in her fingers. Their gazes meet and Lana nods, hoping to indicate that she will be back.

Every few steps Kitty sways slightly, almost lurching. She speaks constantly in a low, rushed whisper, words tumbling out as she gives a chaotic account of what happened. 'I thought I was going to drown. I prayed, Lana. I actually said prayers. From the boat the swell didn't seem as big, but in the water, it was . . . monstrous. Denny – he found me. He clipped our life jackets together and told me to swim with him.

'The paddleboard,' Kitty says, blinking rapidly. 'We'd thrown it overboard to lessen the weight on the yacht. Everything was stripped. Denny helped me reach it. He dragged me onto it – and we clung on. Waiting.'

Lana tries to picture it – the cold ferocity of the sea; the crippling fear of not knowing whether they'd be rescued; the constant howl of wind. She squeezes Kitty's arm more tightly.

'You know what I was thinking when I was on that paddleboard?' Kitty says, looking up at Lana. 'I thought about us.' She smiles a little. 'I thought about that day we paddled out towards the mangrove forest as the sun was going down. We saw that shoal of tiny fish leaping out from the water and I got so excited that I wobbled the board and we capsized. We smacked our heads together as we went under, but it didn't even hurt because we were laughing so hard when we came up. And then we just lay across the board with our legs in the warm water, watching *The Blue* on its anchor.'

Lana says, 'I remember.'

'That's where I pretended I was. If I'd thought about what was really happening, I don't think I could have coped.' Kitty slides her arm free, wiping the tears from her face with the back of her hand.

The medic leading them comes to a halt, saying, 'Here we go. I'll try not to keep you long – I know you've had an exhausting day.' As the medic opens the door for Kitty, she says to Lana, 'You can wait next door, if you like. I'll bring Kitty back to you as soon as we're done.'

She nods. As Kitty steps into the room, something dawns on Lana. 'Where's Aaron?'

Kitty turns back, her eyes widening. 'You haven't heard?'

Lana shakes her head. 'Heard what?'

Kitty's expression clouds. 'He didn't make it, Lana. Aaron drowned.'

*

Lana stands in the corridor, her back pressed against the wall.

Aaron is dead.

Drowned.

The knowledge rocks her, makes her breathing shudder.

Out of everyone, he is the one who Lana would have thought most likely to survive. There was an unbending resilience about him – an invincibility, almost. *But dead?* The idea of it is so cruel when the rest of them have been safely returned to land.

She cannot picture it – his large frame adrift in the sea. How can the water have claimed him when it has been his home for the past three years? From Heinrich and Shell's account, she knows he was the last to climb aboard the life raft, wanting to make sure the rest of the crew were safe first. It was afterwards that the wave came, washing Denny, Kitty and Aaron into the water. The paddleboard saved Denny and Kitty's lives – but not Aaron's.

Her temples throb with tension. She unknots her headscarf and closes her eyes, pressing her fingers against her scalp. She works her fingertips over the hair follicles, trying to rub away the pain. Somewhere in the distance she becomes faintly aware of a door opening, then the sound of footsteps moving towards her.

Her eyes open and all of a sudden, there in the corridor facing her is Denny. His parents stand on either side of him.

'Lana.' The way her name sounds on his tongue makes a forgotten place inside her ache.

They are close enough so that she could reach out and touch him. The thermal suit he was wearing earlier has now been swapped for a pale-green jumper that's ripped at the collar, and a pair of trousers that are slightly too short. They are not his clothes, but dry clothes the centre must have supplied. His face is deeply tanned and she notices that the new beard he's grown is darker than the curls on his head.

Denny, without taking his eyes off her, says, 'Mum, Dad. I'll catch you up.'

His parents hesitate, their gazes moving to Lana. She can feel his mother's reluctance to let her boy out of her sight, but his father says, 'We'll be in the reception area.'

Lana hears their footsteps receding down the corridor. She remains facing Denny, her chest rising and falling. It feels as if everything around them has melted away and all she can hear is the drill of her own heartbeat and the air being drawn in and out of her lungs.

His gaze travels slowly over her face. 'Lana,' he says again. 'You're here.'

She nods, heat rising to her neck.

He steps towards her and a deep fluttering fills the base of Lana's stomach. She cannot do this; cannot stand so close to him. She takes a small step back.

In the months since *The Blue*, she has wondered and hypo- thesized, rubbed her imagination raw with the thought of Kitty and Denny as a couple. She has pictured them lying together in the hammock, Denny's hand tracing the curve of Kitty's hip. She has heard his voice bantering and volleying with Kitty, who'd end the joke sitting astride his lap and kissing him. She has smelt the sun lotion Kitty would rub into the long stretch of his back, paying particular care to the spattering of moles on his shoulder. Her throat feels as though it is closing, but she manages to take a breath and push out the words, 'You're safe.'

'Yes.'

'I thought . . . we thought you were dead,' she says. 'Paul Carter told us.'

Denny looks bewildered.

'Search and Rescue reported that your body was found with the EPIRB attached to it. But it wasn't.'

'No. It was Aaron.'

She blinks. 'Aaron? I don't understand how they got it so wrong. Paul Carter . . . he told your parents. I saw. It was terrible. They were sobbing. Jesus,' she says, running a hand over her mouth. 'To tell someone that their son is dead . . .'

'Lana,' Denny says, his voice level. 'Their son *is* dead.'

She looks up, confused.

'Aaron was my brother.'

*

Lana feels the heat of the corridor raking over her skin, hears the sound of voices somewhere beyond them. Her heart pounds in her chest. 'Your brother?'

'Yes.'

'But . . . I don't understand.' She shakes her head. 'You never said . . .'

'I know. I couldn't. Aaron wanted it that way.'

He and Aaron were brothers?

Impossible. She would have known.

She stares at Denny anew. He is a completely different build from Aaron, taller, wirier. Yet when she pictures them both side by side, perhaps there is something shared in the angle of their jaw lines and the heavy frame of their brows. Yet the two of them are so . . . different.

Her thoughts swim back to *The Blue* as she starts re-examining memories, holding each up to the light of this new information. There were the obvious things that connected Denny and Aaron – like they were both from New Zealand, and Denny was the first to join *The Blue*. But what else? She remembers Denny telling her he decided to study French after spending a family holiday on Réunion island – and now that she thinks of it, when she first met Aaron he joked about something or other that'd happened to him on Réunion island. They must have been there together. Denny even told Lana that he had a brother, but she didn't ask his name – didn't know anything about him.

She looks at Denny as she asks, 'Why keep it secret?'

'It was Aaron's condition for me joining *The Blue*.'

'Why?'

'It's hard to explain . . . but *The Blue* – the whole idea of setting sail and not looking back – that was Aaron's way of leaving his old life behind. I told you about his wife and baby?'

She nods, remembering the tragedy.

'I couldn't tell you all of it when we were on the boat – but I was there, Lana, when Lydia was murdered.' His voice sounds hollow as he says, 'I found her.'

'My God . . .'

'I was helping out because Aaron was having a crazy time of it at work. Lydia asked me to paint the nursery. I was upstairs with the radio blasting when it happened.' His voice is flat as he says, 'I didn't hear anything – not a sound. It was over an hour before I found her. I came out into the garden and saw the washing scattered on the lawn. Lydia was . . .' He pauses, his face grey. 'She was lying on her side, blood pooling from her middle. If I'd gone outside sooner, maybe I could've . . .' She watches as Denny tilts his head back, his eyes cast upwards. Under the strip lighting his expression is raw and exposed – and she sees it: Denny blames himself for not saving Lydia.

She wonders, *Did Aaron blame him, too?*

'Is that why you joined Aaron on *The Blue*?'

He drags his gaze away from the ceiling, managing to meet Lana's eye. He nods slowly. 'I was worried about him. He didn't tell anyone he was leaving, not even our parents. He just set sail.'

'The boat belonged to your dad?'

Denny nods. 'He used to run it as a charter business, but for the last few years it'd just been sitting on a mooring doing nothing. After Aaron lost Lydia and the baby, he quit his job – quit everything. We were all worried. Mum and Dad decided it'd be good to give him a focus again, so they said if Aaron refitted *The Blue*, he could have her.'

Lucy Clarke

Denny explains how Aaron worked tirelessly on the boat for six months, teaching himself how to take engines apart, install solar panels, repair sails. 'He lived and breathed that boat, and once she was seaworthy again, he'd sail her up and down the coast to spots we visited as kids. Then, one day, Aaron went sailing and didn't come back. Mum and Dad found a note saying he was heading across to Australia.'

'He didn't tell anyone?'

Denny shakes his head. 'To be honest, I'm not sure he was planning to make it to land. Only he did. He moored up in a deserted little cove up north. I flew out and tried to persuade him to come home, but he wouldn't. Said *The Blue* was where he needed to be.'

'So you joined him.'

Denny nods. 'We sailed around northern Australia for a while, then went over to Indo. By the time we got there, we were both flat broke – so we decided to take on paying crew.'

'That's how it all started,' Lana says quietly, finally understanding.

He nods. 'And now it's over. *The Blue* is gone, and so is Aaron.' His shoulders begin to shake and he screws up his eyes, but tears still manage to squeeze out, trailing down his cheeks and into the tangle of his beard.

'I'm so sorry,' Lana says, stepping forward and putting her arms around him. She feels his body slacken against hers as she holds him.

38

NOW

Lana leads Denny from the corridor into the waiting room. He slumps into a chair and sits with his head hanging forward, the weight of it held in his hands. Whatever today is for the rest of them – for Denny it will always be the day his brother died.

So many things begin quietly slotting into place, as if the missing pieces of the jigsaw she has been searching for could only ever be found here on land, all these months later. She now understands Denny and Aaron's loyalty to one another – that quiet respect they displayed, and that particular way they functioned, as if each knew the exact moves the other would make before he'd even made them.

She also sees just how important – no, *vital* – The Blue was to Aaron. It makes sense that Aaron was furious when he discovered Joseph had stowed away because it put *The Blue* in jeopardy. She remembers Aaron pinning Joseph against the bulkhead, a vein in his neck throbbing lividly. He was leaning in close to

Joseph's ear, saying, 'Don't forget, I know you, Joseph. I know what you are.'

And then something clicks.

Meth. It's just a word, but the four letters of it unlock a door in Lana's mind beyond which she hasn't been able to see.

Aaron's wife and unborn baby were murdered by Mills Weaden, a meth addict. Then, the day the crew were preparing to set sail for Palau, Aaron discovered that Joseph – a crew member he'd invited into the sanctuary of *The Blue* – was suspected of killing his parents while high on meth.

There's no doubt in Lana's mind that that's why Aaron kicked Joseph off *The Blue*. But what none of them could have foreseen was that two days into the passage to Palau – and on the anniversary of Lydia's death – Aaron discovered that Joseph had stowed away. Trapped at sea with no way of getting rid of Joseph, Aaron's fury seemed to consume him. She remembers how hard he drank that night, and how his mind was elsewhere – somewhere separate from the yacht and the crew. Denny was the only one who seemed able to communicate with him, the two of them sitting close and talking intently.

And then there was Joseph. He didn't keep out of Aaron's way. It was almost as if he got a kick out of antagonizing him. Lana guesses that, at some point that evening, the two men found themselves alone together. Did Joseph push things too far – and did Aaron snap?

Did Aaron kill him?

Perhaps Kitty was there too and witnessed it – and that's what she meant in her email.

'Denny,' Lana says, turning to him, her heart beginning to race. 'What happened to Joseph?'

Denny lifts his head, holding her gaze. His eyes have lost their glimmer and seem dulled, vacant. He doesn't speak, doesn't move a muscle. Denny is the one person who knows the full truth about Aaron's past. The one person Aaron would confide in.

Lana says, 'You know, don't you?'

She waits for him to say something.

Anything.

Denny leans back in his chair, exhaling hard.

She stares at him. There was a time when she thought she knew him so completely that she would have been able to guess where his thoughts had taken him. She could once tell that when he stood at the bow and his gaze turned distant, he was often thinking about home. Or when she was speaking and his lips turned up into a smile, it was because he'd already skipped ahead to something funny he was going to add. Their connection on *The Blue* felt powerful and real – yet perhaps it never was. She didn't even know that he and Aaron were brothers. Denny protected that secret for Aaron's sake, and now she has to wonder what other secrets he's kept for his brother . . .

'What happened?' she repeats, the muscles in her jaw tightening. She has carried her suspicions with her for months, trying to convince herself that she has been making too much of the missing pieces: Aaron's shoulder that he claimed was injured in the shower; Aaron being so adamant that they should not report Joseph missing; the crew's insistence that no one saw anything on their watch; the bloodstain on the deck. Pinpricks of perspiration begin to bead at her temples. 'Did Aaron kill Joseph?'

If it was murder, they are all complicit by not reporting it. What will happen to them now that Aimee Melina is here? Aaron is dead and no one can prove what happened.

'No,' Denny says firmly, his eyes on hers. 'Aaron didn't kill Joseph.'

She waits, her pulse ticking in her throat.

He stares at her, the colour draining from his face. 'I did.'

*

Time slows and warps. Lana hears the faint wash of the wind outside, notices the slow ticking of a clock somewhere nearby.

Denny rises to his feet and moves to the window. He stands with his hands in his pockets, his head thrown back towards the ceiling, exposing the pale skin on his throat where his beard ends.

She doesn't dare speak. She looks carefully at Denny as if searching for something she's missed before. But all she sees is how sad his face is, how deep the shadows are beneath his eyes.

She thinks of what he's been through today: drifting on a paddleboard in the open sea as he and Kitty fought to survive, and then learning that his brother has drowned. He must be physically exhausted and emotionally wrecked; he can't mean what he is saying. 'You didn't kill Joseph.'

'Yes,' he says. 'I did.'

Denny's firm and resolute tone scares her. She waits, afraid to ask more now.

Little by little, Denny begins to recount what happened. As he talks, only his lips seem to move. The rest of him remains rigid, as if the memory of the event has him pinned to the spot.

'You remember what it was like that night,' he begins, his gaze fixed on something beyond the window. 'The drinking. The tensions between all the crew – even us.'

Us. That word. She feels a fresh twist of loss.

'It's strange, but I had this . . . feeling . . . that something was wrong about it. Like something terrible was going to happen.'

Thinking back, Lana recalls how on edge Denny seemed that night – he wasn't drinking with the others and kept himself glued to Aaron's side, talking to him in a quiet voice, his gaze only moving away to look out over the dark water, as if watching for signs that the weather was going to turn. It was as if he was trying to keep a lid on a pot that was slowly beginning to boil.

'It was the anniversary of Lydia's death,' Denny says, 'and Aaron, he was in a bad place, a really bad place. I hadn't seen him like that since the early days when he'd just lost her.' Denny rubs the corner of his mouth, saying, 'He was fixated on Joseph. It was like Joseph had become this . . . this embodiment of Mills Weaden and everything he'd done. He told me Joseph was polluting *The Blue*, destroying it all.

'When everyone had gone to bed, it was just Aaron up on deck doing his watch. I stupidly thought being on watch would be the best place for him. There's this . . . peace Aaron found on the water, and I hoped the solitude might do him good. Only – Joseph came back up on deck. Maybe he couldn't sleep, or maybe he was looking for a fight, or maybe he just didn't realize it was Aaron's watch.'

Denny pauses for a moment before continuing. 'I heard them talking through the hatch in my cabin. There was something in their tones that I didn't like. I'm not even sure how the argument started – I only caught snatches of it – but Joseph began demanding his notebook back, and I realized Aaron must've snatched it from him. From what I could tell, Joseph lunged for the notebook, but Aaron tossed it overboard.'

Lana's eyes widen. She remembers how important those note-books were to Joseph, how he dedicated so much time and care to writing his apologies.

'Joseph just lost it – started raging at Aaron in French and English. Aaron wouldn't listen – he shouted back, calling Joseph a *sick bastard*. I was willing Aaron to shut up, to leave it alone – but he couldn't. It was like . . . I don't know . . . like he was standing in front of Lydia's murderer, finally having his chance to confront him. He kept saying, "I know who you are. What you've done. You killed your own parents! You're a fucking murderer!"'

Beads of perspiration line Denny's top lip and his skin looks deathly white. He swallows and goes on. 'Then I heard a rush of movement in the cockpit – and I knew, I knew then what was about to happen. I should've been up there sooner . . . I was only just climbing on deck when I saw Joseph pulling the helm knife from its sheath.

'The next second Joseph was on top of Aaron, forcing him back against the lifeline. I heard Aaron's gasp as the knife went into him. I lunged at Joseph, grabbing him by the neck of his T-shirt and pulling him off.' Denny pauses, his brow furrowed. 'But . . . I threw him too hard. I heard it – heard the clunk as Joseph's head hit the edge of the cockpit. I turned . . . and his body seemed to slump as he rolled towards the edge of the yacht. He slipped under the lifeline like a deadweight.'

Denny shakes his head, saying, 'I didn't even help him. I went straight to Aaron – he had his arm clamped across his body, and I thought the knife had gone into his chest. I was freaking out, remembering how I hadn't got there quickly enough with Lydia . . .' He swallows. 'When Aaron lifted away his arm, I saw that the knife had punctured his shoulder. It looked bad – but not life-threatening. He kept telling me he was fine, that he just needed something to stop the bleeding. I grabbed a rag and tied it around his shoulder.

'It was then – only at that moment – that I gave Joseph another thought. A minute or two had already passed – maybe more. That's enough to change everything if someone's gone overboard.' Denny looks shaken as he says, 'I should've tried to rescue him straight away – should've left Aaron and immediately thrown out a life ring or done something.

'Eventually I got it together – logged the GPS, then furled the headsail, while Aaron managed to start the engine. That's when I saw someone standing on the foredeck. For a second I thought it was Joseph and that, somehow, we'd got it wrong – he hadn't gone overboard. Only it was Kitty. She'd passed out in the hammock, I think. Must've been woken by the noise.

'A moment later, Heinrich came lurching up onto the deck,

too. He'd heard the commotion and was asking what was going on.'

Lana is struggling to take in everything she's being told. She tries to picture Kitty stumbling from the hammock and Heinrich rushing from below deck – both of them still half-drunk as they took in the scene: Aaron hunched over with a bloodied shoulder, the headsail furled in, the engine running.

Denny says, 'I told Kitty to wake you and Shell, get you both to help search, but Aaron said, "No. No more people! Everyone's too fucking pissed. It's too dangerous! We'll manage."

'So Kitty and Heinrich fetched the searchlights, and I mapped out a search course, then we started making the pattern. Aaron was reading out the distances before each turn, I was on the helm, and Heinrich and Kitty took a side each. The four of us were watching the water, but even with the searchlights it was hard to see. The wind was increasing and we had no idea how far he could've already drifted.'

Denny looks at her as he says, 'We searched and searched, Lana. But we never found him.'

Lana thinks about how she and Shell woke the following morning to find Joseph missing. They began looking for him – rushing through the cabins, checking the heads and sail lockers and hatches. 'Why didn't you say anything to Shell and me?'

Denny's expression is thick with guilt, eyes defeated. 'Aaron wanted as few people to know as possible. Joseph didn't trip and fall overboard – I threw him. I killed him. If the authorities knew that, I don't know what would've happened to me – but

I do know it would've been the end for *The Blue*. And Aaron knew it, too.'

*

For a long while, the two of them stand in the waiting room in silence.

Lana looks down at her hands. They are clasped in front of her, her knuckles white. She releases them, letting her arms hang at her sides as the blood flows back into her fingertips.

Finally, after so many months of wondering, Lana has the truth. She allows it to work slowly through her, beginning to make sense of why Denny withdrew from her in the days following Joseph's death; why Aaron claimed he'd injured his shoulder in the shower to cover for the knife wound; why Aaron, Heinrich and Kitty were so adamant that the authorities shouldn't be informed.

She suddenly looks up at Denny, thinking of the group vote. 'But you voted with me. You wanted to tell the authorities Joseph was dead.'

Denny nods slowly. 'I couldn't live with it, knowing what I'd done. I hated that you didn't know – that I couldn't talk to you about it.' He looks at her closely. 'I knew how hurt you'd been by your father lying to you. I didn't want to be that person, too. It felt like this secret we were all keeping was . . . destroying everything. The yacht. Me. Us.'

She sees the defeated slump of Denny's shoulders, the grey tones of his skin, the flatness of his eyes – and it reminds her of how he looked in the days following Joseph's death. He barely ate or slept, focused only on getting them safely to land. His usual enthusiasm and buoyancy were vanished – and Lana barely recognized him.

'It was an accident, Denny,' she says firmly.

He looks haunted as he says, 'Was it? I'd have done anything to protect Aaron.'

The door to the waiting room opens. Kitty walks in, her gaze flickering between the two of them, a question forming in her expression.

There is a long silence.

Then Lana rubs a hand over her forehead, saying to Kitty, 'Denny's just told me about Joseph.'

Kitty stops. Her lips press together as she shakes her head. 'I'm so sorry, Lana. We should've told you at the time. We thought it was for the best. We thought we were protecting you.'

'Does Shell know now?' Lana asks.

Kitty shakes her head.

'She needs to be told,' Denny says.

Kitty agrees, then she takes a step towards Lana and says quietly, 'I don't know if Denny's explained – but that morning you found me in his cabin – we'd been talking about Joseph. That's why I was in there. Nothing happened.'

Lana stays very still, as if a dawn light is beginning to rise inside her, shedding light over the darkest memories in her heart.

She is aware of Denny nodding, saying, 'I was in such a state about what happened with Joseph. I was reliving every moment, looking for how it could have been different. I wish I hadn't yanked Joseph so hard, wish I'd tried to get the knife from him, wish I'd woken everyone to help search. I just wish every single thing had been done differently.' He looks up at her and says, 'I saw what his death did to you, Lana – and that made it even worse.'

Guilt is scored into the lines above his brow as he explains, 'Kitty was the only person I could talk to. I couldn't go to Aaron, and Heinrich . . . he just shut down – he wouldn't even say Joseph's name. But for me . . . I was the one who'd done it. I killed him. And I just kept replaying what'd happened, needing to make sense of it. I was losing it – totally losing it. The night before we reached Palau, I spoke to Aaron and said we had to tell the authorities when we arrived. The two of us had this terrible fight . . .' he says, his eyes clouding at the memory.

Kitty takes over. 'Afterwards I went to check on Denny – try and calm things down. We talked and talked, right through the night. Eventually we must have crashed out. That was it, Lana. Nothing happened.'

Even after all the hours Lana has spent picturing that morning, replaying the way Kitty's arm was draped over Denny, the guilty expression sliding across his face as he woke, Lana can tell that this is the truth. Now she understands why, at the time, Kitty couldn't explain what she was doing in Denny's room – not without explaining about Joseph.

Lana can't stop herself from asking, 'What about later?'

'Later?' Kitty repeats.

'The eight months you've spent on the same yacht.'

'Nothing went on – not that night, or any nights.'

Slowly, Lana nods. She believes her.

'I'm so sorry for not being honest with you about Joseph,' Denny says. 'For not being honest with everyone. I felt like I couldn't tell you – or the authorities – because if Aaron lost *The Blue*, he'd have lost everything. It doesn't mean I think it was the right decision – it wasn't. Believe me, I know it wasn't.'

But Lana doesn't blame Denny – the whole crew were responsible for what happened on board. Aaron might have provoked Joseph, Denny might have thrown him across the deck, and Kitty and Heinrich might have kept quiet about what they'd seen – but Lana and Shell were on that yacht, too, and neither of them told the authorities. All six of them have to live with that. 'You never meant to kill him,' Lana tells Denny. 'You were protecting your brother.'

But even as the words leave her mouth, she thinks, *Will Joseph's sister see it like that?*

She glances out of the waiting-room window and across the tarmac towards her car. Aimee Melina is still standing there, arms at her side, staring towards the building.

Lana takes a deep breath, steeling herself. She needs to tell them that Joseph had a sister – and that she's here at the Maritime Rescue Centre, waiting to find out what's happened to him.

39

NOW

L ana walks across the port with Aimee Melina at her shoulder. The sky is darkening and there is no break in the clouds now. Neither of them speaks. Their feet move in rhythm towards the group of people standing together at the port edge.

When Lana told Aimee Melina that she and the crew needed to talk to her about Joseph, she stared at Lana with a cool, assessing gaze. 'It is not good news, is it?'

'No. No, I'm afraid it isn't.'

Now Lana looks towards the group gathered at the water's edge, and feels the space at the centre of the group where Aaron should be. Denny stands silently with his hands at his sides, his gaze directed at the water. Shell – who like Lana has only today learnt the truth about Joseph's death – has positioned herself slightly back from the others. Her gaze keeps travelling to Heinrich, and she stares at him with her head angled to one side, as if she no longer recognizes him. Even after everything that has happened, Heinrich still protested that they don't need to tell Aimee Melina a thing.

Denny shook his head, eyes narrowing. 'You can't be serious? She's his *sister*! She has a right to know what's happened to him.'

But Heinrich remained resolute. 'What do you think Aaron would want?'

Denny looked sickened by the question. 'Aaron was only ever trying to protect *The Blue*. If he'd known Joseph had a sister, he would've made a very different decision. We all would.'

'I'm just worried about what'll happen to us if we tell her,' Heinrich had said.

'No,' Shell had cut in bitterly. 'You're worried about yourself.'

Heinrich looked chastened by the remark and after that he said nothing more.

Now, as Lana and Aimee Melina approach the group, Aimee slips her hand into her coat pocket, and Lana imagines that her fingers are pressing against Joseph's letter, the weight of his words resting beneath her palm.

The crew hear them approach and turn. Lana watches Denny's expression as his gaze settles on Aimee.

He crosses the group towards her, stopping a couple of paces in front of her. He introduces himself and tells her, 'I met Joseph in the Philippines when he was backpacking there.' He holds her gaze as he says, 'There's something important we need to talk to you about.'

*

Joseph's sister stands poker-straight, chin lifted, her pale hands stuffed into her coat pockets. She listens silently to Denny, her dark eyes never leaving his face as if she needs not only to hear – but to see – every word he speaks.

Denny's voice is level as he retells the story of Joseph's time on *The Blue*. With a simple clarity he talks to her of finding Joseph sleeping rough on a remote beach; of his spectacular dive from the cliffs; of him dancing around the fire with Kitty; of the long evenings he spent at the bow with his notebook filled with apologies.

The rest of the crew listen just as closely, anxiety settling into their expressions as all of them now know what comes next.

Lana understands that Denny holds himself responsible for Joseph's death – but what he won't be responsible for is Aimee Melina spending a lifetime wondering what happened to her brother. She needs to hear the truth – and Denny needs to tell it.

For all these months, he has kept the secret of what happened to Joseph. It hasn't been to protect himself, but to protect his brother: *The Blue* was everything to Aaron – and Denny couldn't watch him lose that. But now things are different: Aaron is dead and the yacht sunk. Denny is free to tell the truth.

Aimee's expression changes very little as she listens to the details of the night Joseph went overboard. Denny could have told any version of the events, saying that Joseph had too much to drink and slipped overboard and no one else was involved, but instead, he recounts the evening detail by detail in the exact way it unfolded. He explains about discovering Joseph stowed away and the growing tension between Joseph and Aaron; he explains that it was the anniversary of Aaron's wife's death – and the awful relevance this held; he explains how hard everyone had been drinking and how, in the thick of the darkness, he heard an argument break out between Joseph and Aaron; he explains about the knife Joseph thrust into Aaron's shoulder, and how he himself flung Joseph across the cockpit, Joseph's body sliding beneath the lifeline; he explains about searching with Kitty and Heinrich, the bad weather coming in, the acceptance that Joseph was dead.

Finally, Denny explains their decision not to inform the authorities. 'Because Joseph stowed away, he wasn't on the crew list. No one knew he'd left the Philippines on *The Blue*. He'd told us he had no family – so we believed that no one would be searching for him.' His voice breaks off for a moment and he squeezes his thumb and forefinger into the sockets of his eyes.

When he has composed himself, he looks at Aimee Melina and says, 'I'm so sorry – had we known about you, everything would have been different.'

And there it is, the truth finally released.

Aimee remains very still, her face sheet-white. Lana can feel the tension radiating from each of the group, the air thickening between them. There are no sounds except for the light wash of water against the edge of the port and the distant cawing of gulls.

Aimee lifts her hands as if about to brush away a strand of hair, but instead of reaching towards her hairline, she covers her face to stifle the terrible wail of grief that ruptures the silence.

*

The crew watch, horrified. Aimee is hunched forward, her long coat pulling tight across her shoulders, wisps of hair blown around her face.

Lana tastes bile at the back of her throat: they have done this to her, all of them.

Denny steps forward, his face ashen. He moves as if to place his hands on Aimee's upper arms, but she raises her head, lifting her chin and facing him.

'No.'

Denny pulls back, his hands rising as if in surrender.

Aimee does not wipe away the tears that run down her face. They leave glimmering trails against her clear skin as she asks, 'He's really gone?'

'Yes, I'm so—'

She shakes her head. 'Do you believe,' she says, struggling to gain control of her voice, 'do you believe in your heart that Joseph would have killed your brother?'

Denny looks at her for a long moment. Shadows pass over his face as if he is back there on the yacht. 'Yes,' he says firmly. 'Yes, I believe that Joseph would have killed him.'

Aimee allows these words to settle. Then slowly, she says, 'You were protecting your brother. But you see,' she says, her mouth tightening, 'now you've taken mine.'

Denny swallows hard, his eyes closing.

'For all these months I have not known my own brother was dead – so I travel halfway around the world to find him. To tell him that I would like to begin to try to forgive him. But I am too late. You have taken that chance from me, yes? All of you.'

There are tears in Denny's eyes and he struggles with his voice as he says, 'I'm so sorry. I'm so, so sorry.'

Aimee says nothing; instead, she takes out a cigarette and places it between her lips. She flicks the lighter and draws the flame to the tip of the cigarette, which burns bright. She drops the lighter back into her pocket, glances at the crew a final time, then turns and walks away, a trail of smoke lingering behind her.

40

NOW

The crew have no possessions to take home with them – no backpacks or bags, no clothes except for the ones on their backs, no passports or wallets or cameras – not even a single picture of *The Blue*. Everything they once owned is now at the bottom of the sea rolling beneath the waves.

There are no big goodbyes: Shell disappears with her parents; Heinrich calls home to Germany and his parents arrange a hotel for him for the evening; Kitty waits in Lana's car. The only plan that is made between any of them is that they will stay in New Zealand for Aaron's funeral.

Funeral. The word feels too new, too final. Lana is barely able to comprehend that Aaron is gone. The only thing she knows is that somehow it feels right that *The Blue* has gone, too, as if one couldn't exist without the other. She pictures the great hulk of the yacht resting on the seabed, sea water working through the timber, pulsing through the bunks, filling every crevice and nook. Over the weeks and months and years, she imagines that a carpet of seaweed will begin growing around its anchor chain, fish will make a home of its cabins, rich corals will grow up through the deck – and she likes to imagine that it would please Aaron to know that *The Blue* won't be ending its days on a mooring somewhere, but will become a habitat for sea life.

It is only Lana and Denny who stand together now. The wind is at her back, Denny in front of her. Dark shadows circle his eyes and she sees the strain the day has taken on him.

Lana wonders where Aimee Melina is right now. Is she riding in the back of a taxi, ringing a friend in France, someone with a legal background perhaps, and seeking their advice? Or is she, in fact, sitting in a hotel bar, a glass of wine untouched in front of her, relieved to finally know the truth? Lana can only guess at Aimee's thoughts, or what she'll do, but the one thing Lana knows for certain is that she's pleased that Joseph's memory won't be forgotten.

'Denny,' she says, 'whatever happens next, I'm here for you.'

'Thank you,' he says with meaning.

A few moments later he steps towards Lana, leaving only inches between them. 'I know everything is a mess right now, but I want to tell you something. When you left the yacht in Palau, I came looking for you.' His words take her by surprise. 'I took the dinghy to shore and searched the beach for you, then the main village. I went everywhere I could think of – the taxi station, hotels, restaurants, bars – and asked anyone I came across whether they'd seen you . . . but it was like you'd vanished.'

'I went straight to the airport,' she explains. 'Flew here.'

'Why New Zealand?'

This time she knows the answer. 'I couldn't let it go. None of it. The crew. What happened.' She pauses, looking directly at him. 'You.'

He reaches out and takes Lana's hand. A shock of desire pulses through her: it is still there after all this time. She feels the damp heat of his palm against hers and squeezes his fingers tighter.

'I wish,' he says, his hand wrapped around hers, 'that we could go back to when we first met. Do you remember? When we sat on those rocks on that first day? Or that night-swim when we lay on our backs looking up at the stars.'

'I know,' she says, moving a fraction closer so that their hips are touching. A bolt of heat shoots through her and she closes her eyes, imagining she is on the yacht with the smell of sunshine and coconut oil in the air. She wants to dive backwards, sink deep into those lost moments of swimming together in a moon-struck sea, of drinking cold beers on the deck as the sun went down, of riding together on a moped with their bodies pressed close. 'But so much has happened since then . . .' Lana says. 'It's impossible to go back.'

Denny swallows hard, his expression filling with regret.

'But do you remember what you once told me?' Lana says. 'We'd just started the passage to Palau and were standing together at the bow. I was looking out across the empty horizon, worrying about what'd come next – after *The Blue*. You said to me, "That's the thing, Lana. You don't go back. You go forwards."'

Denny stares at her for a long moment – and then his lips

begin to edge into a smile. He leans in close, his forehead resting lightly against hers, and whispers, 'Forwards, then.'

*

It is late by the time they pull up outside Lana's apartment. Lana slips the key from the ignition, then reaches over and gently squeezes Kitty's arm, rousing her from sleep. 'Here we are, Kit.'

Kitty yawns, rubbing a hand over her eyes as she sits up. She looks at the row of illuminated shopfronts. 'You live above one of these?'

Lana nods. 'That one,' she says, pointing towards a tiny wooden doorway painted duck-egg blue.

'Taronga Gallery and Café,' Kitty reads aloud. Then she turns, facing her. 'You live above a gallery?'

Lana smiles as she says, 'I like to keep a close eye on my artwork.'

Kitty's eyes widen. 'Your artwork is in there?'

'Just a handful. And they're on a tiny wall. Right at the back.'

'Lana, that's incredible!'

She shakes her head, saying, 'Not really. I've been working in the gallery for a few months and I think the owner eventually took pity on me and agreed to put up some of my work.'

'Have you sold any?'

'A few.' She's sold seven sketches and five paintings in the past month, and used the money to buy new paints and canvases, as well as a set of expensive brushes she was hankering after.

'Can we go inside so I can see them?'

'Sure.' They get out of the car and walk towards the gallery. Lana unlocks the door and flicks on the lights, illuminating a small space with a tired wooden floor and crisp white walls. There is a single counter, from where they serve coffees and a range of home-made cakes that the owner, Jacqueline, bakes herself. It's an informal gallery, mostly selling the work of local artists, but it has a loyal clientele and does a good trade.

Kitty wanders slowly around the space until she reaches the back of the gallery where a small rectangular wall is filled with Lana's work.

Kitty stops. Her fingers move to her mouth as she stares at the great expanse of sea, of empty bays guarded by thick forests, of limestone cliffs that fall away into sheer lagoons.

Then her gaze trails to a series of sketches of two girls. She stands completely still, looking at each of them in turn: two girls sitting at the bow of a yacht, tanned legs dangling towards the sea; two girls laughing with their heads bent towards one another; two girls lying in the shade of a palm tree, sand dusting their knees. 'I haven't seen any of these. I didn't know . . .'

'I did them later. Here, in New Zealand.'

Kitty looks at the final painting at the edge of the wall, with a 'Not for sale' sticker pinned to a corner. The image is of a glassy azure sea with a hint of coral visible beneath, and drifting on the surface is a yacht with a dark-blue hull, the silhouettes of seven people lounging on deck.

Kitty shakes her head. 'It's so beautiful.'

Lana feels herself bloom with the compliment. 'Thank you.'

They are both quiet for a moment. Then Kitty turns to Lana, asking, 'Did you miss it?'

'*The Blue?*'

Kitty nods.

Lana thinks for a moment. 'Yes. I did,' she says, understanding what Kitty has lost today. *The Blue* drew them far from the routines and patterns of normal life, gave them a chance to see the world, to be whoever they wished to be within the small stretch of that boat. Aboard *The Blue*, expectations weren't heaped on them, questions of earnings or careers were barely talked about, families didn't have to define them, there was no treadmill. 'The thing is, Kit,' she says, finally understanding, '*The Blue* was never a boat. Not really. *The Blue* is a mindset. A place within yourself.'

Slowly, Kitty smiles. 'I like that.'

When Lana looks down, she notices flecks of something clinging to her bare ankle, just near her tattoo. She leans forward, running a fingertip over her ankle, realizing they are specks of hardened paint. Remembering the dropped paintbrush and the unfinished canvas upstairs, she picks off the paint and holds it up to the light. Blue, the colour of the hull. Her palette is always blue.

Kitty slides her right foot next to Lana's left. When Lana glances at their feet side by side, her eyes widen. She turns to Kitty, a huge smile spreading across her face. On Kitty's ankle is a tattoo of an intricate dark wing. 'You got the tattoo! You had it done!'

Kitty shrugs. 'If I say I'll do something, eight years later, I'll usually do it.'

Lana laughs.

'Although I wouldn't recommend Papua New Guinea as the place to go for tattoos. Had it done in a hut.'

'Did you faint?'

'Twice.'

Lana laughs again. 'I can't believe you did it!' With their ankles touching, their tattoos form a pair of intricate feather wings. 'Why?' Lana asks, her voice quieter now.

Kitty looks at her for a long moment. 'You need two wings to be able to fly.'

Lana slings her arm around Kitty's shoulder and they lean their heads together. Behind them the salt breeze flows in through the open door, carrying the night scents of the ocean.

EPILOGUE

A body floats, unseeing eyes fixed on the brooding sky. A pair of cotton shorts has darkened, pockets gulping with water. A shirt billows, then clings to the unbeating chest. The streak of blood across the right temple has washed away now, leaving the skin clear and greying.

Below, the sea teems with darting fish carving through the water in great shoals, while tiny flecks of nutrient-rich plankton spin in the light. Deeper still, milky-eyed predators patrol the sunless depths where the seabed is scarred with the markings of currents, and broken coral lies as hard as bone.

But above there is only a body.

And a yacht.

Eight hours earlier, in the dark hours of the night, Joseph was hauled from Aaron, the knife flying from his grip. He felt the crack of his head against the cockpit floor, then felt himself rolling, rolling . . . his body slipping beneath the lifeline and dropping into the ocean. The liquid world filled his mouth, his nostrils, stung his open eyes. There was no air, just the cold shock of water enveloping him and the cling of wet clothes against his skin.

He didn't fight. He let himself tumble further and further into the watery depths – until eventually his body slowed. He seemed to hover for a moment, weightless, suspended. And then he began to rise upwards, towards air, towards night.

He surfaced, wild-eyed and blinking as the ocean exploded with light. Tiny flecks of phosphorescence lit up the surface of the water, spinning and dancing around him.

Joseph didn't think about the fresh pain at the side of his head, or the blackness of the night, or the disappearing stern light of the yacht. Here, in the ocean, surrounded by infinitesimal lights, he felt as though he was drifting through the most surreal high.

He almost wanted to laugh, realizing that this was how it was meant to end: the middle of the ocean, a moonless night, no chance of rescue. *The Blue* had only ever been a fantasy – one he'd clung to, hoping it was the answer, believing he could sail away from grief and guilt.

But he couldn't.

When he lit that first match outside his parents' house, it was the end of him. He might have been too high to fully know what he was doing; he might not have known they were inside; he might have regretted it with every fibre of his being – but they were still dead because of *him*.

He thought of his sister coming to see him weeks after the police threw out the case. He'd opened the door to her gaunt, tear-streaked face, and she'd tossed an envelope at his feet. 'Hope you're happy. They kept you in their will after everything you did. A hundred thousand euro, Joseph. That should keep you out of your mind for the rest of your life.'

His eyes had stung with tears as he told her, 'I never wanted their money.'

When his sister walked away, he knew then that he had nobody. He grabbed his backpack and passport and took the first flight that had spare seats. He cashed the inheritance cheque on the way, knowing he wouldn't spend it – ever – but he needed to carry the weight of that €100,000 in his backpack, to remind him of what he'd done.

And then *The Blue* had found him. A fresh start, new friends who didn't know about his past, sights so beautiful that he'd sit alone absorbing them and wondering how his world could have turned so ugly when there was all this beauty.

He wrote to his sister, just once. He told her he was sorry for everything he'd done; he described *The Blue*, explaining it was a new beginning; he asked her to meet him when the boat docked, promising that by then he'd be a changed person.

But tonight he'd destroyed his promise.

He should have been able to control himself, but Aaron kept repeating that word over and over – *murderer, murderer, murderer* – and Joseph could feel the raw, unhealed place inside him stretching tighter and tighter, until eventually something in him snapped.

As he trod water, he watched the ghost-white wake of the yacht fading into the distance. All around him the ocean swam with the electric-blue lights of phosphorescence. It was over.

Up ahead, he became aware of a change in *The Blue*'s bearing. The pale wing of the sail was caught in starlight as the yacht seemed to turn. Joseph blinked rapidly, watching. It took him a moment to understand: they were coming back for him.

They thought he was worth searching for, worth rescuing! Something in his heart lifted.

The yacht glided nearer, phosphorescence stirring and shimmering in the bow wave. From the waterline *The Blue* looked like an otherworldly shadow – a majestic hallucination. His clothes clung to his skin as his arms swirled through the water, and he could feel the warm trickle of blood down his temple.

As the yacht drew closer still, he could see the flowing script of its name on the blue hull; he could see Denny at the helm, beside Aaron who was clutching his shoulder; he could see Kitty standing on the far side of the yacht, Heinrich on the near side – both of them scouring the water with searchlights.

Closer still they sailed.

Close enough so that he imagined he could almost reach out and touch it.

Close enough to have a chance of rescue.

Close enough so that the beam of a searchlight made a smooth golden arc that was nearing him.

As the light tracked back and forth, Joseph was mesmerized by the brilliant blaze. Then, all of a sudden, it was upon him!

Spotlighted, he squinted into the dazzling glow. The light held steady, pinned to Joseph. Against the hard glare of the beam he couldn't clearly see the person's expression, but he knew they were looking directly at him.

But then he felt it – a hesitation.

Denny's voice cut across the water. 'See anything?'

Silence.

A whisper of an image floated across Joseph's mind: the €100,000 stuffed in his backpack, left in the cabin he shared.

Then out of the silence, one simple word from Heinrich. 'Nothing.'

The beam of the searchlight swung away.

Darkness cloaked Joseph.

He stared into the blackness.

He could have shouted – perhaps there'd have been a chance he'd have been heard – but instead he only watched as the yacht sailed on. The searchlights continued to glide over the dark rise of the empty waves, a ghost-white wake trailing behind *The Blue*.

There was only one choice left now.

He drew in a long breath, filling his lungs with air so fresh and pure he could taste the ocean in it. He imagined it was his final dive from the high board: his parents and sister were in the audience, sitting close, and the crew were waiting to whoop and cheer as they had done on that sun-gilded afternoon at the cliff jump.

He focused every ounce of his resolve on making this his most spectacular descent. He closed his eyes to the shimmer of phosphorescence and the fading wake of the yacht – and dived. Deeper and deeper he descended, his body an arrow, his hands clasped to a point. A low heat began to build in his chest as a trail of perfect silver bubbles left his lips.

As the burning in his lungs raged into a fire, he cut through the cool layers of the sea into the endless darkness – twisting, rotating, dancing, soaring . . .

AUTHOR'S NOTE

The locations that the crew visit within the Philippines and Palau are entirely fictional, as is the existence of the Bay of Islands Maritime Centre in New Zealand.

READING GROUP QUESTIONS

What does *The Blue* represent for the different travellers? Is it more than just a yacht?

Discuss Lana and Kitty's relationship. How does the journey challenge their friendship?

The Blue seems to offer a sanctum for the travellers, until their secrets begin to surface. Do you think it's possible to ever truly leave the past behind?

Why do you think Lana and Denny are so drawn to one another?

The crew are faced with a moral dilemma during their passage to Palau: hide Joseph's death and sail on, or tell the truth and possibly lose *The Blue*. What would you do?

Discuss the differences and similarities between brothers Denny and Aaron.

What would you say is the real turning point in the novel? When does paradise become something else altogether?

Discuss Denny's statement on page 156: 'You know . . . maybe having some time away is more about letting go of all the things you're not. Becoming the person you were always meant to be.' Do you agree with him?

What do you think about the epilogue? Does it change how you feel about the rest of the novel?

Discover more page-turning fiction from Lucy Clarke

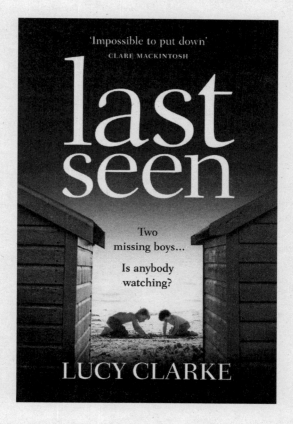

'With twists, turns, secrets and lies aplenty, you'll
have no choice but to devour it in one'
HEAT

Available to buy now

Chilling, gripping, and utterly compulsive,
Lucy Clarke's new novel is unmissable

YOU
LET
ME
IN

Coming September 2018

Inside these pages you will find the tools you need to develop your reflective writing.

I have divided the book into three sections.

○ The first section introduces you to key theories of critically reflective practice, showing how you can use these to gain greater self-awareness and develop your work. Space for writing is provided to help you get started.

○ The second section is designed to support you in writing more freely. Quotations, structured activities and helpful prompts encourage you to write at a deeper level.

○ The final section explores 'where next?' and is designed to help you see what could be on the horizon.

A number of my own students who have studied critically reflective practice have said, 'I knew I would learn a lot on my course, but I didn't realise how much I would learn about myself.'

I hope you will find this journal just as useful.

Signed

Barbara Bassot

Canterbury Christ Church University, UK.

Praise for the first edition:

'This book provides a very useful scaffolding for students to articulate their understanding of reflective writing. The book has transformed the way in which I approach our personal development planning course – indeed, I have revised my marking criteria based on its contents. Barbara Bassot has managed to make sense of a problematic area for students in an accessible, succinct way. Highly recommended.' – **Oliver Sterland, Lecturer in Business & Management, Regent's University London, UK**

'The layout and style of this journal is very appealing to students. It is well thought out and broken into manageable sections for the learner. I am looking forward to using it with my students, and hope that its use will enhance their understanding of critical reflection.' – **Regan Shaw, Lecturer and Programme Director, BA Community Learning & Development, University of Dundee, UK**

'I love this text, and so do my students. It is easy to follow and offers good and practical advice. The students love the way that the key themes are applied to vignettes.' – **Eves Rees, Senior Lecturer, Department of Social Work, Cardiff Metropolitan University, UK**

'This book is very easy on the eye, and subtly inspiring.' – **Marie Ramsden, Practice Lecturer in Social Work, University of Hull, UK**

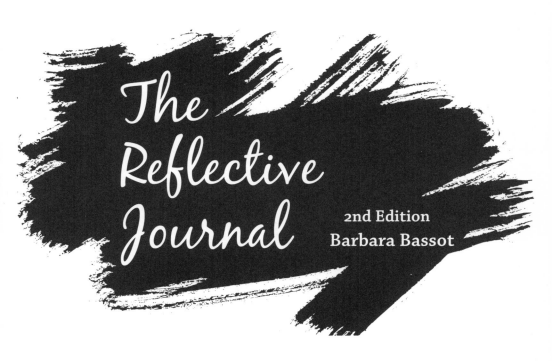

The Reflective Journal

2nd Edition
Barbara Bassot

macmillan
education

palgrave

First edition 2013

Second edition published 2016 by
PALGRAVE

Palgrave in the UK is an imprint of Macmillan Publishers Limited, registered in England, company number 785998, of 4 Crinan Street, London, N1 9XW.

Palgrave Macmillan in the US is a division of St Martin's Press LLC, 175 Fifth Avenue, New York, NY 10010.

Palgrave is a global imprint of the above companies and is represented throughout the world.

Palgrave® and Macmillan® are registered trademarks in the United States, the United Kingdom, Europe and other countries.

ISBN 978–1–137–60348–7 paperback

This book is printed on paper suitable for recycling and made from fully managed and sustained forest sources. Logging, pulping and manufacturing processes are expected to conform to the environmental regulations of the country of origin.

A catalogue record for this book is available from the British Library.

A catalog record for this book is available from the Library of Congress.

Printed in China

Contents

Acknowledgements

The author and publishers would like to thank the following publishers and organisations for permission to reproduce copyright material:

Taylor and Francis for extracts on pages 7, 11 and 53 from Bassot, *The Reflective Practice Guide* (2016: 10, 15, 94). Pearson TalentLens for the extract on page 13 from Honey and Mumford, *The Learning Styles Questionnaire*. Routledge for the extracts on pages 17 and 93 from Moon, J., *Reflection in Learning and Professional Development Theory and Practice* (2000: 187, 191) and pages 81 and 105 from Ghaye, T. and Ghaye, K., *Teaching and Learning through Critical Reflective Practice* (1998: 16, 19). Wiley-Blackwell for the extracts on page 19 from Jasper, M., *Using reflective journals and diaries to enhance practise and learning*, in Bulman, C. and Shutz, S. (eds) *Reflective Practice in Nursing, 4th edition* (2008: 177), page 55 from Atkins and Schutz 'Developing Skills for Reflective Practice' in Bulman, C. and Schutz 'Reflective Practice in Nursing, 5th edition', page 65 from Johns, C., *Guided Reflection: a Narrative Approach to Advancing Professional Practice* (2010: 37), page 132 from Johns, C., *Becoming a Reflective Practitioner, 3rd edition* (2009: preface, xi), page 142 from Johns, C., *Becoming a Critically Reflective Practitioner, 4th edition* (2013: 69) and page 145 from Bulman, C., *Reflective Practice in Nursing* (2013: 9). Wiley for extracts on page 30 from Johns, C., The value of reflective practice in nursing, *Journal of Clinical Nursing* (1995: 23–24), and on page 41 from Schön, D.A., *Educating the Reflective Practitioner* (1987: 26). RoutledgeFalmer for the extracts on pages 43, 69 and 127 from Boud, D., Keogh, R. and Walker, D., *Reflection: Turning Experience into Learning* (1985: 19, 28, 26). Palgrave for the extracts on pages 87, 129 and 140 from Thompson and Thompson, *The Critically Reflective Practitioner* (2008: 27, 42), and on pages 120 and 136 from Rolfe, G., Jasper, M. and Freshwater, D., *Critical Reflection in Practice: Generating Knowledge for Care, 2nd edition* (2011: 7, 209). Prometheus Books for the extract on page 111 from Dewey, J., *How We Think* (1991: 13). Wiley: Jossey-Bass for the extracts on pages 76 and 134 from Brookfield, S. D., *Becoming a Critically Reflective Teacher* (1995: 2, xii). SAGE for the extract on page 32 from Thompson, N., 'Reflective Practice' in R. Harrison and C. Wise (eds), *Working with Young People* (2005: 96), and page 99 from Campbell, A. and Norton, L., *Learning Teaching and Assessing in Higher Education*, (2007: 141). Wiley for Figure 1, Kolb's Experiential Learning Cycle, on page 31. Oxford Centre for Staff Learning and Development, Oxford Brookes University (OCSLD) for Figure 2, Gibbs' Reflective Cycle on page 66, found here: https://www.brookes.ac.uk/students/upgrade/study-skills/reflective-writing-gibbs/. Ed Muzio at Group Harmonics for Figure 4, Argyris' Ladder of Inference, on page 78, from The Ladder of Inference Creates Bad Judgment (2011), found here: www.groupharmonics.com/HelpDesk/Ladder.htm. The Career Development Institute (CDI) for Figure 7, The Career Learning and Development Bridge, on page 153, from Bassot, B., 'Career learning and development: a bridge to the future' in Reid, H., *Constructing the Future: Career Guidance for Changing Contexts* (2009: 4).

Introduction

Welcome to *The Reflective Journal*. Whether you are a student on a professional course in a university or college, someone undertaking a work-based qualification or a professional practitioner who wants to continue to develop their knowledge and skills, *The Reflective Journal* is designed to help you to reflect on your practice and thereby enhance your personal and professional development.

The aims of *The Reflective Journal* are fourfold. First, it takes you on a journey from reflective practice to critically reflective practice. Reflective practice encourages us to review our learning experiences, whilst critically reflective practice means that we begin to engage with our emotional responses and to challenge some of the assumptions we might be making about people and situations. It also asks us to consider issues of power, for example in relationships and organisations.

Second, *The Reflective Journal* introduces you to a broad range of theoretical models of reflection. These models are often abstract and thereby difficult to apply in practice. Some would even argue that knowledge of such theory does not help you reflect. However, Thompson (1995: 29) rightly cautions us against 'the fallacy of theoryless practice' and the practice of reflection is no exception to this. Having an understanding of these theoretical models will help you to reflect at a deeper level by highlighting things that might not be obvious on the surface. This journal serves as a tool to help you build a deeper knowledge of reflective practice by applying theories of reflection to your ongoing learning and development.

Third, the journal enables you to record your learning and development, so that you can return to it in the future. Many of us think that we will remember things that happen in our lives, particularly things that we feel are significant at the time. But in reality, especially when our day-to-day lives are so busy, we can forget even those things that we were convinced at the time we would remember.

The fourth aim of *The Reflective Journal* is to enable you to gain a deeper understanding of yourself and your practice through writing. At a writers' seminar I once attended, the leader of the session said, 'I have to write about things in order to understand them.' At the time, this was something of a revelation to me, as I always thought that people (like him) who wrote a lot did so because they already understood a lot. The process of writing forces us to slow down and to take time to reflect, which allows our knowledge and understandings to grow. Unlike many of the books you will read, this is one that you will be able to write in – and I encourage you to do so!

No doubt you are currently entering a time when you will gain lots of useful knowledge and skills in relation to your professional development. Through this learning process you will also find that some of your attitudes and the way you think about things will be challenged.

'I always knew I would learn a lot, but I never realised how much I would learn about myself.'

Many professional practitioners are aware of the value of reflection in their day-to-day work and most professional courses include modules on reflective practice and professional development. Students on professional courses are often asked to keep a reflective diary or journal, and *The Reflective Journal* will help you as you study these particular modules and also on your course as a whole.

How to use this journal

The Reflective Journal is designed as a tool to help you reflect, thereby enabling you to take a deep approach to your learning and development. When asked to keep a reflective diary or journal by their tutors, many do not find this easy. *The Reflective Journal* shows you how to start writing reflectively and how to develop your writing to enable critical reflection.

Part 1 is broken down into ten themes. Each theme starts with a brief introduction and is followed by five pieces of content based on the theme, where some key theories are introduced in an accessible way. These are followed by a number of blank spaces for your written reflections, including some practical activities to help you to apply theory to your practice. The quotes provided are included for close reading – by examining each word and phrase in detail you can gain a deeper understanding of yourself and your practice.

The theory discussed in *The Reflective Journal* is drawn from a range of academic disciplines, such as health and social care, education, counselling, business and management. Throughout, the word client is often used to refer to the people who you will engage with in your capacity as a professional. If this is not an appropriate term for your particular context, please use an alternative, such as patient or student. You will also find a number of quotes from students interspersed amongst the text. These serve as examples of reflective writing and could act as a source of inspiration.

Part 2 contains further activities and quotes, along with more blank pages for reflective writing. These serve as further prompts for thinking critically about your practice.

Part 3 focuses on CV building and career development. This section contains activities to help you think about your experience more broadly, particularly in relation to how your professional knowledge and skills are developing. It can also serve as a helpful record for the future.

The Reflective Journal introduces you to a wide range of relevant theory. In this particular respect, it should be seen only as a good starting point; it is very likely that you will want to read more and you should always use the reading lists provided by your tutors. At the back of the journal there is a full list of references in the Harvard style and an index of some of the key terms used.

Most people who are new to reflective writing need to know where and how to start. Perhaps most importantly, they need to be assured that their writing is reflective and not merely descriptive. A good place to start is by reading the journal's list of contents and then completing the first two themes. This should help you to begin to start writing reflectively. The journal is written to enable you to think at an increasingly deeper level as you work your way through it. However, you should not feel that you have to follow the order of the themes rigidly, particularly if certain topics and theories are being covered in your lectures or seminars. You should feel free to use it as best suits you. It is important to be aware that there is a danger in using the journal mechanically, for example by writing a specific amount each week or feeling that you cannot look ahead. This could mean that writing becomes a chore that you gain little from. As time progresses you may find that you would like more space to write, in which case do feel free to write in a notebook as well as in the journal.

Many people find that the time they spend writing reflectively is time well invested. Since the publication of the first edition, *The Reflective Journal* has helped many students and professional practitioners to reflect at a deeper level. I hope that you find it helpful in your learning and professional development.

I would like to express my sincere thanks to my family and friends for their tireless support in the process of bringing *The Reflective Journal* to fruition. In particular, I would like to thank Phil Bassot for his careful work on the diagrams, Marc Bassot for his excellent proof reading and constructive comments and Morag Greenwood for her impeccable work in obtaining the relevant permissions. My grateful thanks also go to all the students who gave me permission to include their quotes, which have inspired me and I am sure will inspire others. Finally, I would like to thank my commissioning editor, Peter Hooper, and the publisher for continuing to believe in a new kind of publication.

Barbara Bassot

Part 1

Models and tools for reflection

Theme 1

Beginnings

This section will:

- ○ Help you begin to understand the process of transition and what often happens when you start something new
- ○ Introduce you to the concept of the 'metaphorical mirror'
- ○ Discuss issues of motivation, including the importance of having a personal vision
- ○ Emphasise the importance of time management
- ○ Help you begin to examine your learning styles

Theme 1.1 Starting something new

When we start anything new, such as a new course or job, there are almost always challenges along the way. Change can be both exciting and daunting at the same time, even when the change is something you have been looking forward to. You are probably starting something new at the moment and so have begun a process of transition.

Various words come to mind to describe a transition and some of them are as follows:

- ○ Exciting
- ○ New
- ○ Different

- ○ Scary
- ○ Taxing
- ○ Emotional

You may be able to think of others. During this process of transition you may feel or experience some, or even all, of these.

A useful model of transition is one put forward by Bridges (2004). Bridges argues that all transitions start with endings and finish with new beginnings; it has three stages. Stage one, 'endings', asserts that we all experience loss at the beginning of the transition process as we let go of what is behind us. Even if we dislike our current situation and are moving onto something new and different we experience loss, as most of us prefer what we know (even when we dislike it) to the unknown. This is followed by stage two, 'the neutral zone'; this is generally an uncomfortable place where we can feel anxious and uncertain about what lies ahead. It could be described as a state of 'limbo'. But Bridges argues that we need to spend time here so that we can discover what we should do next. The final stage is 'new beginnings', as we move forward into the next phase of our lives. It is particularly interesting to note that all three stages overlap; so we can still be experiencing loss, whilst feeling uncertain about the future after we have begun something new.

Describe your recent experiences of transition. Have you experienced any of Bridges' (2004) stages? If so, which ones stand out in your memory? Are there any that do not seem appropriate to your situation? There is a space below for you to use, if you want to.

Theme 1.2 The 'metaphorical mirror'

When looking in a concise dictionary for the word 'reflection', you will find at least two different definitions – a mirror image and thinking. Over time you will develop, through a process of thinking and looking at your practice in a 'metaphorical mirror'. This will heighten your levels of critical evaluation and self-awareness, as you examine your knowledge, skills and attitudes. Many of us look into different types of mirror each day – here are some examples that give us insights into reflective practice:

> *'Reflection enables me to process my thoughts and make sense of them.'*

○ **The bathroom mirror** – most of us will get up in the morning and look in the bathroom mirror. We then make a choice; we can decide to leave things as they are or take some action to make ourselves more presentable to the outside world! Examining our practice means that we are not always happy with what we find. However, taking action or not always involves choice.

○ **The rear view mirror** – this is a vital tool that people use every time they get into the driver's seat. By using it we can see what is behind us and assess whether or not it is safe to move ahead. Reflective practice means looking back on experiences we have had, so that we know how to move forward.

○ **Wing mirrors** – these also help us to see what is behind us when driving. Most wing mirrors are convex, which helps us to see what is just over our shoulder, or in a blind spot. Feedback from others plays a vital part in helping us to identify what might be a blind spot in our practice.

○ **The magnifying mirror** – this is indispensable in situations where we need to look at our faces closely, for example when shaving or applying make-up. The close examination of an incident can mean that we avoid mistakes in the future.

○ **The funfair mirrors** – clearly, we do not look in these regularly, and these mirrors distort what we see. Some practitioners always feel that what they did was fine because they did their best, whilst others tend to be very hard on themselves and always find fault with what they did. In both cases it is likely that there is some kind of distortion. This points to the vital role of feedback from, and discussion with, others; this helps to get a more accurate picture of our practice (see Theme 5).

○ **Shop windows** – whilst these are not mirrors per se, we can see our reflection as we walk past. This reminds us of the capacity that we all have as human beings to think about things as we are doing something else. Schön (1983) calls this 'reflection-in-action'.

'learning and reflection go "hand in hand" and it is difficult to imagine one without the other.'

(Bassot, 2016: 15)

Theme **1.3** **Motivation**

When starting something new, particularly if it involves a large commitment of time, it is important to think about what motivates us and what we want to achieve. In his work *The 7 Habits of Highly Effective People*, Covey (2004: 95) urges us to 'begin with the end in mind' (Habit 2). He argues that everything is created twice – first in our minds and then in the practice of our everyday lives. He emphasises the importance of having a personal vision for the future and that focusing on the end result or outcome is one way of helping us to begin to see this more clearly. Interestingly, he also argues that if we do not have our own vision, we could live lives where the vision and priorities of others become more important than our own.

It is worth spending some time thinking about what you hope to achieve in the coming months. If you have recently embarked on a course of study, what are you hoping to gain from it? Think about the following questions:

○ What are your long-term goals? Whether you have a specific career goal or not, imagine you are talking to a friend five years from now; how would you like to describe what you are doing?

○ What made you choose what you are doing at the moment? What do you hope to gain from it?

○ Where does your sense of achievement lie? What are you looking forward to most?

○ What are the key areas where you feel you need to develop? What could hinder your development?

○ How could you overcome the barriers to your development?

Whatever your responses to these questions, having a clear vision can play a vital part in maintaining your motivation and commitment to your personal and professional development.

Try this

Write some notes for each of the questions on the previous page. Which areas in particular do you need to work on to ensure your success?

Theme 1.4 Time management

Being well organised is vital for success in many areas of our lives, and good time management is an important skill that everyone needs for study and professional effectiveness; many people find they need to continually work at it. Go into any bookshop or library, or browse on the internet, and you will find numerous books on time management because there is not a single way of managing time that works for everyone. If you find an approach that helps you, use it, but don't become a slave to it, as it might not work for you forever.

There are several common themes in time management literature; here are some of them:

○ Understand what you want to achieve – this usually involves setting some long-term goals.

○ Think about how you are going to get there – this then means setting some medium- and short-term goals to help you to make progress.

○ Setting priorities – in our busy lives it is important to be clear about what needs to be done and when, so we need to prioritise what we do first and so on.

○ Working through procrastination – this is often called the thief of time. Particularly when we dislike things or find things difficult, we tend to put them off. This means that the time we had disappears, or is stolen from us.

○ Dealing with interruptions – there are many things that can easily distract us and cause us to waste a lot of time.

○ Understanding the difference between the important and the urgent – things that are urgent demand our immediate attention and at least give us the impression that they need to be done now. Things that are important help us to achieve our long-term goals. We need to beware of spending too much time on urgent things to the detriment of things that are important. The result can be that we fail to achieve our long-term goals.

Think about how you manage your time at the moment. Which areas do you feel you need to work on?

'Time management is rather like fishing by hand – one day I think I've got it and the next it slips away from me!'

(Bassot 2016: 10)

Theme 1.5 Learning styles

In order to be able to use the 'metaphorical mirror' effectively and to examine your practice in a thorough and thoughtful way, a high level of self-awareness is essential, and you can achieve this in part through self-evaluation. A vital aspect of this process is to understand more about your learning styles – this will help you to gain more from your course and to understand both your strengths and potential areas for development.

Honey and Mumford (2000) have carried out extensive work on the subject of learning styles and have identified the following four distinct styles:

> 'In order to ensure my journey is a successful one, I believe that it is essential to have a good balance of all four learning styles.'

○ Activists are doers and like to be involved in new experiences. They are open minded and enthusiastic about new ideas. They enjoy getting on with things and can achieve a lot in a short space of time.

○ Reflectors are thinkers who like to stand back and look at a situation from different perspectives. They enjoy collecting data and thinking about things carefully before coming to any conclusions. They often observe others and listen to their views before offering their own.

○ Theorists are analytical people who integrate their observations into sound theories. They think problems through in a step-by-step way. They can be perfectionists who like to fit things into a rational scheme or model. They have an ability to see things in a detached and objective way.

○ Pragmatists are practical people who are keen to try out new ideas. They prefer concepts that can be applied easily in practice. They enjoy problem solving and decision making.

Most of us have a preference for more than one style. Strengths in all styles denote a strong, all-round learner – so in order to gain most from your studies it is important to know your least preferred styles, as this will give you clear areas to work on as you progress.

'Learning style preferences determine the things people learn and the ease with which they learn them. They exert a hidden, but powerful, influence on learning effectiveness.'

(Honey and Mumford, undated)

Try this   Think about your learning styles (Honey and Mumford, 2000). Which are your preferred styles? Which ones do you feel you need to develop?

Theme 2

Starting to write reflectively

This section will:

- ○ Help you begin to understand what reflective writing is
- ○ Enable you to understand the role of writing in reflection
- ○ Show you how writing sharpens your focus
- ○ Help you to start to write reflectively
- ○ Give you a structure for reflective writing

Theme **2.1** What does it mean to write reflectively?

In order to begin writing reflectively, you need to understand what reflective writing is, and equally what it is not. Here are some characteristics of reflective writing.

Reflective writing is:

- Always written in the first person (I ...) with a focus on yourself
- Generally more personal than other forms of academic writing
- Helpful when you are asked to evaluate your experiences
- Focused on your experiences, thoughts, feelings and assumptions
- A form of self-supervision
- Honest and spontaneous
- Subjective
- A record of your thoughts and experiences that you can return to
- An investment of time.

Reflective writing is not:

- Simply a description of what happened
- Written in the third person with a focus on others
- Calculated
- Objective
- Something that can be rushed
- Simply about planning what you will do next time.

Reflective writing helps us to link our ideas together and discover meanings from the things we see and experience. Our understandings become broader and deeper as we question our approaches to people and circumstances. Like any other skill, reflective writing is one that will improve with practice. Indeed, reflection itself is a skill which also improves over time. As you progress, you will find that your learning will become deeper as a result of your investment of time in writing reflectively.

'writing also provides a means by which learning can be upgraded – where unconnected areas of meaning cohere and a deeper meaning emerges.'

Moon (2000: 187)

Theme 2.2 — The role of writing in reflection

When starting the process of reflective writing, it is important to understand how writing in this way can make a difference to your learning and development. Sometimes I hear people say 'but I reflect all the time, for example in the car on my way home.' This kind of everyday thinking is very different from thinking deeply about something as you write about it. Many tutors working with students on professional courses recommend keeping a reflective journal or diary as a tool for personal and professional development.

'Writing seems to unload my mind, clear it of all those thoughts that seem to whirl around with no escape.'

Brockbank and McGill (2006: 282–3) discuss the following benefits of keeping a reflective journal and describe it as 'a map of your learning journey':

- ○ It is always available to you – it is never too busy
- ○ It never answers back – it is always open to listen
- ○ It maintains privacy and confidentiality
- ○ It opens up a continuous relationship with the self
- ○ It accepts everything and everyone unconditionally
- ○ It does not get tired of hearing the same thing over and over again – for example 'I still find this difficult because ...'
- ○ It is written in the moment and is a true reflection of how you thought and felt at the time
- ○ It gives you a chance to communicate with yourself
- ○ It brings greater clarity through the process of writing
- ○ It never disagrees with you
- ○ It provides a record of learning and development.

You may be someone who loves journal writing and may have kept a personal journal for some time. On the other hand, you may be new to the whole idea.

No one is suggesting that writing is the only way to reflect; in fact, people often find reflecting together in pairs or groups to be very helpful too (see Theme 9). However, writing has its own unique advantages.

'As a private document, a journal can include whatever you want it to. There are no rules about personal reflective writing – the important thing is to use it to achieve the purpose you are using it for, and to write in it in a way you want to write in it.'

(Jasper, 2008: 177)

Theme 2.3 It's all about the RAS

So why is writing thought to be important in the area of reflection? There is no doubt that writing is a skilful activity; most young children learn to read more quickly than they learn to write. In general terms, writing is a much more difficult skill to master; hence many students say that the most difficult things on their course are the written assignments. It is important to understand that writing often leads to a significantly deeper level of reflection than thinking alone, as it slows our thought processes down. It is impossible to write about something without thinking about what you are writing at the same time.

The act of writing is not necessarily difficult in itself; for example, writing something that you know already, such as a nursery rhyme that you can recite off by heart, is easy. But other types of writing are much more challenging, as the very process of writing helps us to understand things. This is important in relation to reflective writing – if we want to understand more about ourselves and our practice, we need to write about it. Writing involves thinking about what you are writing as you are writing it, making decisions about what to write, how to express it and processing your thoughts. Sometimes it might mean explaining your approach so that, if appropriate, someone else can read it and understand what you have written. Put simply, the act of writing helps us to develop our understanding.

Research in neuroscience shows that writing stimulates the reticular activating system (RAS) at the base of the brain. The RAS functions as a filter for information that our brain needs to process, and makes sure that we give more attention to what we are actively focusing on at that moment. The act of writing, therefore, sharpens our focus and will usually be a more effective way of learning something than, for example, discussion or reading. You will be much more likely to remember something you have written down than something you have read or discussed. And, of course, you then have a record that you can go back to.

Theme 2.4 Reflective writing – how do I start?

When you have not done it before, writing a reflective journal for the first time can be difficult and many people do not know where to start. Often they ask questions such as:

○ What am I meant to write?

○ Where do I start?

○ What if I get it all wrong?

○ What if I write things that make no sense?

These are natural questions to ask, and you can gain some confidence and re-assurance from Bolton's (2010: 107–18) practical advice on starting to write as part of your professional development. In her work she describes five stages of reflective writing – she calls Stage 1 'the six minute write'. Here she gives the following pointers:

○ Write whatever is in your head

○ Time yourself and write for six minutes without stopping

○ Don't stop to examine your writing or to be critical of it; just keep writing even if it doesn't seem to make sense

'I have decided to maintain this journal whether it is a masterpiece or not.'

○ Let your writing flow; don't worry about spelling, punctuation, grammar and so on

○ Give yourself permission to write anything

○ Remember, whatever you write cannot be wrong – it's yours and no-one else needs to read it.

Bolton suggests other forms of writing in the subsequent four stages. Stage 2 involves thinking of an experience you have had and writing about it as if you are telling a story. In Stage 3, you can then read the story (and the six minutes of writing) and respond to it. In Stage 4, she suggests sharing what you have written with someone else – this needs to be someone you know well and trust (see Theme 5.2 on critical friendship). In Stage 5, she suggests you could begin to develop your work by writing from someone else's perspective – for example, from the client's point of view.

Try this   Now try doing one of Bolton's (2010) 'six minute writes'. Be sure to time yourself and to write freely. What are your reactions to this? For example, was it easier than you thought? More difficult than you thought? Too short a time or too long? And so on. Now check your writing against the two lists of points made in Theme 2.1. Does your writing fulfil the criteria for being described as reflective?

Theme 2.5 A structure for reflective writing

People who are new to reflective writing often find it helpful to have a structure for their writing. This can help them to make a start and will often then be discarded as writing reflectively becomes easier. Knott and Scragg (2013) offer a useful structure for writing a reflective journal, which can be helpful for people who are faced with the question, 'So what do I need to write?' Their structure is based on three stages, each with accompanying questions for clarity, which should encourage a deeper reflective approach.

Stage 1 – **Reflection**

Here the authors suggest that you focus on an issue or a concern that you have in relation to your practice. Like Bolton (2010), they advise that this is done freely and spontaneously in order to capture your thoughts.

Stage 2 – **Analysis**

This is the most complex of the stages and involves responding to the following key questions:
- What is happening here?
- What assumptions am I making?
- What does this show about my underlying beliefs about myself and my practice? What are some of the alternative ways of looking at this (for example, from someone else's perspective)? This particular aspect is similar to Bolton's (2010) Stage 5.

Stage 3 – **Action**

As this suggests, the focus here is on the action you take following the analysis. Again the authors suggest considering some key questions:
- What action can I take?
- How can I learn from what has happened?
- How would I respond if this situation occurred again?
- What does this experience tell me about my beliefs about myself and my practice?

Try this   Now try using Knott and Scragg's (2013) structure for reflective writing. Focus on a concern you have at the moment in relation to your learning and development. Write something in response to each of the prompt questions. Once you have done this, again think about your response to this exercise (see the questions in the previous activity). Which of the two methods do you prefer? What are the reasons for your preferences?

Try this　　Now look back to Theme 2.4 and try moving on to Stage 2 (Bolton, 2010) by writing a story of a recent experience you have had. If this does not come easily to you, imagine you are talking to a friend at the end of a busy day and what you would say. When you finish writing, think about what you feel you learned from this.

Theme 3

Learning from experience

This section will:

- ○ Help you begin to understand how we learn from experience
- ○ Introduce you to a number of theoretical models of experiential learning
- ○ Encourage you to focus on positive experiences as well as problematic ones
- ○ Help you to recognise that as well as making progress we can also regress

Theme 3.1 ERA model

When you are new to reflective practice, a simple, straightforward model can be a useful way of helping you to get started; the ERA model (Jasper, 2003) is one of these. ERA stands for Experience ▶ Reflection ▶ Action and is an easy model to remember when you are in the early stages of your studies. Often it is depicted as a triangle with one of the letters at each point on the triangle with arrows from E to R to A. The components of ERA can be explained as follows:

○ Experience – this can be anything that has happened recently that you feel has some significance. It could also be something from the past that has come to your attention more recently.

○ Reflection – this takes place afterwards and the reflective processes are how we learn from the experience. Reflection can also involve thinking about how we might respond in the future, and as we progress, it can also happen during an experience.

○ Action – this follows the learning and is concerned with the action we then take following the experience, as our new perspectives then feed into the next experience.

The ERA model can be summarised as follows. We have experiences that have some kind of significance and we learn from them by thinking about them. This builds our knowledge and understanding and we take action. As our perspectives change, our practice moves forward and we take all of this into the next experience.

Theme 3.2 Driscoll's 'What?' model

Like the ERA model, Driscoll's (2007) 'What?' model is also a useful starting point. It has the following three steps:

○ **What?** – Step 1 encourages you to write a description of an event that has happened in your professional practice.

○ **So what?** – Step 2 involves carrying out an analysis of the event by reflecting on selected aspects of it.

○ **Now what?** – Step 3 asks you to devise a number of proposed actions following the experience and in the light of what you have learned.

Driscoll's model, which reflects the work of Borton (1970), is drawn as a circle with arrows pointing clockwise, showing how the three stages follow on from one another. However, a number of arrows can be drawn following Stage 3 to illustrate a variety of actions that could be taken following an experience.

Driscoll has also formulated a number of useful trigger questions to help you to use the model effectively, including:

○ **Step 1** – What was my reaction to the experience and what did others do who were involved?

○ **Step 2** – Do I feel troubled? If so, in what way?

○ **Step 3** – How can I modify my practice if I face a similar situation again and what are the main learning points that I can take from this?

Many people who are completely new to reflective practice find the ERA and Driscoll's models very useful starting points for their early reflections. They are simple and easy to remember. However, after a time you may find that you need to reflect at a deeper level in relation to your developing practice. So do not be afraid to use these models in the early days and then to move on to others. This will mean that your skills of reflection develop alongside the other key skills that you use in professional practice.

'Reflective practice can be interpreted as being the practitioner's ability to access, make sense of and learn through work experience to achieve more desirable, effective and satisfying work.'

(Johns, 1995: 23–4)

Theme 3.3 Kolb's Experiential Learning Cycle

Many writers on the subject of reflective practice use cycles to describe how we learn from experience. These cycles enable us to understand the process as well as develop the ability to improve our learning and professional practice over time.

Kolb's (1984) Experiential Learning Cycle gives insights into how we all learn from experience. There are four stages in the cycle, which are depicted as following on from each other, as shown by the arrows in the diagram below.

Kolb argues that this cycle often (but not always) starts with a concrete experience that is reviewed through reflective observation. This is followed by abstract conceptualisation, where new thoughts and ideas emerge, which are then tried out in active experimentation, ready for the next relevant experience. All of this may happen in a matter of moments, or over days, weeks

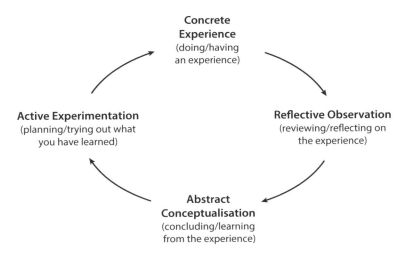

Figure 1 Kolb's Experiential Learning Cycle
© 1975, by John Wiley & Sons, Ltd.

or months, depending on the experience. However, if you have particular learning preferences linked to your learning styles (see Theme 3.1) you may start the cycle at a different point. So, someone with a strong Reflector style will often spend time thinking before they act and start an experience. Theorists will often look for a model they can apply to an experience before embarking on it, and Pragmatists usually like to plan before an experience whenever they can. Activists by contrast will often start at the top of the cycle.

Kolb argues that in order to learn the most from experience, we need to complete all four phases of the cycle, although it is important to understand that this will not necessarily always happen. For example, if we have a strong preference for a particular learning style, we can be tempted to skip points on the cycle. So, if something does not go well, a strong Activist may be tempted just to try again without spending time reflecting. A strong Reflector might spend too much time thinking about what happened, without learning from it and preparing for the next experience. A Theorist might be keen to try their favourite model again, convinced that it should work, and a Pragmatist could be tempted to be dismissive of something that they perceive does not work well in practice first time around.

It is also important to remember that any model that argues that things always happen in a particular order leaves itself open to critique – does it always happen like that? The answer is, probably not.

'Reflective practice is an active process of constructing solutions, rather than a passive process of following procedures or guidelines.'

(Thompson, 2005: 196)

Theme 3.4 Progression and regression

It is easy to fall into the trap of assuming that we always learn from experience when, of course, this is simply not the case. We can probably all think of circumstances where we have not necessarily learned from experience; this might have resulted in failing to make progress, or even a sense of going backwards in our development. Illeris (2014) argues that this can happen in the following two ways:

○ Where we feel we are expected to learn too quickly or too much, or both. Here we feel that the demands made on us are too heavy and, as a result, we find it too difficult to let go of how we see things at the moment. We experience lots of uncertainty and doubt about our capabilities and might feel unable to cope with what is being asked of us.

○ Where we feel that we need to change, but prefer the safety of what we know already. Change always involves risk; at times the risk might simply be too high and we prefer to stay as we are.

In such circumstances our response might be to continue with our current ways of thinking and working, in order to avoid change, or in some situations we might regress into a former position as this feels more comfortable. However, where change is unavoidable, the only possibility might be withdrawal from the situation. If you find yourself in this position (for example, a work placement where you feel the demands being made are too high, or you are being asked to do things differently from the way you are being taught) the best course of action is always to seek support from your tutors before making any decision to withdraw.

Try this   Think of a situation that you have encountered recently where you struggled to engage with learning from experience. Describe the situation and evaluate it, to find out why you did not learn from this experience. Does any of this resonate with Illeris' (2014) reasons? Are there any other reasons you can add which are particular to your situation?

Problematic experiences or positive ones?

When it comes to discussing the kinds of experiences we learn the most from, authors differ in their approach. Here are two contrasting views as examples.

Osterman and Kottkamp's (2004) position is that we learn most from problematic experiences, and they argue that we need to focus on the kinds of situations that we encounter that cause us difficulties. As a result, the first step in their cycle (again based on the work of Kolb) requires us to identify a problem. This could be some form of discrepancy or gap between what happened and what we might have hoped for or expected. The second stage of 'observation and analysis' is the most important stage and the most complex, enabling us to gain a deeper understanding of the experience. This then leads on to the third stage of 'abstract reconceptualisation', where we search for new ideas and strategies, which are then experimented upon in the final stage of 'active experimentation'.

By contrast, Ghaye (2011: 9) cautions against only focusing on problems using what he calls 'deficit-based' models of reflection and urges us to concentrate on positive experiences in order to avoid 'spirals of deficit-based actions'. Based on foundations of positive psychology, his strengths-based model offers an approach that encourages us to build on the positives by asking the following four questions:

'I now feel that reflecting enables me to face a problem.'

1   What is successful right now? (Appreciate)
2   What do we need to change to make things better? (Imagine)
3   How can we achieve this? (Design)
4   Who needs to take action and what will the consequences be? (Act)

Whether we focus on problematic experiences or positive ones, reflecting on them will provide us with opportunities for growth and development. It is easy to see that focusing on one to the neglect of the other could mean that we become too negative or positive in our outlook. This could then be an argument for maintaining a balance between the two contrasting approaches.

Try this   Choose one of the learning cycles discussed in this section. Now try applying it to an incident that has happened recently as part of your work or training. How useful was the model? How would you describe its strengths and weaknesses as a means of beginning to evaluate your professional practice?

Theme 4

The practice of reflection

This section will:

○ Help you begin to think about what it means to be a
professional

○ Introduce you to the key concepts of reflection – on and
in-action

○ Introduce you to the concept of critical incident analysis

○ Help you begin to distinguish between espoused theories and
theories in use

○ Introduce you to the concept of professionalism as artistry

---

The word 'professional' is one that we hear being used frequently, but what does it actually mean? Sometimes we hear people say, 'Well, that wasn't very professional, was it?' You may be on a course of professional training or be engaged in continuing professional development; either way it is worth spending some time considering what being a professional means.

Here are some thoughts. Being a professional means that:

○ You have a body of knowledge in relation to your particular profession

○ You work in a relatively autonomous way, without needing close supervision of every aspect of your work

○ You are expected to show some initiative in your work

○ You understand the boundaries of your role and have a clear grasp of when you need to refer to someone else

○ You have the relevant skills to carry out your role well

○ Your attitudes are in keeping with the profession that you belong to (for example, a caring, supportive or positive attitude, or indeed all of these)

○ You adhere to the code of practice or ethics relevant for your profession

○ Your work is not straightforward and will involve making professional judgements when you encounter situations where there are no clear right or wrong answers

○ You aim to improve your practice all the time, reflecting on what you are doing and engaging in continuing professional development

○ You aim to keep up to date with new knowledge and skills in relation to your practice.

'I cannot allow my relationships with clients to become personal and must be more professional in my dealings with them. I must not allow my judgement to be clouded; I have to work on this if I am going to be truly effective in my role.'

In his seminal work *The Reflective Practitioner*, Schön (1983) discusses Glazer's concept of major professions (medicine and law), near major professions (business and engineering) and minor professions (including social work and education). Major professions have traditionally relied on the application of science, based on the use of logic, or what Schön refers to as technical rationality. By contrast, Schön argues that those in the minor professions occupy the 'swampy lowlands', where practice is messy and often confusing, as there will not always be a logical solution. Whatever kind of profession you are involved in, even a relatively scientific one, when working with people your work will not always be predictable. Coping with this is a central aspect of what being a professional involves.

Reflection-on-action and reflection-in-action

Schön's (1983) work is seminal in relation to reflective practice, and in his text, *The Reflective Practitioner*, he describes two important types of reflection: reflection-on-action and reflection-in-action. Both are important for people working in the minor professions, where typically there is no single correct response to a situation and no 'one size fits all' model that can be learned and applied in all situations and circumstances.

Reflection-on-action involves looking back on an experience and helps you to:

○ analyse what happened
○ think through the event from a number of perspectives (for example, your own and the client's)
○ identify the things that went well
○ identify problems and work towards solutions where possible
○ identify areas for development
○ build your professional knowledge
○ think about what you would do next time in a similar situation.

Another important aspect of reflection-on-action is that it can prevent your practice from routine stagnation, by encouraging you to turn off your 'automatic pilot'. This is not meant to imply that you will need, or indeed be able, to spend time reflecting on everything that happens. However, it is well worth thinking about when and how you will make time to include this in your professional life, in order to keep your practice (and your working life generally) vibrant.

The second type of reflection that Schön (1983) discusses is reflection-in-action. All of us spend time thinking – it is so much part of our everyday lives that sometimes we do not even realise we are doing it. Reflection-in-action is the kind of thinking we all do as we are working, studying and living generally; as human beings we have a capacity to think whilst doing other things. When writing about reflection-in-action, Schön describes it as 'thinking on your feet'.

When working with people, it will often be necessary to try a number of different strategies to enable them to engage with you as you work with them. By reflecting-in-action, you will be able to assess the strategies you are using as you go along, deciding whether or not your approach is working with that particular individual or group. If not, you will need to change your approach to try to find something that will work.

Schön, of course, is not without his critics. Whether or not it is possible to distinguish clearly between reflection-on and reflection-in-action is debatable. Indeed, in his own writing Schön himself is not absolutely clear on this distinction. However, as concepts they are often useful in helping us to analyse practice at a deeper level.

'Reflection-in-action is where we may reflect in the midst of action without interrupting it. Our thinking serves to reshape what we are doing while we are doing it.'

(Schön, 1987: 26)

Theme 4.3 Critical incident analysis

When reflecting-on-action, it is often helpful to focus on a particular experience or event and to examine it carefully. This is often referred to as critical incident analysis. A critical incident is often something which we interpret as a problem or a challenge in a particular context, rather than just a routine occurrence (see Osterman and Kottkamp, 2004 and Theme 3.4). Usually it will be something that gives you some kind of inner discomfort – it can often make you stop and question what you should do next. You may find yourself thinking something like 'OK, so what on earth do I do now?', as some kind of gap in your knowledge is exposed.

Critical incident analysis is an approach to dealing with the challenges that everyday practice brings. If we are aiming to practise reflectively, we need to be prepared to pose questions about our practice in order to problematise it. So, for example, rather than simply describing what happened, you should be prepared to question why it happened as it did, and think about it from a number of different perspectives as well as your own. This will also involve refusing to accept 'what is' and being open to seeing things differently and to making changes. We need to explore incidents that occur in our day-to-day work in order to understand them better and find alternative ways of reacting and responding to them. Such incidents can have a significant impact on our personal and professional learning.

A critical incident is usually personal to an individual. Incidents only become critical (that is, problematic) if the individual sees them in this way; what is problematic for one person may not be for someone else. The incident is defined as critical after the event and it is worth

'In life we all have encounters and experiences which make us pause and possibly re-evaluate how we see and deal with certain events. Professionals call these times critical incidents.'

remembering that we may often feel negative about any such incident. It is important to get beyond any uncomfortable feelings (see Theme 6) this may cause so that learning and development can occur.

'Reflection is an important human activity in which people recapture their experience, think about it, mull it over and evaluate it.'

(Boud, Keogh and Walker, 1985: 19)

Theme 4.4 Espoused theories and theories-in-use

Schön spent a significant amount of time working with Argyris, and together they took some important steps forward in gaining a deeper understanding of experiential learning. In their work Argyris and Schön (1974) argue that two types of theory are at work in professional practice. They are as follows:

○ **Espoused theories** – these are conscious and public. If we are in a situation where we are asked to explain our actions or our plans, we will use our espoused theories to explain what we did and why. Espoused theories are explicit and describe what we say we do.

○ **Theories-in-use** – Argyris and Schön argue that people operate with mental maps that help them to know how to think and act in certain situations. These maps are established over time and are based on our previous experiences and our assumptions regarding such things as what works and what does not. When taking action, we draw on our theories in use. Theories-in-use are implicit and describe what we actually do as distinct from what we say we do.

In practice, there is often a discrepancy or gap between our espoused theories and our theories-in-use. It could be argued that the role of reflection is to reveal the theories-in-use and to explore the nature of the gap. This will enable us to work towards congruence (or genuineness) in our thoughts and actions. Whilst the two remain connected in some way, the gap creates a catalyst for reflection that can lead to change. However, if the gap between the two is too wide this can become a problem.

Our theories-in-use are closely linked with what Schön (1983: 50) refers to as knowing-in-action, which is tacit knowledge. If you ask a very experienced practitioner why they did something in a particular way, many will need some time to think about their reasons before being able to articulate them. Their first response could be something like 'well, I'm not sure; I just did it that way'. In short, their practice has become automatic and somewhat intuitive because of their range and depth of professional experience. Whilst this is immensely useful, it is also worth remembering that this is where bad habits could begin to creep in.

Try this   Imagine you are facing a difficult issue in relation to your professional practice – use a real-life example if you can.

Now write down how you will respond to this under the two headings of your espoused theories and your theories-in-use. Now highlight the similarities and differences between what you have written under each heading.

Theme 4.5 Professionalism as artistry

The idea of artistry in relation to professional practice reminds us of its unique nature and the high level of skill involved. Any painter who is asked to produce a copy of a particular piece of their own work knows that it is highly unlikely that it will turn out to be exactly the same as the one they painted originally. The first piece of art was created in particular circumstances and was influenced by physical things like light, dark and shade, as well as more intangible things like the mood of the artist at the time. In the same way, highly skilled professional practice cannot be replicated at will, as the people, atmosphere and situation will all be different. For example, it is tempting for students to think 'I'll do X because that worked well last time' and they are then surprised when things do not turn out so well second time around.

Schön (1983) saw artistry as being at the heart of professional practice, enabled by reflection-in-action. As professionals reflect on what they are doing while they are doing it, they are able to draw on theory and their previous experience in order to revise their plans, modify their strategies and make adjustments to their actions. Professional practice is complex, messy and can be unpredictable; a high level of creativity and flexibility is needed in order to meet the needs of each client. However, thankfully, this also means that working life is never boring!

Artistry in professional practice is very far removed from any kind of competence-based, tick-box training. However, this is not meant to imply that such things as professional standards have no part to play; by contrast, these are useful and necessary in ensuring that the final painting is skilful, valuable and well produced, rather than simply a rough sketch.

Describe a time recently when you were very conscious that you had to reflect-in-action or 'think on your feet'. How easy or difficult was this at the time? Describe it as a series of steps and then focus on the changes in your thinking and in the strategies you were using at the time. How did this help you to build your tacit knowing-in-action?

Theme 5

Learning from feedback

This section will:

○ Help you to understand what constitutes good and bad feedback

○ Introduce you to the concept of critical friendship

○ Introduce you to the Johari Window model for feedback and self-disclosure

○ Help you to think about the settings where feedback can occur

○ Understand the concept of feed forward

Theme 5.1 What makes good feedback?

Good feedback is vital for professional growth and development, so it is important to understand what it is and what it is not. On professional courses, and in professional practice generally, you will receive feedback and will also be asked to give it to others.

Good feedback is:

- ○ Respectful
- ○ Helpful and supportive
- ○ Honest
- ○ Specific and focused on behaviour that can be changed or developed
- ○ Timely
- ○ Limited in amount – there is only so much feedback a person can cope with at any one time
- ○ Clear and clarified if necessary, to avoid misunderstandings
- ○ Focused on positives with some points for further development to enable the person to make progress
- ○ Motivating.

Good feedback is not:

- ○ Hurtful
- ○ Accusatory
- ○ Unhelpful
- ○ Undermining
- ○ Judgemental
- ○ General and focused on personal issues
- ○ Too much to take in at once
- ○ Vague and woolly
- ○ Only focused on negatives.

Understanding what makes good and bad feedback is important for two reasons. First, it helps you to process feedback when you receive it. Suffice it to say that not all feedback is good, for the reasons identified above. When receiving feedback it is important to examine it in order to discern its validity. Second, it enables you to give good feedback to others.

When thinking about a model for engaging in feedback, the idea of the 'praise sandwich' can be helpful. In other words, begin with some positives, then focus on some areas for development or things that could be done better, and finish with a summary of the positives. Remember that it is very difficult for someone to move forward in their development if they only receive negative messages. Such messages often start with words like 'but'. Changing this by using words like 'and instead you could' can make a real difference to how someone receives feedback and subsequently uses it. Everyone needs positive points to build on.

Feedback given in the form of the 'praise sandwich' boosts confidence, builds self-esteem and helps someone to see where they can improve. Confidence is a very delicate thing – difficult to gain but very easily destroyed. It is always worth remembering this whenever you are asked to give or receive feedback.

The 'praise sandwich' is, of course, not without its critics. For example, once it becomes obvious, people can either focus on the criticism and forget the praise, or do the opposite and focus only on the praise and fail to hear any criticisms. If too much praise is given and little criticism, people can get the impression that everything was OK, when this may not have been the case. This is an easy trap to fall into if you need to give some challenging feedback to someone at any point. If too little praise is given, it can be seen as tokenistic and appear insincere, in which case it is likely to be ignored. Feedback that involves praise followed by development points using words like 'as well as' and 'you could develop this by...' will be constructive, supportive and developmental.

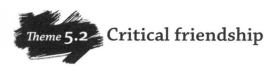

Theme 5.2 Critical friendship

There are things in life that a good friend should and will tell you; as such, a friend is honest whilst being caring in their approach. While you are studying on your course or as part of your continuing professional development, you may be asked to work with a critical friend; this is a person who can help you engage with many aspects of your growing self-awareness. Working with a critical friend will help you gain valuable feedback on your practice, mirroring the kind of relationship you may have with a supervisor. It is therefore important to choose a critical friend carefully.

So, what makes a good critical friend? They should be:

○ Someone who you know and can trust
○ Someone who puts you at ease
○ A good listener
○ Someone who asks good questions that challenge your thinking
○ Someone who acts with integrity
○ Someone who is positive, constructive and encouraging
○ Someone who is willing to point out negatives as well as positives.

The core qualities of critical friendship are:

○ Respect for each other
○ Trust
○ Openness
○ Honesty
○ A good rapport.

A vital key to becoming an effective critical friend is to remember to take a sensitive and questioning approach. A critical friend is not there to be negative or destructive, but rather to help their friend to examine critically their approach in any given situation. Often a good place to start is to ask the important 'why' question. This should not be asked in an accusatory way, such as 'why on earth did you do that?', but in a constructive, enquiring way, for example, 'what made you respond in that way?'

It is important to spend some time thinking about who your critical friend could be – it is worth remembering that it may not be your best friend. It should be someone who you can rely on to give you open and honest feedback, even if there may be aspects that you do not want to hear. In the long run, this will be of greater benefit to your professional development than working with someone who finds it difficult to question the more challenging aspects of your practice.

'I was very relieved when we were asked to choose a "critical friend" to help throughout this journey. Now I felt like I had someone to go to and, equally, they could come to me.'

'Without feedback we risk the possibility of practising in some kind of "bubble" or vacuum where we only see things from our own viewpoint.'

(Bassot, 2016: 94)

Theme 5.3 The Johari Window

Feedback will be important in your professional development, as it will ensure that you are not operating in a vacuum. The Johari Window was developed by Joseph Luft and Harry Ingham and is a model which helps us to gain useful insights into how we relate to other people; this can give us greater self-awareness regarding how we communicate with others in groups.

The Johari Window (Luft, 1984) is a square divided into four panes:

○ Open (top left) – things that we know about ourselves and that others know about us
○ Blind (top right) – things that others know about us that we do not know
○ Hidden (bottom left) – things that we know about ourselves that others do not know
○ Unknown (bottom right) – things that no-one knows.

The model shows how feedback and self-disclosure can help us to gain greater self-awareness. Being open to feedback and engaging in receiving it will enable you to become aware of those things that others know about you in the Blind area, but you do not necessarily know about yourself. Similarly, being willing to self-disclose from the Hidden area will enable others to get to know you better. This decreases the size of the Blind and Hidden areas making the Open area larger.

All professionals need to be open to feedback for their professional growth and development. The right amount of self-disclosure at the right time can build empathy in a helping relationship. But remember, in any professional situation self-disclosure is always a choice, and you should never disclose something unless you are comfortable doing so. Indeed, in some professional settings self-disclosure is seen as problematic, as it could be a distraction from the needs of the person you are working with. So you should always self-disclose with caution.

Giving feedback and receiving it along with self-disclosure always involves an element of risk, so it is important that it is done in an atmosphere of trust.

Some people argue that the overall goal is to expand the Open area as much as possible. However, it is important to remember that it is certainly possible to be too open and to disclose too much. In professional practice it is appropriate that some things remain in the Hidden area; for example, how you might feel about a particular client's behaviour or outlook. Some things are disclosed more appropriately only in supervision or with a more experienced colleague.

'reflection involves reviewing our own values, challenging our assumptions and considering the broader social, political and professional issues that are relevant to practice.'

(Atkins and Schutz, 2013: 23)

Try this   Have a discussion with your critical friend about your progress. Afterwards, think about your discussion in relation to the Johari Window. How did you seek feedback, and what was your response to it? How far were you prepared to engage in self-disclosure? What were the reasons for this?

Theme 5.4 The settings where feedback can occur

We have already established that feedback will be an important facet of your professional development. Eraut (2006) usefully describes the following four different settings where feedback can occur:

○ **Immediate and *in situ*** – this is feedback that is given during or immediately following an experience and is given by a colleague or someone who witnessed the event. It is usually specific and can focus on the factors that influenced the particular situation, which can often be forgotten later.

○ **Informal conversations away from the workplace or place of study** – feedback here can be intentional or unintentional and can depend on the learning culture with in the given situation.

○ **Mentoring and supervision** – here feedback is more formal and related to performance. The mentor or supervisor will not always have direct opportunities to observe the work they are asked to supervise.

○ **Appraisal** – more formal and less frequent feedback, which relates to the achievement of goals and objectives set previously.

Eraut is clear that receiving feedback will not always be a positive experience, and, in fact, at times it can even be distressing. However, it is vital for professional development; without it we can deceive ourselves into thinking such things as, 'I did the best I could in the circumstances', or, 'I must have misunderstood what was required. If things had been clearer, I would have known what to do.' He also points to the need to use feedback, rather than simply receive it. This highlights the issue of choice; listening, taking stock and acting on feedback when we feel it is justified and appropriate will always involve making a decision. Engaging in the feedback process means that we will be able to learn from the experiences of others. This could alter our perceptions and help us to begin to see things differently.

'Reflective practice itself, or even the study of it, can lead you to think of things that you know you should try but maybe are afraid.'

Try this   Now think of a time when you received what you felt was useful feedback on an aspect of your professional development. What was good about it and how did it help you? How far did the feedback fulfil the criteria for good feedback in Theme 5.1? Now go through a similar process focusing on some poor feedback you have received.

Feed forward

The idea of feedback in professional development is very well known, but the concept of feed forward is much less so. Whereas feedback focuses on the past, feed forward concentrates on the future and involves making suggestions for practice. In a feed forward exercise participants work in pairs and play two roles. In one role they are asked to provide feed forward and in the other to accept it, seeking to learn as much as they can. Participants choose a behaviour they would like to change, describe it and ask for two suggestions for the future that might help them achieve a positive change in this area. While receiving feed forward, participants listen carefully and take notes.

When compared with feedback, feed forward has the following benefits:

○ It focuses on the future, which can be changed
○ It is seen as positive and focuses on solutions rather than problems
○ It tends to be well received
○ It requires knowledge of the task rather than the person
○ It is seen as being more objective so is not taken as personally
○ It is quicker and often more efficient
○ It tends to imply more of an equal working relationship
○ People tend to listen more carefully to it

Whilst it is clear that feedback is vital for professional development, it is clear that feed forward also has a part to play. Many students do not always enjoy receiving feedback; by contrast, feed forward can be powerful, dynamic and enjoyable.

Theme 6

Feelings and professional practice

This section will:

○ Introduce you to the Almond Effect

○ Help you to understand that our memories and feelings are stored together in our brains

○ Introduce you to two models of reflection that focus on feelings as a source of learning

○ Help you to understand that our feelings can be a guide to assumptions we might be making

---

Theme 6.1 The Almond Effect

As human beings we all have emotional responses to people and situations. However, we often fail to understand what triggers these responses and why they can be so powerful at any given time. No doubt we have all experienced situations where we have said things or reacted in a certain way and have immediately regretted what we have said or done. Riches (2012) explains that the reason this happens is because of what she calls the Almond Effect.

Neuroscience shows that the human brain is designed to respond to threatening situations with a 'flight or fight' response. These responses are usually automatic and are the result of the hard-wiring of our neural pathways. They have been learned through the process of evolution and have played a vital part in the survival of the human race. Coming from the Greek word for almond, the amygdalae (we each have two of them) are almond-shaped parts of the brain that play a vital role in stimulating and regulating our emotional responses to situations and people, particularly in relation to fear. In short, they prompt a 'flight or fight' response where appropriate. Because of our amygdalae we can also sense emotional responses in other people. Our instinctive emotional responses always happen first, followed by our rational responses.

Riches describes a 'Mindfield', where the Almond Effect prompts us to respond emotionally, before we have had the opportunity to think things through; often this results in saying or doing things that we might regret. In her book, Riches discusses a range of strategies to help us to slow down and to reach a more rational position. These include the following:

○ Noticing any physical signs, such as an increase in your heart rate, trembling or blushing
○ Breathing deeply before responding
○ Being aware of your body language and keeping it open.

It is always worth remembering that, as human beings, we are emotional first and rational second.

Try this   Think of an incident that has happened recently which has prompted a strong emotional reaction in you. Describe the incident and try to identify what might have prompted such a strong response. What does this tell you about situations like this and how you will cope in the future?

Theme 6.2 Memories and feelings

In his early work on Transactional Analysis, Eric Berne was influenced by the work of Wilder Penfield, a neurosurgeon from McGill University in Montreal, Canada. During his career, Penfield carried out a large number of experiments whilst operating on conscious patients suffering from focal epilepsy. He did this in order to learn more about how the human brain functions, particularly in relation to how memories are stored.

Penfield found that by touching particular parts of the temporal cortex with a galvanic probe, patients were prompted to speak about memories that came into focus. They described what they recollected vividly and in detail. In addition, they also described how they felt. As a result, Penfield concluded that memories and feelings are stored together in the brain. In other words, when we remember things, we not only remember how we felt, but also experience those feelings (or at least some of them) again. At times, we might remember something, and this memory prompts us to feel what we felt at that time. At other times, we might have a particular feeling, and it can take us some time to link it to a previous experience or time in our lives. These feelings can often be triggered by an event or by one of our senses – for example, a piece of music that we hear or a particular smell. However this happens, Penfield's research shows that memories and feelings are stored together in the brain, and one cannot be evoked without the other. In relation to professional practice, having an understanding of this is helpful for two reasons. First, we should expect our feelings to come to the surface and not always be able to understand immediately why this is happening. Time spent in reflection, either alone or with others, will often help us to remember our past experiences and the feelings associated with them. This means that we can begin to process them. Second, we should not be surprised by instances where our work with clients causes us to have feelings that we do not expect. These feelings can be linked with reminders from our past that we can then begin to rationalise.

'The expression of feelings is always cathartic. The issue is not so much removing them but accepting them as valid and harnessing this energy for taking positive action.'

(Johns, 2010: 37)

Having considered the role of our feelings in professional practice, we can use theoretical models to help us to understand more about how we process these. Gibbs' (1998) Reflective Cycle is particularly useful and is depicted in Figure 2.

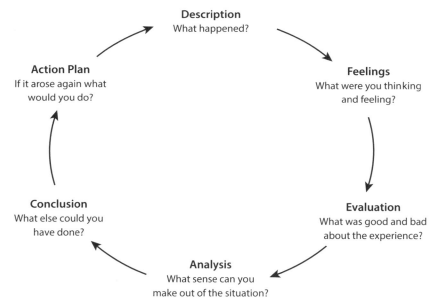

Figure 2 Gibbs' Reflective Cycle

Many people find the prompt questions on the cycle particularly helpful in making the model practical and easy to apply to their work. For those who are supporting people in challenging circumstances, the second point on the cycle, with its focus on feelings, is particularly important. It would be foolish to think that a professional practitioner who is asked to work in an empathic way would not have emotional responses to the situations of their clients. As we know, this is not how we function as human beings.

It is worth noting that the third step on the cycle, 'Evaluation', encourages us to examine what was positive about the experience as well as what was negative. Some people have a tendency to be too hard on themselves, focusing only on the negative aspects of experiences. As Ghaye (2011) argues (see Theme 3.4), we also need to recognise things that have gone well and to build on these. The fourth step on the cycle is also worth noting, as it is different from other cycles we have examined so far. Here, Gibbs urges us to engage in analysis in order to make sense of what happened. The tentative wording he chooses, 'What sense can you make out of the situation' (as distinct from 'What sense do you make out of the situation?') seems to imply that the experiences we have in professional practice and the situations we face will not always make sense. However, he encourages us to try to make sense of them in order to deepen our understandings.

When comparing Gibbs' cycle with that of Kolb, it is clear that there are both similarities and differences between them. Like Kolb's cycle, Gibbs also suggests that learning from experience happens in a particular sequence of steps. However, Gibbs' model is more detailed in that it has

'By reflecting on my own feelings about a situation, I am beginning to feel less stressed about things that are beyond my control.'

six points on it compared to Kolb's four. Gibbs' emphasis on feelings takes reflection to a deeper level and can be seen as a key milestone on the road from reflective practice to critically reflective practice.

Processing feelings

In their book *Reflection: Turning Experience into Learning*, Boud, Keogh and Walker (1985) put forward a very useful reflective cycle that focuses on feelings. As human beings, we all have emotional responses to situations, and Boud et al. encourage us to pay attention to our feelings in order to process them.

Their reflective cycle has the following three stages:

○ **Returning to the experience** – this involves recollecting what happened and could include discussing it with others.

> *'Writing has helped me to make sense of things, especially why I am feeling a particular way. It is something I will definitely carry on, I'm not as stressed as I was which is a positive.'*

○ **Attending to feelings** – there are two important aspects in relation to paying attention to feelings here: building on positive feelings and removing negative or obstructive ones.

○ **Re-evaluating the experience** – this is the most important stage, where new knowledge is added to existing knowledge and incorporated within it.

In contrast to Gibbs, Boud et al. use the term 'stages' rather than 'steps', and their model is designed to be multi-directional – highlighting how professionals often move forwards and backwards within the process of reflection as their analysis of their practice becomes deeper.

It is important to note that unless we attend to our feelings and take action to process them, it is likely that negative or obstructive ones, in particular, will remain and could then act as a barrier to our professional practice and development. Processing feelings involves externalising them and how we do this is a matter of choice, like many other areas of professional development. It is important to work out what helps you as an individual. Writing in a journal like this can be therapeutic and can help you to engage in the process of externalising your feelings. For some people, writing about their feelings on paper helps them to leave them there, literally and metaphorically. For others, discussion and supervision (see Theme 9) have the same effect. The vital thing to emphasise is that it is the processing of feelings that is important, not how it is done.

'Of particular importance within description is the observation of the feeling evoked during the experience. On occasions our emotional reactions can override our rationality to such an extent that we react unwarily and with blurred perceptions.'

(Boud, Keogh and Walker, 1985: 28)

Try this   Now try using one of the reflective cycles (Gibbs, 1998 or Boud, Keogh and Walker, 1985) to evaluate your learning from the incident in 6.1. Which cycle did you choose and why? How useful was it in helping you to deal with the emotional issues raised by the incident?

Theme 6.5 Feelings as a guide to assumptions

Bearing in mind that Transactional Analysis teaches us that our memories and feelings are stored together in our brains, our emotional responses to people and situations can then give us significant clues as to why we think and act in certain ways. In many circumstances our feelings act as a guide to assumptions that we might be making (see Theme 7) and these will often be closely linked with our previous experiences. Here are two examples.

You have been working with a client for quite some time and are not seeing much, if any, progress as a result of all your efforts. Consequently, you feel very discouraged and do not look forward to your regular meetings with the client. You find yourself thinking that your work with them is a waste of time. You begin to realise that your expectations of the client are now very low and that your negative thoughts are affecting your relationship with them. Your feelings of discouragement have alerted you to your assumption that this client will never change and this is something you now feel you need to address.

By contrast you are also working with a client you admire. This client has done so much to overcome adversity, and you feel a huge sense of pride in their achievements. You look forward to seeing them, as they make your work feel worthwhile. However, over a period of time you realise that you want the client to achieve even more in order to live up to your expectations of them rather than living their own life; again this is something you now feel you need to work on.

Here we can see that it is not only negative feelings that can guide us regarding our assumptions; positive ones can do this too.

Theme 7

Assumptions

This section will:

○ Introduce you to the keys terms reflection, reflectivity and reflexivity

○ Introduce you to the concept of double-loop learning

○ Discuss how we can challenge our assumptions by using the Ladder of Inference

○ Discuss Mezirow's seven levels of reflectivity that can lead to perspective transformation

○ Introduce you to a model that helps you to challenge your limiting assumptions

---

Theme 7.1 Double-loop learning

In Theme 3, we examined Kolb's (1984) Experiential Learning Cycle. In this process, we have an experience, reflect on it and draw out some general principles and any new knowledge that can then be applied as we prepare for the next experience. This type of learning is valuable in day-to-day professional practice and can be described as 'single-loop learning' (Argyris and Schön, 1974).

However, in order to take professional learning to a deeper level we need to begin to challenge our own assumptions and our established ways of doing things. Assumptions are things that over time we have begun to take for granted. We do this to such an extent that we no longer question them or even think about them. In many circumstances, assumptions are valuable, as they prevent us from needing to think about every aspect of our lives in detail. For example, if we had to think closely regarding what to do each time we made a cup of tea, life would be exhausting! Instead, we draw on our past experiences and make it somewhat automatically. However, if we apply this to professional practice with people, this kind of 'automatic pilot' becomes very risky, as it is here that prejudice and discriminatory practices can be rooted.

Critically reflective practice encourages us to delve beneath the surface of our long-held ideas and paradigms, in order to challenge our assumptions. Here, the concept of double-loop learning (Argyris and Schön, 1974) is very helpful.

Unlike Kolb's single loop, double-loop learning asks us to bring our assumptions to the surface, to challenge them and to question the things that we take for granted (see Figure 3). This can lead us to question our personal values and beliefs that lie beneath professional practice (see Theme 8). As a result, through this process, our habitual ways of thinking about things can change, and practice can become more creative.

Questioning our assumptions as part of reflective observation is always personally and professionally challenging. It can be done by asking questions such as:

○ What assumptions am I making in this situation? Am I jumping to conclusions?

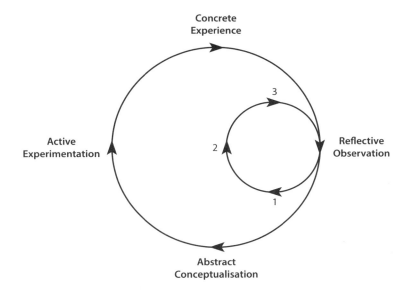

1. Am I jumping to conclusions? What assumptions am I making?
2. Are my assumptions justifiable?
3. How should my perceptions change?

Figure 3 Double-loop learning

○ Are my assumptions justifiable?

○ Do my perceptions need to change?

Like Schön's reflection-on and reflection-in-action, this type of questioning can be done during an experience (in-action) or afterwards (on-action).

Think of a recent example from your practice where you engaged in double-loop learning to question your assumptions. What did you conclude about your assumptions? Were they accurate and appropriate in this instance?

'Assumptions are taken-for-granted beliefs about the world and our place within it, that seem so obvious to us as not to need stating explicitly.'

(Brookfield, 1995: 2)

Theme 7.2 Reflection, reflectivity and reflexivity

In the early part of this journal, we used the term 'reflection' to denote the kind of thinking professionals undertake in order to evaluate their practice. As we now move towards having an understanding of critically reflective practice, two more words require some clarification: 'reflectivity' and 'reflexivity'. This is not straightforward, as these terms are similar and can sometimes, rather confusingly, be used interchangeably in literature.

○ **Reflection** – this is the term used by many writers on the subject of reflective practice, including Schön, his colleagues and his associates. It refers to the thinking processes that we engage in as learners and professionals and can be deliberate or otherwise.

○ **Reflectivity** – this is the deliberate act of engaging in the process of thinking in order to analyse and evaluate an aspect of professional practice. This is sometimes referred to as the 'doing of reflection'.

○ **Reflexivity** – refers to the high level of self-awareness needed to practise in an anti-discriminatory way. It involves becoming aware of our values and assumptions, which are culturally situated. Fook (2004) argues that such awareness demands that we look inwards and outwards, recognising that every part of ourselves, including our context, affects how we practise.

Reflexivity is vital for all professionals who want to become critically reflective practitioners. In all situations this will involve being aware of issues of power in relationships and in institutions and seeking to shift the balance of power where appropriate.

Each of us at some point in time has been guilty of making assumptions and jumping to conclusions. To begin to challenge our assumptions, it is important to understand how assumptions are made. The Ladder of Inference (Argyris, 1982) is a very helpful way of looking at this. In his excellent video clip on the Group Harmonics website (found here: www.groupharmonics .com/HelpDesk/Ladder.htm), Ed Muzio (2011) draws the diagram shown in Figure 4:

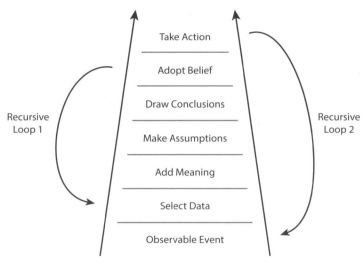

Figure 4 Argyris' Ladder of Inference

At the foot of the ladder, we observe an event as it happens. The human brain receives so many messages each day that we select the data we need or want at any given time. We then add meaning to that data from our current situation and our past experiences in similar circumstances. The meaning we add is drawn from the perspective of our own personal and cultural settings.

This leads us to make assumptions and, from there, to draw conclusions about the person or the situation. These conclusions then become part of our beliefs about the world and how it operates. The action we then take is based on our beliefs.

Following on from this, we can take one of two recursive loops. The first is from our beliefs to the second step of the ladder. Here, our beliefs lead us to make choices about the data we select in the future. In short, we usually select the data that confirm our existing beliefs and ignore the data that do not. The second loop is from action to the bottom of the ladder. Here, we take action to seek more observable data. But the data we gather are also based on our beliefs, which encourage us to see what we have seen before. This makes our approach biased in favour of what we have seen previously. By following either of these recursive loops, our assumptions are confirmed and our existing beliefs are reinforced.

Here is an example. Someone you are working with (a client, patient or student) behaves badly and you select data from what you observe. You only see their bad behaviour rather than anything good they might do. The meaning you add is that you are not surprised that they behave badly as many people you work with in this particular context behave like this. You then make assumptions about the person based on this; for example, that people in this context always behave badly and this particular person is no different. From this, you draw your own conclusions that whenever you work in this particular context, you need to expect to deal with difficult people. These conclusions form the basis of your beliefs, which in turn influence your future actions. In your actions, you are then most likely to select the data that confirm your existing beliefs. Without even realising, you get to the point where you see what you expect to see, rather than what actually happens.

This habit can be avoided by consciously going to the bottom of the ladder, and either regularly questioning the assumptions you make and the conclusions that you draw from them or, alternatively, seeking out some contrary data that will disconfirm your assumptions. In the example above, you could seek out some evidence for positive behaviour to disprove your beliefs. This is a vital step in working towards anti-discriminatory practice, and it is an important element of critically reflective practice.

Mezirow's seven levels of reflectivity

The feelings we have about the people we encounter often stem from our attitudes and values, which can then affect how well we engage with them and the expectations we have of them.

In Theme 6, we examined Boud, Keogh and Walker's (1985) model of reflection. In their work, they take us beyond the acknowledgement of feelings into the realm of examining our attitudes and values and the ways in which these, along with the assumptions we make, can be reinforced through experience.

'I can see I might assume things because of my values and the experiences that I have had.'

Citing the work of Mezirow (1978; 1981), they describe the following seven levels of reflectivity, which help us to examine how we approach people and situations: in particular, the assumptions we might make as a result of past experiences. The first four levels operate within our ordinary consciousness and include an examination of our feelings and values. The remaining three levels lie within the realm of critical consciousness and include becoming aware of the reasons why we might be quick to make judgements about situations and people. The seven levels are as follows:

1 **Reflectivity** – becoming aware of how we see things, and how we think and act. What do I think and feel about this person and how does this affect my behaviour?

2 **Affective Reflectivity** – becoming aware of our feelings about how we think and act. How do I feel about the way I think/act in relation to them?

3 **Discriminant Reflectivity** – questioning whether or not our perceptions about people are accurate. Are my perceptions of them correct?

4 **Judgemental Reflectivity** – becoming aware of our value judgements. What assumptions am I making about people and their situation based on my values?

5 **Conceptual Reflectivity** – questioning the constructs we use when we think about other people. For example, just because the person does X, will Y always follow?

6 **Psychic Reflectivity** – recognising our own prejudices that can make us quick to make judgements about people on the basis of limited information about them. Am I jumping to conclusions?

7 **Theoretical Reflectivity** – becoming aware that the reasons we are quick to make judgements about people are based on cultural and psychological assumptions. What are my assumptions about this person based on?

By examining our thinking at each level, we can begin to question our assumptions, in particular whether they are accurate or not. This means we can challenge our assumptions where we feel they are not justifiable and reframe them where appropriate. Mezirow asserts that assumptions are always culturally situated and that by reaching the deepest level of Theoretical Reflectivity some perspective transformation can happen. In other words, reflecting at this level means that I begin to think about things differently.

'Reflective practice is a process that involves a reflective turn. This means returning to look again at our taken-for-granted values, professional understandings and practices.'
(Ghaye and Ghaye, 1998: 16)

Think of a time recently where it became clear that you had made some inaccurate assumptions. What happened? When and how did you become aware of the assumptions you were making? Now use either Argyris' Ladder of Inference or Mezirow's seven levels of reflectivity to analyse your thought processes and your actions in relation to this. How might the outcome have been different if you had not made these assumptions? What can you learn from this?

Theme 7.5 Challenging limiting assumptions – the Career Thinking Session

It is important to recognise our assumptions, as they can restrict the way we view people and situations. If they are based on negative stereotypes, this can be detrimental to ourselves and our clients. Challenging our limiting assumptions is an important element of learning and development, and it is a vital part of becoming and remaining a critically reflective practitioner.

The Career Thinking Session (CTS) model (Bassot, 2016) gives a framework for challenging our limiting assumptions, and it can be used in supervision (see Theme 9) or with a trusted colleague. It involves intense listening and a series of open questions posed by the Listener to the Thinker. The Listener waits until the Thinker has finished saying all they wish to say before moving on to the next step.

Adapted from the work of Kline (1999) the CTS has the following six steps:

Step 1 – 'What do you want to think about?' Here the Thinker expresses the thoughts and issues they have brought to the session.

Step 2 – 'What do you want to achieve from the rest of the session?' This is an opportunity for the Thinker to express what they would like to focus on in the CTS.

Step 3 – 'What are you assuming is stopping you from moving forward in your development?' This encourages the Thinker to start to address their limiting assumptions. There are three types of limiting assumptions: facts, possible facts and bedrock assumptions. All can act as barriers to career and professional development. Limiting bedrock assumptions undermine confidence and self-esteem, and are so significant that they inform our beliefs and what we see as 'truth'. Finding the bedrock assumption and articulating it is a vital part of the CTS.

Step 4 – 'If you knew that … what ideas would you have towards your development?' The ultimate goal here is to enable the Listener to design the Incisive Question (IQ) in relation to their bedrock assumption. The Thinker is asked to find the positive opposites to all their limiting assumptions and to state these in relation to their future development. The IQ is the positive opposite to the bedrock assumption; it cuts through the limiting bedrock assumption, removes it and replaces it with a new, positive assumption. This liberates the Thinker to think freely about their future.

Step 5 – Writing down the IQ. The IQ is written down and the Listener then poses it a number of times, until the Thinker has voiced all their new positive ideas in relation to their future development.

Step 6 – Appreciation. Sharing limiting assumptions is sensitive and challenging; it demands trust and openness on both sides. This final step keeps people thinking and asks both participants to share a positive quality they have valued in one another during the session. This encourages the Thinker to focus on the positives in relation to their future and to continue thinking after the end of session.

Theme 8

Ethics and values

This section will:

○ Introduce you to the key terms 'ethics' and 'values'

○ Introduce you to the concept of Transactional Analysis drivers

○ Help you to think about the impact of your values on your professional practice

○ Establish the importance of considering issues of power in professional practice

---

Theme 8.1 Ethics and values – what's the difference?

In order to practise in a critically reflective way, an understanding of your own values is important. Often the assumptions we make about people and situations (see Theme 7) are based on our values, so having an understanding of them will be vital in professional practice. Many professional courses include modules on ethics and values and, as part of these, a range of theoretical approaches are considered. The terms themselves are complex and not easy to define, but Knowles and Lander's (2012) work provides a helpful and practical introduction to this whole area.

In discussing definitions of ethics and values, Knowles and Lander (2012) suggest that values are things that we feel are important to us – in a literal sense, they are things that we value. These values are linked with our beliefs about the world and how it should operate. Ethics then, are sets of rules that help us to know how to act and behave correctly in relation to our values. Here is a very simple example: I value honesty and believe it to be important, so I do not tell lies.

Values can be personal and professional. Our personal values are deep-rooted and will often stem from those things that we have learned to recognise as being important, usually from a very young age. Such values can include things like honesty, hard work and the importance of family. Personal values are always culturally situated and reflect the social context of the individual. Professional values are approaches to practice that are accepted by a particular profession as being central to the way work is carried out. Often, these are enshrined in codes of practice that a practitioner agrees to abide by in their work and provide the foundations of professional practice. Such codes often also consider aspects of ethics, which detail how things need to be done in order for these values to be demonstrated.

However, any consideration of ethics and values will always be challenging. Here are two areas for thought. The simple example given above might appear to be straightforward, but does this mean that I never lie? Are there situations where not being honest could be justifiable? In relation to professional practice, you may well be able to think of examples where your own personal values could be at odds with your professional values. These are often referred to as ethical dilemmas, where there will not be a simple straightforward answer as to how you should proceed. Here, taking a critically reflective approach is vital.

'This is another aspect of self-awareness, being able to recognize what feelings are currently affecting us and how significant they may be.'

(Thompson and Thompson, 2008: 42)

Theme 8.2 Transactional Analysis drivers

The concept of drivers is important in Transactional Analysis (TA), and recognising them and the influences they have on our work and lives can be extremely helpful. Put simply, drivers can be seen as consistent messages we received from our parents or carers when we were growing up. They consist of commands about what to do and what not to do, how we should behave and how we should not, plus definitions of people and the world. Kahler (1975) put these messages together into five groups called drivers. Drivers become powerful psychological tools and have a big influence on how we live our lives; in other words, they drive us.

The five TA drivers are shown below. Each driver has strengths and weaknesses associated with it; weaknesses often emanate from strengths that are overdone. Here are some examples:

○ **Be Perfect** – accurate, eye for detail, neat and tidy but will be harsh on themselves and 'beat themselves up' when they don't meet their own exacting standards, and can be harsh on others too.

○ **Be Strong** – excellent in a crisis, dependable, makes people feel safe and secure, but doesn't tend to show their feelings so may come across as aloof and disinterested.

○ **Try Hard** – has a strong work ethic, is persistent and resilient but sometimes does not praise others.

○ **Please (people)** – great team member who gets on well with lots of people, but does not want to upset people so can be unassertive and have a desire to rescue people.

○ **Hurry Up** – enthusiastic, achieves a lot in a short space of time, but can be prone to make mistakes through rushing and lack of forethought.

Recognising our own TA drivers makes us more self-aware. At the same time, an understanding of them can help us become more aware of how others are behaving and communicating. As in other areas of professional development, it is important to focus on the strengths of the drivers, whilst seeking to minimise their weaknesses.

Consider the descriptions of each of the five drivers. Which would you say is most and least like you? What new insights does this give you about yourself and your relationships with others?

Theme 8.3 The impact of values on professional work

We have established that everyone has personal values and that these have an impact on professional practice. One question that then arises is whether or not an individual can be completely neutral (or in other words remain completely objective) in their professional work with people. In the context of counselling, Corey, Schneider Corey and Callanan (2007) discuss the concept of therapeutic neutrality, which can usefully be taken into other professional arenas. They discuss a two-way process; the ways in which our values affect our work with clients, and vice versa, and what can happen when the two sets of values are in conflict with one another.

They also pose some questions that are helpful to think about. First, is it possible to keep our values out of the professional helping process? Many people today would argue that it is not possible because our values are an integral part of our make-up. Second, if it were possible, would it be helpful to set our values aside? Corey et al. argue that this is not desirable, as the sharing of values can in itself be helpful, encouraging people to think through their own positions on a range of issues.

The most important point they make is that if we take the stance that neutrality is not possible, professional practitioners need to have a clear understanding of their own values and the impact these have on their work. These values can then be discussed openly. This helps the client to know where the professional practitioner is coming from and

'I can see I might assume things because of my values and the experiences that I have had.'

means that the person can explore their own values. However, sharing values should not be done as a way of influencing the person concerned. A discussion of values will include such things as clarifying assumptions and articulating core beliefs and this will often be challenging for all concerned.

Now think about instances recently where you feel your values have been challenged, for example through working with clients in particularly difficult situations. Describe your responses to these challenges. How has this helped you gain greater self-awareness?

Theme 8.4 Anti-discriminatory practice

Critically reflective practice involves an acknowledgement of issues of power that are present in all relationships. In order to examine how such issues are played out in society, Thompson (2012) outlines his PCS model, which helps us to understand how inequalities and discrimination are perpetuated in society. This model contains the following three levels:

○ **Personal** – these are our individual thoughts and feelings and the behaviours that emanate from them. Our personal attitudes and values, or our ways of perceiving things and people, are also part of this level and include prejudices that we might hold about certain people and situations. To some extent, this level is shaped by our previous personal experiences.

○ **Cultural** – culture relates to things that are shared by people. This includes shared understandings and meanings as well as the way things are done in certain contexts. All of this leads to patterns of behaviour that are deemed to be acceptable or unacceptable within that particular social setting. At this level a wide range of assumptions are made and much is taken for granted without any questioning.

○ **Structural** – this operates at the social level; in other words it relates to the ways in which society is organised and divided, and it is linked closely with issues of power. People with power usually like to keep it and to stop others from gaining it; in short, this is oppression. This process means that oppression and discrimination become institutionalised, or in Thompson's words, '"sewn in" to the fabric of society' (2012: 34).

Thompson argues that discrimination happens at every level of PCS, with each level being interlinked and reinforcing the other. Critically reflective practice involves recognising our own values at the Personal level, the ways things are done at the Cultural level and any inequalities that operate at the Structural level, particularly within our own institutions. As with all aspects of reflective practice, we are then faced with choices to make regarding possible action.

'exploration of the self and personal constructs that influence how one views the world.'

(Moon, 2000: 191)

Try this   As you were growing up, your parents and/or carers no doubt used some phrases that you remember well. You may remember them as, 'X always used to say … when I was little/young.' A very common example would be something like, 'Work hard at school and you'll get a good job.' Think back and write down some examples of these. How have these phrases influenced your personal values?

Theme 8.5 Issues of power

Reflexivity involves not only being aware of ourselves and the part we play in the professional process, but also being clear about the impact of the context of our work on practice. In all professional relationships it is important to appreciate the influence of power. Issues of power will always be present when we work with clients, who will usually feel that power lies with the professional practitioner rather than with them. In certain professions (for example teaching and social work) this is clearly the case. In classrooms, teachers need to maintain a positive learning environment for all students; this can involve applying sanctions when some are reluctant to engage positively in the learning process. Social workers hold the power when it comes to issues like child protection and when working with vulnerable adults. Issues of power can also be seen at work within other professions. In nursing, Johns (2013) argues strongly that in a profession dominated by women, many nurses experience patriarchal attitudes and practices that can oppress them.

We also need to be clear about the dangers involved in exercising too much power in working relationships. For example, the social work profession recognises the need to be aware of issues of power and its potential misuse; this can lead to discriminatory and even oppressive practice (Thompson, 2012). At times, power will need to be shared; for example, if young people in school are going to progress to higher education, they will need to be strong independent learners, so sharing power in the classroom during their later years at school will become an important part of preparing them for the future.

Theme 9

Reflecting with others

This section will:

○ Discuss what makes good supervision

○ Introduce you to a model for supervision

○ Help you to engage effectively with supervision

○ Introduce you to the concept of the reflective conversation

○ Discuss the value of reflecting in groups

Theme 9.1 What is good supervision?

When examining a particular term, it is usually helpful to start with a definition of it. However, in relation to supervision this is difficult, because how it is defined will depend on the particular professional context. This means that it will be important to check the meaning of supervision within your particular work setting. It is important to emphasise that the kind of supervision we are discussing here should not be confused with that usually provided by your line manager, which tends to focus on the achievement (or otherwise) of set goals and targets. One big issue within the literature on supervision is whether or not it should be provided by a practitioner's manager. Some professionals would argue that this should not be the case, whilst others would argue that it can be helpful. In some circumstances there is simply no choice.

The overall purpose of supervision is to encourage professionals to reflect on their practice in a deeper way in order to enhance their professional development. This is shown in Figure 5.

Figure 5 Professional development and supervision

So far, the main emphasis within this journal has been on reflection as an individual activity. Whilst this is very important, there is no doubt that much can be learned from reflecting with others. This process gives us vital feedback in relation to our development and enables us to see things that we simply would not see otherwise (see Theme 5). It is also important to note that supervision is not always open to everyone who feels they need it or feels they would benefit from it. In the early days of a new job, it is good to check out the opportunities for supervision and to consider making use of them wherever possible.

Like many other areas of professional practice, we cannot assume that all supervision is good supervision. In many respects, good supervisors have lots of the qualities of good teachers and good practitioners. They show respect for those they are supervising and demonstrate empathy. They often take a questioning approach as distinct from a didactic one and have excellent listening skills. A sense of humour is important too. It is good to remember that supervisors need feedback too, and giving this in a positive way can help to cement and maintain a healthy working relationship.

'Reflective thinking means suspending our judgement until we have carried out some sort of systematic enquiry.'

(Campbell and Norton, 2007: 141)

Theme 9.2 Models of supervision

There are many theoretical models that explore and explain the concept of supervision, and one of the most well-known is that of Proctor (1986). Proctor uses the following three terms to describe the functions of supervision:

○ **Normative** – this involves monitoring the work of the practitioner to ensure that they are practising effectively in ways that are competent and ethical. This includes checking that the relevant code of ethical practice is being applied consistently and appropriately. The main question being posed here is: 'Is the practitioner meeting the norms of the particular profession?'

○ **Formative** – the focus here is on the practitioner's professional development, and the aim is to help them to develop their skills, professional knowledge, and appropriate attitudes and values. This leads to a greater and deeper level of self-awareness. The question being posed here is: 'How can this practitioner develop themselves further?'

○ **Restorative** – this is sometimes referred to as supportive and is concerned with the support practitioners need when faced with challenging situations. Such situations cause stress and sometimes distress, and it is important that practitioners have an opportunity to process their emotional responses (see Theme 6). In extreme cases, failing to do so could result in burnout. The question being posed here is: 'How can this practitioner be supported in processing their thoughts and feelings in relation to challenging situations?'

Effective supervision can only happen in a safe space, and supervisors and supervisees have a responsibility to be sure that the circumstances for supervision enable it to take place comfortably and without interruption. A high level of trust between supervisor and supervisee is vital, whilst observing the general principles of confidentiality – that nothing should be disclosed to another party without the permission of the discloser, unless they are at risk of harm or are violating the law. It is also important to note that supervision protects clients, too, in ensuring that practitioners are competent (normative), professional (formative) and able to cope with stressful situations (restorative).

Try this Think about what you would like to gain from your next supervision session using Proctor's (1986) three headings: Normative, Formative and Restorative. If you do not have access to supervision, think about how you might be able to access some support from others, again under Proctor's headings.

Theme 9.3 How to engage effectively with supervision

Supervision can offer a vital opportunity for critical reflection, and it is important to think about how you can engage with the process in order to gain the maximum amount from it. The following points are worth thinking about at the start of the supervision process and before each session.

In order to benefit from supervision, it is important to think about what you hope to gain from it. Before a supervision session it is always good to spend some time in preparation. Going into a session without thinking it through first could mean that you gain little from it, and you could also give the impression that you are not taking it seriously. Understandably, this can make supervisors unhappy! Make sure that you are clear about anything that your supervisor has asked you to prepare or think about beforehand.

Effective supervisors usually make explicit ground rules with their supervisees at the beginning of their relationship, and you should expect to make a contribution to establishing these. Beforehand, think about how you would like to work with your supervisor, including when, where and how often you would like to meet, as well as what your expectations are from supervision. These ground rules provide helpful boundaries to the supervisory relationship. Be prepared to be open and to reflect on your beliefs and values. Any kind of self-disclosure is a choice (see Theme 5), and an effective supervisor will offer a safe space where you can feel free to take some risks, such as disclosing things without the fear of ridicule. The usual protocols around confidentiality will apply.

When writing about supervision, Reid and Westergaard (2013) argue that it is a parallel process. This means that some of the interpersonal skills used in professional practice (such as empathy, congruence or genuineness and active listening) are mirrored in the supervision session by both parties. Remember that supervision is generally recognised as an important process for people in the helping professions and that through it your practice will be enriched and your stress levels reduced.

Try this   Think about how you can gain the most from supervision. Are there any barriers or constraints that you experience? If so, how could these be minimised?

Theme 9.4 The reflective conversation

We have established that reflection is not always a solitary activity, and there are times when reflecting with others can be very helpful. Ghaye (2011) discusses the value of the reflective conversation as an aid to critical reflection on professional practice. With its theoretical roots in positive psychology, at the heart of the conversation is the desire to reflect constructively, creatively and critically, particularly in relation to the values that underpin practice. In a reflective conversation, these values should be questioned closely (Ghaye uses the word 'interrogated' here), in order to enable the practitioner to see if they can be justified or not within this particular context. If not, they will need to be reinterpreted.

Ghaye makes the following points about the reflective conversation:

○ It should always include a discussion of values
○ It can start as a conversation with yourself, but should then progress to a conversation held between two people
○ It often has a question and response format – it is a dialogical process
○ It should not just focus on the past, but should also consider the future
○ Space and time needs to be set aside for the conversation
○ It helps practitioners to make sense of experience and to build collaborative knowledge
○ It is based on experience which happens in a social context
○ It can lead to enlightenment and empowerment and can add meaning to what we know already.

Reflective conversations have much in common with supervision sessions and involve an understanding of the ground rules, active listening and empathy.

Examples of questions that can be asked in a conversation are:

○ What is my professional work like and what values do I bring to it?
○ What is successful about my work?
○ What evidence do I have for its success?

- How has my work come to be successful?
- What is the effect of my work on my clients?
- What do I need to improve and how can I achieve this?

Remember that it is important to think about who you have a reflective conversation with; a critical friend will often be a good starting point.

'Above all else, a reflective conversation is one that involves a discussion of values.'

(Ghaye and Ghaye, 1998: 19)

Try this   Try having a reflective conversation with your critical friend or supervisor using the questions in Theme 9.4. Following the discussion, think about how useful this was. What did you feel you gained from it? How difficult was this and what were the challenges?

Theme 9.5 Reflecting in groups

If reflection is only practised as a solitary activity, it could easily become too focused on our own point of view and we could see things only from our perspective. This would inevitably mean that our views become narrow, blinkered and possibly even biased. Reflecting with others counteracts this and enables us to gain different insights; this means we can then question our practice in the light of this process. Some practitioners often work alone (for example, teachers in their classrooms and counsellors with their clients), so reflecting in groups can be refreshing and stimulating.

Reflecting in groups has many benefits and here are some of them:

- ○ It combats isolation
- ○ It offers different perspectives
- ○ It helps us to be creative
- ○ It combats stress
- ○ It prevents burnout
- ○ It helps us to develop our understandings of practice
- ○ It prevents stagnation
- ○ It helps us to process our emotions
- ○ It helps us to question our assumptions.

Discussing practice in depth with others helps us to develop our understandings of it; this is important, as inevitably there will be no single fixed way of dealing with the situations we encounter. However, as with critical friendship and supervision, the atmosphere must be supportive and safe, so that communication flows easily and freely. Exploring challenging aspects of practice in groups helps us to sharpen our thinking and critique our ways of working, which is both useful for us and for our clients.

Theme *10*

Bringing it all together and moving forward

This section will:

○ Introduce you to the Integrated Reflective Cycle

○ Discuss two seminal theories in relation to the management of change

○ Emphasise the importance of managing stress

○ Introduce you to Johns' work on reflection as a way of being

○ Encourage you to engage in Senge's Personal Mastery

Theme 10.1 The Integrated Reflective Cycle

In this journal, we have examined a range of theoretical approaches and practical issues in relation to reflective practice. We began our journey with an exploration of some seminal literature on reflective practice, which encourages us to learn from our professional experience by evaluating it, in order to improve it. We then progressed towards our destination of critically reflective practice by examining the role of feelings in relation to professional practice, followed by a consideration of how we make assumptions and the importance of challenging these in order to practise in a critically reflective way. To do this, the importance of considering our own ethics and values was discussed and the importance of reflecting with others was highlighted as part of this process.

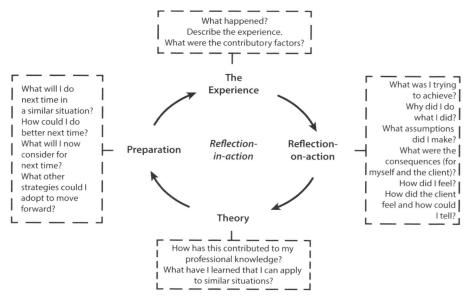

Figure 6 The Integrated Reflective Cycle

The Integrated Reflective Cycle (Bassot, 2013) shown in Figure 6 draws on several of these approaches. It is useful to compare and contrast different theories, as they often have their relative strengths and weaknesses. In this cycle, I highlight the strengths of a number of theoretical models and have posed questions around the cycle in order to prompt your thinking. Taking a questioning approach to your professional practice is an excellent way of delving deeper into not only what you did, but why – a key feature of critically reflective practice. Clearly, this approach is not completely new, as this cycle draws on some of the questions posed by Gibbs (1998) and Johns (2009).

Like any other model, the Integrated Reflective Cycle needs to be critiqued, as it also has its strengths and weaknesses. Critiquing theory and, in particular, its relationship to professional practice is always necessary. Its strengths are the things that will allow you to take your practice forward and its weaknesses are the aspects that could hinder your progress, which therefore need to be discarded. However, it is always important to be clear about the reasons for your critique and to make sure that you can justify these. For example, focusing on a model just because you like it may not be a position you can easily defend. Equally, discarding something just because it takes you into difficult territory is also questionable. Critically reflective practice demands that we accept a level of 'inner discomfort' (Boyd and Fales, 1983: 106) to enable our practice to develop.

> 'Reflective thinking is always more or less troublesome because it involves overcoming the inertia that inclines one to accept suggestions at their face value; it involves willingness to endure a condition of mental unrest.'
>
> **(Dewey, 1991: 13)**

Managing change

Engaging in professional development always involves coping with a level of change in relation to several different aspects of life, both personal and professional. It is often helpful to take an analytical approach to help you to understand more about how you approach change and cope with it. Lewin developed two very useful theories that serve as analytical tools in relation to understanding how change can be managed.

In his field theory, Lewin (1951) used a scientific approach which he applied to social situations. He argued that there are forces that promote change (driving forces) and those that work against it (restraining forces). An issue or situation is held in balance by the interaction between the two forces. Lewin calls this balance 'quasi stationary equilibrium', which represents the present state. In order for change to happen and to achieve movement towards what Lewin calls the desired state, either the driving forces need to be maximised or the restraining forces need to be minimised. When both happen together the amount of change is greatest.

Linked with these ideas, Lewin (1951) also developed his three-step model, which is as follows:

○ **Step 1** – Unfreezing, which involves reducing the restraining factors.
○ **Step 2** – Movement, or encouraging the development of new ideas and practices focusing on the driving forces.
○ **Step 3** – Refreezing: stabilising the changes at the new level of 'quasi stationary equilibrium' to avoid slipping back into old practices.

Lewin's models are very helpful tools for analysing your own responses to change, but also those of your colleagues and clients. Whether these can be applied in their entirety today is questionable. For example, his concept of refreezing could suggest

'My work life is a work in progress.'

the kind of stability that our fast-paced and ever-changing world never appears to have. However, many argue that Lewin's theories have become seminal in the field of organisational behaviour. Bringing them into the theoretical arena of critically reflective practice so as to understand processes of change is also helpful.

Try this   Think about a period of change that you have either
experienced recently or that you are about to experience.
Describe the driving forces for change and the restraining
forces. Evaluate how easy or difficult the change was or will be in relation to
these forces.

Theme 10.3 Managing stress

Practitioners in all professional fields need to be able to manage stress in order to excel in their work and to achieve a healthy work/life balance. Too much stress causes distress, which can lead to burnout, and too little can mean boredom and lethargy. In particular, it is important to recognise when we are under too much stress so that we can take some appropriate action.

Fontana (1989) highlights the following three groups of symptoms in relation to stress:

○ Cognitive – changes in our thought patterns can mean that we become forgetful or easily distracted
○ Emotional – we can feel anxious and become upset easily by simple things
○ Behavioural – we can lack enthusiasm and become cynical.

Recognising when we are experiencing a lot of stress is the first step to taking some action to deal with it. Here are some of the ways that stress in our lives can be alleviated:

○ Good time management (see Theme 1.4)
○ Being assertive and not afraid to say 'no' when the situation warrants it
○ Practising relaxation techniques
○ Getting the support of friends and colleagues
○ Taking good care of yourself by doing some physical exercise, eating well and getting enough sleep
○ Setting yourself new challenges both at work and outside
○ Retaining a positive outlook by focusing on what is going well and by doing something you enjoy
○ Recognising what you can and cannot change and focusing on the former.

In spite of all of the above, it is important to understand that stress can only be managed to a certain extent, and if you find yourself in a position where, in spite of all your best efforts, stress becomes unmanageable, you may need to make some important decisions in order to protect your health and well-being.

'It is problematic when I have no control and the stress turns into unhealthy pressure and everything goes downhill from there.'

Theme 10.4 From 'doing reflection' to 'reflection as a way of being'

In his book *Becoming a Reflective Practitioner*, Johns (2004) examines five different levels of reflection, moving from 'doing reflection' at a surface level to 'reflection as a way of being' at the deepest level.

1 'Reflection-on-experience', where the practitioner reflects on an experience after the event in order to gain insights that might inform their future practice. This is a reminder of Schön's (1983) reflection-on-action (Theme 4) and Kolb's (1984) cycle (Theme 3).

2 'Reflection-in-action', which Johns describes as pausing during an experience in order to make sense of it, leading to reframing the situation in order to move towards a desired outcome; for example, by trying a different strategy.

3 'The internal supervisor', which involves the practitioner having a dialogue with themselves while they are interacting with another person, again in order to make sense of the situation. This could take the form of a questioning approach with yourself.

4 'Reflection-within-the-moment' demands that the practitioner has an awareness of how they are thinking, feeling and responding as an event is unfolding. Importantly, this includes being open to changing or shifting your views and ideas as you practise.

5 'Mindful practice' is the deepest level, where the practitioner has a high level of awareness of self and what they desire from their practice. This links with Senge's (2006) ideas of vision, which will be discussed in the next section.

In his later edition, published in 2009, Johns' understanding of mindfulness has developed, keeping the idea of achieving desirable practice as the aim but also involving what he describes as 'seeing things as they really are' and 'without distortion' (p. 10). Such a statement is always open to critique, in that it is questionable whether this is achievable or not. It is, however, something to aim for.

In reviewing the journey we have taken so far in this journal, from reflective practice to critically reflective practice, it could be argued that we began at the first level of Johns' model and are now considering aspects of 'mindfulness' at the deepest level.

Senge's Personal Mastery

In his book *The Fifth Discipline*, Senge (2006) discusses his concept of Personal Mastery, which involves living life from a creative viewpoint rather than a reactive one. To engage in Personal Mastery, we need to clarify continually what is important to us and where we want to be as practitioners (our vision) and learn to see our current reality more clearly. Imagine stretching an elastic band between your two hands, one hand above the other. The hand above is your vision; this can be summed up as the kind of practitioner you would like to be. The lower hand is your current reality. The elastic band stretched between the two represents the creative tension between your vision and your current reality. This creative tension is central to Senge's concept of Personal Mastery.

Tension is a word that often has negative connotations associated with stress and distress. Creative tension, however, is a positive concept and needs to be harnessed. Creative tension is the source of the creative energy that we need in order to continue learning and developing. It enables our practice to keep moving forward and is vital in retaining a high level of motivation and commitment to professional practice.

> '*I constantly strive to learn more and evolve with every new piece of knowledge that I gain.*'

In the image of the elastic band outlined above, there are, of course, two things that can happen as the tension is released. Either the hand below moves towards the hand above – so I keep my vision and my current reality moves towards it. Or the hand above moves down towards the hand below as I lose sight of my vision and it moves towards the acceptance of my current reality. It is important to note that as my current reality moves towards my vision, my vision must continue to move forward (upwards) in order to maintain the creative tension. People who show a high level of Personal

Mastery continually reappraise their vision, in order to maintain the creative tension needed to propel themselves forward through a continuous process of learning.

Although we have now reached the end of our ten themes, the work of Senge urges us to continue developing through renewing our vision in order to protect and foster our creative tension.

'Habermas suggested that perspective transformation occurs through critical reflection, that is, the attempt to reveal the extent to which self-deception and ideology distort our perceptions.'

(Jasper and Rolfe, 2011: 7)

Try this   Imagine you overhear a group of friends and/or colleagues describing you and your work. Write down what you hope they would be saying. Now use this as the basis for writing your vision for your practice. Now think of some examples of how you can make progress towards your vision.

Part 2

More space for reflection

Part 2 offers you more space for reflective writing and contains a number of activities and quotes to help inspire you. The activities are designed to help you to continue to reflect critically on your learning and development. The quotes offer insights from a number of writers into different aspects of reflection, like the quotes in Part 1. How you use these pages is up to you and you should feel free to use them as suits you best at the time. Remember to date your writing for the following two reasons; first, it is very easy to forget when things happened and, second, it is good to look back and see how your work is developing over time.

Try this   In their reflective model, Boud et al. (1985) discuss the need to process any negative feelings we might have in relation to our experiences in order to remove them. Think of an experience you have had that you felt quite negatively about. Did you manage to process your feelings? If so, how, and if not, what were the barriers that got in the way?

'Maybe just being aware that my assumptions could be wrong and unhelpful is a good start.'

'three elements...are important in the reflective process. Returning to the experience...attending to feelings...re-evaluating the experience.'

Boud et al. (1985: 26)

Try this
Brookfield (1995) suggests that there are four lenses through which we can reflect on practice critically. They are as follows:

1 Our own autobiographies and experiences as learners
2 The eyes of our clients
3 The experiences of our colleagues
4 Theoretical literature

Think about how each of these lenses will give you a different perspective on your practice and bear in mind issues of power in the helping relationship. Now think of times when you have engaged in critical reflection using each of the four lenses. Are there any of the four that you are reluctant to use? Why might this be? Does this need to change? If so, how? If not, why not?

'Every situation is different and requires its own unique way of dealing with it.'

'By critical we mean it in the sense of an approach that is characterized by questioning and not taking things for granted – especially social arrangements that are based on inequality and disadvantage.'

(Thompson and Thompson, 2008: 27)

The most common reason that practitioners give for not engaging in reflective practice is lack of time. Most professionals work in busy environments, where the pace is fast and there is usually too much to do. In such circumstances, it can be tempting to switch on your 'auto pilot' and rely on what you already know in order to cope with the workload.

Working from the premise that we do not have any 'free' time at work – the only time we have is the time we make – why is it important to make time to reflect? Now write down how you could put this into practice.

Having some physical space for reflection can also be very important. Describe your ideal space – what would it look like and where would it be? How else can you gain some space for reflection?

'Rather than acting or responding, I am now taking a moment to reflect in action and refer back to similar experiences. This approach allows me to think on my feet as I am drawing on prior experiences. It means that I am now able to adapt my behaviour in order to gain a more positive outcome.'

'All professionals are concerned with knowing and realising desirable and effective practice, yet work in conditions where, for one reason or another, such realisation is often difficult.'

(Johns, 2009: xi)

Try this   Think of an example from your practice where you have begun to think about something differently. Now try describing how this change came about on one side of the page and how your assumptions were challenged on the other side.

'Reflection gives me a sense of relief, a way to look over a situation, revisit it in a time and place that is relaxed and with a more open mind without distraction.'

Critical reflection 'happens when we identify and scrutinise the assumptions that undergird how we work.'

(Brookfield, 1995: xii)

Try this   Think about your development over the past few months. Now try to depict this visually – for example as a diagram, graph or picture. Remember that you do not have to be artistic to be able to do this, as a simple line drawing can be very effective. What does this show about areas where you feel your development has been significant?

'Studying reflective practice has really had a major impact on my life. I am already much more self-aware.'

'it could be argued that self-evaluation is the highest-level cognitive skill and the most difficult to master.'

(Rolfe, 2011: 209)

Try this   Now look at the picture, diagram or graph from page 135 and try writing a story about what it depicts. Does it remind you of any particular theoretical approaches?

'Writing in my journal is a big help. If I have something going round in my head, I now write it down, it feels like it gets it out there and I can either leave it there, or do something about it.'

'the reflective practitioner is always mindful not to be seduced by any compelling theoretical view but to hold it loosely, until it can be metaphorically chewed over and checked out for its appropriateness to inform.'

(Johns, 2013: 69)

Try this   Find a photograph or image that depicts how you feel about your progress at the moment. Now describe it and try to summarise what it means for you.

'I am beginning to realise that I do reflect a great deal. However, the process of writing in my journal is making me think more about how I acted and whether this was the best method in such circumstances.'

'Reflective Practice is not ... A luxury we
can't afford ... the more under pressure
we are, the more each of us needs to be
thinking clearly and carefully.'

(Thompson and Thompson, 2008: 8)

It is very easy in busy professional practice to succumb to doing things out of habit rather than because those particular ways of working are effective. Are there any areas or aspects of your work where you feel this is the case? If so, what action might you be able to take?

'At first I was a bit uncertain about how I would manage reflecting in writing. It felt strange to write my thoughts, I was happy to think behind closed doors in my own mind but felt slightly exposed putting pen to paper.'

'Becoming mindful ... the antidote to complacency, habit and blindness.'

(Johns, 2004: 5)

Try this　Write a letter to a friend or someone you know well, discussing the highs and lows of your recent experiences. You could save this and post it to yourself in a few months' time to examine how you have progressed since then.

'I realise that I have more to gain as a practitioner if I analyse my experience and understand the meanings behind my action and whether I could have acted differently.'

Try this   Which areas of your work and study are you finding the most challenging and why? Is there anything getting in the way of your development in these areas and, if so, what might you be able to do to reduce its impact?

'My patience has been pushed to the limit both personally and professionally, but having the reflective journal to unload my thoughts into helps me to have some positivity that I can resolve today's situations with positive results for all concerned.'

Reflection is 'concerned with developing people who are able to challenge and question, in order to make a difference in the world.'

(Bulman, 2013: 9)

Part 3
Career development

Part 3 offers you the opportunity to look forward and focus on your career development. It is important to understand that the world of work is changing at a rapid rate, and that this brings challenges to people in all areas of the labour market as they recognise the need to think about the future differently. The Career Learning and Development (CLD) Bridge model is introduced as a means of illustrating this, followed by a number of activities to help you to work towards career happiness, build career resilience and establish career growth.

Career development

In Part 3 we start to look forward and move on to examine some relevant career development issues. You may have already made some career decisions or you may still be unsure about what you want to do in the future. Equally, you may currently be working and thinking about your next career move. Whatever your situation, it is useful to consider your present position and where you might like to be in the future. This could relate to your medium and longer term goals (if you are clear about them), or it could mean trying to establish some. We begin by examining some of the ways that the world of work is changing and the challenges this brings to people in all areas of the labour market. This is followed by a brief introduction to the Career Learning and Development (CLD) Bridge model which explains some of the factors involved in how people make their career decisions. There are then a number of activities that you can carry out to help you to think about your own career development.

In all situations – whether you are on a professional course of study, are already working in a professional context or simply beginning to think about your future – it will be very useful to keep a record of your learning and development. This will be particularly helpful when you apply for jobs in the future. It is easy to think that we will remember what we have done, but in reality we often do not. This means that we can waste a lot of time trying to remember the detail and looking back to get accurate dates for when we did certain things. Part 3 also acts as a useful record of your learning and development and is likely to save you time in the future, whilst also giving you an opportunity to reflect on your experiences at work or on placement.

Change and career

There is no doubt that the world is changing at a rapid pace, particularly in response to the impact of such things as ICT and globalised marketplaces. In the past, the term 'career' was seen as an occupation, or some kind of paid work, which also implied an element of progression. It was something tangible that someone could find by analysing themselves (for example, their interests and skills) and the opportunities available to try to get the closest match. Having found a good match, they could then work to make progress within their chosen area. This view of 'career' was very helpful when times were stable and to a large extent predictable. However, more recently the idea of 'a job for life' has come into question and many have begun to see 'career' as a metaphorical journey through life, moving from one area of work to the next – sometimes with breaks in between. In addition, 'career' is now often seen in terms of life as a whole, not just paid work, as issues of work/life balance become more important to many people.

Many aspects of our lives are changing, not just the world of work, and everyone needs to embrace change in order to progress – some might say in order to survive. This is the case in all sectors of the labour market (public, corporate and charity), and it means engaging in lifelong learning to update your knowledge and skills on a continuous basis. In recent years, the notion of 'employment', with its connotations of security and progression, is frequently being replaced by the idea of 'employability'. The onus is shifting onto individuals to make themselves as employable as possible. This usually means being prepared to engage in training and development, to respond appropriately as the needs of employers change and to be prepared for the consequences of being part of companies and organisations that need to downsize or rebrand themselves in times of recession and budget cuts.

Flexibility and employability therefore go 'hand in hand'. However, this does not necessarily mean that the notion of a career for life is dead, but rather that we all need to be as well prepared as possible for the challenges that change brings.

Career as a journey

The idea of career as a journey can be very helpful, particularly for those people who do not yet know what they want to do. Looking a long way ahead is often difficult, particularly when we live in an unpredictable world. Rather than trying to answer the age-old question, 'What do I want to do with the rest of my life?', many people find it easier to focus on the next step. Even looking a few years ahead can be daunting for some and the classic interview question, 'Where do you see yourself in five years' time?' is notoriously difficult to answer – many interviewers themselves would struggle to respond to it! Whether you are someone who has medium- or even long-term goals or whether you are very uncertain about the future, focusing on the next step will help you to make progress in your career thinking.

The Career Learning and Development Bridge

In my work as a lecturer in career development (Bassot, 2009), I developed the concept of the Career Learning and Development (CLD) Bridge as a way of explaining career and career development in more detail (see Figure 7). The CLD Bridge uses the metaphor of a suspension bridge. Suspension bridges function because the tension in the cables, compression in the towers and the weight of the road are all kept in balance. Without this balance, the bridges would collapse. I chose the metaphor of a suspension bridge because it illustrates the tensions that many people experience between what they want as individuals and the demands of their context. The Bridge harnesses these tensions and relies on them in order to function, showing that in relation to career, tensions and stress can be seen as opportunities and possibilities rather than threats, but without underestimating the many challenges that are involved.

Taking account of the constant and rapid changes in the world at large, the CLD Bridge operates with two-way traffic. It is important to understand that you do not cross the Bridge once, but travel back and forth as your career develops. This illustrates the need to engage in continuous professional development, in order to meet your own needs and those of your employers.

Career, then, is something that you construct throughout your life and is not a 'one-off' decision. To many, this will be a relief, as the idea of making a decision (or, worse, a mistake) that determines one's career for the rest of one's life is a daunting prospect.

We will now focus on the three aspects of the bridge that are highlighted in the diagram.

First, on the left-hand side is career happiness. Career happiness is focused on what you want as an individual and can include such things as maintaining a healthy work/life balance and choosing a field of work in which you will gain satisfaction. This often involves making choices that are in tune with your values, which can affect the sector that you choose to work in (for example, corporate, public, charity). These values can be extrinsic (such as the importance of earning a high salary), intrinsic (such as feeling respected for what I do and making a difference), or lifestyle values (such as where I live and how far I will have to travel to work), or any combination of these.

Second, and on the right-hand side of the Bridge, is career resilience. This is vital in enabling you to cope in the changing world and its turbulent labour market. Career resilience means remaining positive in spite of challenges and being able to 'bounce back' from disappointments. It involves developing a strong underlying belief in yourself, including your knowledge and your skills, by focusing on positive feedback and working on your development points. Having a high level of self-reliance is also important in building career resilience, as is being receptive to change rather than fighting against it or dismissing it.

The road represents career growth (Bassot, Barnes and Chant, 2014) and is based on Vygotsky's (1978) concept of the zone of proximal development (ZPD). Wood (1998: 26) defines the ZPD as 'the gap that exists for an individual child (or adult) between what he [sic] is able to do alone, and what he can achieve with help from one more knowledgeable than himself'. The

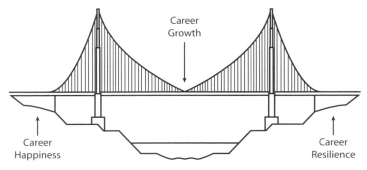

Figure 7 The Career Learning and Development Bridge

focus of learning and development in the ZPD is on what a person is able to do next rather than what lies far ahead in the distance. In relation to career, you can make progress within the ZPD by gaining useful practical experience and by having discussions with others who are more knowledgeable (for example, employers and careers advisers). These activities and discussions enable you to write (in a metaphorical sense) your career narrative, or story.

The following activities are designed to help you to think about how you can work towards career happiness, develop career resilience and maintain career growth.

Try this   Describe the times in the past when you felt happiest. Try and identify some of the reasons that made you happy at those times. Make a list of the things that will make you happy in the future. Is there anything surprising here?

What does the term 'job satisfaction' mean to you? Make a list of the things that are vital for you when you think about a job or career that will give you satisfaction. Now rank them in order of importance. In the light of what you have written, how would you describe your core values in relation to your career development?

Try this How would a good friend describe you as a person? How would you describe yourself? Are there any differences?

Try this   This activity is about career resilience. Describe your core skills under the following headings. Use the right-hand column to note things you need to work on – be as honest as you can. This process will be helpful when you need to write a personal statement as part of a job application.

Table 1 Core skills and development points

Core Skills	Development Points
Communication – oral With individuals With groups In meetings Other	
Communication – written Reports Case notes Course assignments Other	
Communication – ICT Managing e-mails Word processing Spreadsheets Other Numeracy Budgets Expenses Keeping relevant statistics Other	
Team work – your role in a team	
Leadership skills	
Problem solving	
Analytical skills	

Core Skills	Development Points
Organisational skills	
Creativity	
Resilience	

Now write a paragraph to summarise:

○ Your strengths

○ Your areas for development.

Try this   Think about times when you have needed to overcome some difficulties. What strategies did you use at the time? What was successful and what was not successful?

Table 2 Log for work/placement experiences

Dates	Place/organisation	Contact details	Experience gained

Table 3 Training courses attended

Dates	Name of course	Place	Documents (certificates, attendance records)

Try this Spend some time thinking about how you got to where you are now. Here are some questions that can help to guide you in developing your career narrative:

○ Where am I now?
○ How did I get here?
○ Why did I choose to do what I am doing now?
○ How did I make my decisions?

Rank your decisions using the following scale:

5 = Excellent
4 = Good
3 = OK
2 = Not good
1 = Not good at all

What does this show you about how you have made your decisions and how you might make them in the future?

Imagine you are telling your career story so far to a friend. What would you include? Describe the most significant parts of your story so far.

Try this Imagine it is 3/5/10 years from now. Where (generally) do you hope to be and what will you have achieved?

1 Make a list of things about yourself that you feel have changed over the years.
2 Now list some things that have remained the same.
3 What do these things say about you as a person?
4 What kind of pointers do they give you in relation to your career development? This might include the insights they give you into the kind of person you are, the kind of work you might find satisfying and the kinds of things that could be important (even vital) to you in a job.

Bibliography

Argyris, C. (1982) *Reasoning, Learning and Action: Individual and Organizational*, San Francisco, CA: Jossey-Bass.

Argyris, C. and Schön, D. (1974) *Theory in Practice: Increasing Professional Effectiveness*, San Francisco, CA: Jossey-Bass.

Atkins, S. and Schutz, S. (2013) 'Developing skills for reflective practice', in Bulman, C. and Schutz, S., *Reflective Practice in Nursing*, 5th edn, Chichester: Wiley.

Bassot, B. (2009) 'Career Learning and Development: A bridge to the future', in H. L. Reid (ed.), *Constructing the Future: Career Guidance for Changing Contexts*, Stourbridge: Institute of Career Guidance.

Bassot, B. (2013) *The Reflective Journal*, Basingstoke: Palgrave.

Bassot, B. (2016) *The Reflective Practice Guide*, Abingdon: Routledge.

Bassot, B., Barnes, A. and Chant, A. (2014) *A Practical Guide to Career Learning and Development: Innovation in Career Education 11–19*, London: Routledge.

Bolton, G. (2010) *Reflective Practice: Writing and Professional Development*, 3rd edn, London: SAGE.

Borton, T. (1970) *Reach, Touch and Teach*, London: McGraw-Hill.

Boud, D., Keogh, R. and Walker, D. (1985) *Reflection: Turning Experience into Learning*, London: RoutledgeFalmer.

Boyd, E. M. and Fales, A. W. (1983) 'Reflective learning: Key to learning from experience', *Journal of Humanistic Psychology*, 23.2: 99–117.

Bridges, W. (2004) *Transitions Making Sense of Life's Changes*, US: Da Capo Press.

Brockbank, A. and McGill, I. (2006) *Facilitating Reflective Learning through Mentoring and Coaching*, London: Kogan Page.

Brookfield, S. D. (1995) *Becoming a Critically Reflective Teacher*, San Francisco, CA: Jossey-Bass.

Bulman, C. (2013) 'An introduction to reflection', in C. Bulman and S. Schutz (eds), *Reflective Practice in Nursing*, 5th edn, Chichester: Wiley-Blackwell.

Campbell, A. and Norton, L. (2007) *Learning Teaching and Assessing in Higher Education*, Exeter: Learning Matters.

Corey, G., Schneider Corey, M. and Callanan, P. (2007) *Issues and Ethics in the Helping Professions*, 7th edn, Belmont, CA: Thomson Brooks/Cole.

Covey, S. (2004) *The 7 Habits of Highly Effective People*, London: Pocket Books.

Dewey, J. (1991) *How we think*, Amhurst, NY: Prometheus books.

Driscoll, J. (2007) (ed.) *Practising Clinical Supervision: A Reflective Approach for Healthcare Professionals*, Edinburgh: Ballière Tindall, Elsevier.

Eraut, M. (2006) 'Editorial', *Learning in Health and Social Care*, 5.3: 111–18.

Fontana, D. (1989) *Managing Stress*, London: BPS Books with Routledge.

Fook, J. (2004) 'Critical reflection and transformative possibilities', in L. Davies and P. Leonard (eds), *Social Work in a Corporate Era*, Aldershot: Ashgate.

Ghaye, T. (2011) *Teaching and Learning through Reflective Practice: A Practical Guide for Positive Action*, Abingdon: Routledge.

Ghaye, T. and Ghaye, K. (1998) *Teaching and Learning through Critical Reflective Practice*, London: Routledge David Fulton Press.

Gibbs, G. (1998) *Learning by Doing: A Guide to Teaching and Learning Methods*, Oxford: Further Education Unit, Oxford Polytechnic.

Honey, P. and Mumford, A. (undated) *The Learning Styles Questionnaire*, online. Available at https://www.talentlens.co.uk/develop/peter-honey-learning-style-series (accessed 19 February 2016).

Honey, P. and Mumford, A. (2000) *The Learning Styles Helper's Guide*, Maidenhead: Peter Honey Publications.

Illeris, K. (2014) *Transformative Learning and Identity*, Abingdon: Routledge.

Jasper, M. (2003) *Beginning Reflective Practice*, Cheltenham: Nelson Thornes.

Jasper, M. (2008) 'Using reflective journals and diaries to enhance practice and learning', in C. Bulman and S. Schutz (eds), *Reflective Practice in Nursing*, 4th edn, Chichester: Wiley-Blackwell.

Jasper, M. and Rolfe, G. (2011) 'Critical reflection and the emergence of professional knowledge' in Rolfe, G., Jasper, M. and Freshwater, D. (eds.) *Critical Reflection in Practice: Generating Knowledge for Care*, 2nd edition, Basingstoke: Palgrave Macmillan.

Johns, C. (1995) 'The value of reflective practice for nursing', *Journal of Clinical Nursing*, 4: 23–30.

Johns, C. (2004) *Becoming a Reflective Practitioner*, 2nd edn, Oxford: Blackwell Publishing.

Johns, C. (2009) *Becoming a Reflective Practitioner*, 3rd edn, Chichester: Wiley-Blackwell.

Johns, C. (2010) *Guided Reflection: A Narrative Approach to Advancing Professional Practice*, Oxford: Wiley-Blackwell.

Johns, C. (2013) *Becoming a Reflective Practitioner*, Oxford: Wiley-Blackwell.

Kahler, T. (1975) 'Drivers—the key to the process script', *Transactional Analysis Journal*, 5.3: 280–4.

Kline, N. (1999) *Time to Think*, London: Ward Lock.

Knott, C. and Scragg, T. (2013) *Reflective Practice in Social Work*, 3rd edn, London: Learning Matters/SAGE.

Knowles, G. and Lander, V. (2012) *Thinking through Ethics and Values in Primary Education*, London: Learning Matters.

Kolb, D. (1984) *Experiential Learning: Experience as the Source of Learning and Development*, New Jersey: Prentice Hall.

Lewin, K. (1951) *Field Theory in Social Science*, New York: Harper & Row.

Luft, J. (1984) *Group Processes, an Introduction to Group Dynamics*, Mountain View, CA: Mayfield.

Mezirow, J. (1978) *Education for Perspective Transformation: Women's Re-entry Programs in Community Colleges*, New York: Center for Adult Education, Columbia University.

Mezirow, J. (1981) 'A critical theory of adult learning and education', *Adult Education*, 32.1: 13–24.

Moon, J. A. (2000) *Reflection in Learning and Professional Development*, Abingdon: Kogan Page.

Moon, J. A. (2006) *Learning Journals: A Handbook for Reflective Practice and Professional Development*, 2nd edn, Abingdon: Routledge.

Muzio, E. (2011) 'The Ladder of Inference Creates Bad Judgment', www.groupharmonics.com/HelpDesk/Ladder.htm (accessed 19 February 2016).

Osterman, K. F. and Kottkamp, R. B. (2004) *Reflective Practice for Educators*, 2nd edn, Thousand Oaks, CA: Corwin Press.

Proctor, B. (1986) 'Supervision: A co-operative exercise in accountability', in A. Marken and M. Payne (eds), *Enabling and Ensuring: Supervision in Practice*, Leicester: Leicester National Youth Bureau/Council for Education and Training in Youth and Community Work.

Reid, H. L. and Westergaard, J. (2013) *Effective Supervision for Counsellors: An Introduction*, Exeter: Learning Matters.

Riches, A. (2012) *'Where did that come from?' How to Keep Control in any Situation*, e-book, Sudbury, MA: eBookIt. Available at www.anneriches.com.au/almond-effect.html.

Rolfe, G. (2011) 'Education and the reflective practitioner' in Rolfe, G., Jasper, M. and Freshwater, D. (eds.) *Critical Reflection in Practice: Generating Knowledge for Care*, 2nd edition, Basingstoke: Palgrave Macmillan.

Schön, D. A. (1983) *The Reflective Practitioner*, Aldershot: Ashgate.

Schön, D. A. (1987) *Educating the Reflective Practitioner*, San Francisco, CA: Jossey-Bass.

Senge, P. (2006) *The Fifth Discipline*, 2nd edn, London: Random House Business.

Thompson, N. (1995) *Theory and Practice in Health and Social Welfare*, Buckingham: Open University Press.

Thompson, N. (2005) 'Reflective Practice', in R. Harrison and C. Wise (eds), *Working with Young People*, London: SAGE.

Thompson, N. (2009) *Practising Social Work*, Basingstoke: Palgrave Macmillan.

Thompson, N. (2012) *Anti-Discriminatory Practice*, 5th edn, Basingstoke: Palgrave Macmillan.

Thompson, S. and Thompson, N. (2008) *The Critically Reflective Practitioner*, Basingstoke: Palgrave Macmillan.

Vygotsky, L. S. (1978). *Mind in Society*, Cambridge, MA: Harvard College.

Wood, D. (1998) *How Children Think and Learn*, 2nd edn, Oxford: Blackwell.

Index